Eden's Fallen Angel

by

Jaclyn Tracey

Entering Eden Series

Eden's Fallen Angel

Cover Art by *The Wild Rose Press, Inc.*

The Wild Rose Press, Inc.
PO Box 708
Adams Basin, NY 14410-0708
Visit us at www.thewildrosepress.com

Publishing History
First Edition, 2025
Trade Paperback ISBN 978-1-5092-5923-6
Digital ISBN 978-1-5092-5924-3

Entering Eden Series
Published in the United States of America

Dedication

For Eden, my house hippo~cadaver dog~sharer of all edible and some seriously non-edible delicacies~there's no one else I'd rather have staring me down waiting for our next adventure, that once we get out the door you decide you don't want any part of. You, like the characters of this book, keep me guessing all day.

Here's to countless belly rubs, buckets of drool and sloppy kisses... Sorry I'm such a messy kisser.

Chapter One

The floor of the Hall Royal thrummed with the same enthusiasm static energy converged on people in launderettes during a bustling Saturday morning. Elyza St. James tingled from her teeth to her tootsies. The piano's pulse ascended her legs, tantalized all those personal spots that responded to perfection with vibration. She couldn't help but smile. The sensation invigorated her, made her appreciate each breath. Instead of looking for a way to escape her own skin, music soothed her soul and kept most of her charms in check.

These days, with so much chaos destroying the world, being an empath sucked the nice out of her faster than half her family could drain someone dry, and that was saying a lot. Immortality had its advantages until stage four of the hunger games struck. By then everyone was nutty looking for a candy bar.

She cracked open the dense steel dressing room door and slipped through, practicing her strut past the sound stage manager. Before he could protest, Elyza put her finger to his mouth to shush the man. "Don't even think about it."

The tall man donned in a tight black uniform grinned. "Ms. St. James, has anyone ever been able to say no to you?"

With a quick glance back over her shoulder Elyza gave the guard a playful wink. "No one that's lived to say it twice." She peeked around the thick, velvet gold curtain. People in the amphitheater straddled the arms of chairs, some whistling, others busy with their pinky fingers and index fingers stuck straight up hooting and chanting, "Aimeeleigh! Aimeeleigh!" to which Elyza's Aunt Raven graciously announced, "That's an entirely different concert." Under her breath, with the microphone covered she added, "Even if I can evanesce," ending with a killer smile and feisty power fist jab to the crowd.

Elyza scooted back to her dressing room laughing. Aimeeleigh could be Raven's doppelganger, but the huge difference being Aimeeleigh could sing better than the angels and her aunt? That's where the piano came in.

Not a moment later the soundproof door opened. Sydney St. James squeezed through and ducked for cover from the gathering mass of paparazzi outside her sister's dressing room. "Full house tonight, ET. Not a vacant seat. Last one just sold for six whopping G's. The things humans will do to get up close and personal with the supernatural community. I don't get it. Everybody wants to be Sam and Dean or Klaus and Elijah until they are a demon. Then they're all about a cure. Anyway," Sydney paused and took in her sister, giving her a curious once over, "don't you worry about one single strand of your glued-in-place hairdo coming undone." Sydney pointed to Elyza's head, "My gosh that looks dreadful. Why did they do this to you?"

With a ginger caress, Elyza smoothed a few strands in place and licked her fingers. "Nice huh? Artistic interpretation. The hairstylist couldn't get my mop to behave so she made it into a beehive and literally used honey to hold it in place. "

"Seriously Elyza, you look like a leftover in one of those old battery commercials."

Sydney went to touch her sister's head but Elyza warned, "Don't make me zap you!" She watched her sister's chocolate brown eyes widen.

Sydney straightened her stance and with defiance added, "You wouldn't dare!"

Elyza bat her eyelashes as a wide thin-lipped grin spread across her face. "Try me."

Shelby Jane Thomas, Elyza and Sydney's cousin, giggled, adding, "No worries Syd, Elyza knows you're Serina's favorite child."

Elyza mulled over, *Serina's favorite child*, and produced a faux grumpy face.

Sydney attempted to change the subject. "Well, I'd give you a hug, but I don't want to feel your boobies pressed against me. Girl, you're all but dancing in your birthday suit. And did you know there's more paparazzi here than when the Queen and her rug rats go for a stretch on their balcony."

Elyza tossed an uplifted brow to her older sister. "Funny."

Sydney puckered her signature coral-colored lips and blew Elyza a kiss. "You're going to be on the cover of every boo-tay magazine known tomorrow. Did you see all the security? You are smokin' hot."

Elyza shot her thumb over her shoulder and pointed at a table. "Oh, I'm a hot mess all right. Let's just hope I don't burn this place to the ground." All eyebrows raised, the three of them did a synchronized head bob of knowing. "And, Syd, you already know why there's so much security. It isn't my boo-tay as you so affectionately called it, it's my darlin' lil throat."

"Baby sister, how much are this booby trap and threadless thong you're sporting tonight worth?" Sydney went to touch the outfit but she was met with a 'Don't touch the merchandise,' finger.

"The bra," Elyza hesitated and attempted to scratch her head but stopped with the first twinge of pain. "Fecking hair!" She grunted and refocused. "Eight million to hold the girls in place. Got more bada-bing than hookers do herpes."

"That's my sweet tart!" Shelby mumbled as she fingered through her digital camera looking at pictures. Glancing upward she added, "It only cost that much because your ta-tas are huge. Needed more rocks to cover them." A death-defying shot covered the room to Shelby. She laughed. "Oh, Lizzy, don't even try to deny it."

"I wasn't going to, but there's no need to point them out."

"No. No there is not." Shelby whirled around so no one could see her cracking up, even though her body jerked with snickers.

With a snort, Elyza continued, "My string, aka thong"—Elyza climbed up and stood on a chair and with a little spin she flashed the two women her nearly bare bottom— "One mill."

That caught Shelby's attention. "Holy crap, Lizzy, did you know you have a dimple on your tush? Is that cell—"

Gasping, Elyza jumped off the chair and slapped her hand over Shelby's mouth, "Bite your tongue, Shells. Most taboo word in a model's vocabulary."

Shelby pushed the chair backwards away from her cousin. "About the only word other than salad. Cellulite!

Ha! Said it."

Sydney jumped in, "Practically inconspicuous."

"Practically?" Hand on her bony hip, Elyza spewed, "For the record I am not so vain I can't take a little ribbing," while she cranked her neck over her shoulder looking in the mirror.

Shelby added, "Sweet-tart, I can't believe we are sitting here talking about your ass. The dimple is like the elephant in the room."

"Did you just tell me my tush is the size of an elephant's?"

Poker-faced, Shelby answered, "No lovie, just the dimple."

Laughter burst through the confined space, with Sydney adding, "Yup, able to take a little ribbing like a pro and keep on ticking."

"I give up." Elyza fidgeted with the top, straightening it before she adjusted the thong. "We've moved on from having a silver spoon up our patootie to this. And no, it's not any more comfortable unless ya wiggle around a bit and hit that center spot just right. They don't call them G strings for nothing." Teasing, Elyza began to gyrate her hips.

Sydney squealed, "Dear lord woman, I didn't want to see your tush, let alone whatever this is."

Never missing a beat Elyza grunted, imitating someone, certainly not her, mid orgasm. In order to enjoy those spine-tingling titillations, one needed a boyfriend and where she made up in other areas of her life with the finer things, she sadly lacked in the man department.

Sydney asked, "Have you practiced wearing the blue diamond mask?" She picked it up and held it to her face. "It's so beautiful. I can't believe Drac let you borrow it. Lizzy, I can't see shit. Girl, you're going to crash and burn."

"Thanks for jinxing me." Elyza snatched the mask from Sydney and placed it on the table.

Shelby pointed to the necklace laid out on a square of blue velvet. "What about the showstopper, Lizzy, *Le Bijou du Rol*, the Hope Diamond? I'd be more worried over that." Shelby made a cross out of her fingers and held her hands in front of her. "I heard it's pretty—deadly. Some say—" Shelby whispered, "—cursed."

"I heard the same thing," Sydney added. "Stories go whoever wore it, owned it, stole it, borrowed it, thought about wearing it, owning it, stealing it, borrowing it, or touching it—" Sydney slapped Shelby's hand away from the table, "—all seemed to meet the same nasty, Friday the thirteenth type deaths."

Giving Sydney a sideways scowl Shelby begrudgingly retracted her hand. "That hurt."

Sydney concluded, "Hurt more if you get your greedy paws on it. Look at Marie Antoinette. Chopping block. The queen kinda left the necklace dangling."

"Guys, stop fecking hexing me." Her middle finger air jabbed toward the door. "Out!"

Shelby waved her hand. "Oh-oh-oh quick before I forget. You'll never guess who is in the audience. Remember the two fur bags trying to pick us up a few weeks back when we were at the Arcade in Manchester? With binoculars no less."

A smile, devilish in nature, lit up Sydney's face.

Elyza knew that smirk well. "Don't go there, Syd."

Sydney went there. "They won't need binoculars to see the dimple."

"Definitely not the ta-tas." Shelby wiped tears from

under her eyes. "Gosh you're an easy target."

"That's it! Out. The two of you. Right this second."

Sydney did a super-fast lean in to Elyza and kissed her cheek. "Love you more."

A slight grimace made its way to Elyza's face. Trying to downplay the pain Elyza ran to the mirror and blurted, "Sissy, you and that outdated coral lipstick of yours. Now I have to buff a pair of lips off. All I can say is thank God it isn't that neon pink Shelby cakes on."

"My lips are perfect." Shelby puckered up and made a raspberry noise.

Sydney slipped in, "It's better than where that last raspberry noise came out of you earlier."

"It wasn't that noticeable," Shelby added.

"If you say so." Sydney bit her cheeks and went on, "For the record, I will never ever be caught dead in that dreadful pink shade." Sydney blew a kiss to Shelby. "Remember that. If you're at my funeral and the morgue director, AKA Momma, thinks she's funny trying to send me off in that color, please tell her I will haunt her."

"Syd, you haven't got it in you to haunt a fly let alone your mum. This one on the other hand—" Shelby tossed her thumb over her shoulder at Elyza, "—she scares the you know what out of me right now. Can you imagine her as ghost?" Shelby slapped her thigh giggling before she pushed her body into a standing position. "Okay, sweet-tart, you just got your two-minute warning. My vibrator just went off—and no, it didn't give me anywhere near as much of a thrill as you're getting from your gold chastity thong. You need a real man, sweetie. Someone you can sink your teeth into. We'll work on that after the show."

The corner of Elyza's lips dipped down. "That

obvious?"

Both Shelby and Sydney headed to the door chortling. Shelby pointed to Elyza. "Don't freak when the fireworks go off. You just keep to center runway and try not to let your personal crop get singed."

To drown out the noise coming from the main stage, Elyza raised her voice, "It's called a wax job, Shelby Jane. You should try one." Elyza swiped her finger over her eyebrows and pointed back to Shelby. "Unibrow for starters!"

"Don't forget to cover-up the birthmark. And I don't have a unibrow!"

"Actually," some strange fella walking down the corridor added, "you really do, but I find it rather sexy. Let me pluck it for you."

"Go pluck yourself, Dudley," Shelby retorted.

Sydney added, "We call her Bert for a reason."

"You do not," Shelby quipped, nudging Sydney in the side. "You don't, do you?"

"Well, not to your face, Seashells," Sydney teased as she looped her arm through her cousin's. "Come along then Bert."

****

With the patience only the dead can perceive, I waited for the young man assigned the daunting task of feeding the monsters to finally get around to my neck of the woods. My neck of the woods—my humor remains intact. Sadly, only I see the irony in it. Pain ravages my gums as my choppers descend to wrap around the precious metal flower wedged between my lips. This only means one thing, dinner time. You have no idea what I wouldn't give for a spicy shank, the pulse full of verve with a twist of tang. In other words, someone fighting for their life with their adrenaline and endorphins flooding their system. Those extra little additives make everything more succulent. Succulent, if only. If I'd had but a drop of saliva, my mouth would have watered, but alas, here I am, the pinned-up poster boy, barren, confined to a casket for one. My loving jailers being cryptic sadists always make certain I am last in line for the chuck wagon, knowing full on my keen sense of smell will stir up a voracious appetite, only to gnaw at me until my level of lunacy spreads my proverbial wings and demands this mild-mannered mannequin earn his keep. I am the equivalent of Pavlov's maltreated dog.

That's when the real show began. Sections of tattered, worn out red-velvet rope draped across brass poles cordons me from the public getting too close. Their loss. Hannibal had a more secure, elaborate glass enclosure where he could get up and wander about. Me? I lost the feeling in my ass decades past.

The sick reality is I am live bait for natural selection, or as natural as one can perceive when you're on a one-way thread being hand-picked from true monsters, those who smile in your face with grandiose promises only to laugh and regale in your misery as your last breath is caught mid scream. There's an exhibit near the rear of the building filled with photos and a painting called, The Last Laugh.

I don't find it the least bit funny. Nothing here is funny.

Maybe if I were the one getting the last laugh, I'd have a reason to smile.

My being here began as punishment for a night or two of lust which got a smidgen out of hand, but the lovely curator of this joint, please note my sarcasm, found his true calling to be darker than mine. And I'm a hard act to follow. I am now the reason this crypt of mourning all things older than dirt…aka the museum, thrives. People love a true horror story and apparently, I am the first-ever living creature in captivity.

Lucky me! I'd do a little jig if I weren't rusted in place.

Where the hell is Dottie's tiny tin can?

Teeth, also known as dents, canines, or—my favorite, fangs, magically appear when I am taunted adding a certain savoir fair to my already debonair persona. My enchanting black eyes glow brilliant red, the color found in strumpet's windows, only strumpets offer happy endings to loyal patrons whereas I seem to be the only one happy at the end with my patrons. Give and take. It is what life is all about. People give. I take. Right here and now I've taken a lifetime or two of nonsense from these monsters disguised by flesh and bones in fancy suits with white veneers. All masking their true identities. Not I. What you see is what you get.

I am now and have always been the equivalent of back-alley circus spectacles, where those of severe misfortune or disabilities were once hidden in musky tents, only to be displayed and ridiculed by conniving puppeteers who profited from other's oddities and misfortunes. I get it, shock and awe, truly I do, but if I am to be brutally honest, I'm just not fond of being the main bleeding attraction. Everyone around here knows it, and everyone uses it against me.

If only I could make a peep, I would take over the lion's job at the beginning of all films and roar my heart out. What's left of it.

Not so long ago I bustled from the top of the food chain. Gasconaded my good fortune to the point of ridiculous, which well, in hindsight, might have been my downfall. Dear old dad tossed me in a casket claiming I lacked self-control. He unloaded me on Drac who then rummaged me off to this dungeon. And today's youth get bent if they have their phone privilege revoked a day or two. Try spending an eternity tucked in a tin box in the same skivvies you started out with a quarter century ago without being able to flex a muscle to scratch your balls if you have an itch. Whiners.

Slurping and growls echo throughout the building. Others, in the non-petting portion of the zoo are chomping away on the scraps they are allotted. Dare I say I have a slight issue listening to others eat whilst oblivion nibbles at my shell.

I count. I curse. I count again. When the noise proves too much, I find something else to ease my suffering.

Ah, look at that! I'd point if my arms weren't fastened down with lovely, barbed cuffs laced with vervain. A speckle of dust sifts through the last remnant of sunshine catching my eye. 'Tis dull, no sparkle. It's dust for God's sake. Nowhere near as engaging as one might believe. Delirium washes over me in the same manner an oil spill congeals on innocent wildlife; it is suffocating. This is what happens to the mind when you've been denied sustenance for what feels like dawn's early light. It was probably only yesterday. Call me a mite overtly dramatic, but I am trying to amuse myself in the wake of my wake if I don't bleeding get fed. So, I think of philosophical things. Distractions. Things that yesterday when your belly was bloated and your pants too tight you never would have pacified some idle idiocies to cross your mind. Things that seemed trivial. Trite at best, but today if you haven't the answers you fear your brain will pop like an overinflated actor who just won an Oscar nom. My eyes shift left to right, up then down taking in of what I can of my surroundings. If my head weren't strapped in place with some knock off of Jesus's thorny crown entwined with sprigs of the Hawthorn plant, I'd get a better view of the tomb they have me propped within. Mannequins get more attention than I. They get an occasional change of clothes, a good dusting off… dear lord how I'd love a good dusting off. I'd raise my brows in jest if possible but alas my skin has that Botox resting bitch-face going on. If nothing else, I have less wrinkles than anyone else my age. This is me, my vain attempt to remain positive.

A dull headache nags me. I pray for respite, for all the good it does. Ever notice in situations such as this people bow to their lord and savior, ask for miracles for others, for themselves, a cure for cancer, for world peace, for someone to fall into your lap and offer up a neck… Never happen. God's to-do list must be overwhelming. My current tasks are but two; dine and dash.

Melancholy blankets me in the way dew covers the morning grass. I am weighed down, reticent. So bitterly damp inside even mold regrets growing on me. My cankered heart quickens in pace only to realize the struggle is futile. These invisible confines of my mind are more impossible to breech than the silver cuffs and nails through what was once my masculinity.

The true monsters have achieved their goal. Endpoint. Match game. Xanti Sinclair is about to toss in the towel.

My mind helixes in battle to remain solicitous. A song pops into my head from a few decades' past. Something about God being one of us? Would anyone believe him if he waltzed down the avenue disgorging gibberish from the Holy scriptures? I'd shake my head no but again the whole being staked in place…well it is a redundant idea. And why of all the songs out there did this one pop up? I have no other rendezvous to attend so I allow this inquisition since the bleeding lyrics are on repeat now.

Does Jesus truly save souls? Mine perhaps? Maybe I should have a chat with the bloke. As my stomach begs for sustenance this entire scenario may be more plausible than I had fathomed. I could die. Not today but someday. We, Jesus and I would have tea over the whole good versus evil debate where neither of us win. In attempts to save my soul he sprinkles me with blessed water, and I sizzle and fade away. Yeah, I don't fancy that scenario. If I move up the totem pole to his dad, does God give one those pop quizzes with three questions everyone is so in tuned too? Something about your name? Your favorite color? The air-speed velocity of a virgin swallow? I do suppose I would end up here regardless with that question… If you fail, are you cast out of Paradise for eternity? Tossed to oblivion like rubbish as portrayed in that ridiculously silly python movie?

Maybe I should study.

Is there a plan B for redemption? How many of the Ten Commandments must you break before really getting God's goad? Does God believe an eye for an eye? A life for a life? If so, what does he do with the soul once the body no longer thrives? Forgiveness? Entrance to the pearly gates where all will be forgotten—stuffed under the rug perhaps? Or purgatory and if so, then all the speeches of forgiveness and redemption seem bogus at best. Was confession a means to lure unsuspecting children into a darkened booth and then made to do ungodly acts with those claiming to be so pious, but in reality had souls filled with wickedness? "Don't say a word of what we've done, and all shall be forgiven." Yes, even vampires go to church. The roof doesn't cave in when we enter. But someday, one priest's sanctuary will implode as I exit.

The soft shuffle of sneakers mixed with an occasional squeak from the lad who drags one foot across the marble floor sparked my attention. I wish he'd get his leg fixed. People find anything with which to ridicule others. My nostrils flare in delight. I get a whiff of supper… Time to engage in plan B… Determination and desire set the course to one's dreams. There shall be no tossing of the towel today.

Once done with the infusion, the kid hastily removed the tubing and needle from my skeletal arm, jammed everything into a red plastic bucket adorned with a skull and cross bones sticker, yanked off his purple latex gloves and tossed them in with the rest of the infectious rubbish.

There's really nothing infectious about me, other than my personality, oh, and my bite…

As the boy stepped back and away from the strike zone, he removed the two-inch metal plate protecting his neck.

Brave sweet, stupid lad.

With a slight groan, I caught the boy's attention. Pretty certain my cock jerked when he flinched. I had no idea the limp thing still worked. Finally, after months of futile attempts to make eye contact with the red-haired lad, the kid's precocious nature rose to the occasion. The innocence in those baby blues would soon see the world through a kaleidoscope of twisted history, dreams never achieved, and life disintegrated to ash before he realized he'd stoked the match. Resurrection would create a new following. Hallelujah, maybe Jesus found it in his heart to save me after all. Him, saving sinners one at a time. Me creating them one at a time. Circle of life, baby.

There's an oldie but goodie song from the 60s I used to belt out when I got some babe, and I can picture my father plain as day. His thin lips even thinner in a grimace, his neck veins swelled to the point of bursting when I sang the ditty. It made me giddy. We, dad and I, had an insidious love-hate relationship. He hated me and I so loved making him as miserable as he did me. In the moments to come, this kid would despise the song as well.

With everything I had inside me, my sunken, lifeless black eyes pleaded, begged, bribed, and eventually snared the kid. I had to make my move. Today. One more day in this sarcophagus would be my undoing, even though I'd said that exact thing yesterday and every day before. Today the key dangled before me. *Just a little closer kid.*

The only other time the taste of freedom had graced my lips I'd escaped this shrine for a week. The seven days were short-lived, but the most rewarding, satisfying time I ever recalled.

The memories of my escapades that week have fed my forlorn existence here in solitary confinement. Today a handsome little red head will replace old memories, while making new ones. A smile could have worked its way to my lips had some torturous instrument not blocked it.

Once I had the kid locked in on my mental channel, I spoke to him. *Peek-a-boo!* Oh, the look in his wide, horrified eyes. Precious!

Hello friend. Do not be alarmed. Could you please remove the barbed crown and the object blocking my speech, so I don't use all the juice left in my brain to speak to you? I would be most appreciative. I'd kill to have a conversation with someone.

"And that would be why you have that rusty cork jammed in your mouth."

The ghastly expression on the kid's face when he realized I spoke to him telepathically and he'd answered drove my desire. The boy reeled back and stumbled over the hazardous waste bin only to land on his butt. Hands behind him, he tried to back pedal his way out of the tomb-like exhibit.

About ten feet from me, all breathy, he asked, "How did you do that? I heard you were brain dead. How can you talk to me like I'm one of you? I'm not one of you. I'm no monster."

Not yet.

"Stop it!" The kid's voice bellowed throughout the museum. The wolves heard this and took to howling. The lad appears ready to run. Need to keep him engaged.

Brain dead? My father used to call me that, but as you can see, I'm here in the flesh, or what is left of it. I am having trouble understanding why someone would treat me this way? Why am I on display?

It's not like I am clueless or brain dead, but every conversation needs a beginning.

Curious, the boy rose, crawled back over, sat on his

knees, stretched his neck and peered over the edge of the black tin casket. Just out of reach. "Because you are one of the undead? Because you kill people for the heck of it? Because you're cannibalistic beyond Dahmer? Because you are an amoral, cynical, psycho vamp that is no smarter than a fifth grader?"

Could you please remove this metal jam? I'm not going anywhere. I'm staked down with silver for Satan's sake. And bring me a fifth grader and we'll see who gets the last laugh.

The kid chuckled. "You're twisted." His figurine demeanor cracked. "This is true; you are secured down. All I know is you were brought here before I was born. Dracula deposited you if the story is true."

Name rings a bell.

"That's it? Name rings a bell? He's like the king of the underworld, dude. He's the most notorious demon ever."

Damn, I wanted to smile so badly it hurt. Clearly this kid hadn't met my family. *Kid, I know who Dracula is. Met the man. The myth is so much larger than life.*

"Dude, he put you here, so yeah, he's pretty bad ass."

Please, take this device out of my mouth? I'm as harmless as a mosquito right now.

"Mosquitos are killing people these days—West Nile Virus. Bug spray. Ya need lots of it. Anyway, your teeth, they ripped from you. How do you do that? Make teeth? Even alive people can't make teeth. And they grow right around the cock-stop you got in your mouth and then the curator rips 'em out time after time. That's torture. Your teeth-ah-fangs are really gnarly though."

Gnarly?

"Gross? In need of whitening strips?"

Whitening strips?

"Man, you'd never survive the night if I let you out. How did you get on before you were brought here?"

With a little help from my friends. And there it is, another ditty. I want to dance so bad. *Do you believe my family left me to rot?*

"Yup! People think being a vamp is cool. Not me. You're living proof humans will never let you live in our world."

On a guttural level I agree with the child, but with vehemence I will fight and die for my species. God put us here for a reason.

Fodder control is my guess.

I watched in the mirror as a single red sanguineous tear leaked from the corner of my eye. That single drop got the kid to stand up and lean into the casket. A sudden gust of euphoria swept over me. I know beyond a shadow of a doubt I hold a numinous quality. It's what keeps me alive.

Please? Don't make me beg. My face will probably look like one of those Halloween masks in the horror movies when this is removed.

"Already does, dude. So, you're a movie buff? Didn't think vamps watched television."

Love all flicks. Westerns are the best though. Cowboys. Heard someone mention riding a cowboy instead of the horse. I like the concept.

"Well, we seem to have one thing in common."

You like westerns too?

The kid laughed. "Yeah, that's it."

How old are ya kid? Asking for a friend... My laughter remains muffled. *What's your name?*

"Twenty. Hoping to head back to university in a month. Name's Murph."

To my utter astonishment the kid reached in and with meticulous care wiggled the prongs of the crown from my skull and chucked it aside. Then he attempted to loosen the screw to the pear of anguish keeping my mouth occupied. The kid tugged and fought with the release pin pulling my head forward and back. The headache I thought I had earlier is more like the paper cut you get on your tongue licking an envelope compared to this.

Easy! You'll break my neck.

"You are already dead. This contraption is rusted in place. Hang on."

Staked in place here. Not exactly flexible.

In a surprising display of what would be either faith or stupidity the kid crawled up on the casket and straddled me.

Oh, today just keeps getting better and better.

The boy leaned in and said, "Sorry if this hurts," before he yanked with everything he had. My upper half jerked forward. Something snapped. A vertebrae perhaps? Nope, a rib. Kind of hurts to breathe. Dammit. There's a valid reason people need to move and not lie about all day. Exercise equals bone health.

The kid lost his balance when the rusted bulb tore free of my mouth taking with it, I think half of my bottom lip. Scrambling to get up and away, the kid's foot caught on one of the stakes that held my right arm down and loosened it. In that moment our eyes met and in those precious seconds two worlds collided.

"I got you, babe."

Death met Life. They tangoed. Death slipped his

arm around the curve of Life's back and pulled her tight against him, allowed her to feel the life trapped forever within. Death smiled as he dipped Life backwards, whispering in her ear, "The beginning of the end is when we appreciate life the most, don't you agree?" Death stuck his foot out, knocked Life off balance, and leaned in for the final kiss.

And every conversation has an ending.

"Goodbye, Murph." The smile I'd dreamt of for the past quarter century spread across my handsome face the same way lightning strikes. It's not every day someone lands in your lap. Half dead, low on about five liters of type O, and even stiff as a board did not halt my one shot at freedom. My hand latched onto the kid's crotch, my spindled yellowed nails pierced the kid's jeans as if they were butter, sank in, and with the accuracy of a nutcracker I gripped down and crushed the kid's peanuts. In the kid's next breath his body slumped forward and couldn't have landed more precisely than the space shuttle could have on the moon. New dents descended, I ate like it was the holidays with my fat pants on.

When done, I reached into my breast pocket where someone had ever so nicely tucked a hanky, for show of course. I dabbed the corners of my lips dry then looked up to the camera, tapped my hand over my heart and said, "Thank you. Good to the last drop." Recall that from a commercial and have always wanted to say it.

It's the little things.

All dusted off, new clothing donned courtesy of the museum's fashion department, I came to a staunch halt in front of a full-length mirror. My chest now filled out a bit, shoulders back, chin held high, I admired the new look. My choice in fashion dates me. I loved the

Victorian era when I paraded through the dark alleys, so I borrowed a tail coat, and a top hat. I adore it. It hangs just over my brows and balances attractively upon my pointy little ears. My sideburns curve into my lips and tickle. The sideburns remind me of an actor from days gone by who always asked people, "Are ya feeling lucky?" Yes, I am.

A gold pocket watch, slightly tainted green, hangs from one pocket fob. Broken, but it adds a touch of swagger regardless. I swiped a Victorian pair of spectacles, the frames round and small, the lenses tinted red from one of the displays educating the populous that Salvino D'Armati made reading glasses, not dear old Benny Franklin.

As I skip along the marble floor, the heels of my boots make a delightful click, the sound echoing through the museum. The werewolves and shapeshifters are howling as if someone in their packs has been slaughtered. One of my brows gave a thoughtful shift. Feeling rather charitable after such a feast I decided, not on my watch!

And just like that, with the flick of a master switch, one age-old question had been answered: Who let the dogs out?

I tucked the cell phone I'd borrowed from my dinner into my pocket. I'd replaced it with a note in Murph's pocket, telling him to call me when he wakes. It'll be nice to have a mate to enjoy time with. I think we hit it off quite swimmingly. With the notion I'd walked out of a time machine, I took in a deep breath of fresh air; my senses are overwhelmed.

Freedom. I now understand how old Georgie boy felt as I glided through the front doors from my confinement. His music resonates within whatever part of my soul remains.

How long has it been since I've been dazzled by the stars or gotten a whiff of something other than stale mothballs, odious women saturated in bottles of Eau de toilette water or rotted flesh, which oddly smells better than the cologne...

With the cooler wind in my face, I pulled my jacket tighter, snuggled into the warmth the material offered and headed down Cockspur Street, with my newly found confidence a step or two ahead.

Taking in the crowded sidewalks, people out and about for a million different reasons, I can't find a single reason there is so much negative news on fast food. Dieting, now that was where the problem lay. The spices of life strut by me, some in stilettos, some in flip-flops, some in furry sheep skinned boots, all with the basic same ingredients, crunchy bits, and a jellied soft center.

Yes, the dance I've been denied all these years thrummed from my hips to my toes and any second now there would be a new Lord of the Dance. Drum roll please...

Chapter Two

Hearing a pounding on the door Elyza bristled. "What did you guys forget?"

"Elyza, open up. It's Serina."

Elyza tugged the hefty door open. "My queen bee. What a pleasant surprise."

With her turned up little nose in the air and a genuine grin, Serina declared, "It's about bloody time someone recognized me for my true calling."

Elyza quashed her comments. Her mother, hands down was a piece of work, and God how she loved her. Curiosity piqued, Elyza's brow rose while she watched her mother from the corner of her eye. "What brings you back here? Couldn't wait five more minutes?" Elyza highly doubted it. Her mom was one of those instant gratification types. Now or never was her mantra. Life was too short and there were no guarantees. Serina slinked through the door in a black lace evening gown, the neckline scooped and scalloped with black velvet, her endowment there for the world to see.

Heck, it was impossible to miss and lucky little Elyza had the same genetics. Elyza's mother had a triple D strapped to the front of her along with a waist that was well in fashion a century past; basically non-existent— eighteen inches without a corset strangling her. She wore a necklace of emeralds and diamonds to match her eyes, green and glittering, but Serina's eyes held more beauty

23

than any piece of jewelry in the room. Elyza might have been a tad bias. When her mother gave you her attention, she made you feel like you were the most precious person alive, even if it was a simple, 'Hi'.

"I had to see you… before all the insanity began. Stand back. Let me look at these ice cubes."

Elyza choked. For all her years and intelligence her mother never seemed to pick up on the decade's lingo. It was one of the qualities that made Serina, well Serina and made Elyza love her more than anyone or anything. "Just ice, Momma. The saying is ice."

"Well ice is cold, and you are sizzling."

Elyza buried her face in her hands laughing.

Serina gave Elyza a dismissive shoo of her hand. "Whatever. Show me the outfit. There has to be more to it than this, right? Where is the rest of it?" Serina circled her daughter searching the room for more clothing. "A robe, a paper bag…a moo-moo…"

"A moo-what?" With a gentle shake no of her head, Elyza added, "This is it. All of it." Elyza gave her mother a quick spin trying not to flash her backside too much. "What do you think?"

"Even though the judges knew what they were doing when they picked you, your dear papa is going to have a heart attack. I didn't know one could make bras and thongs from diamonds and gold dust. A lot of diamonds." Serina produced a mischievous grin. "You are stunning. Now, about the choker…"

With her hand tossed in the air and her index finger pointed at the table, Elyza accused, "And there is the true reason for the visit. Aren't you the least bit superstitious?"

"Baby, the only thing any of our family fears are my

spells."

Elyza's mom approached the Hope diamond with a mixture of standoffish caution and unhealthy curiosity. She mirrored a little kid who had been told not to touch something and they were debating whether or not to listen. Serina went for it. Elyza shrieked, "Mom, you're so cheeky. You only came here to get a glimpse of that didn't you?"

Serina cocked her head sideways and winked. "You're using that line on me? Cheeky? Look in the mirror, little girl." Serina slapped her daughter's behind. "Did you know your tush has a dimple?" Serina bit her cheeks when Elyza rushed to the mirror and cranked her head backwards checking out her backside.

"It can't be that noticeable." Elyza's voice came out drenched in anxiety.

"Vanity, kid. The girls told me to tease you when I passed them in the hall. This piece, my little princess, it's surreal."

Serina hoisted the blue diamond from the velvet cloth and placed it against her throat and glanced in the mirror with a gleam of approval. "This is truly stunning. What do you think?"

Elyza gasped, "Mom, good grief! Put it down. The curse, remember?"

"I have at least eight more lives. No worries! No one's tried to off me in this century." Serina carefully placed the necklace back on the table. "Never did I think I raised a superstitious child."

"Growing up in a household of witches I learned caution the hard way." Elyza squinted, her lips thinned, and she pointed to Serina's chest. Elyza reached over to her mother and with her index finger and thumb plucked out a purple nitrile glove tucked in the crevice of her décolletage. "Ewh! When did you turn into Gram? She's always tucking tissues down her bra."

"Nice catch." Serina took the glove from Elyza and headed for the rubbish bin. "I got a call just before heading over here. Another distant cousin was murdered. Well not quite dead, but dead all the same."

"Who?" Elyza had to know. "How distant? Not quite dead?"

"Queen's niece, Delaney. Queen Devona's child from my time. She's a vamp but someone attempted to take her head from her shoulders. I've got her on life support until the Family is notified and arrangements are made."

"I had no idea Devona had more children after her son, Devon. Bet the Family pulls the plug."

"Never made public knowledge for fear another child would go missing. Devona stepped down and relinquished the crown to her cousin, Elaina, so she could raise her child out of the public eye. The girl attacked today is Devon's sister. I'll bet he doesn't even know she exists. Beautiful girl. She was an up-and-coming gem about to outshine the current majesty and her brood. And we know how much the paparazzi are willing to go for a good kill shot and headline. God rest our beloved Princess Dayanna. The world will never be the same. She passed the year you were born."

"I know, Momma. Assassinated at a charity event raising money to save elephants and slaughter the poachers. Anyway, we know how much the queen hates to have the spotlight shine on another. Momma, I hope history isn't repeating itself."

Serina cupped her daughter's cheeks gently. "Just be

aware of your surroundings at all times. We don't know who is behind the murder or how many trees they're willing to burn down to wipe out the family forest. Today's crime scene left me uncomfortable."

Elyza butt in, "Of course it would, Momma. A woman was murdered." Serina tossed her arm around Elyza, but Elyza ducked and backed away. "Sorry, you're pulsing with distress right now."

"Understood." Serina went on like Elyza's needing space was no big deal. "Other things were going on at the crime scene. The assault happened in the same area where all those young girls keep going missing from. I noticed a few men eyeing schoolgirls in a disturbing way that set my alarms off. I asked the cops to investigate the men. I know it's a long shot, but it can't hurt. Oh, one last thing," Serina held her hands out in front of her, pointing to Elyza, "don't call me crazy—"

"Crazy's such a harsh word. Passionate perhaps?" Elyza blew her mom a kiss.

"Funny. Could have sworn I noticed Avery at the murder scene." Serina waited for a response and waved her hand in Elyza's face. "You really think I'm nuts, don't you?"

"No, but Momma, Avery's been dead a long time. If he were alive, don't you believe he would have made his way to you. He so loved you and daddy and Sydney."

"I'm being silly. When you don't have a body, you lack closure."

"Not silly at all."

"I asked the cops to look into him too. As for Princess Delaney, if anything should happen to me, your father knows where she is."

"Momma! That's so cryptic. Stop it."

Teasingly Serina added, "You're the one worried about the choker." Serina leaned in and kissed Elyza's cheek. "Your Auntie Jovan texted me earlier saying I needed to get to the heart of the matter. Said she'd been scrying—more like day drinking, but either way, we both know that's not a good thing. I have no idea what she meant. Anyway, I suppose you need to finish getting ready. Are these things strapped in place?" Serina made a V with her index and middle finger and pointed to Elyza's breasts.

After a huge huff Elyza mumbled, half-joking, half-praying, "They will be." But just to be on the safe side she added some handy-dandy double-sided sticky tape. After a few jarring tugs and no spillage, Elyza felt confident no wardrobe malfunctions or overexposure moments like the one that happened at Super Bowl XXXVIII would mar her evening. The girls seemed to be as well behaved as her hair. "All right Momma, go make sure Lucian isn't laid back in a chair snoring to the heavens."

"Seriously, my love, we're talking about your father. Give him a chair and two seconds and it's lights out. I love you, Elyza. Remember that always. You have my heart. You have given me more joy and laughter and grays than any one person has ever had the fortune of."

"Serina, what the heck? I've never seen a gray on you. You sound like you're trying to say goodbye. I'll see you in like twenty minutes and we'll go eat. I'm starving."

"You know my rules. Never miss the opportunity to tell someone how you feel. Dinner after this is done sounds perfect. I prayed for you to knock 'em dead, baby."

"Momma, the saying is, 'Break a leg,' not knock them dead."

Head twisted slightly, her brows slightly pinched, Serina gave her daughter the once over and then landed her sights on the stilettos Elyza had to wear. "In those heels, Elyza, you stand a very good chance of that happening. There is a reason you work for the Fallen Angels." Serina headed out laughing.

"You're so not funny!" Elyza yelled, even though she was laughing.

Lips scrunched, she bent at the waist and slid one foot into the sandal and secured the strap on her five-inch death trap. Second foot nearly secured, the triple secret coded knock-tap-knock-knock-tap sounded. Elyza hopped over, opened the door to an entourage of men honed from granite and then somehow Pinocchio'd into sheer brutal deliciousness, armed to the hilt with what appeared to be every illegal version of a rifle known to mankind ready to escort her to the main stage. One of the men placed a royal velvet purple cape over her shoulders and with a slight hand gesture offered her the door.

"Time to bring the house down, Ms. St. James. Shall we? You'll have two men in the front of you. Two on your sides and two at your backside. We got you covered since your garments don't."

Elyza elbowed the guard in the ribs. "Frankie thinks he's funny."

"Frankie does too," The guard answered with an innocent grin hoisting his gun in the air.

She knew the routine. They'd practiced it all day except then she'd had real clothes on and sneakers. Things you could strut your stuff in and not spill it. Modeling wasn't what it was all cracked up to be.

Smiling in these shoes should win her the Oscar tonight. Not toppling over?

The night was young, and she wore a four-century old curse around her neck.

Chapter Three

By the time her feet hit the stage, the only thing between her and thousands of fashionistas lay a gold thread and some polished coal. *Here comes Eve in a flashy fig.* When her teeth began to chatter Frankie slipped her a small travel-sized bottle of whiskey.

"Chug. It'll save the porcelain pegs from shattering."

"They're mine, thank you very much." Elyza produced a snarky grin and with one tilt of her head backwards, she downed the liquor.

Once she had the mask secured to her head the view was like looking into the eye of a firework's grand finale. Sydney wasn't joking. She couldn't see shit. Flash after flash branded her retinas as photographers swarmed her. Elyza steadied herself. "Let's do it." The two front guards, Elwood-nicknamed Woody, and Kelvin-probably named after the temperature due to his inhuman ability to heat up a person with a simple glimpse, slinked to the end of the catwalk, their every motion sexy and synchronized. Woody went left and Kelvin to the right. The men hit their spots, held up their rifles in one arm and pulled the triggers back. Paintball baubles filled with colored glitter exploded. Sparkles sifted through the crowds and coated everyone. And all this time Elyza thought the guns were real.

She felt a little foolish until...

The two front guards disrobed. Elyza gasped. One of her favorite movies was about a guy named Mike, who had magical abilities to bring women to their knees performing on stage…These men missed their calling. Ladies in the front rows jumped up waving singles all too enthusiastically. All that remained were buff bodies decorated in skin-colored speedos. Clearly Elyza hadn't been briefed or debriefed about this event. She wasn't a girl for surprises, but in the grand scheme of things, this one had its finer points. For a moment she found something else to gawk at, as did the audience. Only thing better than a man with a tight tush happened to be a stage full of men. From Elyza's vantage the men carried no concealed weapons. The audience's enthusiasm continued as the men flexed their muscles and showed off their physiques. Maybe they had a divergent weapon tucked away, to the left, or right—or possibly straight up? Judging from Shelby and Sydney's reaction she got her confirmation. Both women were nudging each other, eyes bright, jaws wide open, pointing. Even her grandmother, Olivia Spencer joined in the fun. She stood, opened her arms and yelled, "Come to Grandma boys."

"Oh. My. Goddess," Elyza mumbled. Subtlety, it didn't exactly run in their genetics.

Wearing a newly found confidence, Elyza didn't feel anywhere near as naked as she had moments ago. Frankie on her left and the other guard on her right, Bruno took the center stage and followed suit. Shelby's camera appeared and flashes dispersed getting angles that should only be in anatomy books, or a porn magazine. Elyza shot her cousin a nod of approval. Shelby jammed her index finger and thumb in her mouth and whistled. Others in the audience followed.

Frankie turned to her. "Blinging beautiful. Go get 'em, Princess."

"That's not my name," she said sternly.

The announcer backstage cued her start. "And now, here in one of the most majestic halls on earth we welcome our very own Fallen Angel, Elyza, wearing a one of a kind…"

The voice on the intercom faded into white noise. The first few steps she held her breath, then choked when her parents jumped up in the front row waving. Shelby sat casually in her chair, her legs crossed, cowboy boots perched on the edge of the stage. She gave a 'who knew' gesture with her hands just before she gave the nod aimed at Lucian St. James. He pointed at Elyza and yelled, "That's my baby." That's when Serina got on her chair, threw one arm around Lucian for balance and blew kisses at Elyza.

"Show 'em what you got little girl," Serina yelled, "just not all of it. Oh dear lord, Lucian, she's showing it all." No intercom needed.

Lucian pat Serina's behind. "You made a funny, love."

"I wasn't joking. Cover your eyes," Serina shouted at Lucian while her hands blinded the man. Sydney and Olivia were thick as thieves, wrapped in each other's arms laughing.

In the twenty-odd years Elyza had been on this planet, this had to be the first time they ever let their defenses down in public. Facades were hard to keep, but necessary for their survival. Literally and physically, her family were a melded combination of royal pains, witches, werewolves, and vampires. And there were rumors of a crown and a skeleton or two in the closet! Didn't everyone have the essentials tucked away for a rainy day?

Parents! What to do with them? Especially when you look the exact same age even though a century and change split the difference.

As if wearing nothing at all in front of an entire theatre and television cameras wasn't enough to get you noticed. With a subtle glance to her hip, she made sure the concealer still covered the birthmark. That stupid little blemish acted more like a bullseye. Everyone born of royal blood carried it. More like branded with it.

Nothing but skin showing. Regardless, something was off.

One foot strategically placed in front of the other, Elyza executed long sexy strides praying her feet remained grounded. She scanned the amphitheater and found her focal point and wished she hadn't. Duncan Thomas, Shelby's father, perched himself on the balustrade of the upper balcony, his feet dangling over the edge, waving with one hand, holding a video camera in the other.

Even with all the background noise of the crowd and the music blaring she heard him yell, "Lizzy, you shine brighter than that zirconia, baby."

Duncan, she yelled in her mind, *you daft imbecile, get down.*

Your father is the daft imbecile little girl, not me.

At this exact moment I beg to differ. Please get down.

The fool would fall to his death if not careful. What the heck was wrong with her family tonight? She'd done modeling jobs before where they'd all behaved. It was the after parties where everyone let their hair down and fangs flash. She sought Shelby out through their telepathic channel.

Look at your dad, Shells. It may be the last time you see him if someone doesn't get him down.

Shelby stood and aimed her camera at the balcony. "Daddy!" She waved. Flashes went off in that direction. *He's such a character. Isn't he?*

Shells, get him down.

He's fine, Lizzy. Watch your own butt. Oh wait, I think the guards are. Hahaha!

If she hadn't found out the first time how much it hurt to shake her head, she'd do it again, but pain had a memory. Frustration and worry were about to take center stage. At the end of the catwalk she spun, her royal purple cape flowing like soft liquid waves on a moonlit lake around her slender figure. She did what she was asked to do, give the audience the slightest tease of what lay beneath. With one hand on each side of the cape she slowly opened it, cocked one hip forward, edged her leg out, flipped the mask up and winked to the crowd before she snapped the edges of the cape closed, lowered the mask, and spun on those spikes with perfect balance. On her way back to the beginning of the stage she let the cape drop to the floor and spun just as another song began. Two more trips to the end of the walkway and she was done with her Lady Godiva stint.

She had this. The crowd went wild, got her juices flowing. Okay, maybe she overreacted earlier. Maybe her nerves were toying with her but being a witch and an empath, she could pick up catastrophic events due to her precognitive abilities, and right now her inner voices were acting more like Cybil with her imaginary friends having a brawl at the Running of the Brides dress sale. A moment later the audience began a chant of, "Rock the runway."

Yes, the 'O' she'd teased of earlier just might happen. This aphrodisiac, standing in front of a live crowd having everyone's attention and pleasure, soaked into her skin better than any bottle of champagne, oysters, berries slathered in dark chocolate, with a seriously hot male massaging her where the sun didn't ever stand a chance at shining over could have. She shucked oysters; they were slimy and gross. The hot guy massaging her? She did a quick glance of the audience and noticed a young man busy jotting down notes. He looked up. When their gaze met his smile shot like a poisoned arrow between her legs. Embarrassed, Elyza barely was able to smile back. Then before their staring contest got awkward, she gave a slight sway of her hips and veered to the left of the runway for all the photographers to get their one in a million shot while she did a slow spin. She looked back to see if she still had the man's attention. When they connected, a second arrow pierced her heart.

Passing her family, Lucian got his last laugh in. *Lizzy's got a dimple.*

You're an imbecile, Daddy.

See, told ya he is and always will be the imbecile. Duncan chuckled.

Together, all her family, Serina, Lucian, Olivia, Sydney and even Shelby told Duncan, *Get down ya daft old man.*

Elyza crossed the stage and repeated her actions for the cameras on the right side. When she hit the last two feet of the runway, she glanced up praying Duncan had come to his senses, but no, the silly man now thought he was some high-wire tight rope walker.

Getting a sharp pain in the center of her back, Elyza touched her back. Her fingers came away covered in sparkle paintball goo. She attempted to brush the glitter away but it soaked into her skin.

About to shout, "What the f...?" Elyza glanced at Kelvin on the front right corner of the stage. He was laughing with the gun aimed at her. "Did you just ping me?" Mad one second, the next? "Oh, that felt really good. Holy crap, you are scorching hot." Elyza waved her fingers in front of her face pretending her hand was a fan. Then she shot a quick glance at Elwood and found out fast why they called him Woody. The man had a tree trunk tucked in his speedo...a tree trunk she might consider climbing. With the erratic ride of her emotions racing around a speedway she twisted back to the crowd and glanced up. Duncan teetered on the balcony. She had precious moments left before whatever just hit her like a fully charged dildo would take total effect, to get him off the ledge. "Get him down," Elyza pointed and screamed, but it was too late. Some guy sat behind Duncan yelled, "I can't see around you, mate," and shoved him off. In an attempt to suspend him Elyza thrust her powers at Duncan with as much animation as she could muster and in doing so realized she appeared like a demonic high priestess in a cartoon. With a quick glance down at her silhouette she added X-rated, graphic, to demonic high priestess.

"Marshmallows!" Elyza decreed. Why? She was fresh out of spells and thought of the ridiculous marshmallow giant in the old ghost movie that busted into NYC to save the day. Duncan needed something big and spongy to land in. The sugary confection she conjured left the theatre to resemble the aftereffects of a fluffy avalanche. A little overkill. That's how Elyza rolled—all or nothing.

Regardless, Duncan slipped through all the fluff. Faces, forever captured on film, mouths open in full scream mode, eyes wide with horror, some clamped shut trying to block out Duncan's image crushing the people below, would haunt her till the end of her days.

She spun to Shelby, ready to run to her, but Shelby stood there in a trance, her camera clicking frame after frame, lost in the moment. Elyza on the other hand, posed for countless photographers, her hand on her hip, her chin held high, her little turned up nose even higher. Ah, the wonders of mood-altering drugs.

There Duncan's broken body lay forgotten, blood leaking from where there shouldn't have been holes. The people he landed on, in no better shape.

Pouring on a sultry swagger, rolling his shoulders backwards, his pecs and ab muscles defined, Frankie slinked over to Elyza. He leaned into her and whispered something in her ear she couldn't quite make out, but with the effects of the splat guns potions her imagination went into overdrive.

When he reached down into his speedo and removed a second tiny bottle and held it up, Elyza groaned, "There goes that fantasy. Packing, huh Frankie?"

"I'll unpack for you later. Drink up and save the world as you know it." He wiggled the bottle in her face.

Elyza reeled back, confused. Right now she should be hopping mad, not wanting to hop the hot guy, who oddly had an antidote to whatever the paintballs held in them. "How come I can touch you and not want to die?

That's never happened. I've never been able to touch a single person without experiencing something. Usually pain."

"It's the potion in the paintballs."

Was it time to listen to that annoying inner voice instead of telling it to bugger off? She felt so fecking fabulous right now all she wanted was, well…Frankie, Woody, Kelvin and maybe a few others on the stage, giving the audience an entirely different show. The Vagina Monologues would look like a Sunday sermon by the time this charade ended.

"Elyza!" Frankie gave her shoulders a jerk.

"What?"

"Look at your friend, Duncan. Snap back to reality, Princess."

"Don't call me that. You trying to get me killed?"

He untwisted the cap and shoved the bottle in her grasp. "No, but someone else is. Chug!"

"Seriously the last thing I want my lips on is something cradled next to your junk." Regardless Elyza slipped the mask from her face and then spun so her back was to the audience, wiped the top off the bottle, and guzzled. The drink, whatever it was, had a nuclear effect on her system. People can talk all they want about sobering up in the face of adversity, but this concoction took Elyza to the extreme. Never in her life had she experienced anything so mind-blowing, so targeted on the present and how to react. Her vision became that of a hawk, lethal. A second aftershock shook her like Santa stuck in a Christmas snow globe.

Sparkles. She was over them.

Elyza grabbed Frankie's shoulders for balance. "Why? Why would you give me a drink before I came out here and then give me another? You trying to take advantage of me?"

"It's not like that, I swear." Frankie spun Elyza around. To everyone watching the show, they dirty danced. He slid one leg through hers and yanked her close to him. He grabbed her around the waist, slid his hands behind her back and rocked her upper torso left to right so she appeared to sway in his arms. He pulled her back into view and whispered, "They weren't supposed to shoot you."

Her voice splintered in anger. "But the audience was ok? Who's they?"

Frankie swung Elyza out, their arms fully extended just before he tugged and reeled her back to him with an underarm spin to boot. She crashed into his chest, his hips, his manhood, his one arm hitting her in the small of her back. "Don't touch me." She attempted to get away from his touchy-feely fingers.

"Look Princess—"

Elyza snapped, "I said not to call me that. Why shoot the audience with drugs? They're innocents."

"So whomever won the bidding wars on the jewels wouldn't recall us stealing them. We're running out of song, sunshine. Another ten seconds and the bell will chime twelve and you my dear, are going to turn into a hot mess and I'll bet you can't run in those heels…"

"Stop it. Get away from me!"

Frankie gave her a final spin and let her go but he remained close.

Hand to her face she ripped the mask off and rubbed her eyes hard, hoping to clear not only her vision but also the fogginess she seemed to be swallowed by. Euphoria one second, paranoia the next. Why on earth, she wondered, would people willingly do drugs? Not having control of thoughts, emotions, or plain old smarts to distinguish right from wrong? Pain filled her soul for all those who did drugs to escape whatever Hell they were trapped in, not realizing they were digging a direct route there in the process.

Elyza took a calming breath and scanned the audience. People swayed, sang, and chanted her name. The effects of the paintball's juju were no longer affecting Elyza, thanks to Frankie's little potion, but the audience? From what her parents had told her she envisioned Woodstock being something like this; happy, stoned, having sex in the balcony… She did a double take. Yup, there were couples bumping uglies to the song covered in—well, Elyza was hoping it was the marshmallow—white, creamy.

The crowd cheered louder, "Take it off. Take it all off." Seriously? There wasn't much more the imagination needed to elaborate on. Fist pumping, lighters were held high as if she were at the encore of a concert.

Brandishing his weapon, Bruno yelled, "Frankie, step back, we don't want to get you accidentally. Elyza, strip. Show us what you got."

Elyza sized up the last two guards on stage who were blocking the exit from the stage. Dick Junior, and Nugget, were both aptly named. In Elyza's mind there were only a handful of men equipped to wear speedos, and these two weren't it. They demanded the same thing. "Take it all off, Ms. St. James. Show us the goods."

"Be careful what you ask for. I warned ya." Prodding her fingertips into Frankie's chest she allowed all the powers she curtailed most days to travel through her to her dance partner. He was about to do more than the two-step. Sparks sizzled from his ears, eyes, nose and mouth. He took a few off-balance steps before he fell doing two backward summersaults, landing on his belly, his speedo now down around his thighs. Shelby fled to the edge of the stage making certain she got all the angles of him on her camera. "Shelby, for the love of God, get to your dad."

Elyza stomped over to Nugget. Before she could say a word, he jammed the gun in her face. Pissed? Outraged? No one word summed up her fury. She crammed her finger in the barrel to plug the opening. Later, if she lived, she'd worry over the repercussions. "You're next."

Laughing at her, Nugget demanded, "Shut up and hand over the goods and just maybe you can get to your fallen friend's aid. Procrastinate and everyone dies."

About to blast him into oblivion Frankie made it to his knees and caught her attention yelling. "Princess!"

What bloody part of not calling her Princess did he not get? She turned in Frankie's direction dislodging her finger from the gun's barrel. Frankie scrambled, stumbling over his thong, trying to get to her. Bruno ran straight at her leaping at the very last second over her, going for Frankie.

A deafening rush of air exploded. Instant headache, eyes watering, the suffocating scent of gunpowder left her in a proverbial mushroom cloud. The entire amphitheater looked like photographs being shown through an old View Master, one frame after another...gunshot—picture of someone dying. Gunshot—someone falling from the balcony. Gunshot— someone's arm blown completely away flying haphazardly through the crowd and landing in some horrified woman's lap. The process continued until a bullet pierced her mother.

Mid-lunge, Frankie screamed, "Drop, Elyza."

Frozen in shock, Elyza couldn't move. With the emotions in the hall ranging from panic to hysteria to disbelief to a full out frenzy, she was about to decorate the stage with nothing that resembled a girl's best friend. Bruno tripped and rolled to an awkward stop at her feet with two jagged holes in his chest. Frankie came at her, staggered, his hand covering his neck. Blood gushed through his fingers, dripping down his chest. His knees buckled and he fell.

"What the hell is happening?" Trapped in a hellish time continuum, Elyza took in the hall. Not thirty seconds ago the theater had music filling people's souls; They were dancing in the isles, enjoying life. Now those souls took flight to higher grounds. When a rapid spray of gunfire exploded, Elyza screamed and didn't stop. She tried to find her family, but unshed fury blinded her. All the guests in the audience, magazine publishers, clothing designers, models, photographers, merchants, media, caterers, philanthropists, street urchins, innocent people, everyone that had come to see her, come to help benefit such a worthy cause to find a cure for vampirism, lay in discombobulatcd hcaps, thcir clothing saturated in death. Small fires from the lighters that were used earlier for encores set the white confections Elyza created to buffer Duncan's fall into an all-out bonfire. Glitter from the paintballs still coated most of the people. Those still breathing and able to flee had been turned into live sparklers scramming for the doors; others were dowsed with melted sugar and engulfed in flames. So many distraught figures screaming for their lives, it reminded her of a scene from some pyrotechnic horror flick where she was the star, and the villain all in the same breath. And then there was her mother.

And it was all her fault.

"Stop, drop and roll people!"

Desperation swallowed her words as body after body succumbed. Why hadn't the sprinkler system kicked in? Surely this place had to have one. Just because it was built in 1871 there had to be some code ordinance the city used to update the safety features. This was present day England, not the Stone Ages.

Her mother, her best friend, her everything, had a hole in her chest big enough for a bowling ball to roll through and not hit a single pin. Serina's head lay flopped on the back of the chair, her gorgeous green eyes somewhere in Never Land. Blood splatter covered Lucian. Olivia held her bloody hand over Serina's chest and went to work doing what she did best, healing people without the need for conventional tools or hospitals. Olivia was the most powerful mage on the planet and if she wanted something, she got it by any means possible. Aided by her sidekick, Elyza's grandpa, Father Thomas Butler, a true fallen angel, a white lighter, Elyza had hope.

"Bra, leaf and mask now, Ms. St. James. Oh, and the paperweight around your neck too, if you please." Dick Jr. waggled his fingers under her nose. "Do it or the next round takes out the back of your dear father's head." Nugget poked her in the back with his rifle.

Elyza gave an indignant snort before she spun and slammed her fist into the Nugget's crotch and gave him her own personal version of being tased, adding a little juice of her own. He doubled over and went down. Kelvin jammed the end of his rifle in her chest.

"That wasn't very nice. Give us the goods, love."

"Whatever!" The jewels weren't hers and no one else's lives were worth this. Elyza ripped the bra off taking a top layer of her flesh with it no thanks to the double-sided sticky tape. She chucked it off the end of the stage. "You want it, get it yourself." Kelvin didn't waste a second and did a header into the crowd after the garment. Elyza didn't notice if Kelvin got up, but she hoped he didn't. "Why the feck did you have to shoot all the women? I'd have given you the crap."

Wheezing after having been shocked, Nugget bragged, "Because there's nothing worse for a man to know he can't protect his family, Lizzy. Lucian is experiencing this now."

"Then your family must consider you the biggest loser ever." She wiggled the golden thong to get it over her knees and off. The garment dropped to the floor with a weighty clunk. She kicked the bedazzled raiment into the first row of seats.

Woody came up behind Elyza and with one hard tug ripped the Hope Diamond from her neck. "Ta, babe."

Without a split second to spare, Elyza squared off to face the guard. Her finger tapped her bottom lip. "Woody, have you ever heard of a spitfire? Did you know there are people out there with the ability to accomplish just that? I'm not talking about circus acts where people inhale flammable ingredients and then are stupid enough to add a match to it or swallow a flaming sword pretending to be a human shish kabob." Elyza crooked her finger bringing the assailant closer. "Woody, watch closely," she whispered just as she pulled her powers from deep inside her. Her hatred for this man and the others on stage consumed her. They'd killed innocent people and one of them put a bullet in the one person on this earth she loved more than life. Her mother. Elyza inhaled. Her chest expanded then contracted a few times, her energy growing more violent than the Great Fire of 1666 that began on Pudding Lane. Tonight, history would reign down and leave that night in ash comparatively speaking when she finished with these heathens. She opened her mouth and made some gross hacking noise cats make before she spit out a ball of fire. "Fire and Wood—You're about to go up in smoke. Ta babe!"

Horror crossed the guard's smug demeanor seeing a huge ball of flames smack his abdomen. "You're a..."

An evil snarl formed on Elyza's lips. "A hot mess? Yes, I suppose you could say that."

Fingers splayed, he dropped the necklace as flames began to devour him. Another moron that didn't know the necessary combo of putting a fire out and she'd die a slow death before she spewed one word to him as how to. The sight wasn't pretty, and Elyza knew she'd overstepped her boundaries using her gifts for nefarious reasons, but right now, torching this murdering scoundrel was all she could think of before he killed someone else. With a second to spare Elyza spun back to Nugget. His fate would be the same, but she was too late. He'd vanished along with Dick junior... the necklace and the mask.

"Dammit!" Stood in all her glory for the world to see, Elyza stomped over to the purple cape kicking Bruno's dead body in passing. She reached over him, grabbed the cape, wrapped it around her shivering, naked body and forced her lungs to work. At the end of the runway she slid down to the floor to make her way to her mother. "Lucian, get her out of here. Where is everyone?"

Almost incoherent, Lucian pointed to the door. "I think Raven grabbed Sydney. Savanah and Ethan went for the car."

Elyza couldn't figure this catastrophe out. People were corralled into the venue, a stampede happening as hundreds vied for the same exits at the same time. Bodies under feet, people were being crushed like half-smoked cigarettes as others attempted to flee the inferno. "Brick and mortar crumble and fall. Be gone wall. Make an escape route before all is moot." Once more she went deep inside her chi and gathered her energies. When the trickle of energies grew until she could no longer contain them, she pointed at the wall just to the right of the exit where most of the crowd had gotten sardined into. She directed her powers in a direct line, like a laser pointer and drew an imaginary door much wider than the current exit. The wall exploded outwards making room for people to get out. Hopefully, it would save some. She looked back on her mother's lifeless body and gulped down hope.

Lucian latched on to his father-in-law's shoulder. "Thomas, we need to move."

Father Thomas Butler's white hair stuck to his forehead dripping with a mixture of blood and sweat. His huge blue eyes were streaked with worry. Father Butler pointed. "Lizzy, go to Duncan and aid Shelby."

"Are you certain Serina is ok? Because seriously," Elyza pointed to the hole in her mother's chest, "I'm no doctor but I don't think that," and she screamed the next part, "fecking hole isn't supposed to be there."

"Lizzy, go baby. Shelby needs help. Thomas will be over in a minute. Now go. Your mum would be upset if she saw you worried."

"I am upset, Daddy. I've never seen so much blood or ribs!" Elyza wiped her eyes and gasped. "I'm going to pass out."

A bloodied hand settled lightly on Elyza's arm leaving a tingling sensation all the way to her toes. "Lizzy, you're stronger than this." Olivia softened her tone, "Sparky, get away so I can focus on saving your mother's life. Can't worry about you too."

"Liv, don't you let her die."

"She will get my last breath, baby. Go help Shelby with her dad." Tears welled in Olivia's eyes as she grabbed Elyza's hand and kissed her goodbye.

"Elyza!"

She used my real name. As if this cluster fuck wasn't enough evidence to make the situation undeniably real, Shelby used her real name. There was never a day she did that. Elyza kissed her father's cheek and began the daunting task of climbing carefully over bodies to get to Shelby.

Duncan. The woman he'd crushed when he'd fallen lay lifeless. The man beside her, possibly her husband, sat in a total state of shock rocking her and sobbing, the two of them covered in a tannish-brown melted mess.

"Daddy, someone will be here in just a minute. Hang on." Shelby's hands were shaking while she tried to soothe her father. "What the hell happened, Lizzy?"

In a rush of words Elyza blurted, "I think they used some crop-dusting potion in the paintballs to let everyone's guards down. Kava perhaps? Or Valerian or

Passionflower. Or a combo of all three? They're all relaxants. Or Skullcap. That one knocks me out."

"You're babbling but you're still standing, Lizzy."

Elyza pointed to the ruins of the amphitheater choking back tears. "Why? Why did they go to all this elaborate mess? All they had to do was get me in the dressing room. Frankie gave me the antidote before they killed him. I don't understand."

"Lizzy, stop thinking and help my dad."

"You know I don't have those abilities, Shells. I can't save people like my mom and gram. But I can kill them. And not with kindness."

"What you did to that guard, I would have too if I had that ability."

"I'm literally the black sheep in the family."

"I call bull on that, Lizzy. You're the best out of all of us. A heart of gold. Willing to do whatever it takes. Now help me."

Regardless, Elyza knew the truth. She'd murdered a person.

"Lizzy, I need to stop the bleeding." Shelby ripped her jacket off and tried to tear it into strips to bandage her dad's head. Head wounds: Even paper cuts resembled a machete slice.

His face disfigured from pain, blood running into and around his eye, Shelby used her sleeve and dabbed at his face to clear his vision. Duncan placed his hand on top of Shelby's. "Sweetheart, stop. I'll be fine." He pointed to the exit. "Girls, get out of here. The fire is out of control. Go now."

Elyza grabbed Duncan's arm. "There is no way we are leaving you, old man. Can you wiggle your toes? Walk? Please say you can walk."

"One way to find out."

Elyza grabbed under Duncan's arms and Shelby reached around her father's lower back and together they carefully lifted him from the rubble and got him to his feet.

"You ok, Daddy?" Shelby asked when Duncan yelped with his first step, but he kept going.

Elyza addressed the man cradling the woman Duncan crushed on his fall. "Mister? Come on. Follow us out."

"I'm not leaving my wife."

The resolve in the man's eyes, Elyza knew he would never leave her, and he would willingly die beside her. Truest of love. Elyza could not let the man die. Period. She used her mental lines of communication and pinged Savanah's husband, Ethan, who was helping others get out of the building. *Ethan, there's a guy and his wife beside Duncan. He'll die.*

Ethan showed up before Elyza finished asking for help. Careful with the woman, Ethan draped her in his arms. "Sir, follow us out of the building. I have her." Sniffling and wiping his eyes, the man followed.

The overwhelming blare of sirens replaced the once joyous music that filled the amphitheater minutes past. Duncan's pain, coupled with every other person's fear in this building flooded Elyza's soul. She bent at the waist and held her head and screamed something inaudible.

Shelby reached over and placed her hand on Elyza's arm. "Breathe sweet tart. Don't lose your superhero powers now. I need you."

With a tight-lipped grimace, Elyza mumbled, "I love you, Seashells."

"Ditto. Now move that dimpled ass."

Chunks of the once ornate ceiling caved in around them.

The wall she'd expanded moments earlier now had a ring of fire blocking the exit.

"Fabulous! We are so not jumping through that. Grampa!" Elyza's voice bellowed, "Rain. Make it fecking rain in here."

And the droplets fell with as much as enthusiasm as standing at the bottom of a waterfall. Drenched, the cape Elyza wore clung to her better than her own flesh. Made it tricky to maneuver in. Smoke and steam rose from burnt bodies, clouding the path. If Elyza survived this night with so much raw madness it would be an absolute miracle. Stepping over a body her heel caught on the hem of the cape and before she could do anything, she went down taking Duncan with her and walloping her head on one of the chair's arms. Trying to get her footing and hands under her for leverage she slipped again in a glob of paintball glitter. "No! Shells, get Lucian to help you. I'm seeing stars. Duncan, I am so sorry. Tell me I didn't hurt you?" Flattened on the mucky, dank floor Elyza's fingers brushed up against something rough and chunky. Snagging it she spared a quick glance; it was one of the articles she'd worn on stage. She jammed the jewels into the pocket of the cape and waited like a damsel in distress to be rescued.

Duncan attempted to assure her, "It's all right, Elyza, the head's the one thing on me ya cannot crack. Trust me. Your dear daddy and uncles have tried countless times."

"Mine isn't as hard as yours." Right now Elyza had double vision. Was it the drugs? The concussion? The alcohol? Her head meeting the concrete floor full force?

Or a not-so-comical parody of ill-timed events that culminated with the discharge and authority of some cataclysmic event? "Knock 'em dead baby," Serina had said to Elyza, instead of breaking a leg… Frustrated tears and sobs filled her eyes and throat. Why couldn't her mom have gotten it right the first time?

And then the guilt settled in for making this mess all about her mother's misuse of the English language.

After what seemed like an eternity, Lucian bent over and picked up Duncan from atop of Elyza. "Shelby, help Lizzy out of here. Follow me girls and don't lose me. The smoke is thick. Olivia wiggled her nose getting Serina and Thomas out."

"Are they okay?"

Lucian reiterated, "Stay close."

The fact that he didn't try to quell Elyza's fears spoke volumes of just how dire the predicament really was. Like she didn't already know life and death hung in the balances. He could have lied to her. But then she'd never have forgiven him. Their relationship from day one was all about trust.

"Lizzy, my camera! I can't find my camera." Shelby let go of Elyza's hand and got down on her knees and hands in search of it.

"Shells, forget the blasted thing. We gotta get outta here. And I got more of that fecking sparkly stuff all over me."

"Not to worry, Lizzy. Vamps don't really sparkle. They glare and even though you have mastered the sneer I am not leaving without it." Shelby stammered adamantly, "It's got the faces of those goons on it. I'm gonna hang them to dry."

"Forget it. You and I are the only ones hanging out

to dry if we don't get moving."

Lucian's voice filled the hall. "Elyza, Shelby, the place is starting to cave. Duck!" He barely finished saying that before the upper balcony made its final decent to the lower level. Velvet chairs spilled onto the amphitheater below, bodies included. Dust mixed with smoke made it nearly impossible to see or breathe.

Was this what it felt like to be buried alive? Elyza thought back to all the terrorist events in the recent past and said a prayer for all the lives lost to ignorance, racism, tragedy, and hatred by people who held greed and prejudice in place of God, their family and love. Elyza shoved a heavy hunk of plaster out of the way and kept going.

"Found the camera! And I found the top half of your outfit." Shelby stuffed the diamond bra into Elyza's hand.

Elyza jammed the garment into a pocket on the cape. At least she had the outfit. "Shells? You with me?" With a tug to the back of her cape, together they proceeded toward the door. "Don't let go. I think we're almost out."

Chapter Four

With swift purpose, Zander Templar bolted toward his one-bedroom flat. The one that looked exactly like every other cottage along the avenue, baring mildewed, white brick exteriors, chipped slate roofs, and in all likelihood, buckets or pans sporadically placed throughout the flat to catch a leaky drip. The only defining difference going down the lane? Everyone else had gardens versus withered dandelions, had grass in place of dirt, took meticulous care of their shrubbery, and had real curtains hung instead of bed sheets.

Inconspicuous throughout his jaunt home would have been splendid instead of the outlandish mess he had going on. The sirens in the background might have had something to do with his rapid retreat yet did nothing for his current state of health.

If he were to drop dead here and now the mortician would probably discover an acidic swamp growing in his gut. He had no idea what was going on, but he had this new pain every sunrise as of late, or when he went to eat, drink or the saddest most aggravating part, every time sex crossed his mind. And seriously? How many times a day did that happen? He was, after all, in the prime of his life.

Frustrated, he raked his fingers through his thick mop and grimaced finding a tender lump on the back of his head he didn't recall acquiring. The pain had him doubled over dowsing a nearby shrubbery with his last meal of fish and chips. Wiping his mouth, a loud gasp caught his attention. An elderly woman, her head adorned with pink spongy curlers, donned in a pink shaggy robe, stood on her stoop staring him down from the tip of her judgmental nose. The paper she'd only just acquired she dropped. With haste she scurried back inside her flat, losing one of her slippers in the process. His hand up in retreat to flag her down, he heard the lock of the door snap in place. Since the slipper was not made of glass and since he had never been dubbed Prince of Anything, she would not receive someone knocking her up asking for her shoe size. Damsels in distress weren't his thing.

Zander glanced down the front of his body. Perfect, a witness that knows diddly squat and a victim, him, who had even less of a clue about his predicament. Blood leached his clothes. In this current state of dishevelment, he resembled an extra in a zombie show. No one could be wearing this much blood and still be alive. Thankfully it wasn't his. Would have been nice to know who's it was and how he ended up covered in it. The priest costume would be a good one to figure out too, since holier than though he was not. *What the hell happened to me?*

As he continued by, he bent down and pinched the woman's Daily Mail since she had no use of it. First thing that caught his eye—the date. Losing an hour or two was one thing, but the past day? And second, the headlines: The front page looked like a grid map with linear black lines quartering sections to signify the stories equal importance. One last picture blocked in the center: All that was missing was mug shots.

Soon, if the coppers found him, he would be

glamming the covers of all the posts.

Top left corner byline read: The Hall Royal is a royal loss thanks to a Fallen Angel. Recovery efforts in progress.

Top right byline had a photo of an exhibit at Museum Piccadilly: Vampire flees, taking with him all the fleabags.

Bottom left photo showed the fleabags, which most people believed were the fabricated, over-active imaginations of Hollywood and authors—vampires, shapeshifters and werewolves in London. This town was about to get fun.

The bottom right picture had Zander's full attention: a local priest drained of all his blood. DNA galore amongst all the gore. Zander wiped the raindrops from his eyelids and strained to look through the plastic wrap covering of the paper again. With a sparing glance at his new attire something visceral sucker punched him. Finally, the center photo had a picture of a stunning woman, green eyes, dark blonde hair, and ruby red lips. The caption read: A Pine Box for the Princess.

The page showcasing the priest put his mind into a tailspin, talking to himself. "You've gotta be kidding. There's no way I did this. Did I? I'm not a monster or a vamp. Am I? No, I'm just an insane wanna-be journalist without a valid tagline or alibi! Or job, hence the word wanna-be." With a quick look over his shoulder he opened the front door to his flat and slammed it behind him, latching the lock in the process. He flew to the windows and peeked out behind the makeshift curtain-bed sheet to see if anyone followed him. A streamline of sirens and police sped by. He drew the sheets' edges together and resting his head on the wall, practiced breathing. Freaked out over the paper's depiction of a vamp attack and unable to catch his breath, he fled for the bathroom, yanking the withered string to the overhead light. Lips peeled back, his dentist would have been proud of the care he took of his teeth. No fangs. That would have made his mother happy.

If he had one.

He exhaled one hefty sigh of relief before he made his way to his darkened bedroom and started to strip off the stolen blood-soaked clothes. Not stolen. He reneged that, didn't like the sound at all. Borrowed perhaps. Pilfered from a box the rich donated to the poor?

Charity it is.

He balled up the bloodied clothes and tucked them in the corner. Later, he would discard them. Bury them far, far away.

After he burnt them. In a hurry to get back into the bathroom to take a quick shower he fumbled over a very sparkly sandal and kept right on going.

This, whatever it was, whoever's it was, blood, had to go. Down the drain. Followed by a gallon of bleach. If he learned nothing else over the past few years, he knew this from watching all the forensic shows on television. Murderers should clean up after themselves. Nothing like teaching inmates the latest ways to commit the perfect crime once they're free to rove. *Aw, jeez, I just categorized myself as a murderer. I didn't kill anyone.* He glanced over at the wad of clothing, the frock—not his. The pants that were two sizes too big? Holiday turkey pants perhaps? His shoes—a smattering of red fluid stuck to his trainers. Something in his gut sank.

His freedom once caught. Parole board would have

him strung up before a lynch mob before teatime. He could not, would not, never ever set foot in jail again. Not for anything or anyone. Ever!

He glanced back at the blood-stained clothing.

He snuffed out a groan.

Blood was supposed to stay inside the body. Not be worn like he'd mutated into the devils incarnate flaunting some masochistic ritual. *So now I'm the Devil's cohort. This day just keeps getting better and better.*

He removed his Celtic cross and hung it on a small tack on the wall. Out of the shower and mostly dry he put the chain back on and turned the light off in the bathroom. There was no need to look in the mirror. There was never a day the reflection smiled back at him. The physical picture had been painted over the past years like an apartment that got rented, painted, rented again and painted again. Lost dreams, insecurities and loneliness were well hidden under the layers of marred flesh. Shallow yes, but reality dictated his world and everyone else's. Like it or not life's glory belonged to the pretty people and sadly, from his perspective beauty went no farther than skin deep. He could dig all the way to Shangri-La searching for someone to change his mind and still only end up with slugs. His scars were a constant reminder, both inside and out, that everyone wanted something. Some wanted his hide. Some, his soul. His heart had yet to be claimed. Loneliness hurt more than the scars. The keloids on his back read better than braille in a book; they told his story. One no reader ever wanted to crack the spine open to journey inside.

One scar seemed to be the focal point of his life, where his past collided with his present and like an exploding star went their separate ways. No one could explain it, the doctors, nurses, priests, or police. The linear jagged-edged mesh of thickened skin ran from beneath his Adam's apple to his navel. Its width measured three inches. That scar initiated him into the foster system. And his last memory of his life before it happened. At four years of age most kids have families, friends, someone to hold their hand across a street, or to sing them to sleep, teachers, a life of picture books, a stuffed animal to cling to for comfort in their darkest hour, memories, even if it's bits and pieces; something. Zander had a plastic wristband with the name Jon Doe. And his Celtic cross. For all he knew a nurse probably gave it to him while he lay in a cold room in a crib with a mattress covered in a plastic binder in case he had an accident.

Someone wiped his slate clean. He didn't even know his name when he woke up in the hospital. The nurses in the pediatric intensive care unit saved not only his life, but soothed and comforted a scared little boy as best they could right up until he'd been dragged away kicking and screaming by a social worker. She delivered him to one of many temporary houses. Not homes. The places he resided had nothing warm or inviting about them.

Along his back, buttock, and legs more scars lay concealed from being whipped. He wore them as a badge of honor, having survived the brutal savagery of those entrusted to care for him. Yet deep down beneath the surface, wounds festered. He wanted answers. Needed them. Deserved them. It was one of the reasons he wanted to become a journalist. Reporters had great access to anything, and all legitimately done under the First Amendment. Well, most of it anyway.

He ran his hand over the scar that passed across his

heart. A foreboding loss enveloped him when he touched it. He couldn't explain it and it, the feeling never diminished. Was he ripped from a loving family? Was he thought dead and missing? He never noticed a photo of himself on any milk containers. Did his family give up on him? Or maybe his family detested his very existence and tried to eviscerate him. Someone came bloody close. His head started to pound.

He made his way to his bed. The thick flannel black sheets were worth their weight in gold. The room was blacker than any charm he'd ever been made to perform when he was being bounced through the farming system. Illusionists didn't hold a candle to his mad magical skills.

Energy dwindled down to what equated to a shock when scuffing feet across a carpet, Zander flopped his spent body on the bed and closed his eyes. Exhaustion, mega puzzles to solve and the possibility of police busting in his door had his mental amps completely fizzled, but so far all had eluded him. He chanted a quick spell to encase his house, so no one could get in or out, unless he deemed it so. Let the cops have fun with that.

Sleep, tranquility, and rest were his for the taking. Right up until someone's breath slapped him in the face at pillow-talk level.

Adrenaline. Nothing on earth like it. Did someone stab his voo doo doll in the heart with a Goliath-sized syringe full of the hormone jump-starting it? Zander bounced backwards in between heartbeats and pounded the light switch. A dim, flickering bulb in the center of the ceiling made the room look like a cheesy back room of a brothel.

Naked girl on bed. Brothel it is! "Holy… who the hell are you? How'd you get in here?" Mind games. He shook his head. Blinked a few times. Squinted. Rubbed his weary eyes. Blinked again. Was he in the right flat? For God's sake the row of tenement homes were identical. Eyes refocused, he scanned the room to his mountain of dirty laundry, shoes strewn, a poster of Winston Churchill with a quote reading: If You Are Going Through Hell, Keep Going, and… lastly, a naked girl still there on his bed, with slender legs, bountiful breasts, slim waist, biceps with enough punch to knock him on his keister and an angry beehive of jet-black hair sticking straight up in the air with some stray strands skewered in different directions. Bridezilla's picture popped into his mind.

With the exception of bad hair day, he had a really beautiful girl in her birthday suit handcuffed to his bed.

Happy dance or heel toe express?

Hold the happy feet. Sex hit the radar and with that he tapped those unhappy tootsies to the bathroom, and again tripped over Ella's stiletto. *How the heck did I miss it the first time?* Hopeful his insides couldn't produce another gastric drop, he rinsed his mouth out, and made a quick surveillance of his flat and then made his way back to the bedroom.

He peaked in the doorway and there she was… still handcuffed to the headboard like a girly magazine pin-up, eyes-glaring, thin-lipped with a mask of attitude times infinity. "Who are you and how did you get into my flat? And why did you handcuff yourself to my bed? Are you some kind of sacrificial poser?" There, he beat her to the punch.

"Are you kidding me?"

Venom all but shot from her mouth. Was there a spark? A flame? Zander rubbed his eyes again. Just how exhausted was he?

"Why did you tie me up? Did my sister and cousin put you up to this?" Elyza glanced around the room. "Sydney, Shelby game's up. Not funny anymore."

"What? Who?" Zander ran to the closet to see if he missed someone hiding.

"My sister, Sydney? Really sassy little southern belle? My cousin, Shelby Jane? The redheaded ginger snap? Where are they? Tell them they can come out now. Come on! I gotta tinkle."

"Lady, I don't know you from Adam." Zander then made some hand gestures as he pointed to her slender body. "Maybe I should say I don't know you from Eve."

"Stop playing me, Father. Undo me. You fecking, stupid moron. Unless you want your bed sheets soaked get me outta these cuffs. Kinky fecker! Oh, crap. I did it again. I'm sorry. I don't usually swear at priests unless they restrain me against my will. Let me go!" Elyza's voice filled the tiny flat.

Father? Absolutely dumbfounded Zander scratched his head and searched his room for anything else out of the ordinary about to spring a prank on him.

"This is a joke, right? One of the guys put you up to this? My parole officer?"

"Your what?" Her teeth clenched, Elyza struggled to free herself. She bit out, "Undo me, perv!"

"No, really, how did you get in here?"

"Seriously, I'm going to have a bladder malfunction in like five seconds. My dignity is moot at this point. Four, three...if I get to one..."

"All right all ready. Gosh, you're a hot mess. Stop with the drama and just tell me who the hell are you?" Zander reached over and grabbed his key from the top drawer of his nightstand. With the slight twist of the key the cuffs fell to the floor.

One hand meagerly trying to cover her dimple and backside, her other hand went to conceal a full-frontal exposure. She fled for the bathroom mumbling things no good Catholic girl would ever dare say.

Zander's jaw dropped. Whether it was due to the body the little tempest with a strange tattoo on her left hip stomped past him with or the fact that he indeed had a woman held against her will in his bedroom remained to be seen. Either way trouble had found him. Lynch mob it is! Any minute now…

Just exactly how long have I been parading about as a Priest?

"Lady, you have to forgive me, but I have no clue who you are or how you got here."

"Really? That's your story?" Elyza yelled, "Nothing?"

With the sound of the toilette flushing Zander stepped back away from the door and got out of her way. "At least tell me your—"

"Elyza." On a mission she marched straight to his closet. "Yours?"

"Zander." He followed one step behind her. "What are you doing?"

"Covering up my tush, as should you. I've been bleeding naked too long."

"And from the looks of it chilled." Whether he intended it or not the index finger shot up and aimed at her breasts.

"What are you, in second grade?" Elyza fished through his clothes until she found a flannel shirt and pair of sweatpants. Being naked in her skin was one thing.

Being exposed with his naked skin was another story, one she hadn't opened the book on yet. "What the heck is wrong with you?" she asked as she tugged on the sweatpants. "I wake up handcuffed in fecking silver rimmed in Brim. Really nice! If I ever reach my family, you're toast. And since when do priests wear cool clothes. And hex a home so no mental channeling can hit the airways? And keep Brimstone? Hello! It's illegal! Like everything else you've done so far. You wanna go to jail?"

"Just got out."

Whether Elyza ignored his answer or never heard it, she had buried herself in his closet rifling through his belongings. She yanked a designer suit off the rack and jiggled it in Zander's dazed face. "Looks more mobbish than religious." She shoved it at him. "Get dressed."

"What? Put that back. That's my court suit."

"Wait. What? Court suit? You weren't kidding when you said parole officer? Father—oh, Jesus, you're a fecking pedo."

Index finger back in motion, he interrupted her. "About that... I'm umm, I'm not a priest. Or at least I wasn't one till I met you. I'm not known for impersonating men of the cloth...until today."

She drawled out, "Nooo..." to the impersonation gig.

He had to give her credit, she mastered sarcasm. "And I'm definitely not a pedophile." Eyes squinted, lips thinned, head twisted slightly, he gave a slight shrug of his shoulders. "When did we meet?" Trying to ease her fears and be cordial, the smile he attempted died when she rolled her eyes until only the whites were visible.

"Just let me leave. What's with the house guarded

with hexes?"

Zander tossed his hands in the air and dropped on the edge of the bed, his hands strategically placed over his naughty bits. "I am at a loss, lady. I'm sorry if I hurt you. I didn't, did I? Beginning to think I was drugged. The fashion show yesterday is the last memory I own and how everything went so astronomically wrong… and the entire audience had been exposed to some mind-altering drug and—come to think of it—" Zander's eye grew wide, and he gasped. "There's no way!" He jabbed her shoulder with his index finger "—You're her, aren't you?"

Head thrown backwards in annoyance, Elyza's sigh hissed out of her little turned up nose while one brow shot for the heavens. "Is this your plan? Play dumb? Feign any lack of knowledge to the kidnapping and wrongful imprisonment of yours truly?" She fist pumped her chest. "You just put yourself at the scene of the crime. And guess who the star witness is." Elyza spread her arms out and then pointed back at herself. "Me, sunshine!"

Angered, Zander bounced off his bed and towered over her. "I am not a kidnapper! I would never hurt another person, especially a lady."

Skepticism painted all over her, Elyza stepped back and nodded to the bloodied pile of clothes in the corner. "Really? Unless you work in a slaughterhouse or had a nosebleed to end all nosebleeds, I don't think the police are going to buy that. Now, clothes on? Please?"

He no longer cared if he was flashing her. This was his flat and he could flaunt his scarred-up body any time he felt like it. Then he noticed tears filling her eyes and his heart sank. He'd scared her. He hadn't intended to.

Hell, he hadn't intended to find a woman in his bed either, but there she stood, all five feet of her, if that, with eyes that reminded him of the Mediterranean Sea on a stormy day. Hands to his sides, he stepped back to give her some space. He offered, "Maybe I was trying to save you." He gave her his best award-winning grin while batting his lashes trying for cute or anything to calm the woman down. Her set jaw and narrowed gaze never changed. "Nothing?"

Arms crossed snugly under her breast she warned, "Don't even."

"My wiles are worthless."

"Indeed."

He pouted.

"Really? Pouting? You think your full-out pout could win my trust over?" Elyza sucked in her cheeks and bit them. Had this naked nincompoop somehow bewitched her? That pout of his made her heart skip a beat.

"It's all I got." Talking to himself more than Elyza, Zander prodded his memory, hoping for a spark. "People were being picked off and discarded the way I toss the peanuts out of my caramel corn. Then some bloke fell from the balcony and took out the lady next to me. That's my last memory. Pretty certain the paintballs were laced with Ecstasy and Devil's Breath."

"Devil's Breath?"

"Scopolamine. Given in high doses it knocks out memories and people do all kinds of things they don't recall. Maybe that's why you're here? Maybe you followed me home?"

"If you've touched me, you'll burn long before you arrive in hell."

"Elyza, you would know if I did anything to you. Right?"

Elyza thought about if for a minute and decided he had a point. Nothing felt sore and she wasn't bruised or bleeding. Or feeling languorous in the least. She crossed her arms tight under her breast and mumbled, "I guess."

"Good. As for the extra security in the house? Doesn't everyone hex their homes these days? Thought it was common practice to keep sexy, naked strangers out. Seriously, Ms. St. James, I have never held a woman against her will. Honestly, I haven't held a woman in forever."

With her left hand she bent and snagged the silver bracelets off the floor and dangled them in his face. "Then why the brimstone cuffs?"

A playful smile spread across his face. "They were a going away gift from the guys on my cell block."

Mischief for the briefest of seconds stretched the tiny walls of the flat and oddly, her heart. He held a playful side to him; he tried to ease her fears in a delicate manner. She was grateful. But they'd only just met, under the most unique circumstances no less. Did she bite? Literally? Is that why he said it? In hopes of her reaction? One glance into his mesmerizing dark eyes, Elyza turned away. He, simply put, personified male masculinity and beauty. She'd never seen another man that literally made her heart beat one stimulating contraction after another. Her perfect imaginary man didn't stand a chance against this one. He was different and yet he was so much more. But something about him made her inner senses want to shed endless tears. He'd suffered, but from what, or at the hands of who? Out of nowhere she wanted to end his torment. Tell him everything would be okay, and just maybe they'd both believe it.

Trying for a nonchalant glimpse, he came in around five foot ten, which worked to her vantage because out of twenty people living under one roof in her ever-growing family, she held the title of the most petite woman. His feathered black hair lay slightly on the longer side of short and yet it held waves, and a silkiness she wanted to run her fingers through. His body seemed to be honed from an assembly of romance writers all vying for smoldering perfection. Solid in all the right places, with the head to toe second glance she confirmed all the right places... His arms, biceps and triceps had lifted a weight or two. Corded muscles stretched like rebar across his chest and defined him with every subtle flex made or breath he took. He had a few scars on him hidden below a religious cross, possibly an auto accident or skiing or he fell into a woodchipper? His neck had some rather thickened pockmarks. Reminded her of sustained abuse from a vamp. The thick linear scar on his chest made her think someone tried to rip his heart out or possibly gut him. It hurt him deeply. She could feel his pain as if it were hers. The scars only added to his handsome rugged appeal. She couldn't help but lick her lips when she glanced from his chest to his hips. And lower. His body mass index had to be close to zilch with one exception. His crowning jewels held some heft. Those she'd seen a few times now since the fool refused to dress.

She would not gawk.

One white lie wouldn't toss her into the seventh level of Hell. Purgatory possibly. It would be time well spent.

Flashing her a playful smirk, he asked, "Who's the perv?"

"Really? You're going that route? You had me restrained against my will and now you're butt naked, might I add by your bed, with a priest cassock and bloodied collarino calling me a perv." And yet even trying to deny it she felt like one because taking her eyes off him seemed impossible. Somehow, he had turned into the chocolate cake and she the frosting, ready to slather her over-heated, over-stimulated body all over the baked goods. What a mouth-watering delicacy. And calorie free. With that thought a pang of hunger gnawed at her belly, but food wasn't on the menu. And out of nowhere it hit her the way a wrecking ball took down a building. "Did you and I make eye contact during the show yesterday?"

His cheeks blushed. "I was wondering if that was me you were checking out."

Elyza straightened her stance and jut her chin out. "I wasn't checking you out."

Stood there with his head cocked sideways, one eyebrow raised told her he wasn't buying white lie number two.

A slow grin poured over his face, and he bobbed his head. "Nice."

She inhaled and tapped her warmed cheeks. This had to be a residual effect of the paintball drugs she'd been accosted by. At least she had something to blame for her spiral into the gutter. "You're a dork." *Did I seriously just call him a dork?*

Something or someone toyed with Elyza because there was never a day in her life, she turned into a hormonal pubescent teen ready to jump the hot naked guy just because he stood a mere foot away in a solid stance. Very solid stance. With an indifferent shift she crossed her legs.

Elyza took a moment to examine her surroundings and gather what wit she had left. First off, what the heck was she doing standing in a man's bedroom she didn't know while he stood there in the best birthday suit she'd ever seen, looking all steamy and she, lest not forget, had been tied to his bedpost earlier? She tapped her head with her fist and immediately wished she hadn't. Her headache roared its ugliness. "I need air."

A quick trip through the small flat revealed sparse furnishings. No family photos hung. No pictures of children, animals, wives, priests, or girlfriends... She fought elation.

There was the bed, to which she'd become one with, a nightstand with three drawers and a small television. She jabbed the power button on the television. White noise and fuzzy-squiggly lines controlled the box.

Perturbed, she grumbled, "No cable?"

"You are a quick one."

"Whatever."

In the main room a plaid chair sat in need of stuffing and a new cover. The front arm of the chair looked like a wild cat had its way with the fabric. Shredded to bits. A few pairs of trainers in various stages of new to should already be in the dumpster were scattered about.

No table or chairs in the kitchenette. No modern conveniences whatsoever. Blackish-green fuzz scaled the top and sides of stacked Chinese take-out cartons in a small dorm-sized refrigerator. Burn marks from cigarettes completed the look on the outdated cream with gold speckled countertop. All that seemed missing were the roaches. Afraid to look closer, a phantom tickle bristled her leg. Arms tight by her side for fear of touching anything, she aimed for the back door. The deadbolt was indeed dead. She couldn't unlock it.

Fecking fabulous! She walked back out to the living area. Tears, one by one slipped through tightly shut lids. "I want to go home."

Zander approached her and very gingerly wiped away the tears. Feeling his hand on her face, Elyza jerked. His touch, she'd never experienced another human's touch without being consumed with pain, or heartache or fear. When she had touched Frankie at the show she'd been drugged. This man's touch was as if a feather caressed her. Light. Meaningful. Loving?

Concussion for sure.

"Hey? I'm really sorry this happened to you." His voice held such sincerity it rocked her to the very core.

She stepped backward away from him. "You followed me out here and you're still not dressed. Dear god man, what does it take for you to realize I'm uncomfortable?"

"I heard the back door rattle. I wanted to make sure no one was breaking in."

Hands in front of her, palms up, Elyza's voice went up an octave or two. "Or out."

Zander's pitch matched hers word for word. "You are free to go. So go already. It'll be one less thing I have to worry over. And I didn't latch you to the bed for the last time."

Embarrassed, she turned away from him, her arms wrapped tightly to her sides.

"Elyza, I shouldn't have raised my voice. I realize you're petrified but I don't have a clue how you ended

71

up here. Forgive me? Please? Are you okay?"

She whipped her head around and glanced at him over her shoulder, sarcastically asking, "What do you think?"

Without hesitation Zander blurted, "I think you are the most gorgeous creature to grace this island." A small giggle filtered out and he bit his bottom lip. "That," his hands were talking up a storm, "I got nothing. It just kinda came out of nowhere." He ended with a full grin and a snort.

Chapter Five

Mouth open, with a confounded guise, Elyza found herself speechless. After a moment of the two of them in a staring contest Elyza prodded his shoulder. "You are more complex than a puzzle missing pieces. Dear, sweet, not really a priest, not really a kidnapper, handsome as feck ex-con, tell me what you recall about yesterday because right now each tick of the clock rips away our freedom. Maybe we can piece this mess together before the two of us are making our one and only phone calls."

"Handsome as feck?"

She put her hand on her hip. "That's all you heard?"

He chuckled. "No one shall ever accuse you of mincing words. Tell me your last memory of yesterday."

She glanced upwards and got lost in his thick black lashes. "Thinking I had my cousin behind me coming out of the building and then waking up here."

Fingers deep in his hair, Zander dug his scalp. "Your memory is as shoddy as mine."

Unable to help herself, Elyza took a step closer to him. "Can I try something with you?"

Zander's broody regard manifested into a wide smirk spread across his lush pouty lips. She slapped his arm playfully. "No brimstone cuffs."

His smile vanished and he grabbed his gut. "Hold that thought," and with that he ran for the bathroom without a single second to spare.

When he came back Elyza pointed to his stomach. "What just happened?"

"If only I knew. I puke at the thought of sex, full moons, and my hearing is impeccable. Too bad the memory is gone!"

Now, more than ever Elyza wanted, no, needed to know what had happened to this man. Her tone much softer she admitted, "Well, it is more than apparent you know some form of witchcraft, so I'll share a secret with you. I can read people's minds, but I must touch you and sometimes the intensity knocks me out and sometimes both of us. It's called, psychometry."

"I've heard of it. Elyza, I am beginning to think I'm cursed. This purging started after I was released from jail." Seeing her color pale and blue eyes widen he was quick to add, "It's a long story. I was forced into a lifestyle I couldn't get out of by foster parents. Swear on my life. But this? Puking all the time? I need to see the physician—"

"Sit." Elyza shoved Zander to the only chair in the flat.

"— Or witch doctor." An ill-fated smirk masked his dismay.

"I've been called worse."

"I can see why." He winked at her startled expression. "It's the hairdo."

Elyza warned, "Brace yourself. This can get intense."

"Trust me little cherub, I would expect nothing less of you. Why do I feel as if I'm about to get electrocuted?"

"Even though I probably should and could, I'll try not to kill you." The, *please tell me you're kidding expression,* Zander gave her made her laugh more. She decided to play it up a bit more. "Do you have a sex toy you can bite down on, ya know, to muffle the pain? A safe word? Or a teddy bear to hug?"

"Not funny!" Zander started to push himself into a standing position when Elyza placed her index finger to his forehead and gave him the slightest zinger. He fell back into the chair stunned.

"So electrocuted it is. For the record, I've never owned a teddy bear."

She quickly added, "Nice dodge on the sex toys," to hide the hurt she felt for him hearing he'd never owned a teddy bear. It broke her heart.

Zander laced his fingers and covered all his private parts from Elyza's line of vision. "Now or never."

She looked him over before she wrapped her hands around his head. Then she did what she'd thought about earlier, she sunk her fingers through all those silky layers of his jet-black locks stealing a private second to enjoy the sensation. Tingles, rapturous in nature delighted every sensual spot Elyza owned. Who was getting electrocuted? She had her very own living, breathing vibrator. Right here and now Elyza wanted to lose herself. Forget the past twenty some odd hours, all the misery and pain she and her family had suffered and enjoy meeting this man, but life's game plan had other ideas. Reality struck better than a freight train missing its designated stop and slamming into a crowded station.

Zander grit down, clamped his eyes shut and only a small, "Ugh," escaped.

Images whipped through her mind so fast she could barely stand. Her equilibrium had the balance of a toddler on its first day of figuring out where to put their feet for purposes other than sucking on toes.

Going in reverse she skimmed Zander's mind. The charitable outfit of the priest he so deemed? Not exactly how it went down. Zander tangled with a vampire. He intervened attempting to save the priest, taking the vampire head on. A savage struggle ensued until the vampire picked Zander up off his feet and tossed him atop the priest and walked away laughing. The humanity this man seemed capable of blew her away, along with his lack of self-preservation. He could have been slaughtered but he jumped in headfirst while others stood there videoing everything instead of helping. He had however, lost his clothing in the fight.

And… so it seemed, he had yet to find any as he sat there very gentlemanly with his hands folded over his personal joy stick.

Skimming his visions further she couldn't get a clear shot of the monster that killed the priest, but vision wasn't the only sense people had in their bag of tricks. She understood many times the sense of smell, hearing and touch play into putting conundrums together. An overwhelming aroma of mothballs overcame her followed by a sense of utter astonishment between Zander and the vamp, almost as if they were acquaintances and shocked to see one another. Did Elyza's naked knight, as she now thought of him, know the killer personally?

Then there was the horror show of the guards on the stage peppering the audience with bullets. Elyza really focused on what Zander retained from this. The guards were aiming at her cousin Savanah, not her mother. Serina dove in front of Savanah saving her. The last memory Elyza witnessed was being flung over Zander's shoulder and running at an unfathomable speed from an upside position until pain exploded in her head.

The discomfort proved too much, and Elyza lost consciousness. When she came too, she was flat on her back looking up into the most soothing tranquil black abyss she'd ever seen. "How long was I out?"

"Geez, I didn't think you'd ever wake up. A good day."

"What?" Elyza fumbled trying to get up. "And you just left me on the bloody floor?"

Laughing, Zander barely answered her. "I'm joking. Only about a minute. What happened, little cherub? Did we learn anything, or am I truly brain dead?" He held his hand to her and helped her to a sitting position.

On her butt with her knees to her chest and her arms hugging them tightly a cheeky grin made its way to her lips. "You can't handle the truth."

"I'd say stick to the day job, but I bet The Fallen Angel company will clip your wings after last night."

"I'm not certain whose jokes are worse."

Zander gave her a deadpan stare. "Sorry love, I wasn't joking."

"Whatever! What I learned from your visions…" Elyza told Zander everything he projected to her.

"I think I know why you have a headache. Got my memory back. You have magic fingers."

"You'll never know how magic." Elyza wiggled her brows playfully.

"That's just mean." Zander stood, his belly grumbling loudly. He pat her head in passing and added, "Duck," and went straight to the kitchenette and hit his little refrigerator.

"I'll goose you alright."

"What?" He asked, returning with a handful of raw

hamburger.

"Dear lord I said that out loud?"

He bent down to her eye level and grinned. "I heard nothing…other than something about being goosed?"

Elyza buried her face in her hands and groaned.

"Okay my little gander, I'll let you off the hot seat for now."

"For now?" Elyza found herself nibbling on her bottom lip this time wondering what would happen later? Mid fantasy of him doing the goosing she heard his voice popping her little daydream like a pin does a bubble.

"Elyza? I seem to keep losing you. Someday I hope you share with me where you go."

She met his gaze and her heart fluttered. "Perhaps a secret garden."

"Well, perhaps at some point, after you and I are out of jail, we can go on a real date where we get to know one another inside out." Zander brought his hand to his mouth and licked the blood dripping down his arm from the raw meat. "Apologies, I know this appears dreadful but it's the only thing that settles my stomach."

"So, we're going to play a quick game," and before Zander could get another cheeky comment in Elyza beat him to the quick, "still a big fat no on the cuffs." With a few wiggles, Elyza crossed her legs and then massaged her thighs. "Say the first thing you think of when I say for example…" Elyza hesitated watching Zander closely, "Dracula."

"Misunderstood." He smiled giving her a contemplative head-bob. "Right?"

"Yeah, pretty much." She'd met the man. The myth. The monster. And she liked him. Hopefully he would still reciprocate the feelings once he found out the mask he'd lent her for the show had been swiped. "Blood."

With his finger still in his mouth he popped it out and answered, "Bitter."

"That it is." Elyza watched Zander's brow furrow, his head cock sideways and before he went down that road she asked, "Sunbathing."

"Depends on if it's a nude beach. No!" Zander fled for the bathroom again.

"I give up." Elyza's voice chased down the short hallway after his naked butt. "I was trying to see if you burn when you're outside."

"Quicker than bacon under a spaceship during the launch," echoed from the bathroom. "I'm bleeding English, Lass. There's no real sun to speak of. Webster added the word *pasty* to the dictionary because of me."

Elyza didn't bat an eyelash. What was one more dilemma to handle? Clearly the poor chap had no idea he was in the midst of a life altering change. When he walked back Elyza studied him. What or who was the catalyst that would eventually take over his current life and give him a bat's eye view of life? His inability to withstand sunlight, along with the unfortunate side effects of his libido, and his new love of a raw diet were the prodromal signs of what was to come. Out of the three she wanted the libido rectified without further ado. The other two she could live with. Maybe he wouldn't freak out.

How much time did she have before he turned? Enough to get out of this flat and back to her family? Which led to the larger question… could she leave him? People on the verge of having their life flipped upside down needed someone to buffer the blows. She'd already begun to grow fond of him. This could only happen to her. Family gets shot up, jewels worth more than those locked in the tower get stolen, she wakes up chained to a bed with a guy about to grow a new set of dents or a fur coat or both and she finds she has feelings for her possible kidnapper. *Stockholm Syndrome it is.* Laughter burbled out from nowhere until she noticed a purple hickey with teeth marks on his bum. "Have you been bitten by anything or anyone lately?"

Zander answered a very unconvincing, "No?"

"You have teeth imprints on your tush. I have no bleedin' idea how I missed it all morning."

He darted down the hall to the full-length mirror. "What?" He yelped trying to crank his head over his shoulder and twist his hip to get a better view. "Which side?" He asked, facing her giving her the full-frontal again.

"Dear lord." One hand immediately clamped over her eyes and the other hand pointed. "Left."

He checked his left. "You're seeing things. There's nothing there."

She peeked between fingers. "Other left."

Zander gasped. "No way. Why don't I remember getting bit in the ass? It's not like it happens every day."

"You were most likely compelled to forget."

"That's a real thing?" A low string of nervous giggles filtered out. "This is freaking insane. Am I going to die? Turn into a zombie?" He tugged at his hair. "Oh, God, I don't want to eat people's brains or sleep in a casket…"

So much for him not freaking out. "Take a deep breath. You watch too much television or read too many fiction books."

"Well, it's not like there's an Idiot's Guide to

Vampirism. Is there?" The poor sod looked baffled to the nines.

He began to pace around his compact living room, stopping at the window. He peeked out the between the makeshift curtains. Watching him she found the easy part. Taking her eyes off him? Mission impossible. "Tell me what you recall. We'll compare notes." Maybe this could take his mind off the current situation and give her time to think.

After a few minutes of silence, he finally answered. "I accidentally slam-dunked you in the fountain in Hyde Park. Your hair was literally smoldering. Your noggin may or may not have taken on the solid cement sidewall." He produced a guilty grin. "Sorry. And you also took a bloody good conk to the head when you were attempting to rescue the man who fell from the balcony. I was about to help you up when some giant came along and picked him up." Zander shrugged his shoulders and added, "Anyway, you were sticky and slippery and one degree away from spontaneous combustion. When I first caught a glimpse of you, you were wearing a cape drawn tightly to your body. Your teeth were chattering, blood ran down the side of your face, ya had one shoe on, and you were doing that ugly crying thing. Hot mess. So, me being the brilliant firefighter-slash doctor-slash-savior of a hot, messy, racoon-eyed woman donning a medieval cape, I gallantly came to your rescue and dunked ya in the fountain to cool off that steaming little body. And nowhere in that wild story, did anyone bite me bum."

Elyza buried her face in her hands and groaned. "Not quite the romance I dreamt up. Getting swept off my feet and tossed headfirst into a fountain."

"Those are the best starts, little cherub, ya know,

minus you being restrained against your will or me tangoing with a vampire."

Curiosity piqued. "Why were you at the Hall Royal? Death wish? Most people don't go to venues where vamps hang out willingly."

Elyza had already come to know one of his signature moves, the shoulder shrug. Every muscle coordinated a flow and movement Elyza found fascinating. She really wished she had all day, heck all week to ask him ridiculous questions just to watch him shrug the shoulders, or smile, or waltz around in the birthday suit to end all suits, but life had other plans. His body had scorcher written all over it. No wonder he called her a hot mess. This was completely his fault, or at least the part where she needed a new cooling system. One piped into her with his long thick hose filled with special coolants. Okay, so this line of thinking was getting her where? Trouble.

"I had hopes of getting my foot in the door of a magazine, doing a freelance shoot, but I lost my camera in the rubble so there goes that. Anyway, you were running blindly screaming, performing your very own magic tricks, just before the broken dude crashed. Want to tell me about that?"

"I have a very ugly temper when people I love are threatened."

With a slight finger-plink to her nose, he admitted, "At least you are gorgeous when pissed and you're making me all hot without any added magic."

Upper lip scrunched Elyza rubbed her nose. "Not five minutes ago I believe you called me a hot mess."

"I don't usually admit this, but I was wrong. Scorching is more accurate." He waggled his brows at her.

She tried to ignore him but found out this would prove impossible. How can you ignore your destiny when it looks you in the face and offers, humor, empathy, safety, concern and possibly some of the most satisfying, worthwhile sex on the planet? Or at least that seemed to be the path her over-imaginative brain took.

Zander leaned in and whispered in her ear, "You and I are in trouble aren't we, little cherub?"

His breath sent sparks down her spine. Seems she wasn't the only one able to heat up a room. With a slight nod, Elyza admitted, "Trouble, sir, is my middle name. You've been warned."

His gaze devouring her, Elyza watched with much enthusiasm as he ran a finger across that plump lower lip, the one she wanted to nibble on. Trying for inconspicuous she did a head-to-toe taking in countless other juicy tidbits that would need tending to for a rainy day. He caught on and played it up slightly, wetting his lips and giving her the eyebrow wiggle. *He's such a tease.* Looking at him filled her with yearning and lust, the last thing she needed, but damn the thrill of being alive coupled with that all-encompassing sensation of first love exploded inside her. *First love? Oh God!*

All this frightened the bejesus from her. "You should really put some pants on. Look, I have to find Serina, and this not being able to channel her or anyone in my family is making me nuts. Things don't go very well for me or anyone else in the vicinity when I get nutsy. They probably think I'm buried in the rubble." Out of nowhere tears filled Elyza's eyes again. "Zander," the hands flew out to her sides, "I never told my mother I loved her." She stood up and grabbed his shoulders.

Looking him in the eye she asked, "Why wouldn't I do that? Say that? People tell each other they love them all the time. Why didn't I? What the hell is wrong with me? Am I that fecking callous? I should have said it. Said something. Anything." She wrapped her fingers around his biceps and shook him. "I could have called her mom. Kissed her goodbye, but I did nothing. She died thinking I didn't care." She flung herself into his chest sobbing. "Zander, she's dead. Her chest had a gaping hole in it."

Delicately trying to console her, Zander reached around her and pulled her closer until she went limp in his arms. His state of affairs, however, was anything but limp.

When she realized his fondness for her rising, Elyza reeled back, her face buried beneath her hands. "I'm so sorry. I really need to go."

Zander pried her hands from her face and dabbed at a stray tear slinking down her cheek. "Never say you're sorry for loving someone. The heart loves who the heart loves and once it has decided someone is worthy there's no going back. You don't know she is dead, Elyza. She knows you love her. Heck, if I can feel it and have only just met you, there is no way she doesn't know your feelings."

"Zander, I can't reach her. This has never happened before. She's always in my thoughts, always! I have to get home."

"I promise to get you home. On the way there can you tell me how you brought back my memory?"

One ounce of dread diminished. He was going to help her get home. With a big sniffle and wiping tears from her eyes she explained, "Hmmm, it's like when you're talking, and you forget the one word you need and then someone says or does something, and the light bulb goes on. Consider me your AC/DC jump." For a moment Elyza let her guard down. Somehow this man she'd only met calmed her storm. His gentle nature, caring touch, and his heated gaze eased her torment.

"You can jump me anytime." He playfully bat his long lashes in her face.

Her jaw dropped. Time to change the subject. "So who are you? What's your story?"

"Wish I knew who."

"You don't know who you are? I hit a brick wall trying to scan your thoughts. They only went back so far and then it was total darkness."

With a sigh, he replied, "The synopsis is, Zander. Zander Templar."

She fought off a smile. "You sound like Bond."

He added a small smirk. "Nah, my lady. More like the Saint."

Arms spread wide she added, "Yeah, I don't think saint is what I'd call you. Too bad your name isn't Simon." The two of them exchanged a brief glance. Head bowed, she bit her bottom lip because her little devil incognito still looked like da Vinci's, Vitruvian Man, in his entire splendor. "So other than the fact you had to have been raised on a nudist colony do you know anything of your past? I'm guessing today is your birthday?"

Zander shrugged his massive shoulders. "Why?"

Index finger in motion, Elyza pointed south of his belly button and gave him a stern look. "Well, if it's not could you please put some fecking clothes on?"

"Oh, hold up, a bit's come back to me. I believe I was supposed to drown you in that fecking fountain." He scrunched his nose at her as he mimicked her vocabulary.

And so it seems, sarcasm slinging 1-0-1 had begun.

A spirited glint crossed his face. "You worried you might take advantage of me?"

"As if!" Truth be known yes, yes, she was. It was all she thought about.

"The bod is rather hard not to ogle over." His mock laugh lacked all sincerity.

She tossed her head back to take him in. "Or kill you. You weren't the one who woke up in cuffs. For the last time, dress that thing?" She pointed to his personal scepter, accidentally poking his penis. The muscle sprang to life. Immediately she clasped her hands over her eyes. "Oops. I—ah, I didn't mean too." Or did she? No telling what might happen if another second went by. He did say she could jump him anytime. Would now be appropriate? Her mind went into overdrive, with him steering that thick gear shifter into her personal parking garage. Forward. Reverse. Forward again with a little more pressure on the pedal… And so on until he ran out of gas. She inhaled sharply. With zero finesse left, her tongue rested between her lips.

With a little grunt he left the room. "My apologies, Elyza. I'm so used to being stripped of my clothes, humanity and dignity from time spent in her Majesty's home for criminally inept that putting on pants seems foreign. We were made to go naked for days at a time to break us down. I wouldn't want to look at this body either if I didn't have to."

"I'm sorry, what?" blew out as she followed him down the short hall all but tripping over his heels. "You have a body gods would envy."

He stopped, his bum a true work of art, muscles

flexing with each stride, his legs completely toned, smooth and nowhere near as hairy as hers could get after missing a shave or two. He spun to her and gave a sweep of his hand down the length of his body. "Nice try. It's pretty mangled." He didn't wait for her response and turned back headed to the closet.

"You mean ripped."

Zander glanced back over his shoulder and implied, "Exactly. I didn't mean to offend you and I wasn't fishing for compliments. There isn't a fish alive smart enough to bite this worm."

The man truly hated his physique. He was ashamed of his body. Of the person he was. He had no clue how to take her.

"You didn't offend me. I didn't mean you were awful to look at—in fact quite the contrast, but I don't know you from Adam, even though you both started out like this." Her audacious nature had her point at his groin and smirk.

"Touché, Mrs. Frankenstein." He pat her hair.

Elyza snorted with a shocked expression on her face. "That bad?"

"Worse." Zander pointed to a few of his disfigurements. "These scars are hideous." His truth weighed his words.

"Not at all. Honest. In fact, I bet they define you. They tell a story that maybe someday you'll share with someone. Maybe me. Barely noticeable." She made a cross over her chest. "Cross my heart and hope to die."

"Truly not the smartest thing to say to someone who had you shackled to their bed. Although, I suppose I could do last rights on you." He bowed to her just before he disappeared in his closet.

And why do I want him to cover that?

Exiting the closet dressed in a pair of black tight jeans, a Manchester United hoodie, and a pair of trainers dangling from his fingers, Zander went and retrieved the paper from earlier and took it out of the wet plastic wrap. Once the paper was in Elyza's hands they shook, the paper crinkling with each tremble. He grabbed her hands to steady her. "We'll be all right. Trust me."

His wild, exotic fragrance enveloped her stirring emotions she had no idea how to act on but oh how she wanted to figure it out.

He tapped on the paper and redirected her. The Line read: A fallen angel for sure! "You made the headlines. There's a picture and details on the third page."

Nose wrinkled, hands thrust palm up she mumbled, "Really? The third page is all I managed? I burn down one of the oldest historical buildings from Londinium times and they can't squeeze my dimpled tush onto the first page?"

They flipped to the section. And there in the lower right hand of the page was a very tiny mug shot of Elyza. Or soon to be mug shot.

"Ego deflated you didn't make the front cover? Glad to see you're taking it so well." Zander went to ruffle the beehive but stopped short. With her current scowl he might get stung.

With a quick flip of a page or two Elyza pointed out the story of the local priest's horrific demise.

Eyes closed, Zander turned away and gagged. "I can't look at that." He walked to the front window and peeked out. "Anyway, where are the jewels? You stole the Hope diamond? Do you have a death wish? And the sparkly outfit? I can see why you'd want that. You looked—" Zander caught his breath, "—hot."

"The murderers on the stage swiped the necklace and mask. I have the outfit. Oh, by the way, you might want to get rid of the evidence in the corner of your room. I can smell blood from here."

Eyebrows furrowed, Zander took a long look at Elyza. "What are you, a blood hound?"

"Hmmm, I suppose that's one way of calling the kettle black without actually calling the kettle black."

The shoulders rose. The shoulders fell. She followed. Damn he was her focal point for meditation. "What kind of answer is that?"

"I have an extremely sensitive sniffer. Why did you attend a charity event for vampires? I know you said you were hoping to get into a magazine, but really, I don't know many people who do that for fun unless you have a death wish, which clearly you seem to."

"It seems we both do."

Elyza realized she had herself a true daredevil. *He'd so fit in with the family. I did not just think that. Now I have the guy coming home with me.*

"As you wish." He waggled his brows.

Elyza dropped her voice to just above a whisper and gave him her full attention, "Did you just read my mind?"

The shoulder shrug went into play followed by a killer smile. "You'll never know. Besides, I've had worse happen to mc. Vamps don't scare me. Humans are far scarier."

"Well, that might be a good thing because I have a feeling you'll turn soon. Your body is prepping you for a life altering change. Your raw diet, sensitivity to the sun and the sex? I got nothing on the sex one. Usually, it's the other way. People turn into nymphs. Sorry."

"Figures I screw up the best part. Damn." His expression going dark, he took to pacing his flat. Elyza followed him like an imprinted duck. "The three successive bites—" Zander paused a second running his fingers over a few scars on his neck— "is there a timely fashion for them or are they like freaking herpes? Like you're stuck with them forever." Zander stopped midstep and spun to face Elyza. "Am I toast? What the hell is going to happen to me?"

Their bodies collided in perfect synchronicity. Her arms caught him at his waist and his arms flowed around her shoulders and captured her to him in a warm embrace. They stood there, neither one moving, their hearts pounding. Elyza closed her eyes and leaned her head onto his chest. Zander rested his chin atop her and nuzzled in.

So this is what perfection felt like. Sharing yourself with another person and feeling completely at ease being you. No pretense, no judging, no lying to the other person or yourself, just trusting the other person has your back and your best interests at heart.

It wouldn't last. Perfection of this nature had to be an illusion. People don't fall into one another's lives coming from a disastrous incident and wind up in love over the course of a few hours. Do they? Elyza's mother and aunt seemed to believe in true love at first sight. Right now, Elyza understood what it felt like to be caught in the eye of the storm. Falsely secure, knowing without warning all could and would change. Elyza craned her head back and looked up at him from under those thick black lashes. "Technically, I am a hybrid. Witch, vampire, and love a juicy steak and anything

chocolate. And technically yes, three times the charm...
or more apropos a curse. If you turn, I will be right beside
you. I promise not to leave you and help you through the
transition."

"This can't be happening to me." Zander dropped
his head and let go of her.

And there it was, the beginning of the end. The
disconnect button had been activated. She knew it would
happen, just not this fast. She needed to change that.
Elyza grabbed his hands and held him until the tension
drained. It was what she did, took other's pain and
suffering so they could get that breath of fresh air or take
that first step after something bad happened. When he
looked back at Elyza, those stunning black eyes sparkled.

"I just had a flashback. You bit my ass, Elyza. When
I was lugging you back to the flat. I thought vampires
were all about the jugular or femoral. Neck nibblers,
upper thigh that leads to happy endings. They make it
look so sexy in the movies. You went for the rump."

"Concussed. Drugged. In shock. Do you want me to
keep going? If I'd bitten your neck I'd have left a wicked
hickey. If it was your thigh, you'd have accused me of
having lousy aim and being a perv."

"I could have lived with the lousy aim." Zander
leaned down and bumped his forehead into hers. "You're
a lousy vampire, Elyza."

Elyza's smile returned. She entwined their fingers.
"I promise, I'll be right here with you if and when you
change. Now I don't mean to sound callous, even though
we've covered that I am earlier, but I need to get home.
Where's the purple cape? There's a pocket I stuffed the
goods into." Elyza let go of Zander's hand and headed
back into the bedroom.

Zander followed, turning on the light in the closet.

Stood there, a sudden phase of nausea and wooziness swept over Elyza. She staggered and hit the wall, while her knees buckled. Zander took a step toward her, hands extended. She shook her head. "Don't! I'm just famished. I need food. Or blood. I haven't eaten in days. And you are one giant sidetrack. The cape? Where is it? You must think the worst of me setting fire to the hall." She stood, determined to get the cape and go home.

"Let's eat first. I'll order curry. Then you can tear my flat apart…" Zander grumbled as the woman ripped things from hangers, flinging shirts, pants, and sweaters over her shoulder into a heap. He was one step behind her folding his clothing into a pile as she made a mountain.

Defeat weighed her words. "It's not here."

"Between you and I it looks like the world's out to get us. Elyza, do you remember any of last night?" He grabbed her hands and looked into her eyes. "And I would never think the worst of you. I think your survival instincts took over."

One ounce of tension drained hearing his words. Eyes closed, Elyza tried to think back of her last moments in the hall, pulling from Zander's memories. "It all happened so fast. I got nothing."

"I believe someone followed us and finished screwing with us. They probably knew you had the other jewels."

"But your house is hexed. How would anyone get in?"

Shaking his head, he answered, "No. I safeguarded it this morning when I got back from wherever I was." Moving his hands in circular sweeps, Zander whispered,

"Let down the guard, no longer need the safeguards. Enter welcomed, leave loved." He looked at Elyza. "Free to come and go as you please, little cherub."

"Zander, I adore that unbinding spell. Very original." Zander gave her a curt bow. "But my nerves are really wired here. I need to be home. Like yesterday." She could no longer pretend everything was hunky dory even if he was. Too many bizarre unexplainable incidents kept happening. Elyza headed for the front door. "I honestly don't care what happened to the outfit. If you find it's yours. Just don't try to sell it around here. You won't be able to buy your way out of jail and your parole officer won't be pleased. I don't even care if I get arrested. I can't breathe. I need my family. Thanks for trying to smooth over the most awkward merry meet and greet in history."

He reached for her. "Don't leave yet. I promise I'll get you home."

"Do you have a car? Money for the Tube?" He shook his head no. "Then this is where we part ways, love. Take care."

"Thanks for being here with me when I turn."

Could she be any more of a cad? Two minutes ago, she'd promised him she'd be there with him, but her family needed her more. She felt it in her soul. Barefoot, she placed her shaking hand on the knob and twisted. She took a step back as the door swung inward and she inhaled, hoping for fresh air and a renewed sense of self. Instead, she was overcome with a dreadful mildewed wormy odor that always seemed to saturate the air after a heavy downpour. If that didn't have bad omen stamped all over it, nothing did. She stepped outside of the confines and wanted to cry finally having the freedom she so needed. One step off the stoop torrential rain battered her better than a boxer taking his frustrations out on a punching bag. She took another step. Freedom. He really let her go. Free from the confines of his flat. His flat that he was able to place some of the most intricate wards she'd ever seen. She couldn't break them. Lord knows she tried. Instinctively she reached out through her mental channels for any family member. Time to crank up the volume on the radio silence.

Serina, Lucian, Shelby, Sydney, Olivia, Thomas, can you hear me? I'm alive. Haven't got a clue where I am. Mom? Dad? I'm alive. Hello? Please answer me? She got halfway down the walkway, lifted her face to the sky and half crying, half laughing she asked, *Can ya hear me now?* Then she heard Zander hollering. Her heart sank. Not the voices she needed. No one from her family responded.

"Elyza, get back in here. It's hammering. You're barefoot. Go take a shower, breathe, and for God's sake let your hair down."

She glanced down at her soggy predicament. She hated to admit it, but he seemed to have a few valid points. Stood in the middle of his path she turned back to him. "Funny."

"Wasn't joking. You look hideous—from the neck up. Come on. Get back inside. I'll order curry and then we can get you home. Deal? It's the least I can do for keeping you last night. Come back in?"

"I thought you didn't have any money."

"I have a tab at the local take-out. The girls there think I'm cute."

Out of nowhere a jealous jab sucker punched her. *This can't be happening to me.* She took one apprehensive step toward him and stopped. "No one can touch me here, right?"

With his right hand he made the symbol of a cross over his body then shrugged his shoulders. "My child, you have my word. Praise be to God." A huge grin followed. "How'd that look?"

"Not funny."

"Was too. Come on then, little cherub, get back inside."

She saluted him with her middle finger. "If you still had the bloody chasuble on I'd never be able to tell you're a pretender. So, a shower, munchies and a ride home? You promise?"

"Cross my heart and hope to die."

"If my family finds you before I get home that's pretty much a given."

After seeing her reflection in the tiny bathroom mirror, Zander's tagging her as Bridezilla and Mrs. Frankenstein seemed spot on. One dull light bulb dangled over the sink with a string as an on/off toggle. The toilette sat crunched between the sink and the metal shower stall. When she peered around the shower curtain, which still had that new plastic scent to it, she squealed with elation. The shower was spotless and smelled like bleach. They now had two things in common. Shoes and showers. It was an odd combination, but other relationships started on far less. *Relationship?* She rolled her eyes.

On the tiny radio perched on the toilette's lid, she found a station with heavy metal. Music, the second-best stress buster. The first? If she knew the man outside the door a heck of a lot better, some company in the shower.

The knock on the door shook the walls. Soap

cascading down her face, she plunged her face into the spray to get the suds out of her eyes. With her fingers tight on the edge of the curtain she pulled it back just enough to peep out. "What's up?"

Zander stuck his head in. Steam rolled out of the opening. "Other than my water meter, your food will be here soon. Chop, chop, Buttercup."

"Hey, you wouldn't happen to have any conditioner, would you?"

"No but I have the next best thing. Mayonnaise followed by a vinegar rinse."

Laughter rolled from behind the curtain. "You making a salad out of me?"

"Don't tempt me. I am famished too."

Less than a half a minute later Zander reentered the sauna. "Here, my eyes are closed. Promise." He tapped the curtain and shoved the mayo jar inside the stall brushing his hand across her breast accidentally. "What was that? Is it what I think it was?"

"You have great aim for a blind man."

All too quickly he babbled, "Really it was an accident. A nice one but…"

"Hey, we have first base covered." An image of him sliding into her home plate had her turning the hot water completely off.

"I found you a pair of jeans that you could get away with rolled up with one of my belts and one of my shirts and a tee shirt under it. Sorry, no bra or undies. Commando will have to do. And I cut the ends off a pair of flip flops, so they don't look like you stole them from some ogre and you're not hopping around on one sandal."

"Wow, thank you. No one's ever offered me their

clothes or fashioned a pair of sponges for me before but then I've never actually been in a position like this unless you count the time my cousin and sister stole my clothes when we were skinny dipping in the woods, or the time I was in the changing room at the mall and the same two women ran off with all my belongings. That went well." His laughter warmed her. He had one of those deep belly laughs that could always make someone smile.

Zander slid down the outside of the bathroom door in the hall and waited for her to come out. "Your sister and cousin sound like trouble."

"You have no idea. As for commando? I appreciate you're not giving me your tidy whities."

"Well love, that's the thing… they weren't really so white."

She fought laughter and cut him off with, "Ewh!" His generosity took her by storm. There was no way this guy locked her up. She knew it from the bottom of her heart. Something happened here last night. Someone compelled them to forget everything, but why? Her grandma Olivia could undo any compulsion she was under.

Fecking cursed choker.

Once dressed and her hair combed, she gave a slight tug on the door. Zander fell in backwards looking up at her. "You're worse than my cat and dog, always waiting on the opposite side waiting for me to exit." With her hand extended to help him up she said, "But you are a prince."

His hand swallowed hers. And at the exact same time it fit better than any glass slipper in the history of glass slippers. She tugged him to his feet but didn't release his hand.

He almost lost his train of thought. If he worried about having amnesia earlier, he would worry even more now seeing this woman with his clothing on, pants rolled up, cinched at her tiny waist and her bosom free to roam under the almost see-through white dress shirt. Her soaked ebony locks hung in ringlets to her waist. She didn't put the tee shirt on. He bit the smile from his lips. "You really are a fallen angel."

"You say that now."

Zander glanced down at the proximity of their hands and didn't want to let go either. "I think I'll say it later too." With the chime of the doorbell, he reluctantly let go and gave a sweep of his hand showing her into the other room. "Lunch, my lady. Go pick a spot on the floor and get cozy. Sorry for the lack of amenities. I only moved in a few weeks ago and haven't had a chance to pretty the place up."

Chapter Six

When Elyza walked out to the living room her heart flip-flopped. This guy, although a diamond in the rough held more radiance than the choker she'd been accused of snitching. He was a hopeless romantic. Never mind the gems she'd been accused of swiping, this guy was stealing her heart.

In the center of the room, he'd spread a plaid blanket with pillows from his bed for cushions. Paper towels were folded into little doves. Paper plates and plastic utensils were set, an open box of Zinfandel and two plastic cups. "Wine this early?"

"It was that or clotted milk."

"Let the day drinking commence." Legs crossed, Elyza plunked her butt on a pillow and got comfortable. She poured two cups of wine. "Cheers." She took a sip and licked her lips. "Just how long was I in the shower?" Smiling one second, the next an overwhelming sensation of doom swarmed her. As he reached for the doorknob she yelled, "Don't ope—"

The force alone of the door blowing in shoved Zander in the corner nook behind it. Two masked men forced their entrance. Elyza took one look at them and the word *moron* skyrocketed to the top of her vocabulary. The headgear covered only the top of their heads and ears. Face was wide open for viewing, or in their cases, identifying morons. One of the morons aimed a handgun at her, and the other assailant pointed a similar weapon at the door Zander landed flattened behind.

"Hey, ain't she the broad the bobbies is lookin' for that done the heist? Wasn't paying much attention last night, but she looks like that St. James's chick." The shorter of the two hooligans nudged his partner in the side.

The taller one dismissed him. "Nah! They pulled a body out of the ashes and think it's the model. And that chick would never spend time with this loser." He tapped the gun on the door. "Turn around and get Zander."

"Sure looks like her," the shorter one pressed.

*They think I'm dead? Oh, god. I have to let my family know I'm alive, bu*t... she thought for a moment. Being dead might have an advantage. *Yeah, it'll delay my stint being incarcerated a day, maybe two.*

"What do you want?" Zander shoved at the door to get free.

The taller thug jammed the nuzzle of the gun in Zander's mouth. "Bring back fond memories, Zan? Having something tickle your tonsils? You will speak when I ask and not before, during or after. Got it?"

"Don't plug him yet. We need the goods first." The shorter moron nudged his accomplice again.

The taller thug smirked. "After then."

Zander bent over gagging when the man yanked the gun from his mouth.

Elyza's heart shattered. She made a move to go to him, but Zander held his hand up, stopping her at the same time the shorter intruder brandished his weapon in her face. These men were true predators. Scum. The polar opposite of Zander. He didn't have a mean streak in him even though trouble seemed to surround his ankle

100

better than a tracking device.

****

Zander snuck a glance at Elyza, expecting to see disgust, shame, hatred, or a combo of them all but instead she stood silently, assessing their newest situation.

She mouthed, "You okay?"

He gave up the smallest nod. The woman just heard some very vile things about his life in prison and she didn't cast him away. Instead, she showed compassion.

"Don't hurt the girl, please? I'll give you whatever money I have. We can leave now and go to the bank. Just don't touch her. I mean it's not like she can identify either of you." Elyza shot him a look of disbelief for calling them out on their idiotic disguises.

"We ain't here for money. So where are they? Boss wants them now. You were supposed to have them last night."

"My boss?"

The taller man tapped the barrel of his gun off Zander's chest. "No one walks out of the HRM Prison in Liverpool without a charge. No one. Take the girl in the bedroom and tie her up. Better yet, make Zander do it. That way we got 'em both covered."

The shorter goon motioned to Elyza. "Get up. Slowly."

"I can't take this another second." Furious, Elyza stood and turned to Zander. "What is this about?"

The shorter invader answered, "Priceless. Or did she cost you a pretty penny?"

"Angel, meet Max and the Ax. I turned state's evidence on them. Got me a reduced sentence for a jewelry heist." Zander stood helpless as Elyza's cheeks reddened. She was pissed and he didn't blame her. He started to cross to her but the barrel of a gun in his chest stopped him dead in his tracks. "Please, I know it sounds bad with everything we have going on, but I swear, I didn't take them. Years ago, I'd just got my license and they made me drive. These criminals are my last foster mom's brothers. I don't know how they're standing here because they each got life for killing the guards and robbing the vault, and then killing the couple whose car they jacked to get away after I drove off and left them stranded."

Zander's confession left her barren. There's no way this was a coincidence. She was marked from the get-go. Humiliation and embarrassment overwhelmed her for believing this guy could be anything other than a man who was using her. She placed one foot behind the next, to inch her way out. "I think I should go home now. Hanging out with jewelry thieves was not on my to-do list today, or last night. Or tomorrow. Or ever! So, with that said, ta!" She spun moving like lightening, around both men headed straight out the door.

"Get her."

Freedom, she'd had it. Could taste it like sea salt on the tip of her tongue, instead she gulped so hard she choked.

Zander. Fecking jewel thief.

She didn't know squat about the man, but she knew all she needed to. She was second guessing herself. To care about him as ridiculous as it appeared. She couldn't leave him alone to face whatever these two scoundrels had planned. He'd told her of his life. Hell, he had the scars to show it. 'First instincts are always right,' her mom told her over and over, 'listen to your gut,'. She swung around to face them, hands in front of her, palms up.

"Do you remember I said when I get upset things happen, Zander? You've been forewarned. Watch!" She didn't ask. Both of her palms began to turn from a natural light shade of fleshy pink to a deep red color a burner on an electric stove gets on high. A flicker of orange and yellow grew in her right hand and then arced to her left hand. Next, she tossed the power into the air and caught it just like a baseball a few times. With each toss the ball expanded. All three men watched, mesmerized.

"What black magic is this?" The shorter man yelled.

"Elementals," Zander mumbled just loud enough for Elyza to catch. "Pretty awesome."

"My temper," Elyza answered as she juggled her fury. "I've had a rather devastating twenty-four hours and I don't see yours turning out any better."

"Shoot," the taller idiot demanded, but before his words finished Elyza tossed the fireball at him, accurate to the point the Sand Man would be proud. Sparks ignited the man's mask in an all-consuming frenzy. Hideous cries for help along with the pungent odor of burning flesh filled the tiny room. His groans lessened as the fire fed its insatiable appetite.

If there were ever a romantic inkling between them, that too went up in smoke, seeing the horror in Zander's eyes.

The shorter thief fired off a bullet, but his shaking hand skewered his aim. A second bullet pierced Elyza's right hip and with the backlash of the firing, the man's arm jerked upwards, and another bullet bore through the ceiling. His momentum continued to spin him with the gun wildly out of control. A fourth bullet ripped through Zanders right flank as he dove in front of Elyza to block her from any further harm. Unfortunately, one last blast rang out. The bullet burrowed through Zander's left flank and continued to forge a path beneath Elyza's rib cage.

Somehow, Elyza managed to send another fireball smacking the moron in his gut. The hitman turned into a helpless caterpillar entombed in a fiery cocoon. Taking their chance at freedom, Zander scooped Elyza up and ran out the door. Flames and smoke followed them into the street.

"How bad is it? How badly were you shot?" Zander asked breathy as he ran with her draped in his arms. Rain-flooded streets reached his knees. It took more effort than he would have thought to get the two of them moving.

"Not sure but with all the bouncing I'm going to be sick. Please stop. It really hurts. How badly are you hurt?"

"Flesh wound. I'm good but I can't—won't stop running. Once the police and fire department get there, I'm a wanted man. Hold on for another minute, please?"

"Stop running!" The intensity of the wind in her face made her feel like a dog with his head hung out a window, cheeks peeled backwards, all teeth bared from the g-force breaking all human limits. "Fecking stop!"

"We're going to get caught. You got bail money? What's that you say? A diamond bra and glittery thong? Gone baby gone."

His ability to regale her with witty sarcasm as they ran blindly through the mistral whilst peppered with holes, and yes, still look incredibly sexy infuriated her more. She had yet to master walking and talking without incident.

And he continued his rant. Men!

"Don't really think the bondsman collects stolen jewels for a get out of jail free ticket anyway. And your sandal will probably melt too." His legs kicked it up another notch.

"You're inhuman," she screamed. "No one runs this bloody fast. What are you?"

"You tell me. You bit me. What did I taste like?" After he'd covered a few miles of scaling fences with her clung to him, leapt over a moving car, horns blaring, and hopped the train tracks in one single bounce with the train passing beneath them he finally slowed down to a stroll. His chest heaved against her side. When he was able, Zander panted, "I'm inhuman? Me? What in the devil are you? I had them ya know. I could have handled them without your black magic torching yet another building while killing two more people and us getting shot. Son of a gun, Elyza. We got shot. This really hurts."

What he said hurt more than the bullets lodged inside her. Her torching yet another place? Black magic? Killing two more people? They were bad people. About to do bad things to them. Self-defense. But he thought she caused the fire at the hall. "I didn't." Her voice barely carried over his wheezing. "Not on purpose. I wanted them to stop hurting people, my mom. It got out of control."

"I didn't mean it. You and I are burdened with circumstances out of our control. We need to get that control back."

"I think I can do that." She had to get him to safety—wherever that was. Had to keep him focused because right here and now she wasn't feeling too hot. And then her innate need to have the last word kicked in. A true trait of her mothers. "Seriously? I don't think you had them unless your plan was to outrun them. They were going to kill us. What I did was self-defense."

"Bullet holes. Good chance they'll get their wish." With a subtle twist he turned his head and coughed, bringing up a large glob of bloody mucus.

She gripped his chin and pulled his view to hers and made him look at her. "Have you ever evanesced?"

His lips squashed together, he muttered, "No?"

"Me either, but there's always a first."

Chapter Seven

"The canning jar! Did you find it? Top shelf behind a paisley hatbox in the closet. The one with a lock." Lucian's frantic voice carried up three flights of stairs.

"Keep her spirit, Lucian. Don't. Let. Go!" Ethan infused every ounce of will and determination he had back to his uncle by marriage as he scaled the stairs three at a time headed for his aunt's bedroom. Inside the dressing room, a massive walk-in closet by today's design, despair settled over Ethan the way snow blanketed the Tundra. He stood frozen taking in Serina's keepsakes over the past century. Hoarder extraordinaire would be her new nickname, if she survived. Comparatively speaking, this place made finding Al Capone's vault easier. For all Ethan knew the vault could be hidden in here too. He chucked shoeboxes aside, plowed through an endless stack of sweaters, blankets and when he got the hatboxes, he didn't see one bloody paisley hatbox, but fifty or more and not one had a lock. Flipping lids from each box he swore as he emptied the contents of every headpiece Serina ever adorned. He came up short. "It's not here," he howled. "Where else would she have put it?"

Savanah joined Ethan, her nerves no better than anyone else in the home. "Where would you hide something you never wanted to look at again but couldn't destroy?"

"I don't know, Savvy. I don't own anything so vile. The only thing I ever put in a box was a frog to scare you that one time and well, I learned the hard way not to scare you. You pass out with the slightest hint of *boo*! I always thought it, this, was a freaking joke."

"Not this time. Gram needs that canning jar and we can't go down empty handed."

"She'll use one of ours if we do. That's a given. That's her baby spread out on the table lifeless. Heartless. Jesus, Savvy, those bastards blew Serina's heart out of her chest. Any other family and she'd be given Last Rights by now." Ethan looked at his gorgeous wife, the mascara in lines down her cheeks, her gorgeous blackish-blue eyes now fiery red with a lethal mixture of anger and fear. Her pain ripped his heart in half. If this continued, they'd need more than one canning jar. Tears disabled his tough demeanor regardless of the efforts to control his emotions. "We gotta find it."

Savanah turned and pointed to a portrait of King Henry Vll and his beautiful wife, Elizabeth of York, hung above the bed. "The wall safe. It's behind it. It has to be."

Ethan bounced onto the bed. Without giving the historical masterpiece a second thought Ethan flung the delicate canvas aside. They watched as the irreplaceable painting smashed on the floor. Defeat written all over his face, Ethan glanced at his wife and then the wall safe. "I don't care, do you? Your mom can fix it, right?"

Tight lipped Savanah shook her head no.

"Seriously, the painting creeped me out anyway, Savvy. The eyes follow you. Probably the White Witch of the estate." Ethan tapped on the wall safe. "Any possibility you know the combination?"

Uncle Lucian, the combo to the safe. Now. Savanah sent that to her uncle.

Lucian passed out, Savanah, Olivia answered. *I'm losing ground. Rip it from the wall. I don't care what it takes to get that safe open, get me that bleeding canning jar now!*

Savanah's grandfather, Father Thomas added, *Savanah, I'm holding on to Lucian's and my daughter's spirit as we speak but I'm growing weary. You know what happens when we lose someone.*

Then I firmly suggest you hang on with your last ounce of light, Grampa because I will not go through what we went through when my papa pulled this sleepy time stint. Have you felt Elyza's presence? Has anyone? Is this why both Lucian and Serina are trying to leave this world? Because their daughter died? Well, other than the more obvious reason of the hole in Serina's chest. "Crap, I feel sick, Eth." Savanah stumbled and clung to the end of the bed, swaying while her fingers dug into the knob on the footboard.

"Father Thomas!" Ethan's voice bellowed throughout the manor. Beyond upset, beyond worried, he no longer needed the mental channeling to be heard from the upper third story of the Tudor mansion. Voices carried when you put every last ounce of life into it. "Savanah crashed and burned. I can't reach my boy, Daelyn, either. They're dropping like flies. Who hasn't yet?" Ethan prayed for all his worth, while he changed over from man to wolf. He needed the wolf's strength to get the bloody door off the safe. And may the devil make peace with his father because that is all that would save him if there's no canning jar in there.

Thomas finally answered Ethan telepathically. He

had no choice. His energy now equated to a flashlight with old, corroded batteries, flickering. Fading.

Ethan, hurry. Shelby and Sydney went looking for Elyza. They aren't answering me. Payton is with Raven right now because she's slipped as well. I haven't heard from my Jovan or your beloved father-in-law, André so I fear the worst. Tell me you found that—

Beloved? I'd laugh if the circumstances were different. With the jar firm in his grasp Ethan descended the stairs gingerly, in the same manner a handmaid from a few centuries back carried a tray of tea without the contents sloshing all over the sides. Only this time he'd lose more than a finger if he spilled a drop. The noxious contents could erode his fingers or Olivia could take his head if anything upset the contents of the jar. He lifted the jar into Father Butler and Olivia's view. Slumped over her daughter's lifeless body, Olivia raised her head slowly with a grimace Ethan understood all too well.

Hopelessness filled her vacant eyes. Ethan had to help her find her fighting spirit with a bit of hard love and reverse psychology. "You can't be serious. Look at it. Really, look at it, Liv. There's no way this is going to work. You might as well just let her pass. This will kill her. Dead." He didn't need to try to be convincing. He was serious.

Her cold glare went from the jar and then settled on Ethan. "Bite your tongue child, before I do it for you. Don't you ever steal away hope. Especially mine. Hope is the one constant on this earth that allows us to go forth. To live. To dream. To imagine a world so precious that tears fill your eyes from the beauty alone. Do you have any idea who you're talking to? Do you have any idea what I am capable of?"

Ethan gave himself an invisible pat on his back. Father Thomas snuck in a nod to him.

Fury didn't only radiate from Olivia's body, it encased her. A living sheath of red waves cloaked both Olivia and Serina's body. Ethan knew if he even tried to penetrate it body parts would be severed or fried. Olivia Spencer's powers, her magic, the spells, the healing abilities, all failed to compare in her ability to knock off someone should she get miffed.

"But—"

Thomas cut him off. "She knows what she's doing, Ethan. Have faith in her. I do."

Olivia turned a cheek and gave a weary smirk to her lover. "I'll have to remember you said that. It's a first I do believe." Her attention back on Ethan, she directed, "Now, very carefully twist the lid. It's rusted. I can see that from here. Once it's open, we must move fast. The liquid must be boiled. Don't get it on you. It's far more toxic than any black charm I've ever used."

"Find that hard to believe." Ethan's brows raised the question.

Olivia slighted his rantings and continued. "Add salt. A lot. Add bleach, a dash. Add some Epinephrine. You'll find a vile in Serina's medical bag in the cold room."

"The walk-in cooler?" Ethan questioned, just to make certain he wasn't wasting precious seconds looking in the wrong room. These mansions had multiple rooms with multiple names.

Olivia nodded. "The Epi, that goes in at the last second. And lastly bring a shot of whiskey. That's for me."

With the vast knowledge his culinary skills weren't

up to par, Ethan did the next best thing. "Payton, get down here. You're needed pronto in the scullery."

Olivia elbowed Father Butler. "I see he does have an ounce of genius after all."

"Livvy," the older man snickered.

"I'm joking, sort of. I was beginning to wonder what Savanah saw in you."

Olivia winked her mischievous green eye at Ethan, but he just stood there, terrified to move.

"It's going to be all right, Ethan. I promise. I'm just trying to lighten your mood. I do love you. If I didn't, we would not be having this or any conversation at all. Now twist the jar over the sink. No need for century old sludge all over the floor. You might want to don some gloves, an apron and a mask too, dear."

"She's calling me dear," he mumbled to no one as he made his way to the scullery. "This can't be good. She's never said a nice freaking word about me. To me. Always teased me about how old dogs and new tricks don't go together. How they're neutered for a reason. We're doomed," Ethan babbled on. With a step backwards Ethan wiggled his arms and tried to shake off the nerves. "So, it isn't my old boss's then? It's his son's?"

Thomas smiled, but not one crinkle reached his brilliant blue eyes. "Your old boss's went through the sink's disposal grinder in the kitchen at Yaddo in Saratoga. The day Savanah nearly died."

His stomach in knots, Ethan begrudgingly added, "I don't see this one being any better."

Thomas tried to ease Ethan's concerns. "It is all in the person, Eth. What their soul brings to light, not their physical attributes."

"Thomas, he beheaded you. That's so not a good soul."

"The organ is going to Serina. She has a soft soul. And you don't have the whole story, Ethan."

"Savanah told me about him, his soul had more tarnish than the silver in this old house."

Thomas answered, "Raven and I sat down one evening and she told me he was nowhere near as violent as his twin. Donovan body-snatched Xavier the night it all went down."

"You mean the night Serina was almost burned as a witch and you lost your head and Xavier, his life."

"At least two of us survived the night." Thomas pat Olivia's back lightly. "She is many things to many people, but she is my light."

Mumbling came from Olivia as she worked with due diligence to try and repair what she could on her daughter before the messy part began. "Thomas, your emotions will be the death of you."

Thomas squeezed Olivia's shoulder. "Then it's a damn good thing I have you, my love."

"Daft sod. You're damned right you're lucky to have me. First, I had to turn back time and then I had to put you back together once as if you were Humpty freaking Dumpty. Second worst night of my life."

"The first?" Ethan asked.

Huffing a strand of hair from her vision, Olivia swept her hand the length of Serina's body.

Footsteps bounding, Payton skidded and came to a complete stop with a few steps in reverse. "You yelled?" Payton pointed to Serina's body and turning his head away declared, "This is catastrophically wrong."

Ethan shot a cautious glance to the man. Payton

didn't look much better than anyone in the house. His amber eyes were the color of a blood moon. His usual bouncy sun-kissed blond curls hung drenched in sweat.

"What's going on in the Banqueting room?" Ethan asked even though he had a pretty good idea.

"The entire house has fallen, apart from this room and Julian and Jonah. They're tending to everyone. I don't know how I'm even standing. This all for one and one for all guys, it'll crumble these walls sometime. Where's Savanah?"

"Down too, so before we lose you or I, let's do this." The canning jar firm in his grasp again, Ethan ran through the directions given to him by Olivia. "Does it bother anyone that the thing actually has a slight pulse?"

Thomas, Payton and even Olivia all turned their immediate attention to the canning jar.

"What?" Olivia bit out tersely.

"No way!" Payton walked over and peered inside the jar. "I can't see anything other than what looks like old black molasses."

"Put your hand on it," Ethan suggested.

"I don't even want to see it, let alone put a hand on it." Begrudgingly he put his index finger on the jar and pulled back rubbing his arms. "Oh shit," Payton's voice shook. "The freaking jar is vibrating, Livvy. The canning jar would be doing the Rumba across the countertop if we let it. It's picking up intensity." Payton waited for Olivia or Thomas to respond.

"Dire circumstances, my dear Payton, shall occur if you do not get that thing prepped immediately. I shall not allow my daughter to pass when I have the solution sitting in front of me." Olivia lifted one hand and through pursed lips commanded, "Do it. Now!"

"Livvy," Payton's hands went out in front of him like he was being held up, "I'm just saying, what if Serina starts to grow a beard and balls?"

Thomas answered, "Then I'll rip mine out and you can use that."

Head cocked sideways and lips taut, Payton finished with, "You won't have to Father Thom. Lucian will do it for you."

Ethan smacked his lips together and nudged the jar to Payton. The canning jar shimmied across the shelf like a Mexican jumping bean. Payton caught it before it smashed to the floor. "Sometimes the things that go on here creep me out."

"Sometimes?" Headed in a backward direction, Ethan announced, "Good luck with this. I'm going to check on my bride and see if I can't reach my son."

Olivia glanced upward to the men. "What? Wait! Ethan, this more than anything, only proves how swiftly we must move. I need you, Ethan. Please? Don't leave."

He had one foot out the door when he heard the frailty in Olivia's voice. She'd begged. Dammit all to hell. Olivia Spencer had never spoken those words to another living being. Ethan knew it with every ounce of life he held. The woman, plainly put, was the sheer definition of pride, self-assuredness, and the ultimate control freak. For her to ask for help, one-things were indeed grim, and two-she was losing ground. For the most magical mage in the universe to be asking for help and from him no less, when she had a true fallen angel, Thomas, by her side, Ethan figured Doom and Gloom were about to strut in with their suit cases, kick off their blood-stained boots, whip up a few steak tar-tar sliders along with a Bloody Mary or two to wash them down then make themselves comfy for the duration until the Apocalyptic crew joined in. And why not invite Pestilence, War, Famine, and Death to the gathering? Why should they be shunned from such a gathering of absolute insanity? Letting loose a guttural groan Ethan rolled up his sleeves and did an about-face.

"Livvy, do a wiggly finger at the pot of water and make it boil. I'm going to grab Serina's bag while Payton prepares us all for judgment day." This time Ethan didn't walk out of the great hall. He ran.

Chapter Eight

Eyes barely slits, my lust sated for the time being I took in my surroundings. A cracked mirror tacked lopsided to rotted plaster and broken bricks detailed a blood-lusted stupor camouflaging my handsome face. This scene before me has my crimson calligraphy stamped all over it. My first night of freedom took its toll on me.

And from the looks of things, those around me.

All spiffed-up, I tiptoed through the tunnel beneath the Tower Bridge to the exit. The breeze from the Thames has more of a bite to it tonight than I.

Hands tossed in the air, my cane out in front of me like God's scepter, I kicked up my heels. The overcast sky didn't allow for a trace of light. The perfect bewitching hour. Street lanterns cast shadows in the alleys. My shadow of course appears tall, ominous, badass, able to make others retreat with haste. The hat alone might add to the allure, but I prefer to believe in myself, since no one else does. Storefronts along the avenue are lit better than Christmas trees and are packed to the gills with patrons, mostly due to the inclement weather. Would no one come out to play? The Tower of London has been closed for hours so the visitors that remained are either famished or foolish. I know which way I'm leaning here.

After walking for nearly an hour I stood outside my

old stomping ground in Piccadilly. Memories flood me. Most, unkind. My father and brothers always taunted me for being odd, the queer redheaded stepchild even though my hair is blacker than the night. Never a kind word went my way. Well, if it came right down to it, I am different. I embraced my inner beast and never looked back. And to top it off, hands down I am the most handsome of the brothers. Dear old dad even admitted it that one time. Said, "If you weren't such a freak of nature Xanti, you'd have this street lined up with women. Your brothers have to glamour, drug, or coerce women to get their attention. If only you'd bat your long, black lashes they'd converge on you like vultures to roadkill. What a waste of sperm. Mine for creating you. All the glorious dark powers and beauty your mother held, given to you through birth and this is the thanks we get. Should have deposited you in the trash the second your mum died." To this day it hurts. The old saying, 'Sticks and stones can break your bones, but words will never hurt you,' is outright rubbish. Words hold the ability to create life or end it. To make your days planted here enjoyable or miserable. I love you. I hate you. You are worth more to me than the air to someone's last breath. A shoe covered in dog shit has more worth than you. You are my greatest gift. I wish you were dead. I now opted for the latter two of these. Death and misery. Wicked combo. As old as the ages. My dear brother, Xavier, used to shadow our father in his words and mannerisms. His parrot, I called him. Xavier always yanked on my pointed ears and yelled, "Abomination." I do not miss him. Or my father. Or my brother Donovan. And why did he get the normal name? My name may mean saint, and is pronounced like Santi Clause, but I think everyone would concur I run a parallel course with Krampus.

In the center of the square the statue of Eros remains erect with broad shoulders, flaunting his masculinity for the world to crave. The empty eyes of the god glanced down upon me with a come-hither look.

If only!

With a cautious eye I searched the plaza and further to the building I'd once called home. No one in their right mind would think I'm a a stone's throw from the place where cops, the security, and the PEON's, a group of militants who exterminated anything preternatural with no questions asked, all hunt me. Heard they have since changed their name to Garlands of Garlic.

Both names are as ridiculous as are the fools running the militia. Sounds more like an Italian bistro. One I might fancy a meal or two from. Maybe some evening I'll invite the leaders to dinner and let them pick up the check. Blood money... I have a new meaning for the word.

Crossing the square, I caught a rather scrumptious whiff. My nostrils flared. I stopped. Sniffed. Gazed around. The miniscule scent trickled up my hooter and tickled my fancy. Made something in the back of my brain attempt to dig through years of perfumes, colognes, men, women, life, death—different odors to place this being. Someone holds a phantom aroma. My eyebrows danced.

Finally, some fun.

The smell, I can taste it. My head whipped around as I take in every person in the vicinity. Could it be the gent who'd just passed by with a glint in his eye and a cell phone at his ear? At a quick glance everyone has one glued to their ears or in front of their face as they walked, talked, or texted. Understandably, my patience thinned. I don't get it. People. Don't they realize their time is precious? They're milk cartons for Pete's sake. Expiration dates—hello. People settle. Some for things they never dreamt of or expected—a loveless marriage, a job that pays the bills but leaves one bankrupt in happiness, or an abusive relationship that leaves ugly discolored bruises verses smudged lipstick? Or a partnership fueled on greed and misgivings. Humans scurrying through the rat race wasting time on their electronic devices instead of talking to the person sitting next to them. This race will become extinct if they don't learn to live in the moment, take chances. Stop watching and start doing. Why do I care? Hello—sustenance.

With my feet in fast-forward, I weaved through the crowds better than a witcher looking for his next coin. The strongest teases to make my eyes water and nose run are semen, blood, pheromones, and sex. Piccadilly smells like a mass orgy. *Gosh it is good to be home.* Sadly, a strong breeze carried with it torrential downpours which dampened my elation. The last of those out trying to enjoy the evening scattered like the rats they were for safety.

As I thought I'd lost the tracer due to the rain a second tiny vestige of burnt brimstone hit me. My crooked smile grew. Fingers to my mouth I fondled a twisted fang, or was the new wordage gnarly, regardless of my vocabulary I stroked the dent in the same manner a gentleman masturbated a moustache; I played with it, twisted it, tugged it, enjoyed the sensation until the damn thing fell out in my hand.

Bone loss. Who knew vampires had health issues? Really? Once you've kicked the proverbial bucket what else could go wrong? At some point I plan to sue the museum for cruel and inhumane punishment. Wrongful imprisonment, no health care, and the worst of all—bullying. My current list of woes is endless. But bullying? I detest bullies.

Vampires more so. We have feelings too. We get such a bad rap. People need to learn if you stopped struggling, you'd most likely survive our attentions. Our prey drive is off the charts. It's the fight that spikes our innate need for dominance. Just give us what we want, play dead if you must. Although, some vamps are true necrophiles so it might not help your cause. A pint or two and we'll be on our way... Pfft! Said no true vampire ever. Someday, I must thank the author of all those sparkling vampires for making my life easier. She has young girls believing we all glisten, we're only interested in true love. Those books and movies paved the way for those of us who stay the true course, believe we are the righteous rulers of the universe and young girl's necks look better with two festering holes in them than some dainty gold chain. I can't wait for the day I get to thank the museum curators for dowsing me in sparkles just for shits and giggles. We will see who shits and who gets the last giggles.

Across the avenue a young man, tall, with a wicked buff silhouette cast a curious glance my way. Did the idiot not know a vamp could snare someone with the wink of an eye? A bat of long, lush lashes? A welcoming smile? A little thing known to many as beguiling? I have all these qualities mastered. Ask Murph... Maybe hold off on that for a day or two until he's not so pissed at me when he wakes.

Across the way, the lad stood roughly twenty feet at

best from me, his azure eyes roiling like the North Sea on a rough day. His tussled hair makes him look like he's just climbed out from the sheets after a good romp. Lucky sod. One slightly damp curl dangles by his temple. A juicy little artery near the surface of his skin pulses next to his eye. I licked my lips in response.

How I love blood. My destiny in life could not have been better. Pretty certain others have a different opinion of me.

The young gent's darker blond mustache and goatee give the illusion he is older than his true age. He's wearing a leather bomber jacket with no shirt beneath it. There's a nasty jagged scar running the length of his chest that vanished beneath the waistband of his jeans. He yanked the edges of his jacket together as if I'd intruded on his privacy. If he didn't want others to take notice he should've worn a shirt. His eyes flashed to iceberg blue. Interesting. He's a wolf. Only a few things can change your eye color that fast. A vamp's eyes usually bleed black or red. Witches get an eerie neon glaze to them and were-animals usually go a few shades lighter than their natural color. I knew a werewolf years past, his eyes reminded me of dewy grass in the morning. When I pulled his tail, those eyes could have pulled Santa's sleigh they got so bleeding bright. I hope to never see the scoundrel again. I will euthanize him given the chance.

A chain hanging around wolf-boy's neck made me do a double take. Antique Celtic cross. Worth a pretty penny. I would know. I bought a few just like it eons past. My gut tells me we are acquainted. It'll come to me. Hopefully I didn't dine on his family in the past. Those conversations never tend to end well.

The man's set jaw along with the determination his eyes held as he watched me makes me ponder who hunts whom. About to cross the cobbled pavement to introduce myself to the feral pup, a cyclone of discombobulated bodies emerged out of thin air. In a twisted heap of bones, skin, and cursing, the mass of flesh fell to the pavement with less grace than the house did that crushed the poor misunderstood wicked witch. Bodies rolled about ten to fifteen feet before coming to a bloody stop. The scent of bitter copper permeated the air. Interest piqued, the big picture enlarged ten-fold. My vision went from what equated to watching a black and white television on a six-inch screen to a sixty-inch flat LED HDTV screen with surround sound sprinkled with a scratch and sniff remote to enhance the entire exhibition. A new fang poked my bottom lip. Kind of to be expected. The old black box in my chest picked up its pace and the saliva flowed better than an avalanche chasing skiers. From the corner of my eye, I noticed the blond not looking any more civilized. I know I know this kid… It'll come to me. That cross he wears…

****

"What the heck? You could've warned me. Like, 'Hey Zan, we're coming in for landing now. Buckle up butter cup. Might be a bit of turbulence. Hold onto your ass.'"

"You, get off me." Elyza struggled to free herself from the solid musculature flattening her into the wet, cold, unforgiving pavement. Stuck on her belly, her face submerged in something she didn't want the answer too, the scent of stale coffee, bubble gum and urine triggered her stomach to tighten. One arm ended up jammed behind her back and somehow looped through Zander's

123

hoodie. There was a new hole in the material he wouldn't appreciate in a minute or two. His arms were secured to her. One went down the inside front of her jeans, and the other with a strangle hold around her neck. One of his legs straddled her hip and his other got wedged between her thighs.

"All gripes aside, I kind of like this position," Zander whispered.

Elyza fidgeted. "Get up!" Rain or no rain, her voice covered the entire plaza. Onlookers gawked and pointed. With a giant huff, Elyza tried to get her hair out of her eyes. "Zander!"

"You passed out midflight. Who does that, little cherub? Come on. We had a deal. I agree to fly with you, and you don't kill me. Look where we freaking landed. And it's dark. What time is it? We aren't in Kansas anymore, Dot. Looks like Piccadilly. And this could be one dilly of a mess."

"Get up and hang on. I won't pass out again. I promise." Elyza struggled to get her feet under her.

"Hey!" Some random woman wearing a bright red hat with a plume of feathers yelled from the sidelines, "Isn't that the model everyone's looking for? Look, she's on the cover of that magazine." The woman then pointed to a small storefront where a collage of magazines, tabloids and what looked like Wanted Posters of Elyza sat.

"I liked page three better." Elyza raked her fingers through her tangled mess and then wiped her face. A glob of gum stuck to her cheek. "Oh this is beyond gross." Zander apprehensively went to remove it. One eyebrow up, her current state of pissed off at the world showed through. "Just band-aid it. Fast."

With a quick tug the gum tore free. Zander quickly placed a chaste kiss on her cheek. "I'm sorry."

To her sheer astonishment and complete dismay two things happened. One, the kiss stole her breath in the most fabulous, sensuous, caring way. And secondly, while she was looking over Zander's shoulder as he kissed her, she stole a second glance at the storefront. The shop didn't miss a single shot of her. Yup, there she was, in all her glory, every last naked inch of her, with her eyes almost a neon blue, the mask in one hand with a straight line of fire streaming from her mouth like a dragon on every freaking cover. And let's not forget that God forsaken dimple. "Am I fecking hot or what?" She buried her face in Zander's shoulder and groaned.

Zander slid his hand under her jaw and then grabbed her cheeks. "Look at me. It's going to be all right. Trust me, okay? I know that isn't what you expected to see but the dimple's not that bad."

A tiny spark shot from Elyza's mouth. "You did not just say that!"

"I'm sorry but your thoughts projected to me, and it came out of thin air, literally. Kinda like that spark you just shot at me. Calm down, Sparky."

"Put your naked, fire-breathing dragon, dimpled arse up there for everyone to see and then say that. My gram calls me that, Sparky."

"You've already caught a glimpse of my arse, love. I would never say mine's not that bad." He winked at her. Had to try to lighten her mood, get her fears under control so they could vamoose. Their circle of trust was rapidly shrinking. It was just the two of them. And about twenty others closing in.

Under her breath she mumbled, "Pretty fecking

amazing actually."

A cocky smirk made its way to Zander's lips. "I know. It's why I show it off like I do. But mostly it's due to lack of clean laundry."

Elyza swatted him. "Get me outta here, Zander. God, Grampa I wish you could hear me. I need help."

Strangers encroached on Elyza and Zander just as the winds whipped up a notch and sent everyone off balance. Jolted into motion, people staggered and fought to remain vertical. A few individuals went rolling backwards down the sidewalk, taking out other pedestrians, rubbish bins, restaurant menu stands, anything not nailed down. Others clung to the person next to them unable to fight Mother Nature's wrath.

Or maybe it was Father Butler's.

Elyza said a quick thank you to her grandfather on the off chance he somehow heard her pleas. The man's ability to manipulate the weather had proven to be a true godsend.

With a quick hand Zander made it to his feet, spread his legs to try and withstand the gale-forced fury. He extended his arm to help Elyza to her feet. "Hang on!" He had to yell to be heard above the storm. "Don't look at them. Just me. We're going to run again. When we're free from eyes, you can make us disappear. No need to prove the covers are correct. Right now, we can say it was photo shopped."

Just as the winds calmed, she blurted, "Who's the character from the eighteenth century? He looks like he just walked out of a museum."

The few remaining pedestrians in the plaza followed her pointing finger. Lips pressed together, the man in the top hat and long black coat waved. "Hello little angel.

You're leaking. I can smell your scent from here. Delicious!" His entire body shuddered in delight.

Elyza tugged Zander's arm "Get us out of here? I lack the energy to fight anyone."

When the blond in the leather jacket closed in and met Zander's eyes a spark of recognition slammed Zander in the heart the way vampire hunters off their prey. Pain seared his insides. His grip on Elyza, he lost. Down they went again. He keeled over hugging his sides, panting. Eyes clamped shut, Zander gasped, held his chest, and prayed he didn't die right here and now. He needed to get Elyza to safety. In all his existence no amount of suffering ever consumed him like this.

Elyza grasped Zander's hand. She flipped his hand over to see his palm then she kissed him in the dead center of his hand. The warmth her lips produced instantly relaxed him. He'd never experienced any phenomenon like this. He was able to think, to focus. He stole a second glance at the two odd men closing in. Who the hell were they to him? Reluctant to let go, he said, "I owe you," and gave her hand a gentle squeeze. "You are a true blessing."

"You say that now. Is that why you call me little cherub?"

His breath still shaky, Zander looked up to her and bit back a weary smirk. "No. You work for Fallen Angels, but you're much smaller than most models, cherub-sized. When I look at those two guys, Elyza, I feel like I'd been left for dead."

Concern clear in her tone she kneeled before him. "Do you know them?" She dabbed at his tears with the cuff of her shirt.

Zander's nose twitched once, twice and his gaze

immediately zoned in on the source. His black eyes became pure onyx. Gleaming. No pupils, no whites. Ah, but there was a glint of trouble lurking in those mesmerizing orbs.

"The scent of your blood, Elyza... I swear I won't hurt you, but like the Victorian goth said, you do smell delish."

"Zander, don't be a creeper."

"Don't judge. There's something in this area that's got me strung up like some loser at one of those hypnotic shows. If I start quacking shoot me."

"I do love a roasted duck with orange glaze." Elyza snapped out a mischievous nod. "Zan, they look about as friendly as Max and Ax. Time to skedaddle."

He had no memory of them. Nothing. It was like sending him off on a scavenger hunt with the treasure more cleverly coveted than the disappearance of the two York Princes. Maybe it would come to him at two in the morning when he was in a deep slumber and he'd jerk into a sitting position and sputter the stupid answer into the darkness with no one to tell it to, unless this crazy little woman decided to stick around and get to know him instead of trying to get as far from him as she could.

He couldn't blame her. He'd found her chained to his bed with no viable explanation, and then two thugs showed up and well, that ended poorly. Being shot truly held no redeeming qualities, not to mention all his belongings turned to ash. He stole another glimpse of everyone in the plaza. Took a mental snapshot of them and stored them away for a time where he could afford to dig inside his past because right now, this very moment, a giant shark frenzy was about to play out if he stuck around and he and Elyza were the chum.

"Come on, Zander, later, after we've survived this, you can tell me all about that which you do not know. Should be an interesting one-sided conversation of me asking all the questions and you just sitting there looking all hot and bothered."

His head cocked a bit to the side a glimmer of amusement met his eyes. "Finally! Something I can do."

"Stop being a drama queen. That's my roll. Can you still run? I can't believe we're still breathing." Against her better judgment Elyza placed her hand over Zander's heart. The pain stymied her, transported her mentally to a place no one could survive. How he had come this far said volumes of his character. And he coveted his pain so damned well behind a mask of poor humor amidst rugged handsomeness. In comparison, the suffering Zander hid to what she felt about her family just before she passed out in his arms, may have even surpassed hers. She knew then the two of them were damaged goods. She needed to help him, regardless of the cost to her and he needed to get up and run, carrying her sorry excuse of witchery, because hands down she was going to pass out again. Soon. Between his dreary past and a few bullet holes, they were a few seconds short of a minute.

"You're a true empath, aren't you? Able to heal through touch. That's your superpower, lil cherub." Zander brushed her soaked tendrils from her face and looked deep into her ocean-blue eyes. "Let's boogie."

A smile, if it could be called one, tried to form on her lips. It fell short. "Head for Bramall, the Tudor mansion." And with that, Elyza went limp in his arms.

***

129

With one eye on the blond and the other on the couple attempting to flee, I took a few more steps toward them, my heels making a delightful clack off the cobbles. Again, a new scent rose. Something familiar. It made my gut twist, and to be honest, that takes a lot. I can't take my eyes from the man with the black hair and black eyes with a girl cradled in his arms. With a nonchalant shift I checked to see where the rugged blond went. To my surprise he too is making his way to the couple.

Distressed cries cut through the storm's howl bringing passersby to a halt with their heads turning in all directions to see where the dilemma lay. Before me, two women appeared from thin mist on the heels of the man trying to flee with the girl flopping unnaturally in his arms. The women plowed down anyone and anything from their path. I stepped back.

Movement caught the blond man advancing. With the boldness only a Sinclair could muster, I held my hand up to halt the dolt. "They're mine, mate. Don't bother," I inferred with a wink going for a friendly warning. He mouthed something back to me I shan't repeat, complete with an angry fist shooting in my direction. And then, as if his animosity weren't enough, one of the two ladies yelled to the other, "Check out the emaciated Goth Abe Lincoln wanna-be."

A petite red head yelled, "Syd, seriously, he's not your style. Stop it."

"Not funny, Shelby Jane."

"Wasn't kidding, Syd. Lizzy! Lizzy *stopppp*! Sydney, that guy has Lizzy!"

"You do realize I am right here and can hear you, Shelby Jane…" My voice trailed after the ladies in pursuit of the couple who crash-landed moments earlier. At least now formalities aren't an issue. I have names. The floppy girl, Lizzy perhaps? The blond kid budging the line looks less pleased than I as everyone rushed off in a huff. The redhead, Shelby, gave it her all yelling at the other one, Syd, "This guy is inhuman. I'll never catch them. Stop looking at the mothball."

"I think I know him," Syd yelled back slowing her pace before me.

I offered a gentlemanly tip of my hat to the girl in passing. "Quite the compliment."

"Douchebag." Shelby shouted out, "Do you have any idea how ridiculous you look?" She kept running, gaining speed the farther she went but not before doing a double take at the blond man. He went to say something but stopped. Now I wondered if they are acquainted. Or want to be. I want to be.

The cuckoo bird in the feather hat chirped, "There," she pointed at me, "the escaped vamp from the museum, Xanti Sinclair," while she snapped her camera frame after frame. Regardless of my current circumstance, I cheesed big, all fangs and flamboyance. I am who I am, Xanti the man. Expect nothing less. And lose so much more.

Sydney came to an ultimate standstill and yelled, "Oh, crap!" before she leapt on me. Why? I doubt it's because I'm the hot dude she wants to shag. More like bag and tag.

The insane little southern bell put to rest all those stories of hospitality, charm, and a refined sense of self as she tore away my jacket, vest, and shirt and attempted the unthinkable, to make me a living heart donor. Not a fan to the ending of this story, I gouged my talons into

Sydney's scalp in an attempt to peel her off me. I winced as she tugged and scratched at my flesh. She on the other hand is one tough cookie. Not a peep from her.

Oddly, the blond man came to my rescue, to separate us. The three of us went down in a tangled mess, so much so that it appeared the laws of physics had been totally skewered. Newton would be pissed. I know I am.

Sydney freed her arm and plunged her fist through the wall of my chest. I winced. How could I not? Ribs broke. What little blood I'd squandered earlier now soils my clothes. A hideous plea of, "Stop it," blared in Sydney's ear. Hasn't been the manliest of sentiments to ever spew from me, but then I've never been on the receiving end of a vicious woman hell bent on assassinating an innocent bystander.

Fighting to save my vampy life, I solidified my grip on her. Her gaze intent on what lay coveted within my chest, her fingers poked, prodded and grasped my lifeline.

"It's not your lifeline scum wad, it's a defunct, corroded, slimy broken pump."

Apparently, she's a mind reader. "Who are you?" I had to know.

"Sydney St. James." She clamped down and tugged with each drop of her sweat saturated in sheer determination.

"I am not my brothers!"

She scathed, "You're far worse."

So, this was how it would end? Poorly from my new borrowed shoes. To have my heart ripped out, and by a woman no less. A St. James woman, nonetheless. What the hell is it with these St. James women that they desired the Sinclair's heartless? Now I know exactly how my brother Xavier and my father felt the day they died.

Not so good.

One last hope, I angled my head just so and bore into her neck. Two could play this game.

Blond man, my savior, bit out, "Release the heart or you lose your arm, Syd."

Squirming, Sydney managed to defy both of us. "I have another arm, you giant heartworm. Release me, you freaking leach."

"Aye, Lass, but only one pretty little neck," The blond mocked.

Sydney cranked her free arm up and poked determinedly as hard as she could until she found my eye socket. We both reeled in pain. I was forced to withdraw my fangs yelping, but this hellion remains steadfast and she squeezed my heart harder. For the record, heart attacks are not fun. Chest pain, shortness of breath, nausea, the overwhelming fatigue to stay in the game, seeing stars… *Shite!*

Sydney wriggled into a kneeled position and leaned into me, her forearm buried within my chest cavity. How funny would it be if my rib cage turned into a Venus fly trap and clamped down on her bleeding greedy phalanges? That would be a moment to remember. Instead, the next best thing happened.

Before my very blurry eyes the young blond man changed. At this juncture I might be hallucinating. Blood loss, lack of O2, does that to a person, even vamps. A thick coat of fur covered him from his elfin ears to his wagging tail. Claws broke free from his flesh, staining his fur red. His back legs remind me of a centaur. Thick muscles flexed as his paws dug through the cobbled pavers for traction, kicking bricks loose, sending one through a windowpane of a restaurant full of gawkers. Glass shattered. People screamed. My adrenaline spiked. Even about to get my ticker ripped from me I still enjoy fear. Maybe it's why I connect to it. I'm bloody well used to it and it's now other's turn to know firsthand what it feels like when death pounds your door down with more enthusiasm than the three little baconaters experienced. I'm not scared. I am furious. There's a huge difference. Wolfie gave it the old college try getting this little goblin off me. That set jaw I noticed earlier now has gleaming canines and incisors barred. I'm a little jealous. My gnarly dents don't compare. I'll sulk later, provided there is one.

The wolf pleaded, "Come on Syd, let him go. I don't want to hurt you."

Twisting back and giving the other man a not so friendly glance Sydney bit out, "Do I know you?"

"I'm sorry," he professed before one sickening crunch stole her thunder. He'd bitten all the way through her arm. Sydney lost the strangle hold on my heart. Thank you, stray mutt.

Except for the woman with the camera and her morose fascination for nothing short of a satanic ritual, most of the crowd dispersed. There is a peculiar fondness taking seed in my gut for this being. Is that bad? I think I want her.

From a café along the walkway an old acquaintance of mine sauntered over to my little ménage. My endearing name for the ingrate, Mr. Pomp-ass, Devon Badcock, stepped off the sidewalk and strut over as if London owed him a life. He's one of those who cry, "Oh, poor woe is me," and expects the world to coddle him just because he has royal blood flowing in his riddled veins. Well, newsflash Badcock, with all the philanthropy the royals were/are known for probably half of Britain has a claim to the same damn electric chair. Honestly it is nowhere near as enticing as the Iron throne. Or so I've heard. People talk about the telly shows while they wait in line to see me in the museum.

When close enough Badcock kicked me in the head with his shiny shoe, the heel two inches. Trying to make himself appear taller too. "Pussy," he accused.

Clearly the man's sentiments for me run along the same venue. "No cock!" I barely spit out his name, but I did manage a gob of blood. Why he changed his name is beyond me. Guess he is attempting to disassociate himself with previous family. Once upon a time Cambridge was a solid name. Badcock makes me think of someone who's dipped their willie into a ripened petri dish.

"Sinclair!" He churned.

Our formidable tones matched.

In the next move Devon added, "You're a moron, Xanti. Middle of a busy avenue acting as a newbie for all to witness. No control. No finesse. No morels. No brains. It is more than clear why your dear daddy locked you in the casket and chained it afterwards. Damn Drac to Hell and back for sparing your worthless carcass. Such a drain on society." Devon yanked a hankie from his pocket and bent at the waist to shine his shoe.

Massaging my jaw, I offered, "No security. No entourage. No paparazzi. No castle to hang your crown. Oh, hold on—no crown either. Pity. At least I am no poser."

"Your chimera slithers close to the surface, Badcock." The blond wolf spun fast on him, lips peeled

135

back, hackles up.

I need to identity this pup. He feels so familiar. Like family. Can't be family if he is trying to save me. History is a good representation of my predecessors. Possibly he is one of the wolves I freed from the museum?

Badcock addressed my wolf boy. "Son, you are in the wrong place at the wrong time. Consequences shall be costly."

The boy snarled and went to lift his leg, to pee on Badcock's shoes.

"Such defiance." Before the wolf got any closer, Badcock pulled a small vile of black dust from his pocket, popped the top off and blew the contents on the three of us.

Dare I utter a few foul words of disparage…

Furious, the wolf cursed, "Go back to magic school and learn a few new tricks that are marketable. Child's play."

"Hold that thought." Badcock grinned, his teeth blindingly white. My nerves bristled. He plinked off fingers counting… "There it is…"

Sydney went down first. Flopped over sideways in my arms. Whether it was due to the black dust or blood loss remains to be seen. I did have a splendid sip before being so rudely interrupted and her arm wound is nasty.

The wolf fought for composure, his huge head lolling in circles, his front legs slowly slipping sideways until the potion Badcock dowsed us with hit him with the same force a piano careening down forty stories to the ground floor flattens a person. His tongue dangled limp to the side of his mouth. His entire body swayed as he went down. I think he said, "Screw you." It came out garbled. He plunked his head in Sydney's lap and lapped away at the excess blood on her arm. "Don't hurt her."

Disgust weighing his tone, Badcock snipped, "You're marking her? Dream on, son. If you seriously think the St. James's want you of all people going doggy style on their daughter you're more delusional than this sad excuse of a vamp. She's mine. I won her fair and square."

"What are you going to do with her?" The wolf questioned, "Kill her?"

"Dine with her. Not on her. Unlike this moron, I am a gentleman," Badcock quipped, nudging me with the tip of that oh-so shiny shoe.

If I get out of here in one piece, I'll give that shoe to the wolf to chew up—foot included.

"You have never, nor will you ever be mistaken for a gentleman, Badcock. Money cannot buy manners or morals."

Badcock responded, "I'm not the one on the plaza animal control will be picking up any minute now, or the deranged vampire everyone on this island is searching for. You and your little puppy will be back in captivity soon enough. Have a good night. I have places to go, a masquerade to get ready for in two days' time and you are so not invited. Cheerio."

Challenge accepted!

Sitting very still, like I had any other choice... I added, "St. James's won't care she's missing. She's adopted ya know. She's not one of them. Not pure bloodlines. Guess you two have more in common than you thought." Gosh I hoped that remark rubbed him the wrong way. "Just saying when push comes to shove who do you think they'll rescue first? Their own flesh and blood or a loaner kid? You were never searched for.

Never found. Royals can be rather snippety that way."

"Adopted kids are probably more wanted than biological ones, Xanti. Think about it. They wanted Sydney in their lives. They went out of their way to make a home for her, a life. Do you truly believe her family is so shallow that adoption would mar their love for this beauty?"

I watched Badcock's regard for Sydney. For a moment envy crept in. No one has ever looked at me with such desire or admiration. Now I feel bad for the girl. If she survives this, she's in for a true haunting. With me what you see is what you get, a monster. With Badcock? He's like ordering an all-beef hotdog, but instead you receive the ass and other body parts of the hog that have been emulsified before being stuffed into a sheep's skin casing. He is total *shite*.

Badcock rambled on, "Sydney is Serina's first love. And look at you. Your father handed you off to the most notorious villain ever to glide around this planet without a single teardrop shed. It isn't the blood Xanti, that defines family. It's the relationships people have. The bonds they build. The trust. The love. The sex. The laughs. The heartache. The tears spilled. When you care more about someone than your own useless shell."

"Things you know nothing of," the blond wolf mumbled.

"And that's what you're bargaining on hey, Badcock? Using her as a bartering chip?"

A momentary drop in his facade answered my question. I could see the cogs churning. He is up to no good.

"I won't dignify that with an answer. The only thing you've ever had is a trail of corpses in your wake. And as always, you didn't listen to what I said, only what you wanted to hear."

"Badcock, you are the definition of a sack of fertilizer. You were castaway, deemed useless by the royals because you have buckets of contaminated blood thrumming through your veins. And I too recall a story of a dungeon, you side by side with my brother Donovan, murder, attempted rape, and near incest on your behalf that really got the St. James's ire up. Fine standards of a supposed gentleman."

A tiny muscle in his jaw twitched. My tarred insides melted. Badcock never acknowledged my accusations, but that twitch says volumes. With a spin that could make dreidels dizzy he stopped in front of the wolf and planted the tip of his fine leather shoe into the wolf's flank. The wolf curled up in fetal position panting. "Not so tough now are you, son? Maybe daddy will take care of you for once." Badcock bent over and scooped Sydney in his arms, touting, "Possession is nine tenths of the law. Mine." He stuck his nose in the crook of her neck and inhaled. When he looked up his eyes had gone three shades of ebony. Sydney's gaze had a perfect mixture of horror and confusion.

Drugs. They're worse than monsters. At least you see us coming.

Badcock had the nerve to knock my top hat off my head in passing.

My strength waned to the point I can't even flex my muscles to give him the middle-fingered salutation— something he can no longer due thanks to Savanah St. James's witchery when Badcock tied her to a dungeon table and threatened to be more than kissing cousins.

Badcock headed toward a sleek black 1930 stretch

Roadster with Sydney's limp body draped in his arms. There was no second glance back. Sydney's helpless stare made my heart ache as she looked between her captor and myself. Yeah, tough call—who is the bigger evil to get stuck with? Him or me? I'd have killed her without taunting her. Put her out of her misery. He jammed her into the trunk and got into the driver's seat and pulled away.

Like I said before—no chauffeur or staff at his beck and call. I hope he is thoroughly put out.

I know I am.

As this potion started to wear off, I made it to a kneeled position. With more effort than I expected, I extended my long lanky arm and snatched my top hat back. My bicep burned. I have an excuse for the emaciated shape. Twenty plus years of lock down atrophies muscles. With my free hand I raked through the tangles of my hair and removed a few stragglers from my vision then plopped the hat back in place. I don't do disheveled well. The catchphrase *neat freak* has been murmured many a time in my presence... Okay so I added the *neat* portion. Freak goes without saying. I scrambled in search of my red tinted shades, but they'd been crushed into the pavement. Someday Badcock will have the same outcome, crushed. I need help getting out of here. I can't, won't go back to the museum. Ever. There are fates far worse than death. My bite. Being immortal and starved in front of the world as life passes you by. Watching your nemesis drive off knowing he bested you. That damned girl. She attempted to kill me and yet knowing her fate is total shite, my feelings are tethered to her. Her fucking family will be the death of me.

I swept the area for anyone with enough empathy, stupidity, stupid empathy, to help me out of my dire situation. And there she was, my partridge in the pear tree. "Madam," I gave the woman in the red feathered bonnet my best innocent regard, batting those alluring black lashes in her direction. "Would you be a dear and help me up? Did you witness this heathen's maltreatments? He just kidnapped that poor woman. You should call the bobbies." I added a slight dash of enthrallment to entice the lass. "Right after you help me get out of here."

"You tried to kill her." And yet she took a step toward me with an extended hand.

Mine! Crap, now I sound like Badcock.

"No dearie, you are mistaken. I have no desire to kill her or anyone." And with that confession I snagged her arm and yanked the woman to ground. Hormones cursing through her petrified shell enhanced my sugar rush. I now appreciate the meaning. When finished, I stood, still slightly off from the black dusting, but I am up. Of my own accord, thank you. "You coming, son?" I straightened my pant legs and pulled the jacket edges tight to cover the holes and bloodstains on my shirt. Chance encounters. Are they truly chance? Is there such a thing as coincidences? Beginning to think not.

"I'm not your son."

"Read between the lines, kid. Get your wiggle-butt up."

****

"Back off and get away from her. I have a gun aimed at your head, buster. I mean it. Stop running with her. You might be able to outrun me but not a bullet."

The menace in the woman's voice came across loud

and clear. He understood it all too well. A stranger under duress would not lead to a happily ever after.

A what? Happily ever after?

Zander stole a glance at the beauty he held crushed to his heart. Stopping was no longer an option. He had to get Elyza somewhere safe. To the hospital. Away from all these strangers that seemed to pop up better than relatives with greedy fingers once someone hit the lottery.

Did he have feelings for his fallen angel? She certainly hit his radar. She didn't just hit it, she short-circuited it. The woman held everything, every quality he'd ever desired in a person. Honesty. She knew nothing else. He could tell she'd never lie to him. Humor, she'd tried to get him to smile even at the direst of circumstances. Sincerity. Compassion. She'd shown a great deal of both, so far, over the past hours of their relationship.

Relationship? He mulled the word around and almost laughed at the absurdity of their predicament. He needed to straighten this mess out before things escalated again. Before Elyza did. And she had a temper. A toasty one. A smile spread across his face when he recalled her standing in his living room juggling a ball of flames. He'd have to remember to never get her mad at him. If she stuck around once he got her home. He'd never had feelings for anyone. Couldn't afford to. What could he offer her? Other than a life on the run? He had no past and right now the only thing his present held was this limp beauty in his arms. He had no job. Yet. Once he got away from this madness, he would seek gainful employment as a journalist or selling newspapers door to door until he got his foot in the door of a publisher.

Determination and desire set the course to one's dreams. He'd heard it before—from someone, just couldn't pinpoint who, but it made absolute sense. He'd finished his degree behind bars, gotten his master's in literature. He had some story lines he was saving for a rainy day. One would be clearing Elyza of all wrongdoing. He knew what it was like to be falsely accused. To lose precious hours, days... years of your life for someone else's immoral deadly sins. Pondering it, he still had to meet his parole officer and get that awkwardness out of the way. Funny thing being he swore that's where he was headed yesterday, before all this insanity fell in his lap. He knew better than to stop back at the pub before going over to the posh building but sometimes nerves are steeled better with an old friend named Jack who offers small shots of self-assuredness at a minimal cost.

Well, JD cost him more than he could afford. Alcohol. He couldn't hold his own anymore. Jail was supposed to toughen one up, not turn them into a teenage girl slurping down shandies to get a quick buzz.

Speaking of buzzes...

A shot whizzed past his head.

"Stop or so help me the next one hits you, you kidnapping mutant."

Not waiting to see if her aim was accurate as her accusations, Zander left skid marks in the pavement.

Footsteps trailing them withered. Zander knew the girl couldn't keep up with him, even carrying a little extra lead and bleeding didn't slow him down. Running was his livelihood. He ran up to twenty miles a day in jail. He ran from everyone and everything, including himself. "Elyza, we have a maniac chasing us. Please wake up. I can take pretty much whatever is dished out, but I can't handle you being injured further."

Her voice barely audible Elyza asked, "Is it a red head chasing us or a blonde? If it's the red head keep running. Her aim is as good as my mom's magic. Not a compliment." Elyza produced a lopsided grin that melted Zander's worries.

Sparing a glance over his shoulder Zander couldn't tell what she looked like with the rain battering them. "I don't know. I can't make her out. You think you're up to transporting us into another zip code yet?"

She nodded or he thought she might have. Her body being jolted with each step might have attributed to the head bob. So out of breath he barely got out, "I got to set you down before I fall." His chest heaved and his lungs sounded like a whistle clogged with spit. He continued until he could no longer hear or see the woman taking shots and screaming profanities at him. He stopped near a small alcove in the back alley of a row of pristine mansions where the servant's entrances most likely were.

Dense strands of coiled ivy concealed a wrought iron gate making the entry almost invisible. A paint chipped stucco wall, roughly eight feet in height, ran the length of someone's property for a block or more. Deep purple roses, tiny violet blossoms with more ivy blanketed the wall. The flowers and wall coveted a plot fit for the royals. They'd stumbled across a secret garden. Just how far had he run? He fumbled to set Elyza inside the alcove by the gate. Raindrops dripped into his eyes and his nose ran. He jammed his hand in his pocket rooting about for a tissue. When he brought the flimsy paper up he noticed it saturated in blood. Patting down his leg his hand came back red and gooey. A sinking feeling engulfed him. He wasn't going to make it. Wasn't going to get Elyza somewhere safe. His legs were about to snap. He leaned into her for support but fast realized her legs weren't working either. Somehow, she managed a slow controlled slide to the ground. With her head resting on the flowery wall and through droopy eyelids, Zander realized her struggle to stay with him wouldn't last much longer either. "Hang on little cherub. Working my magic here." With blind faith he fished through the flowers and found the handle to open the gate. A few jiggles later the latch released. The gate squealed behind his weight. Lifting her from the ground he asked, "Can you walk now?"

Elyza nodded but held the wall for support. Each step of hers resembled Zander's, slow, calculated, off.

"Miss Doolittle, you and I are on a crash course. As strange as this is going to sound, I feel as if I've known you my entire life. How's that for the randiest pick-up line ever?"

Her surprised turquoise orbs staring at him with her ruby lips, looked like a kiss would be the best thing to ever happen to him.

"Please tell me you aren't a fan of that movie as well?" Elyza's head lolled backward and then snapped forward while she fought to remain conscious. "It's all good," she added while she bunched her fist into his hoodie for balance.

He forced a smile. When she swooned and grasped at air, he threw his arm around her waist to steady her. "Elyza? You got all starry-eyed. I know I have this effect on women all the time but don't leave me now."

She went to waggle her index finger in his face but her hand sort of flopped forward. "That's one of my nicknames, Doolittle. Guess it's not as randy as one would think given my name."

"You mean random."

"Yup, that. Although if I were feeling a little less dead randy might be fun."

Oh, if that wasn't music to his ears. His stomach, however, had other ideas. Zander plunked Elyza down and crawled a few feet before dry heaves left him doubled over.

"Ouch! Zan?"

She sounded miles away. Nothing brings you back from the brink of death like hearing someone you care for in trouble. She'd completely toppled sideways. Didn't even attempt to straighten her posture. He made his way back to her and squatted down in front of her then placed one hand on her hip and slid his other under her rib cage to get her back up.

"God that hurts." She grimaced holding her side protectively.

"I'm sorry. I must have grabbed where you got shot." He gripped her other arm and helped her to a sitting position. Getting her mind off the fact they were dying he asked, "I thought models were the picture of perfect posture and balance?" He got very close to her face and tapped her nose. "To which you currently lack both."

She went sideways again and laid there. Her head cushioned on her hand in the grass, her eyes barely slits, she whispered, "I am trying to look at things from a new perspective."

"Poor humor still intact. Good! No sleeping on me, Doolittle. Sleep is for the dead." He gave her a little wiggle. He had to keep her awake until he got her to a hospital. So, he kept talking. "Well, if you were to tell me you spoke to animals, I'd probably believe you."

"There was that one time…"

"No way." Absolute astonishment carried his voice. "I was joking," he conceded while he straightened her.

"I don't know why I'm telling you this. Maybe it's a dying confession?"

"Stop that, Elyza. No dying here. Not today. Promise me."

"Will you be quiet if I agree? I'm kidding about communicating with animals but as for the knowing you part, I feel it too." She placed a wobbly hand on his shoulder for support while she tried to stand, but her legs buckled. "Whoa!" From the ground she tilted her head and glanced at him, a giant moue covering her face. "I'm just gonna sit here for a bit if that's okay with you? I'm comfy."

"It appears you leave me no other recourse." Zander reached over and wrapped his arms around Elyza's backside, beneath her bottom and he hoisted her over his shoulder. He bucked sideways almost making the two of them tip over.

"Ugh! I am going to die."

"We already discussed the no dying thing. Hang on. Christ woman, your ribs feel like blades in my shoulder. We have to get some food in you." With a slight shift he had her right where he wanted her, her head dangling by his butt and her butt cupped safely beneath his hand… so she wouldn't slip of course.

"Oh, Zander, I know every man believes this caveman impersonation is romantic, but all kidding aside, Imma bite ya again if ya don't flip me right side up."

"Maybe the aim on the bite will improve." He pat her bottom which got his slapped. Inside, the garden stole his breath. A maze of flowered paths weaved this way and that through the grove with colors of every flower known and some he'd never seen. The path was lined with a carpet of lush, green grass. Each step his feet sunk into the soothing loam to comfort his weary legs. A little farther up the trail he noticed a gazebo set off to the right. Lace curtains hung to form a smidgen of privacy. He made his way there. Under the wrought iron dome, a queen-sized day bed draped in white linens and lace held an invitation he couldn't refuse. Carefully he plunked Elyza on the mattress and then fluffed a few pillows behind her head.

"Really? I said I felt like I'd known you forever, not I wanted to get into bed with you this second. Let me stop bleeding out first?" Her index finger air-tapped her frustration toward him.

"Okay, so later." His devil-may-care grin multiplied when he noticed a tray of food under another canopy. "Elyza! We hit the jackpot." There were glass pitchers filled with juices, orange and possibly apple. Chilled bottles of champagne sat tucked in silver ice buckets with crystal-fluted glasses begging to be filled with the bubbly thirst-quencher. Steam rose from a tray of scrambled eggs. A tier of plates held bagels, scones, croissants, and brownies with chocolate icing. He punched his chest in triumph and immediately regretted it, roaring in agony, "Ouch."

A slab of beef, rare and bloody, sliced thin, lay decorated by a dollop of horseradish sauce. *Zander?* Was that his name being called to the feast? He crooked his ear toward the table to get a better listen. *Zander?* Fist pump—invited! The table with all its glory gave him an embossed invitation to dine with the Gods. He strolled to it, ran a finger along the edge of the white linen, and picked up a hefty silver fork.

Didn't have these babies in the big house. Kind of hard to stab someone with a spork.

Plastic utensils all the way to the landfill.

An array of yogurts, fruits and little condiments mingled between the spread. His eyes shifted left to right to see whose picnic they'd crashed. No one here but them. A slight plink in his gut warned something was off but what? Other than they had wandered in on someone's party and were about to enjoy a smorgasbord at someone's expense. Zander hadn't eaten like a king in forever. Come to think of it, he'd never eaten a meal like this, not a day in his life. This was a dream come true. Food. A bed. A beautiful woman and well, a beautiful woman on a bed. "Thank you, God," Zander mumbled.

"You're welcome, Zander."

"Okay… that was funky. You never answered me before and God knows, or you know I've done insurmountable talking, pleading, begging, bargaining with you, and never a peep from ya there, big guy. Why now? If I'm not quite dead don't answer that." With a glance around Zander half expected to see a man donned in a white robe, with long white hair and giant serene eyes staring him down. He laughed at his foolishness. He wasn't just speaking to God. God had a universe to run, people to save, animals to love, demons to demolish and the list went on and he knew he didn't make the list. And as the steam from the eggs and steak stoked his appetite, he had some food to devour. Back to reality.

"Elyza, wake up. This food is amazing." He nudged

her side. She grunted. "I did promise you lunch earlier. Here, I made you a plate, pretty lady. I didn't know what you like to eat but judging from all the bones on you, I'm guessing you won't be picky. Damn you're so tiny." Zander set the plate down on a side table beside the daybed. He got up and left and returned with a handful of champagne grapes, tiny, deep violet in color and a glass of apple juice. "Open those wavy blues for me and then chomp on these. Not one sour grape in the bunch. They're pure magic."

When did she turn into a baby bird being hand fed? She felt foolish not being able to lift an arm to help herself and she really needed to thank Zander at some point for caring for her the way he had. He surprised her at every turn. Caring. Compassionate. Tender. Handsome beyond logic. Out of thin air an angelic voice sounded in her ear, but exhaustion beat her head back down into the soft fluffy pillow. She was done talking for a while. Maybe clouds felt this cushy. She didn't recall being this wiped out ever. Must be coming down with something. The voice, it called to her again. *Lizzy, wake up. Wake up, lovie, Momma needs you. I'm hanging on by a thread little girl. Where are you?*

Her chai flooded her to the point of drowning. Anxiety. Death. Sorrow. The unknown. Why would anyone want to wake up to that? Then a male voice snuck in there. Wrapped all that masculinity around her in one giant hug. Solid. Real. Heavenly.

"Doolittle, I have something you'll love if you open those gorgeous eyes for me."

Fingers caressed her cheek, brushed her hair back from her face and traced the outline of her lips. She didn't want him to stop touching her. She really might die if he did.

His voice soothed her. Cuddled with her in the dark. Held her safe. Devilishly. Claiming her. Soul to soul. Left her wanting. Needing… so much more. His smooth lips placed a kiss beside the corner of her mouth. She tried to turn into him, but he'd already backed away.

"I can't believe we found this place. It's just you and I in paradise. How random is this? There aren't even any bugs trying to spoil my first picnic."

Jubilance oozed from him with such innocence. But his hold on her? His grasp held dominance. Kindness. Lust. Playfulness. And curiosity. A true male letting his woman know his intentions in a gentlemanly manner. He curled around her body, his leg over her thigh and they snuggled. This is what she'd always imagined being in love encompassed. Feeling safe, warm and cared for unconditionally. His arm crossed her chest and tucked under her arm. He pulled her back against his chest, wiggled his nose into the back of her neck and placed another small kiss there. She snuggled back against him, his warmth radiating through her cold body.

"Don't leave me, Elyza. I've finally found my future."

Then the softer female voice whispered again. *Elyza, please come home. Where are you? I can't see you.*

Momma? Is that you? Don't worry. I'll be home soon. I love you.

Elyza, I can't hear you. Please answer me.

Grief replaced harmony. Why couldn't anyone hear her? When Serina's spirit waned one of Elyza's eyes fluttered. The pillow her head lay cushioned in blocked her right eye. An arm donned in sweatshirt material held her close. She smelled food. Her stomach gurgled. When she went to sit up his grip on her tightened.

"One more minute?"

Dear lord, the man's voice! His sonance held hope and sincerity. Two things she valued in life. "Where are we?" Lifting her head took way more of an effort than it should have. This enchanted garden looked like a dreamscape. Nowhere in London had a place this freaking beautiful. Not even the palace grounds. She'd been countless times, not that the current queen had a clue. Right here and now it was just the two of them. Zander kissed the back of her head again and she melted into his embrace. This moment between them had its finer points. It felt good to be in the arms of someone who genuinely had her back. And as his hand slid across her breast and cupped it, and so it seemed, he had her front too.

"Nice try. I really don't want to move but I can feel my life draining from under me. I haven't eaten in days." With a little help Zander shoved Elyza into a sitting position.

"I made you a plate, but you fell asleep on me. Probably cold now."

"Actually, there's steam coming off the eggs." Lifting her arm was more like lifting fifty-pound dumbbells. Her hand shook knocking the food off the fork. Her second attempt she loaded some eggs onto it, leaned in quick and shoveled the food into her mouth. Her taste buds exploded in delight. This tasted so divine, tears leaked from the corners of her eyes. Starved, she didn't even remember chewing. There had been a flaky pastry on her plate and that too disappeared.

Thank God there's no fashion shows this week.

She chugged the glass of apple juice and popped grape after grape into her mouth. Each one burst with a delicate flavor when she crunched down on it. The bottle of champagne caught her eye and she found enough energy to get up and make her way to the table. She poured two glasses. With the flute to her lips, she waited for the bubbles to stop tickling her nose before she took a sip. How did they go from nearly getting killed by two henchmen in his apartment to becoming the main attraction at the Piccadilly Circus Plaza to this heavenly place of rest?

Oh, no, no, no, no, no, no, no!

Her feet spinning and her body fighting to catch up, Elyza spun one hundred eighty degrees in a heartbeat, the champagne spilling over the sides of the glass. The beautiful white linens they rested upon were soaked red. Zander's clothes had holes in them. Against better judgment she looked down at her body. Holier than thou. *Feck! Now we're twinning.* She ripped Zander's hoodie off him. Holes. She was so sick of holes.

"Zander, we need to get out of this really pretty garden. Picnic's over, sweet man. The ants are trying to carry you away. I'm so not joking, Zander, wake up! There's some freaky-ass giant ants crawling under you and shoo…" Arms flailing, Elyza screamed and kicked at the bugs. She even stomped on one of them and when the insect crunched beneath her foot her stomach clenched. His lids with those ridiculous long lacy-black lashes remained shut. Not feeling so hot she sat back down beside him on the bed of bugs.

Chapter Nine

"Where is she?" Daelyn Kitt struggled to contain the gruffness his tone conveyed, but raw emotion filled the room, more so than all the family members sprawled out on cots in temporary comas in the great hall.

Shelby rattled, "I lost them both. Sydney told me to get Elyza no matter what." She gripped Daelyn's arm. "Who would take them? And if it's kidnappers, why hasn't there been a ransom call?" Shelby looked out across the large room in search of a friendly face. No one met her lost gaze but Daelyn. And his was anything but comforting.

Daelyn had never witnessed anything like this in his lifetime. The scene before him came right out of some mash unit. Bodies spread out on makeshift beds, the floor, chairs, most of his family lost in transition. Daelyn knew the tales of 'one for all and all for one' but he thought it was just that, his family's over imagination acting up. Each of the elders conjured up stories none of the children truly believed, until today. One family member went down—the dominos toppled.

He paced the same way his grandfather, André did, all legs with resounding thumps with each stride. They were two peas in a pod. Ethan might have contributed his genetic makeup to his son, but from that point on, Daelyn was every bit St. James. Bluish-black eyes like his mother, Savanah's, stole many a look from the ladies and dark straight hair like his great aunt Raven's had them running their fingers through it. His long, lean musculature he gained from running marathons. And his one downfall, he had a temper that could rival his great Uncle Julian's—aka Grimmy.

"So, tell me again how you left Sydney in the plaza alone with a werewolf, a deranged vamp, and an estranged serial killer that tried to rape my mum years ago? And then you fired shots and you don't think you hit anyone but now there's not a stinking trace of Sydney, Elyza or the man that carried her off into the night? You said he looks like he could be the guy from the hall last night?" His fists in knots, Daelyn yelled, "How the hell did this go so astronomically wrong? All she had to do was walk the length of the stage three times. Five minutes exposure tops and now this?"

Not an ounce of tenderness in his tone to be heard, but frustration and helplessness? Daelyn made a pact with Elyza long before anyone realized they could communicate that they would forever watch out for one another. Not only was Elyza his cousin but she was his best friend. And he'd let her down.

Sniffles and tissues in constant dabbing motion, Shelby answered, "I was right on his heels. There was no way he lost me. I followed them through an old iron gate that landed me in a cemetery in dire need of a caretaker. The place was overgrown with weeds and headstones were flipped and broken. I looked all over. They weren't there. They freaking vanished."

With a softer tone, he suggested, "Maybe Elyza finally learned how to evanesce?"

Shelby shook her head no. "She's tried but hasn't had much luck. Her vanishing act is about as good as her mother levitating a feather."

"I can't just sit here with my finger up my…"

"No cursing. I'm just filling in for your mother until she's done pretending to be the Briar Rose." Ethan threw his arm around his son's shoulder. "I'm glad you're home, son. Missed you tons." A huge bear hug followed.

"Same here, Pop." Reluctant to let go, Daelyn broke his embrace with his father. "How is mom?"

Ethan dropped his head, his eyes for the moment shut. "Just left her. We can't fail." Ethan straightened his posture and took Daelyn's hands in his. "Look, in less than an hour this procedure is going to happen. The brine solution is working its magic. We don't have to like it, but we do have to live with the outcome, no matter what. Father Thom will be in shortly and we will begin the ceremony when everyone is here."

"Except Lizzy and Sydney." Daelyn's voice trailed off as he walked out of the room. Moments later he returned lugging a backpack filled with healing stones, herbs, gauze and normal medical first aid items one might find in a home cabinet. And then there was the one thing he held tightly to, a small silver flask. He jiggled the antique container in Shelby's direction. "Great gramps special concoction. Come on, Shells. You and I are going on a space trip. Lizzy may not have mastered the different zip code traversing, but I have. Let's go get our girls back. Keep your mind merged with me and hang on. Show me the way."

Shelby's facial expression said, "There's no way in Hell I'm dancing through days with you," while she reluctantly grabbed the satchel, and followed on his footsteps. "I've lost my marbles to be doing this with you."

A little snippety Daelyn countered. "Maybe we'll find them scattered along the way."

Shelby kicked the back of his leg.

Ethan held up a quick finger to Daelyn and Shelby. "Do you have the stun gun? Bauble gun? Holy H20? Do you have the other ammo as well? Instant snooze alarms? You may need them!"

"I got them all, Pop. Don't worry. I promise I'll keep in contact with you." Daelyn gave a stiff nod, grabbed Shelby's arm and gave her a "Three, two, one, blast off," and they vanished.

****

Zander glanced around to what moments before had to have been his Garden of Eden. He'd never seen anything so breathtaking or tasted food that melted in his mouth. Or, the best part, the woman beside him. That much he could get used to. But then the freaking ants marched in one by one then two by two and the next thing Zander knew he'd been hoisted up and was about to get carted off like sacrificial lamb to slaughter. They meant business. All of them with their tiny little jaws nibbling on him like he'd died.

"Oh, shite!" Skittish to say the least, he wiggled a ginger finger through two holes he'd received at his apartment. "Crap! Elyza? Did we?" He couldn't bring himself to say it, because if he said it then it was true. This was a dream. A nightmare to be precise. Plausible deniability. If he awoke, would he be fine?

Exhaustion consumed him. Sleep seemed a luxury he couldn't afford and remaining awake would take winning the lottery.

He'd wake up soon enough. Couldn't let yourself die in a dream. It was like falling. You always jerked awake just before you splat all over the pavement. He slapped his cheek a couple of times.

Still here bleeding out. Fabulous!

Wearing a grim scowl, Elyza murmured. "Zander, you don't look so good."

He shrugged his shoulders. "I must say," he attempted his best Ed Grimley impersonation with a very groggy voice, "neither do you." He even attempted the little hip gyration dance the character was famous for—and failed miserably.

"Eddie, you've got moves, I've never seen on a man before."

"You're jealous."

Elyza, you need to get back here. Today.

Elyza's mother spoke to her again. The tone held a frantic edge to it.

Serina, I don't want to worry you, but this time I might not make it home. I met a guy. Delicacy and diplomacy entwined. Nailed it. *You always told me I'd experience the typical beginning for a St. James woman, and you are of course right. There, I said it. You are right. You'll love him to death. I probably shouldn't have said that. Anyway, I'll tell you all about him when I see you. Love you more, Mom.*

Hope. She wouldn't succumb to less.

Doo-doo where are you?

Another nickname she'd been labeled with. Daelyn's shorty to Miss Doolittle.

Dae, where art thou my overbearing, handsome cousin?

Doo-doo, I can't hear you. Where are you? Shells and I are coming. Hang in there. Don't leave me, Lizzy. I can't handle Sydney and Shelby alone.

Why couldn't anyone hear her? Pain slinked through Elyza's veins easier than a worm in a rotted apple. Her chest hurt. Really hurt. Like someone was jumping up and down on it. Ribs cracked. She heard them snap. Felt them break and prod into her lungs.

Breathing ability—gone.

Holy co-ouch.

"Get her intubated this second or we'll lose her. Her pulse is thready, eyes dilated and she's nonresponsive. If this is all hers, she's lost a good amount of blood."

"What about the guy over there with his feet sticking out from under the mausoleum? He's covered with ants. He's barely clinging to this world. This is the model everyone's looking for." The second paramedic pointed to Elyza. "Don't let her die. She knows where the jewels are."

That's all they worried about? The jewels? The voices, Elyza didn't recognize them, but she sure as hell understood every impossible word they uttered. She was dying. Zander too.

Mom!!!

She'd wanted, needed the healing touch of her mother's voice. Then she'd know for certain she was all right, but this confirmation of not being able to mentally connect to anyone had all the effects of popping a cyanide pill and hoping it was only Pop Rocks candy giving off the illusion of being rabid. She knew better. Hope fizzled out of the corners of her lips one red drop at a time.

"She's not going to make it."

"Call the coroner."

"The coroner was one of the people at the charity show that died."

A guttural implosion stunned Elyza. Deep beneath her, slight tremors vibrated the ground. Each one wiggled into Elyza's body. The earth had a distinct way of letting mystical powers travel throughout the veins far below, the ones that nourished the planet, ley lines. Most of her family held the ability to tap into them and share the elements, to utilize the magic this world offered. Her family was sending out S.O.S. signals through the ley lines trying to reach her. She tapped back only to receive the same message: Out of service.

"Officers radioed ahead saying we need to add silver cuffs to them both, although this is a done deal. They aren't going to make it. Found a wallet on the man. He got out of jail two weeks ago. I rang his parole officer, but he hasn't met him yet. Thinking he skipped out."

If Elyza weren't busy trying to water the dead, she'd have laughed at the absurdness this situation offered.

Do I know how to keep the family tradition intact, or what? Bad boys! Well, Mom, at least he doesn't have ties to the Sinclair's like Ethan did when Savanah fell for him.

Once the cuffs were placed any hilarity Elyza was able to scrounge up evaporated. Somewhere in her subconscious the reality of this penetrated her thick skull while the pressure of someone compressing her ribs into her heart did. There she dangled in purgatory, a giant fish on a hook, waiting for a hydra to leap up and take a huge chunk out of her tush and then drag her the rest of the way down. Maybe they'd gnaw off the dimple. She would have laughed if it didn't hurt to breathe. And to top it off, the cuffs burned. Well, at least she still had some feeling. All was not lost.

Noise escalated. Harsh voices blared as Elyza's

body lifted from the ground.

To where? Not heaven... *I'm not ready. Hey! Put me down. Please tell me I didn't die. I can see you, ya know, the opposite of the kid that claimed he could see dead people... Hmmm... Do dead people see alive people? I don't want to find out. Help!*

"Did you see that?" One of the paramedics shrieked, "Look there." With a loud crunch and shocking jolt, the gurney she lay secured to fell back to the ground. On contact with the ground her soul exploded into the atmosphere. *Oh shite!*

Well, purgatory, if this was indeed where she was, at least offered a panoramic view of her former life. An out of body experience. Astrophysics 1-0-1. *I'm so not doing this, whatever this is, ghosting. Must I always take things to the extreme?* Above her physical form, Elyza glanced around at her surroundings. This clearly was not the place she and Zander shared a moment. An almost kiss. Held one another. Acknowledged their feelings for one another. This cemetery was hundreds of years old. Unkept. Forgotten. Neglected. Befitting of the dead.

More yelling came from one of the men caring for Zander.

"Son of a b—"

The guy's face went from someone who knew his profession of caring for sick, injured people to backpedaling and tripping over a gangly tree root, landing flat on his butt with his complexion void of color. Then Elyza glanced at Zander. And wished she hadn't. Grey was not his color, not even fifty different shades of it. Those luscious full lips were a putrid hue of blue. His onyx orbs had rolled into his head to view his brain giving him the classic, freaky fifty's porcelain doll look. Those things haunted her. Oh how the tables had turned.

Her little life energy floated over to the gravesite where Zander lay half crushed. She closed her eyes, or tried to, but in her current condition of being stuck like a ghost, in a freaking cemetery no less, she realized all too well someone had a morose sense of humor. Zander's body lay squashed beneath the tombstone of one of the family members the St. James had done away with over a century and half ago.

The stone read: Here lies my son, Xavier Sinclair, loving twin brother of Donovan and halfwit Xanti. Rest in peace son once the deed is done.

Are you kidding me? Her anger escalated to the point her head pounded and she was coated in red.

With a quick glance down at the body, the red was hers. *Crap! Zander, don't you dare leave me.*

Utilizing her psychokinetic powers Elyza blanketed Zander's body and from sheer will and stubbornness she gave him every ounce of energy she could muster. *Live for me you foolish man, or so help me I will ghost you.*

The paramedic stammered, "Where, a—how is that even possible? Quick, get these two out of here."

Elyza's body shook again as the gurney went up and rolled her over the uneven ground in an exaggerated manner.

Her astral essence finally noticed what the two healthcare workers freaked over, Daelyn and Shelby appeared out of thin air a few feet away from them armed to the hilt with splat guns and stun guns. This time she could laugh. These gents probably thought they'd witnessed a true ghost hunter's sighting.

Doo-doo, I'm here. Don't worry.

I see you, Dae. Might I add your attire is a bit overkill?

I'm here too, Lizzy.

Dear Lord, Shelby... you finally can hear me? Shells, you look like some femme fatale that wound up in the slush pile of the edit room.

God, Lizzy, where are you? Please answer me.

Dae, Shelby Jane, I'm right here, right in fecking front of you. The body is kinda hard to miss. Elyza jumped up and down, arms flailing to get their attention. No such luck. Somehow waving invisible body parts lost the efficacy of a real body. Body, mind and spirit, yes, they all worked great together. Separately, not so much. Elyza attempted to hoist a chunk of broken headstone with the intent of hurling it toward them to get their attention. She came up empty of hand. Fecking ghost movies made moving objects appear so easy.

Daelyn grabbed Shelby's shoulder. "The guy over there. Is that the one who stole Lizzy? The one the medics are working on? Shells there's so much blood. It's like a freaking crime scene. Lower the paintball guns. These guys look petrified. From the looks of this, they're being taken to the emergency department for anything preternatural. It's the only explanation for the brimstone silver cuffs."

"Stop you two," One of the paramedics yelled, pulling a pistol out and aiming it at Daelyn.

"Daelyn," Shelby elbowed her cousin, "time to fly."

Elyza tried again, this time to get the gun in the paramedic's hand to misfire. The guy twitched when Elyza slammed her life force into him. Daelyn and Shelby's bodies vanished as shots rang out.

Noting the ambulance guy's urgency to leave this

place, Elyza's spirit streamed inside the ambulance. She attempted to hop back inside her body but she got bounced out. *Crap.* No where to go she sat on top of her physical form as best she could with her legs crossed, protecting herself should someone else try to attack.

A ghastly face with wide eyes and arms came fast at and directly through her invisible being. It reminded her of poking a soap bubble. A slight tinge of pressure followed by a splat of wetness left her queasy. Her physical form shuddered too. Fingers, nimble and fast ripped open the shirt she wore. Noting her breasts were out there like shining beacons, the next time Zander offered her a tee shirt she would take him up on it, provided there would be a next time…

Stickers with cold gelled backs were placed on her chest. *Why is everything in the medical profession ice cold?* Wires ran from the monitor in the front of the cab to her. The EMT rubbed some more gel on a set of paddles and yelled, "Clear!" Instant juice. Nothing like being kick-started with a few joules rattling the old ticker. And since there was nothing other than a flat line streaming the monitor….

Shite! She wasn't one for cuss words all the time, but when the occasion rose…

Shite!

"Charging. All clear. Go!"

Elyza's little ass-tral form skyrocketed into the ceiling of the bus better than a squashed bug once the swatter connected. So, this was what electrocution felt like.

Not quite the blast she'd envisioned.

"Nothing. Still flat line. Recharging."

Shite!

"All clear. Go!"

That one took her out. Even her spirit fizzled into the atmosphere.

Chapter Ten

Voices coming through the intercom jarred Zander's drug-induced sleep. Groggy, he hadn't figured out how he wound up both with cuffs on his hands and shackles on his ankles basically staked down inside a shallow hollowed out hole in a floor wearing only what God gave him when he entered the world. He'd been packed in ice cubes like a bleeding dead fish at the market. A blanket would have been nice. A disgruntled pout made its way to his mouth. IVs hung from the ceiling and see-through plastic tubing pumped something into him. But what? He couldn't see the labels on the bags. One bag had clear liquid being piped into his right arm and the second pouch looked a lot like blood going directly into a vein in his left arm.

A transfusion? He strained to lift his head and look over his body. Everything in his neck and jaw tensed. Why did they have him positioned like he was on a crucifix?

His cross? Where was it? A moment of panic shot through him when he didn't see or feel the necklace hanging from his neck. He strained searching around the room for it. In the far corner of the room a woman sat behind a desk eyeballing him over a pair of thick black cat-eye shaped spectacles. His cross dangled from her thieving neck.

Nothing short of her losing her head would stop him

from retrieving it.

The woman reminded him of an Eskimo hunkered down for a blustery night. She wore a raccoon hat, tail included. Her boots were school bus yellow with fur tufts popping out the tops. Her mittens held finger holes showcasing calloused fingertips and grimy nails. He glanced back at the yellow boots.

My, what bloody giant feet she has.

A blood pressure cuff sagged from a portable shopping cart. Sat upright in a small plastic cup, a thermometer caught his attention. Unfortunately for him, the little glass tube with mercury had red writing on the side of the small intrusive instrument. He knew what red meant. Rectal.

Glutes automatically tightened.

Trying to clear his voice, the woman peered over the top of her glasses. She stood and crossed to him.

"Hello, sunshine. Nice to see those striking black eyes. Wasn't certain you'd pull through or not and once you hear everything you're up against you may not want to continue your journey."

His throat raw, his voice cracked. "Where's the girl I was with? Is she all right?"

"She would be the least of your worries, lad. You're in a pickle."

"Feels more like a freezer." Zander studied the woman. Nice disadvantage too, being spread out on the floor like a doormat for anyone to waltz all over. This had all the makings of jail. Zander glanced out the window to the hall. Yup, just like prison. Two guards held up the doorway to his cell.

Her nametag read Nurse Hagatha. How apropos. What a ghastly hag this nurse appeared to be with her eyebrows drawn on in thick black liner and her lips smeared with something red. Hoping it was lipstick wouldn't make it so. He eyeballed the red pouch slowly draining into him and noticed an empty pouch on the floor beside her.

She wore a strand of garlic with sprigs of purple blooms intertwined around the garlic. The little cloves acted like pepper spray. "Vervain and garlic? Nice combo. Making certain no one mind taps you? Or comes close to you? I am confident you need not to worry about either."

Where was Elyza? As strange as it sounded, only knowing her a day, Elyza stole his heart. If fate stayed this unfathomable course, she'd most likely get his soul too. She could have all of him if she wanted him. He sure as hell wanted her. Alive. Healthy. And by his side for as long as he could have her.

"So, where is she?"

"In a holding pattern."

"What's that mean?"

"You need to be less interested in the murdering-thieving model and more in your own predicament."

Had he not been tied down he'd have shrugged his shoulders out of aggravation. Instead, he attempted to huff a chunk of his hair from his eyes. "Okay, I'll bite. What predicament?"

"You nailed it."

"Nailed what? My wrists to the floor? My feet as well?"

The angel of death as he now thought of her tapped a finger to her pointy, grey teeth then pointed at his mouth.

"Wait! What? I bit someone?"

"You really have no idea, do you? Cute as hell yet clueless." She shoved her thick glasses up on the bridge of her nose with a look of condescension.

"I realize it appears I have all the time in the world to play twenty questions with you, Nursey, but any minute now my girlfriend is going to ride in here on her broomstick, incinerate your you know what, and set me free."

"Your little witch and her broomstick crashed and burned, bat breath. How have you been feeling lately? Have you been able to sleep? Eat? How's the sex? Do normal man things?"

"Hoping you're asking for a friend and not yourself. Kinda hard to when I've been incarcerated the past six years. I'm going out on a limb that you found out I got out of jail and this is why I'm looking like a poor dumb girl in a black magic sacrifice flick? And stop looking at my balls. A blanket would be a decent thing to offer. What's with the ice? It's a little frigid in here. And where is my girlfriend?" The part about Elyza he yelled.

"Templar, we have you on ice, in lock down because you had a fever most people fry their brains on. One hundred thirteen steamy degrees and you were fighting the entire hospital staff. You now hold the record for still being able to enunciate after this."

"No way!"

Her look said she wasn't kidding.

"Why would I get a fever that high and not die?"

One of Hagatha's eyebrows crept toward her hairline. "Do you really need to ask?"

"Apparently!" Even though in the back of his mind something sinister needled him. The conversation he and Elyza had about being bitten took over his thoughts.

169

Elyza thought he was on the verge of turning. She thought she also might be the catalyst having bit his bum.

She continued her interrogation. "Who are your parents? Are they fangers?"

"I don't know my parents. Look, I had a reflection this morning. Vamps don't have reflections, right? And I sure as hell don't sparkle and yes, I'm still able to bask in the sun." For about five minutes.

She laughed. "You watch way too much television, son."

"I'm not a vamp and not your son."

"How do you know you aren't my son? You just told me you didn't know your parents."

His gut tightened at the very notion. "No!" His distressed cry brought the guards into the room armed with stun guns and needles. And a silver-spiked garrote.

"Seriously? A garrote? Bit overkill."

The nurse waved the two men away. "We're good but stay outside the door should there be need."

"Why haven't you euthanized me all ready?"

A little burble escaped the nurse. "Where's the fun in that? We plan on experimenting with you and the fallen angel you came in with."

Zander's temper skyrocketed. No one would hurt her, not if he had anything to do about it. "She's innocent. Let her go. Tend to her wounds. Call her family. I admit it. I kidnapped her and tried to flee with her. Just let her go. I have the jewels at my pad."

"Sorry, Templar. You two are more like Bonnie and Clyde right now. Jewelry heist, killing a priest, arson with two more deadbeats toasted beyond recognition and inadvertently killing a dozen or more people in the venue? Let's just say neither of you are going anywhere.

Your girl certainly isn't. Witnesses saw the two of you fleeing the hall." With a tap on the glass, Hagatha spun on her faux fur, yellow rubber boots. She went to the door with the two guards to meet a gentleman with wispy white hair. Reminded Zander of one of those flowers one makes wishes on. It bugged him that he couldn't recall the name of the yellow flower most thought of as weeds. While the gentleman was cloaked in wealth and vanity, Zander resembled a bearskin rug, his hide momentarily intact.

Every so often they'd all turn and glance over their shoulders and cast a dismal glimpse his way. What did they have planned for him? His mind began to race. Shame his feet couldn't.

Tales of places like this were widespread, but until now no one had proof they existed. *Lucky me to find the Garlands of Garlic secret hiding communal. Oh, Elyza I wish you could hear me. I'm so sorry I got us into this. Dandelions, that's the bleeding flower. Wonder if whitey over there would mind if I plucked a hair so I could make a wish or two. Elyza, I wish you could hear me.*

Chapter Eleven

"Go up to the desk and ask where she is." Daelyn nudged Shelby through the old, rickety elevator door so hard she tripped. "Go on Gracie, get up there." He shooed her off completely ignoring the no visitors sign.

Not having it, Shelby turned on him. "Pfft! No! You go ask." Shelby reached out and latched onto Daelyn's arm and dragged him out of the antique metal cage. With a shove toward the desk, she said, "Do what you do best, Romeo." The door to the elevator creaked as it closed behind them. "We're doing stairs out of here. That thing belongs in a museum. Go."

"Yeah, that thing's got final destination all over it." They both looked back at the elevator and then each other. "The stairs it is. Shells, you're cute, petite, innocent—looking enough and as far as they know, harmless. I'm going to go hang by the nurse's station at the opposite end of the hall and see if I can't pick up any—"

"Nurses? Daelyn! I was kidding when I called you Romeo. You freaking jerk!" Shelby punched him in the gut. Her hands flying in anger she bit out, "Are you serious? Could your timing be any absolute worse?"

Bent at the waist, Daelyn gasped. "Whoa girl! You pack a mean right hook." He straightened his stance holding his stomach. "I was going to say pick up some info. Eves drop."

Shelby closed her eyes in shame. "Oh, gosh, I'm sorry. Just a bit wound up, Dae." She glanced up at him with tears filling her eyes. "I can't believe this is happening." Shelby slumped into Daelyn's chest.

He wrapped his arms tight around his cousin. "I know," he cajoled. "Now go find out where they have her. The sooner we can get to her the sooner we can get the heck out of here."

"Don't you leave me, Daelyn Kitt or I swear—"

Daelyn let Shelby go and reached up and ruffled her red curls. "I know better, Shells."

She strut up to the main reception desk like she owned the place. A few people stood huddled in groups, some holding coffee cups, some red-eyed and red-nosed. Distress, fear of the unknown and worry weren't three things to wear if you're trying to put your best face forward. Hospitals were supposed to be all about hope, not a gateway to the pharmacy for some anxiety meds. Daelyn wondered if any of these people were here to see the man that came in with Elyza. He certainly wanted to see him. He had questions that demanded answers. The man put his cousin in grave danger. Someone used real bullets on them.

"Could you please tell me what room Elyza St. James is in?" Shelby wiped her sweaty palms down her pant legs. She tried to swallow but instead produced a loud gulp that backfired into a belch. Shelby's nose scrunched when she inhaled the aftermath. "Apologies!"

The woman behind the desk looked up with a grimace. With one hand she fanned away the fumes Shelby burped out. Her attitude snooty, the secretary answered, "You could do with a breath mint. And there's no one here by that name. Perhaps she was taken to another hospital? And did you miss the no visitors sign?"

Shelby ignored the woman. "No! She's here. I followed the ambulance. Look again at the roster." Hands tightly at her side, Shelby's nails dug into her palms. She even went as far as to spell, "E-l-y-z-a," slowly but the secretary shook her head no.

"I'm sorry. There's been no one admitted in the past day."

Shelby leaned across the desk and latched onto an old-fashioned, tarnished microphone used for the intercom system. She yelled into it, "Lying bitch! Lizzy, we're coming for you," and she dropped the mic on the floor. Blaring screeches rang out through the halls. People's conversations died as suddenly as someone getting blasted to bits by a firing squad. All eyes settled on Shelby, which is exactly why Daelyn asked her to go there. He knew fully well that when Shelby Jane got upset or frightened or God forbid both the little ginger would snap and a commotion would ensue. His divergence. While chaos kicked up its boots, Daelyn moved swiftly in search of anything with Elyza's name on it. He found an abandoned laptop.

In the background Shelby kept the people at the desk occupied. She demanded to see the list of patients admitted. The secretary continued to spew HIPPA laws at her and all the legal suites that would be brought against her should Shelby not let go of the woman's laptop. Shelby continued to list the bodily harm that would come should the secretary not cower to Shelby's demands. Okay, so maybe Shelby's outrage took it one step further than expected, especially when Daelyn noticed guards rushing toward the desk along with other hospital personnel, all arguing with her.

Way to go, Shells. Keep pissing them off, just don't get tased. This place ain't what it seems. The guy with Lizzy, did he have jet-black hair? Black eyes?

Yes! When he turned to see who was chasing him his eyes looked like Lizzy's favorite color, Goth Black.

He is crucified to the floor and guarded by what can only be called the ugliest creature I've ever encountered.

Daelyn, unless it's five-ten or better with giant brown eyes and long blonde hair nothing hits your radar. I know you think you're funny placing me in this position, well so do I, but hurry up!

"Miss, I am going to ask you one last time to release the computer. I'm going to count to three and then the nice man with the stun gun is going to knock your little ass right out of those cowboy boots." The secretary had her fingers welded to half of the computer and Shelby held the other half with a death grip as they tugged away over it.

"Tell me where she is, and you can have it."

"Let go or you'll get it. And I don't mean the computer."

From the sidelines the security guard began his countdown. "Three, two…"

The secretary gave one all or nothing tug just as Shelby added a bit of a forward shove, declaring, "Fine. Take it!" She watched the secretary's eyes widen, her balance vanish, arms flailing to stop gravity. The computer went air born while the woman flipped over her chair, legs going over her head in a backwards roll. Shelby took off running with the security guard torn between helping the woman up or chasing her.

"Get that witch!" The irate, red-faced woman demanded. The guard immediately let go of the lady and down she went again.

The accelerated click of Shelby's cowboy boots down the hall got Daelyn's attention. He stuck his arm out the door, and whispered, "Don't freak," a split second before he snagged Shelby into a vacant room and slammed the door shut. "Find her and I'll hold the door closed then we'll disappear to wherever she is."

"You scared the crap out of me."

With his back braced against the back of the door Daelyn caught his breath and grinned. "That was fun."

"You're the true idiot Elyza claims you are."

"She's never said such a thing."

Shelby's look said otherwise. "This room. It's padded, Dae."

"Custom made just for you."

"Moron. Look! Leather straps and chains hanging from walls? Really? What the heck is that thing?" Shelby pointed to some sort of metal box with paddles, electrical cords, spring-loaded needle nose clamps with metal tips and rubber handles and a bottle of blue gel.

"Hurry up, Seashells. We gotta find the room number and get out of here. This looks like a scene out of one of the documentaries that closed a boatload of institutions back in the 70s. That is what tasers were fashioned after. The trump card of electrocution. Sizzling grey matter."

"That's so gross."

Banging on the opposite side of the door caused the structure to judder, the frame surrounding it, to splinter. With the notion it was about to be busted down Daelyn widened his stance and braced himself. When Shelby made a small gasp Daelyn watched her color drain before his eyes. "What is it? What did you find?" Daelyn waited all of two seconds before he shouted, "What is it?"

Tears filled Shelby's eyes. Her lips began to tremble, and the computer ultimately slipped through her fingers and smashed on the concrete. "She's in the bloody, fucking morgue."

"Shells, don't do it, sweetie. Don't pass out on me. God damn it, Shells, your freckles are turning white. Please don't pass out."

"I won't. I prom—" Before her words hit the universe she buckled at the knees, and did a backward butt bounce. A dirty blanket all wadded up on the floor broke her fall and cushioned her head where she landed.

"Are you kidding me? What has the universe got against my family?" He timed the moments in between the door being slammed against his back. There was less than a split second of a window to cross the room, hoist Shelby's dead weight over his shoulder then evanesce them to the morgue.

The morgue.

When the doorframe broke free from the encasement Daelyn had Shelby's limp body and the two of them evaporated to thin air. The stunned look on the guard's faces?

He missed it and had no plans of looking back.

Having never been in the building before Daelyn sifted through the corridors scanning each sign. He had a clue the morgue would be in the basement and his instincts were dead on. Down four flights of stairs the air temperature cooled which made it easier to stay in the form of gas. The hotter it got, well science and nature took over and everything expanded making it harder to be invisible.

With a scan of the entire area, the morgue had a lot

more going on than he would have imagined. In most mortuaries people died, they were bagged and tagged, wrapped in plastic so body fluids wouldn't be an issue, then tucked safely in the cooler so the fermenting process wouldn't make your nose twitch, eyes water, or your gut wrench. And as always before closing the door you said a prayer for the lost soul and their family.

In the center of a large room sat a thick glass cube, maybe eight feet by ten feet, made from many smaller glass cubes. Reminded Daelyn of an igloo, only framed in tarnished silver and brimstone. Distorted images of bodies lay stacked one atop of another inside it. A large keypad outside the door locked the enclosure.

Was it to prevent dead from getting out or others from getting in? Zombies or body snatchers? *Ugh! I just called myself a tomb raider. And I may or may not have called Elyza a zombie.* Either way Daelyn needed to get the code so he could get Elyza out of there.

Six rooms, two on each side, made up the outer walls of the morgue. The rooms looked a lot like the ones upstairs. Torture devices hung from walls: Axes, picks, rusted gardening shears, Ash stakes, pliers, and the pear of anguish were all displayed, and all with blood coating them. Blood-splattered masks, shields, overcoats were hung on hooks by the door. Bloody galoshes were shoved beneath them on the floor.

In their current states Daelyn and Shelby floated around the outside of the igloo searching for Elyza's body. His heart sank again. Inside the glass enclosure he counted eight bodies, seven of which from the looks of things had ribs cracked open, organs harvested, and blood being drained and bagged. Couldn't let it go to waste, there were creatures out in the world whose sole survival counted on it. Daelyn fast realized the Garlands of Garlic fanatics might be the biggest hypocrites to roam the earth. They despised the preternatural community, yet they sold their organs and blood products of these supernatural beings for blood money, literally. How many people in hospitals were the recipients of organ transplants? Would the person with the new organ turn into some supernatural creature due to the virus living in the newly placed body part or from a transfusion? And once the Garlands of Garlic had their profits, they in all likelihood lured new unsuspecting creatures back here to get their blood fix and continued the recycling.

The door behind them blew open. Two security guards stopped and scoured the room. The guard that was going to tase Shelby earlier asked the other man, "Where are they? You see them? Is the fallen angel still locked up?"

So, Elyza was in there. Daelyn's will unraveled causing his invisible stature to shimmer. When he and Shelby started to take form, the guard pointed. "There," and charged him holding a stun gun aimed between Daelyn's eyes. Daelyn passed behind the second guard coming at him. The needle-tipped wires penetrated the guard.

His body hit the floor seizing in erratic jerks. Gurgling and choking sounds poured from the man's throat. His tongue lay severed beside his head. Daelyn clasped his hand over his mouth hoping to quell a scream.

"Holy mother," an assistant whispered as she ran to the guard's aid. "I got this. Get in that vault and make sure we haven't lost the model. I don't want to answer for this."

Daelyn waited, trying so very hard to internalize his fears and control his powers so he could remain unseen and keep he and Shelby safe. This was the longest he'd ever been invisible and taken another person with him. His strength waned. Other hospital personnel gathered in the hallway gawking, but none entered. No one enters Hell willingly.

A set of silver cuffs jingled from man's back pocket as he approached the glass door and bent to the keypad. Lips were the new fingerprints, and some institutions were using them instead of retinal scans. Too many people were losing their sight to criminals lately. That fit right in with his recycling organs theory. Sick bastards.

The guard pressed his lips to the keypad and then stepped back.

An alarm sounded just as the airlock made a *poof* and the door blew outward. Daelyn had to get in that vault and get Elyza and Shelby home. May God help him, because if he didn't, he'd answer to the devil. Or Olivia. The devil would be easier to deal with because Olivia loved her granddaughter more than life itself. The guard went in.

The odor that escaped the confines had to be the foulest insult to have ever accosted Daelyn's system. A pungent cloud of blood, bowel and decay seeped out. He internalized a gag and gulped hard, shuffling Shelby's body around so he could wipe his eyes. The temperature was close to zero. His cells contracted even farther. Gave him a little added energy he truly needed, right up until he laid his sights on Elyza's body. His heart faltered. Being invisible had its qualities but it also had a downside. Emotions ruled the mind regardless and when turmoil hit there was a serious mind over matter battle to be played.

Daelyn enveloped Elyza's body with his and Shelby's. When he went to turn her form into a molecular state nothing happened. He tried again and still the same outcome; she remained the top corpse on a pile of bodies with tubes jammed into manmade openings draining her blood into a bucket. Bloodied jeans and a shredded white shirt barely covered her.

"She's dead as they come," the man inside the cube yelled out.

Hearing the ugly truth, Daelyn screamed, "Fuck."

The guard spun on him. "Who the—how the— where did you come from? Lock it now!" The man lunged for Daelyn's fading form, grasping at him through thin air. The door to the room closed with the deadbolt clanking down before the man finished screaming. "Come out. Show yourself."

Great Grampa, she's gone. I'm with her, or at least her body. Elyza is gone. I can't shift her to bring her home. Great Gramps? Hello? I've just been locked in the morgue's vault.

Nothing. From anyone.

Hands tightened around Daelyn's throat. Choking, Daelyn dropped what remained of his invisible façade. Shelby's limp body fell between the two men. Daelyn fought the man with his last ounce of strength but went down on his knees in the struggle. With one last attempt at freedom, he thrust his arms upward and punched straight up through the inner side of the man's arms attempting to break the hold. In doing so he punched the underside of the guard's jaw. The man's head jerked backwards and slammed into a shelf holding a few bodies. The guard lost his footing. Daelyn stood fast and face-planted him. The guy's nose ended up crushed under the pressure and went into his skull. What was one more body? At least the guard landed in the right spot. Daelyn however didn't.

Conundrum: How to get out of an airtight room with two bodies and have no one notice? Daelyn slumped down the chilled wall, brought his knees to his chest and held on, burdened with the knowledge he'd failed everyone he loved.

****

After the man in the money laundering suit left, the nurse came in ready to play doctor. Only this game far exceeded any game Zander ever conjured up. "Don't touch me. You sick psychobabble nurse. You've done way too many drugs if you think there's a chance in Hell of you and me doing anything together. You freaking warped turd. Back up, Gramma."

"Gramma?" The nurse questioned.

"Red's rabid wolf." So badly Zander wanted to point out all the grey whiskers she sported and her enormous feet, but once again—being tied down did nothing for his hand-talking. He gave a triumphant wiggle to his middle finger. "I swear once I'm out of here you're dead." Zander's patience died in that secret garden. Stripped of her roadkill headgear, rubber boots and wearing only the garlic and vervain strand along with Zander's cross, she'd plunked her nakedness on top of his armed with a set of pliers and went to work, trying to rip perfectly good teeth from his mouth. But that was only after she'd unloaded a syringe full of silver nitrate mixed with vervain into his system. It held the same qualities as a person getting their veins stripped when using

Polidocanol. Acid rain's evil twin—able to kill off everything in its path. Vervain added lethargy and a queasy turmoil to the mixture. As if getting shot, having bullets dug out of you, and then turned into a popsicle wasn't bad enough.

Elyza, where are you? God help these animals if they've hurt you.

****

With her spirit intact, Elyza floated through the hospital in search of her physical body. She'd lost it the last time they electrocuted her trying to jumpstart her heart. After she peeled her ghostly astral projection from the roof of the ambulance her body vanished as did the men who'd driven her there. Inside, this institution had to be hands down the worst place on the planet for an empath. Pain, suffering, crying, dying… Voices bounced off her, clung to her, begged for help. The pain equated to a siren going off in headphones with the volume amped all the way up past ridiculous while you had a migraine, stuck in the dessert at high noon, with no coffee, chocolate, aspirin, or shades. If she weren't already dead, she would be soon.

Zander? Where are you? I can hear you. Can you hear me? The saying goes your hearing is the last sense to leave your body. Noooo! That really sounded fecked up. I'm not quite dead. Am I? Can anyone fecking hear me? No one directly answered her, but she did hear a familiar voice screaming as if his life depended on it. She followed the distressed sound down a hallway. Outside the room police, healthcare workers and men in yellow suits with HAZMAT boldly embroidered in red on their uniforms blocked the entrance. They held canisters with white steam rising from each container. Everything it came in contact with crystalized and shattered.

Zander. Without thinking twice, she sailed inside the room and wished she'd had a body to let loose the pain. This little entity she now took refuge in wasn't going to cut it. She needed some meat and bones.

Body snatching or the techno term—mediumship, the ability to take over one's body for a limited time and control everything they did until the poor slob figured out how to get their body back, or the entity in question had used and abused the body and evacuated the flesh in the same manner a virus or bacteria offed its host. *I can't believe I placed myself in that category.*

What did she have to lose at this point?

Everything.

Like a poisoned arrow Elyza plunged through the naked lady's back, going deep, invading her chai. The woman hiccupped once.

Hagatha stopped her advances on Zander and set the pliers down. With a dumbfounded appearance she studied him and scratched her head. She didn't say anything, just stared. And stared until he spoke first.

Full of confidence Zander again promised, "I'm going to kill you when I get out of here."

"I think someone beat you to it."

The voice. Zander couldn't have been more aghast. He coughed, cleared his throat. "Speak again."

"This is a sweet position. You look pretty fecking hot cuffed. Turn around is fair play, huh? Looks like we will get to use the cuffs after all." She smirked. Hagatha's eyes flashed turquoise just long enough to confuse the dickens out of Zander.

Using the nurse's body Elyza slid her hips one time over Zander's personal ice pick. "I think you will be fine

Templar, once out of here. Shame we haven't really had a first date yet. This could be more of a hot spot instead of a polar plunge, although…"

"Elyza? If that is truly you stop with the foreplay because in that body, it will be the end of the beginning." The nurse made his skin crawl.

One second a glimpse of someone he cared for more than he understood, the next the insane plier-wielding, no-dental skills whatsoever nurse reached for the pliers. Then out of nowhere she flipped gears and turned the pliers on herself. The pliers latched onto one of her front teeth and with a few toe-curling grunts, she bucked, fell off Zander, kicked her feet in the air, screamed inaudible mishmash and lay there panting, with blood puddling beside her cheek. This had all the makings of B-rated dragged-out death scene. Zander had never witnessed anything like it. Faces pressed against the pane in the hallway, noses flattened, breath fogging their view. One person on the opposite side of the window drew a heart in the fog and peeked through it. All Zander saw was an eyeball. No one opened the door to see if the nurse was all right, if she needed help, if she was totally bollixed. Zander found this peculiar, but then again maybe these people were used to her toxic antics?

"I'll undo the IV's. Then we need to flee. I'm not sure how long I can keep her mind tapped, Zander. Or how long I can stand being in her. She's a monster."

Hagatha rolled over, got on her hands and knees and crawled to Zander's side, her huge breasts swaying like untapped udders. She bent down so close, so kissably close before she hissed, blood spatter hitting his face.

Elyza teased, "Awe, that wasn't nice. Give him a kiss. No biting."

"No, really. No need to kiss and make up." Zander craned his neck so hard it ended up cramping. "I'm good. Hey, while the good witch is listening could you find it in your heart to undo the restraints. Elyza, I don't mean to sound like a prude, but where's your body? Don't tell me you're a ghost. I'm not taking her with me even if you are inside. I've already kidnapped one woman in the past twenty-four hours. I ain't going for two."

The nurse's face contorted. Her nostrils flared and her lips thinned. Laughter roared from the deepest area of her bowels. Zander decided right then and there this nurse had watched one too many cuckoo flicks and spent way too many hours perfecting the psycho nurse's part.

"Zander, I seemed to have lost my body. I'm pretty certain it's in this place somewhere."

Then the nurse found her voice. "The morgue, witch, and when I get you out of me, you'll be a permanent fixture there."

"Well then, there you have it, to the morgue we go. Zander don't move a muscle until I say to. We have to get all the onlookers occupied." Again, Elyza forced the nurse's compliance, battling her stiff fingers as she fought everything Elyza did. Zander's restraints fell away one at a time. "One last request, my ungracious host—" This time Elyza laughed and hers sounded pretty much as evil as the nurse's did "—Pick up the gun off your desk and aim it at the window. Just above all those idiots out there watching us. Shoot the window out and then you're going to put a bullet into that vaporizing tank. It'll be a blast. Trust me."

"Ah, Elyza, we'll all get blown to bits."

Zander, the voice of reason.

"I got this, trust me. On three, Zander. One, two, two

and half."

"Wait!" Zander whispered. "Where's my clothes?"

"Are you serious?" Elyza's voice reached a new level of perturbed. "I lost my body and you're worried about clothes? You weren't concerned back at your flat!"

"At least grab the chain around her neck. It's my chain."

In a fluid movement Elyza directed Hagatha to slip the chain from her neck and toss it to Zander. "Better?" she asked once he had it secured to his body again.

"Ta."

"Get ready, one-two-three!" Elyza commanded the nurse to reach for the gun while Zander struggled to get his legs under him. The silver and vervain definitely took a toll on his ability to ambulate and being pinned down on an ice bed only hampered his retreat.

"Jeepers, I feel like I have polio." He wobbled to the pair of yellow boots and donned them. "Your feet are even bigger than mine, you ugly wench. Not you Elyza."

"You'll wish polio's all you had when I'm done," Hagatha threatened.

"Shut up, ugly wench." Elyza copied Zander's nickname and winked at him with a devilish half grin.

"This is so messed up."

"Tell me about it. Now before this gets real, I suggest you step back." Elyza didn't wait. Her thumb slid up the outside of the gun and flicked off the safety. With a slight squeeze of the trigger, glass shattered and everyone on the opposite side of the wall dove for cover. Not a second later alarms blared. She—the nurse with Elyza infused inside her—spun toward the steaming tank as Zander limped in an exaggerated fashion from the room. With vehement vows of retribution, one last shot fired at the same time Elyza slipped from the hag's body. The explosion shook the entire floor. Zander fell, crawled a few feet and grasped a walker in the hallway. It took his last bit of resolve to pull his spent body up again. From there he slumped over the walker for support and headed away from the fireball rolling into the hallway. Butt naked with the exception of some fancy galoshes, poisoned and shot up, he was the newest, baddest version of the honey badger. He no longer gave a crap. Fire grew, spread with exigency, and left nothing but ash in its wake, other than a few singed hairs in areas no one would really notice once he got his pants back on.

"Come on, Lady Godiva," Elyza teased.

"No love, I'm Adam before Eve met him. Remember? We had this conversation back at the flat. Don't tell me just because you're a ghost, you're losing your memory." He continued gimping down the hall talking to a spirit he couldn't see, but feel? He hiccupped once and his body shook the way a dog did coming in from the rain.

Oh, yeah—she jumped him.

"You didn't!"

"Oh, but I did!"

"This is weird."

"Tell me about it," Elyza countered. "Didn't we just cover this? Well, now you can never tell me I don't know how it feels to walk in your shoes." Elyza giggled but the sound came out like Zander's masculine burble.

"Technically, Casperella, these ain't my Wellies."

"No. That's a big fat no on the name."

"But it works. You're a cross between a ghost and some poor waif who lost her shoe."

"No."

Zander got all itchy inside when she started laughing. "You're going to give me my body back, right? I mean you can't keep me?"

"Shut up and help me find mine. I don't have the vaguest idea what to do with one of these things." Elyza made Zander grab his penis and give it a tug.

"Dear lord woman! What are you doing to me? I think you know exactly what to do with one of these."

Elyza gripped him harder making Zander double over. "We're going to have fun."

"Stop! Please?" Zander pleaded, breathy as he struggled to loosen the grip his fingers had wrapped around his penis. Whether it was due to his current deteriorated health or his little spirit trying to get a rise out of him was left to be seen. The rise, however?

"Look what you've bleeding done to me, lass. I bet I look insane hobbling through a hallway talking to myself in different voices wearing a woody. I so owe you."

"A woody?" Elyza laughed for both of them. "Again, shut up before anyone notices."

"Well, if I do say so, it's almost impossible to not notice."

"Men. If you haven't noticed pretty much everyone's running the opposite direction and thank God they could care less there's an overheated naked guy trolling the halls. What do you think happened to Hagatha?"

"Don't really care. Hope she rots in Hell."

"I did see a giant ball of fire converge on her. And before you say anything, technically this time I didn't do it."

"You're splitting hairs, little ghost, and you know it.

You made her shoot the tank."

"It got you your freedom. Could we not talk and just find my hide?"

"Works for me. What if we can't find your body or get you tucked back inside? Not crazy about having a split personality."

"At least you have one to split."

If Elyza had a collar, she'd be getting hot under it. The fact she didn't, contributed to her soured state of nothingness. This guy had a body, had legs, was mostly able to get up, and limp down the hall, yet he had the audacity to complain because she hitched a ride spiritually? Then his words sank in. What if she couldn't find her way home? What if she really did croak? What if she did wind up a ghost?

What if?

"It'll be okay, Doolittle. Trust me."

There was the man she'd fallen for. The one who above all, against all odds and they were bourgeoning, found it in him to put her feelings above his. To make sure she didn't fall apart. Well, mentally anyway. Physically? Her gaseous existence equated to a raunchy fart that made your eyes water and your stomach turn before it finally dissipated. Just like her.

"Elyza, stop it. You'll be fine. You're still with me for a reason. I got your back, okay little ghost?"

"You don't have my back. You have my soul, bud. No more split ends. I am with you because I invaded your space, Zander. I'm so sorry. I had no right."

"Elyza, if I didn't want you beside my heart, I could've stopped you. You aren't the almighty Oz ya know. That wizard ain't got diddly on me or my yellow galoshes."

Zander laughed but Elyza didn't. Her conscience got the best of her. She went quiet while they searched for the morgue.

"What's on your mind, Lizzy?"

"Can't you read me?" The idea dumfounded her.

"Yes, but I enjoy our chats more. More intimate."

If she'd had a heart, it would have fluttered. Instead, his did.

"Elyza, stop it. What are you doing to me? First you man-handle my manhood and now my heart." He thumped his chest. "Giving me angina?" He huffed then cringed. "You made me huff? How unmanly is that?"

Elyza laughed. "Pretty!" A little playfulness couldn't hurt in this situation. "Here, this should boost your testosterone level." Elyza took control of his hand again and with due diligence scratched his balls. His cock reacted in true form. "Better?"

"Thank you. When you get your own bones back turn around will be fair play."

The man had feelings for her. Real ones. She knew everything he was thinking. Experiencing. And it scared the heck out of her. She'd never felt this way. Ever. Never expected too. She had no idea how to react. Touching people always hurt. Physically filled her with pain. Until this dingbat kidnapped/rescued her.

About that... She didn't want to filter through his grey matter, but she couldn't help herself. When she had attempted to read him at the apartment, she'd hit a wall. Elyza glanced through his past and immediately wished she hadn't. Loneliness, pain and torment forged a great barricade around his mind and heart.

Zander's life wasn't one for fairy tales. His entire existence to date had been one atrocity after another.

Betrayal, lies, abuse, and hatred for a little boy who did nothing to deserve the life he'd been subjected to.

She'd seen the families who'd taken him into the foster system. All in it for the money, certainly not the child's benefits. Lowlifes, every one of them. They'd beaten Zander, scarred him both emotionally and physically, yet not one of the scars related to the one on his chest. That one he coveted. It had nearly killed him when he received it. Elyza fought the urges to break down in tears and just hold him forever, until the pain and hurt dissolved. She knew otherwise; it never would.

How he held no hate toward the people that harmed him left her in awe of the man. That's where she and her gracious host parted their separate ways. She hated them all. What they'd done to him. People, fosters were supposed to put the welfare of the child first. He'd never been made to feel special. Never had a birthday party or a cake. Never been held or kissed or told he was loved. Or that he was beautiful. So beautiful.

Her heart fragmented. Tears fell regardless of her best intentions. Zander choked and wiped his eyes.

"Missy, what the hell are you doing to me?"

"I'm going to change your world, Zander Templar."

"Trust me, Casperella, you already have. Complete and utter sissy at the moment." Zander and she tiptoed into one of the hospital rooms where a woman's body lay forgotten, bare in a pool of blood, her bruised and lacerated hands and feet bound by leather to the bedframe, with complete disregard and respect for human life. A pillow lay across her face with bloodied handprints on the top of the pillowcase. Another life snuffed out. Zander stopped in front of her and made the sign of a cross. Then he turned and grabbed a pair of her jeans from the tiny closet and slipped them on.

Or attempted to.

Zander kicked off his sexy booties and lay on the floor with his legs in the pants trying his best to squeeze into the taut material. Wiggles and grunts followed as he wormed across the floor trying to jam his thighs into the pants two sizes too small. Once he got the waistband over his hips he sucked in his breath and held it while he tugged at both sides of the material to meet somewhere in the middle and get a few buttons latched.

"Welcome to my world, Mr. Templar. This is a daily occurrence on the runway." She laughed and for a moment it felt so good, so right.

Legs straight out in front of him, Zander bent forward to grab the mattress frame to help him get off the floor. "People in body casts probably have more mobility." The top button on the jeans popped off faster than a cork from a shaken champagne bottle. They both laughed as he finally got his feet under him and stood, still worried the material would split. "How do you strut around like a goddess in these things and not pass out? Did you learn nothing from corsets in years past? Little ghost, do these things make my bootie look fat?"

"You have to get into the metrosexual gist of it. Let's add a little swagger to the hips and there isn't an ounce of adipose on your glutes."

"Well, this is by far the strangest date I've ever had." Once the boots were back on Zander buckled over in hysterics. "The guys on cell block C would die if they saw me."

"I can arrange for a trip." Zander's little snicker eased Elyza's guilt about body snatching him. So far life or death—wherever her balances hung, held promise.

She loved being this close to him.

"Every relationship should be so lucky."

Elyza smiled. "You say that now. Stop reading my thoughts."

Teasing yet serious, Zander said, "Impossible when you're projecting everything through me. Whatever you do, don't go rearranging my thought process or deleting any old girlfriends you find stuffed in my memory."

"Old girlfriends?" Elyza raised Zander's voice to a new level of soprano.

"Ah jealousy?" Zander coughed his way through each word not used to having his cords tighter than the jeans he wore. "Elyza, men's voices are attached to their scrotum. On that note you might have given me a vasectomy. Please be gentle."

Their laughter melded into one harmonious mixture certain to sooth withered, battered souls.

Once they reached the lowest level of the building a sign with an arrow pointed to the morgue. "Dead ahead," Zander announced.

"Really?"

"Too soon?" Zander chuckled, even though he worried he might have hurt her feelings.

"Someone has a twisted funny bone."

"Sorry. You can twist my funny bone all you want once we get you put back together. You ready to go in there, Humpty?" Zander went to take a step forward, but his legs didn't budge. "Doolittle?" Out of nowhere, tears slid down his cheeks one by one. "I take it you need a minute, since you're making me cry again. You so owe me, love. Come on, it'll work out. And if the worst happens, you and I can perform ventriloquism acts in cheesy night clubs. I'll even dress up for you occasionally. Think how fun the sex will be."

"For you maybe." Said with a pound of sarcasm.

"I can live with that." Zander shoved the heavy metal door inward and stood in the doorframe.

"Holy roadkill. Do you see that?" His stomach bucked and he choked. "Ugh! Do you smell that?" Zander had a hard time believing his eyes. His olfactory senses had a harder time adjusting to the scent of death. He spun around the room looking for the one thing forensic detectives and morticians used, eucalyptus ointment. Two feet away on a tray loaded with stuff he never wanted to see again (bloodied instruments, an eyeball…) he plunged his fingers in the goo and rubbed it under his nose. Once he could breathe, he took in the rest of the room.

Corpses lay strewn across the floor, eviscerated, organs harvested, every last drop of blood drained. "These boots have a purpose." Regardless of the rubber soles, Zander took well-anticipated steps toward what he thought resembled a giant ice cube.

"Little ghost, you've gone quiet again. Even though I've only known you a short time I have come to realize when you're silent you're either scheming or about to make me look like a sissy. Where are we, my little body double?"

"You have on girl's skinny jeans and Wellies. The sissy goes without saying. It's in there, Zander. I'm inside that glacier. Why am I so cold?" They did a walk around the glass enclosure, looking for an entrance while looking for Elyza's body. Zander rubbed his arms the way someone does two twigs hoping to ignite a fire.

Rounding the last corner of the cooler Daelyn's pasty body impacted the glass, his face hard-pressed against the unforgiving wall, his nose squashed, nostrils flared while his breath fogged the inside of the glass. His fingernails dug at the glass tomb trying to get out. His mouth wide open amid screaming something inaudible, Elyza forced Zander's body to the opposite side of the wall mirroring Daelyn's actions.

"Daelyn!" Elyza used up every drop of Zander's adrenaline yelling his name as she pounded the wall to break through. No luck. Not even a chip. Fear and confusion obvious in his wide, expressive eyes, she watched Daelyn back away. "Daelyn it's me, Lizzy." Elyza yelled again but there was no spark of recognition from him. Her worst fears were in this room. She was trapped here. No one could see her and none of her family could hear her. Could this be the end of her line? Her life? What would happen when she saw her body? Could she slip back in and go about her merry way? What if she couldn't?

Zander took a sharp breath. "Elyza, what the hell? I'm about to have a panic attack. And who is he?"

"Who the bloody hell are you and what did you do to my cousin?" Regardless of the frigid temps he'd been trapped in, Daelyn's face reddened. "What kind of sick joke is this? Hurt her and you're dead."

Zander's lips moved before he could think. "Past the point of moot, I'm afraid." With that realization his body shook. "I'm sorry, Elyza. It was a crass thing to blurt out. I've never been an astral surrogate before. Just an ass."

Elyza conceded, "Crass, ass or not from the looks of it, you might be right. Dear goddess I'm ghosting for real."

Shots whizzed past Zander's head, one catching his ear. He fell trying to protect his body and Elyza from any further harm. With a quick spin on his knees to see who was after them now and how much precious time they had, he landed at the end of a 38 in his face.

"Not again. What is with everyone wanting me dead?"

"This is going to hurt boy, but only for a second." The guard pulled the trigger back, but the bullet jammed. Zander and Elyza were already one step ahead of him.

Elyza's voice superseded Zander's. "Bet this hurts more."

Zander found himself with a fire extinguisher in his hand. It literally appeared. He had no idea how it got there.

With the nozzle of the extinguisher aimed between the guard's eyes, Zander squeezed the lever. In the end the guard looked like he had a cream pie squashed in his face. Trying to get the caustic material off him, the man fell losing the gun. Obscenities followed.

With Elyza still reigning control over Zander's movements she attempted to get him to pick the weapon up. Zander awkwardly kicked the gun away from the man's reach.

"I'm not shooting the man, Elyza."

Don't want you to but keeping it out of his hands is a great idea. Aim it at the igloo and blast holes into it.

"Who's the dude on the other side?"

My cousin. He's harmless.

"Easy for you to say. He has no idea we are the ultimate Yin and Yang. I don't need to be able to read his mind, Elyza. He thinks I want to kill him."

Then I suggest you shut up and shoot the surrounding door and miss him. Please make it a priority since the security guard is making headway. For whatever the reason Daelyn can't read my thoughts.

Zander went to answer her, "I—"

Elyza made him bite his tongue. "Just shoot." Quite honestly, she knew what happened and why she could no longer reach any of her family. She'd gone so far beyond the rainbow she passed OZ, Dorothy, the flying monkeys, the wicked witch, Go, and missed her get out of jail free card all together. Damn, that one she really could have used. The only thing keeping her semi-grounded had to be her gracious host.

"Elyza that hurt my tongue. How would you like it if I bit you?"

For a split second she found no fault with the idea. To have his lips softly pressed against her flesh, his teeth drinking her in, one drop at a time, would be a fantasy she could not deny.

"You hesitated, love. What God-awful timing you have on sexy daydreams. Did I say God-awful timing? I meant it." Zander reached down, grabbed the cool metal weapon, aimed, and squeezed the trigger on the gun. Each bullet bounced off the glass leaving not even a nick or scratch. With lightning-fast reflexes, he dislodged the mag holding the ammunition and inspected one. "Freaking rubber bullets."

When no more shots rang out, Daelyn pounced at the door, screaming things neither Zander nor Elyza could make out.

"We have to get to him somehow." Desperation saturated her plea. "We must let him know you're not some random beefcake armed on a killing spree."

"Beefcake?" Zander scratched his head with the barrel of the gun. "Not sure if—"

"Compliment? Yes. Zander, set down the gun and

walk up to the door."

"Why, so if he does break it down he'll have my throat that much faster? Elyza there's got to be a password here somewhere. Why lock the bodies up? They aren't going anywhere."

"Unless they're in my predicament."

"Love, did you look, really look inside there?" Zander tapped on the glass with the gun. Daelyn recoiled and slammed head on into it, bouncing backwards when the unforgiving wall didn't splinter beneath his will.

"Didn't anyone ever teach you not to taunt the tiger?"

"Sorry. Little ghost, those bodies have been autopsied. All for the one on the top, yours." Zander gasped. Oddly he was beginning to get used to the little things his body reacted to on her behalf. Women were lousy poker players.

"I can whip you at poker, Templar."

"Yeah, because you're sharing my brain. That's an unfair advantage."

"No kidding," Elyza tried to lighten the somberness of the situation. "How do you know it's my body?"

"One flip-flop is still on your foot." His hand came to his jaw, and he rubbed the stubble over his chin.

Within an arm's distance of the glass, Elyza had Zander tap his index finger to the cold wall three times. Daelyn snarled.

"I come in peace. I enter in peace. I leave in peace," Elyza recited a spell her mother had taught her with a few slight tweaks. Hopefully this one would work, but knowing her mother's casting abilities, or disabilities as the family teased, she held little faith, but she had to do something. "Break these fetters binding this unholy union. Allow my body and soul reunion. Bring forth the power from my runes."

Mentally Elyza instructed Zander to look at the palms of his hands. To his astonishment dynamic symbols moved just beneath the surface of his skin, like cartoon characters coming to life on a pad of paper as you flip each page a different shape takes form. "Place your hands firm on the wall and don't move them. No matter what."

"Seriously? No matter what? This tickles." Zander fought the urge to run his hands up and down the length of his borrowed skinny jeans.

Ignoring him, Elyza continued the chant, "Break these fetters binding this unholy union. Make these walls crumble and fall. Bring forth the power from my runes. Goddess, I beg of thee, have mercy on me. Make me whole, body, mind and soul. Blessed be." Creaking noises filled the room. The clamor reminded Zander of splintered, weathered piers being battered by unforgiving waves. The walls exploded outward, the force blasting Zander backward a good fifteen feet. Snug against a far wall, cross-eyed and breathy, Zander started patting down random body parts checking for damage control. He got back on his feet and looked around. "Whoa! Pretty certain I went farther and faster than Marty McFly."

Somewhat snippy Elyza added, "Can we focus on my future?" Her tone beguiling and her will determined she finished with, "Reawaken the light in my eyes and any other spirit left in this place to die. Daelyn—" Elyza stretched the limits of Zander's vocals one last time to the point he leaned forward coughing and grabbing his crotch. She squeaked, "I'm sorry, Zan. Last time I promise."

"Don't ever promise me something you don't intend to keep." Hands down he knew Elyza had to have the last word in any given situation. He'd spent one day with her and knew her better than most married couples ever thought they knew their spouses over a lifetime together.

Zander, if we live through this, I'll give you the extended uncut version of my life instead of the fast, furious one we're crashing through.

We'll take a slow ride. Nice and easy...

For as much as I adore your voice, could you serenade me after I'm no longer looking like roadkill?

Daelyn uttered, "Buddy, you're a dead man," just as he, Shelby's flaccid body and Elyza's stiff corpse vanished before their disbelieving eyes.

"How did he do that? Are you kidding me? You learned to evanesce before me? You swiped my body, Dae." Elyza screamed at the top of what was left of Zander's voice thrusting his arms in the air, fists clenched, silently cursing the existence of any deity eavesdropping.

"Stop!" Zander choked. "I need water, but first let's get this letch secured so he won't come after us." Fumbling as he regained control over his own movements, Zander reached down to the guard's waistband while the man still tried to wipe foam from his eyes and dragged him across the sloppy floor. Before the guy could protest Zander had the man secured to a gas line that piped in Oxygen to the room. If he broke the line to free himself the chances were good another explosion would occur.

"You won't get far, Templar. Police got your number," the guard hollered.

"And I am going to make certain they have yours," Zander added with confidence. To his side kick he asked, "Where to?" Zander braced himself for flight, knowing full well they were about to rocket through space, wormholes, time…your basic everyday Sci-Fi get away. Eyes clamped, he waited. The warp speed, or the odd nothingness he'd experienced when they'd evanesced before didn't happen. One eye peeked around. Same busted up room full of dead corpses and a deadbeat guard. "Elyza?"

"I'm trying. It isn't working. This place must be warded to the nines."

"One more time. Your cousin did it. Hurry."

A few disgruntled cuss words were heard, but no G-forces made his cheeks pucker or flap.

"I can't evanesce in here, Zander. How come Daelyn could?"

"Please stop making me sound like a whiney girl. Probably due to it being my body? Well, I supposed the old-fashioned way will have to do." He would keep his one thought to himself. They couldn't zip through time because Elyza's time expired. How he prayed he was wrong.

"The idea crossed my mind too," Elyza admitted aloud.

Zander's shoulders slumped, and he sighed. "It'll be all right. Promise."

"Same goes for you, Zan. Don't make promises you can't keep. You keep saying it'll be all right, but honestly, nothing is right."

One pair of borrowed skinny jeans, the equivalent of a nerf gun tucked securely into the waistband of those pants, a sky-blue scrub top pinched from a laundry basket-mostly clean, all while styling sunburst yellow booties, they exited the morgue in true fashion and didn't look back.

Chapter Twelve

Profusely sweating for the two of them, Father Butler continued his vigil of prayer, while dabbing Olivia's misting forehead as she continued to keep her daughter's heartless body from desiccating and her soul from flying to higher grounds. Down for the count were Elyza's parents, Serina for obvious reasons, and Lucian because he and his wife were linked metaphysically together, blood bound. Then there were Elyza's aunties, Jovan (Serina's half-sister), and her Aunt Raven, her Uncle André (her father's triplets), and her cousin Savanah all for the same reasons—blood bound. Elyza renamed it Hell bound. Elyza's uncles, Jonah and Julian (Jovan's bothers) and Payton were hanging in there by the grace of God, and a little thing known in the family as pigheadedness.

"How are we holding up my lovely necromancer?" Father Butler asked even though he knew better. Idle chitchat was all he had left to keep her going. Keep Olivia on point.

"Necromancer?" Olivia turned and gazed into Thomas's tired, red-streaked eyes and barely afforded him a grin. "A white lighter and a necromancer working side by side."

"Opposites attract, my queen. Forever."

"Thomas today feels longer than forever."

Thomas leaned in and kissed Olivia's forehead.

"Have faith. I do in you."

Olivia didn't pull away. She continued to lean on her partner, gaining his strength and never wavering faith in the heavens and apparently in her. Hearing the squeak of wheels Olivia took one breath and reluctantly looked up. Payton and Ethan carted in a serving tray filled with knives, retractors, sterile sponges, sutures, and an AED, automated external defibrillator, to get the party started, or more apropos restarted after the surgery, just in case. Sat in the middle of the tray in a crystal ice bucket, one quivering bleached out pink organ. Eyes narrowed, a scowl brewing, Olivia stood and set her skeptical gaze on Ethan. "Did you follow the directions?"

Finding a sudden interest in his feet, Ethan nodded.

"To a bleeding tee?"

She appeared miffed. Ethan swallowed hard and moved his gaze to meet Olivia's. He gave a half-shoulder shrug.

Her head cocked sideways, her index finger rubbing her lips, she asked, "Odd coloring, don't you agree?"

Ethan and Payton spared one another an ill-fated peek.

Olivia leaned in a little closer, making both Ethan and Payton step back. "Pink? An hour ago it was the color of tar. Now it's peeenk?" She really enunciated the word to the max. "Savanah would love this if she were here to mock it."

"We did follow your directives to a tee, although," Payton tossed a thumb at Ethan apprehensively, "one of us may or may not have added sugar instead of salt to the recipe."

"Whatever!" The tendons in Ethan's neck tightened. "They both look the same and honestly, this hunk of defunctness needs a little sweetening up. An entire sugar cane field perhaps."

Wearied, Olivia asked, "Did the salt ever get added? It's a spiritual cleansing agent."

Payton nodded yes.

"I still can't believe we are doing this." Ethan looked between the remaining people in the room, Olivia, Father Thomas, Payton, hoping for a spark of camaraderie but then he glanced at Serina's lifeless body, her pale face drained of its usual vibrant gaiety and knew this had to happen no matter how insane. He refused to look at the obvious, the gaping hole in her chest. Serina, simply put, was the heart and soul of this household, the linchpin who had this ridiculous family either in hysterics or running for their lives when one of her castings backfired. "So what do we do?"

Olivia held out her hands. "We begin in prayer and then end in it, because if I do not get the outcome I wish for, you'll need all the help you can muster. Let us move my baby to the chapel and begin."

****

The bus ride to the mansion seemed more like a nice Sunday ride through Sherwood Forest. Shrubbery and foliage in every imaginable hue of light, dewy green to well, forest green pathed the thoroughfare. Sleep deprived, Zander would have bet his astral hitchhiker, he witnessed Robin of Loxley groping a vine, swinging through the trees with Maid Marion's legs wrapped securely around his waist getting two rides for one. That type of hitchhiker Zander could have fun with. The one currently testing his patience had him stuck in a traffic circle. Closing his eyes to rest and Elyza popping them back open to look out the window proved a test of wills.

"Can we have a truce," Zander asked aloud? "For the love of God, woman I need sleep."

The woman occupying the seat beside him on the bus leaned away from him, nearly landing in the isle. She eyed Zander head to toe taking in the yellow stained boots before deciding whether to give him the time of day. "Look lad, I get the arm rest. There's your truce. Keep to yourself. And you have a really gross runny nose." Her face scrunched, she added, "And you smell like that goop people used to rub on their chests when they had a cold fifty years ago." The woman then dug in her bag for a wad of tissues and tossed them in his lap.

"Ta." Zander gingerly picked the flimsy papers up and tucked them into the crook in the seat. He decided against telling the woman he was talking to the little poltergeist currently taking up space in his mind… and if he were honest, his heart and soul.

You truly are nuts. One moment you're praising my existence and the next calling me nothing short of a demon.

Well, my fair lady, you are a woman, and women are the devil in disguise, capable of making men insane.

Short trip if you ask me. Don't make me squeeze your nozzle.

You wouldn't dare.

In disbelief he watched his hand march over his thigh headed toward his groin. Muffled from the loudspeaker came, "Hazel Grove, next stop!" Zander bounced to his feet.

That's us. Saved by the bell.

****

About to enter the room, Daelyn paused and prayed; one; to find the wits to tell his family what he had found and two; the courage to tell them who he had lost. The upcoming mistral would be a battle of bravery, strength and resolution.

Candles lit, white to clarify purity and hope lined the two sides of the shale walkway leading up to the sanctuary of the Chapel. The nave itself, to this day, remained simple, truest to the intent of the first owners, the Davenports, a place of worship. Dark wooden pews, aged with dings, divots and some with carved initials lined both sides of isle, facing a large rectangular leaded window. Stained glass images in each pane depicted biblical scenes. Near the chapel bay window rested the Davenport pew with their personal Bible, both the dark meticulous artisanship of the seat and the holiness of the book restored to divinity. On the west wall of the room, The Ten Commandments are scrolled and beneath them is an older pre-Reformation painting of Jesus, in the midst of repair due to whitewashing, when centuries past Catholicism wasn't en vogue. Carved roses from the Tudor era, decorated the dark timbers that supported the ceiling. A fire in the hearth stole the chill from the room but did nothing to lessen the iceberg in his heart. A few chips from the fire went askew, fading from a brilliant fiery orange to a dull black before even hitting the floor. Daelyn looked around the room, his heart broken, his soul much like the dying embers. No one looked up when he came in. No one noticed him covered in blood. There was enough bloodshed already to go around. He simply blended in. Serina's lifeless body waited like an extinguished wick to be reignited with a flame. Beside her, a crystal container with a vibrating organ inside it waited. He couldn't un-see this abomination no matter how badly he wanted to. Had anyone waltzed in off the street this place would resemble a Devil's sacrifice. Truth be known, this had to be Satan's hand with these circumstances mounting.

Rising from a kneeled position Father Butler went sideways, his balance awry. "I'm fine," he stated, as Ethan rushed to his aid. Father Butler shooed him away. "Just been on my knees too long. These days I'm not sure which is worse, kneeling or standing."

Noting only a handful of family, Daelyn asked, "Livvy, Great Grampa, Payton, Ethan, are we it? Are we the last men standing? No offense, Livvy."

Olivia cleared her throat. Father Butler raised a brow. Daelyn attempted an ill-fated smirk and finished with, "Seriously Livvy, you've got more balls than any of us in this room. Where is everyone?"

Olivia nodded in the direction of the banqueting hall. "It is where we have everyone currently resting. Julian and Jonah are tending to them."

Olivia never lost focus of Serina's body. With her head hung over her daughter's chest, one hand covering the hole where her heart should have been and her other hand on Serina's forehead, she inclined her head sideways, resting her icy glare on Daelyn. "So where is my granddaughter?"

"I found Elyza's body. And shortly thereafter I found her spirit. The two are as disconnected as Serina is to her heart."

Father Butler was quick to snap, "She has not crossed. I would feel it." He added as he rubbed Olivia's back, "I would know if my grandbaby was gone."

Olivia asked, "Daelyn, where is Elyza's body? Bring her here beside her mother. Where is Shelby?"

"Shelby is beside Elyza."

"Make sure Shelby is comfortable. Then get back here. We have work to do."

****

Coming down the walkway that courted the stream through Bramall Park, Zander caught his first glimpse of the manor. His inner child, the one that desperately wanted to run through the mansion, see all the hiding spots, the hidden staircases, secret rooms, experience the history instead of reading about it in books, he could barely contain. Get his hands on a piece of history. See the White ghost.

Haven't you had enough of ghosts? Me?

Don't believe I shall ever grow weary of you. How come you stopped using my voice to talk with me?

Figured I gave you a sore throat.

Zander's head bowed sideways with a smirk he hadn't intended.

So, you're a history buff? Have I got a surprise for you. My family are walking, talking curators of the past century.

I can't wait to meet them.

You say that now.

Elyza, I've never really been anywhere or done anything and clearly the HM Liverpool's palace for the criminally inept does not count.

Could we not mention your last address right off the bat when introductions are made? It might make a few of my family members batty. In our current state of togetherness, I think they'd have a better chance of catching us in bed together and getting over that than me holding you hostage ... and your past.

And who's the criminal?

I promise to somehow make it up to you.

Casperella, I shall hold you to this.

Eyes full of wonder, Zander took in the mansion, and the all-around beauty. The outside of the Tudor design with the dark wood and white stucco awed him. What would the inside be like?

Move the tush or we'll never find out. Walk around to the opposite side of the building, where tourists are allowed in. The place is closed to the public while my aunt does the restoration on the paintings.

"And then what? Wait for the police to arrive after they find a strange man skulking about pretending to be a woman trapped in a man's body?"

It wouldn't be the first time. Well... that scenario yes, but the strange men...not so much.

A pang of jealousy blindsided Zander. He had to ask, "Are you accustomed to bringing strange men home?" He held his breath while Elyza continued to laugh.

"Stop."

Stop worrying. Shelby Jane has a habit of meeting all the wrong men and smuggling them in only to get caught.

Once they'd cleared the stairs to the main level of the grounds and walked the perimeter of the home Zander found himself with his grip on the handle of a huge cathedral-shaped oak door. A small explosion detonated in his gut. What was he getting himself into? These people would want his blood, his heart, his head or most likely all three. Anyway he looked at this he did not see a favorable outcome.

"Okay little ghost, now what?"

What do you usually do when you enter a chapel? We pray. We pray these guys believe us. We pray they can get me back in my body. We pray we save my mom and then we work on clearing you and I from any wrong doings.

"I've never been in a church."

What about the priest outfit?

"Ah, that!" Zander closed his eyes and shook his head. "Allow me to rephrase. I've never been in a church that I recall. Better?"

Let's bypass that story too, okay?

"Maybe you should go in yourself."

Not funny. Zander, open the door. I got your back. No worries.

"As I stroll into the valley of death, I ask you, Lord, please afford me the wisdom, patience and fortitude to not piss off anyone I cross paths with that would ultimately accelerate my journey or send me packing in the opposite direction. Yours truly, Zander Templar."

I do suppose a prayer can't hurt.

"That wasn't reassuring."

Before he knew what hit him, Elyza discharged a surge of energy through Zander's body. His fingers clamped onto the knob and with a hard jerk the handle twisted downward, the latch releasing. A toe-curling creak filled the room as door slowly opened inward. Zander peaked around the frame of the door. "Still got my back?" First impressions being everything, he smoothed out his leggings and attempted to tuck in the hospital scrub he'd borrowed. Still no luck. The jeans were unforgiving. He ran his fingers through his hair and let loose a breath of air. One foot in the door, he focused on the room, the people, the shit show before him, and decided comparatively speaking he looked amazing. Resting on the altar of the chapel a naked woman's body with another woman stood above her, her arms buried elbow-deep in the lady's chest cavity. The woman with a pulse spewed chant after chant coming off like a broken record. A reddish-black aura completely encased the two women. Orange sparks dispersed and hit the others in the room. Only the slightest of flinch gave away the woman's steeled focus that she realized the dynamics of the room had been altered.

The woman with blazing green eyes pulled a bloodied hand from the cadaver and pointed to where a light pink heart sat. In a quopping crystal vase. With steadied hands the woman plucked the heart out and placed it inside the woman's chest cavity.

What in Hell did we waltz in on, Elyza?

One stream of bluish-red energy surged from the woman's fingertip and slammed into the corpse. Question one answered—where did Elyza get her hot little temper? The body on the table twitched, the back arched and then flopped back onto the surface with a heady thud. The cadaver's arms flopped to the sides limp, the tips of the fingers the color of an eggplant. Zander knew enough to know that blood pooled in the tips of limbs of when people's hearts no longer worked. Gravity! It always had the last word.

Dear lord, is this what they would do to Elyza? Zander had all he could do to not turn and run.

The woman looked up and set her heated gaze on Zander, almost daring him to intrude. Game on. He took a step closer.

"One is for love, Serina. Never doubt my or anyone's love for you. You will love again. Fiercely. Passionately. With your new heart. With your family. For your family." Another blaze of power slammed into the body.

"Two is for laughter, Serina. You will laugh again. With us. With your family. At us, myself excluded."

A small burst of nervous laughter filled the room. Apparently, that was meant to be a bit of comic relief during a very intense moment, but Zander had the feeling the woman meant it—no laughing at her.

A third surge of power left that ever so lovely odor of burnt flesh in its wake. Zander rubbed his nose and fought a tickle that would lead to a sneeze.

The woman continued, "Three is for health, Serina. Your health will be restored. Flawless. Absolute perfectness shall reign. You shall live a long life with your imbecile husband, your children, all of us."

More soft chuckles filled the room. Zander figured this woman and her son-in-law must have one hell of a relationship for her to joke about him here and now. Zander found he really liked this lady. Had respect for her.

She's my grandmother, Olivia Spencer. She is the most powerful mage on the planet. No, make that the universe. She's the best lady to have on your side, or the worst person to ever have miffed at you. Tread lightly.

I have a way with women, Doolittle.

Like I said, tread lightly.

Olivia spared Zander a reprimanding shot hearing him snicker before she continued. She placed a chaste kiss on the woman's cheek. "You will do this Serina because I mote this be, with the powers vested in me. There is no one higher than me, so breathe for me, my baby. Breathe. Live. Love. Laugh."

It is called psychic surgery, Zander. My mother and grandmother are true healers. No need for conventional equipment or hospitals. Just mind over matter.

Finger tapping to a nervous tune, Olivia grew impatient. Concern weighed her words, "Only half of her heart is beating. Something is wrong. Look! The left half beats, the right half remains stagnant." Payton, Father Thomas, Daelyn, Julian, and Ethan all took a step toward the table, each with their right hand on the next person's left shoulder forming a circle of strength. "No! Do not move." Olivia's panic stifled everyone leaving Zander with the impression this woman never panicked a day in her life. Until now.

"You forgot her memory. The brain has memories, the heart does as well and muscle memory." It just kind of blurted out. Zander had no idea why the words formed or where they came from, but his voice resonated throughout the chapel.

An angry lethal blackened fingernail jabbed in his direction. "Templar?" Olivia's voice held disbelief. Her bloodshot eyes bulged. Contempt painted her mood. Her face blanched white. "Approach the table."

He backed up. "You know me?" His voice cracked. She didn't appear happy in the least they were acquaintances. When in Hell would he have had a chance engagement with the high priestess? As shoddy as his memory had been this made zero sense and for this one particular line in the woman's incantation to spark a connection to something he'd heard at some point only God knew when left him baffled. Of all times why now? It also had others in the room more than aware of his presence. His voice no more than a whisper he said, "I hope we parted on good terms, Mistress," and he meant every word.

"I am amazed you do not recall me, Templar. That

scar you own is more telling than a fingerprint."

This time Zander stepped forward. "How do you know about my scar?" Before he had a chance to get closer two men came at him faster than Cerberus could snag a demon trying to jump levels in the Ever After. One he recognized as Elyza's overbearing cousin, Daelyn. The only thing the second man had missing was a tattoo saying, "Badass." He did a second take on the man's set jaw, lethal choppers bared. He wasn't fully human.

And to make things so much more awkward a few of these people had not a stitch of clothing on. How Zander missed all the excess baggage when he first entered the chapel he didn't know, other than what appeared to be the carnage of a woman's corpse spread out. Not to mention the heart transplant going on and one woman with neon green eyes literally tossing a mini tornado from one hand to the other and then making lightning spark from it into a dead body to reanimate it. Yeah, no reason whatsoever to miss the naked mass of muscles and testosterone. And boobs. Yes, the woman on the table had been blessed by the dreams of many a man. "Elyza," Zander whispered, "I can't believe you gave me a hard time about running around my flat nude."

Seriously Zander? The dreams of many a man?

Zander quashed his laughter.

Daelyn tapped Julian's arm. "Don't hurt him, Grimmy," came out a second too late. Julian had Zander dangling in front of him by the back of his scrub top, snarling in his face. Daelyn grabbed Julian's shoulder. "He has Elyza. And a gun?" Daelyn yanked the weapon Zander had tucked into the back of his jeans when they fled the infirmary. He set the gun down in a pew.

"It shoots rubber bullets," Zander offered, hoping it would lessen the perceived threat.

Julian snarled. "So you basically brought a toy gun to a witch hunt?"

Frantic, Zander squirmed. "I'm not hunting anyone."

"Where is she?" Julian barked, scouring the room. "What have you done with her?"

"Don't hurt me, Uncle Julian." Elyza tweaked Zander's voice and in the next instant Zander's black eyes flashed turquoise.

In a clumsy shuffle Julian dropped Zander and stepped back, tripping. Daelyn's quick reflexes saved him from landing beside Zander.

"Grimmy, it's me, Elyza." That's when Elyza made a cute shoulder-head bob with a coy smile using Zander's resistant body. The movements came off spasmodic.

With disbelief conveying his tone Zander half-asked half-joked, "Doolittle, tell me you didn't just make me look like a zombie in that Halloween thriller dance video? Coz that's what it felt like."

"Ha!" Elyza roared still borrowing Zander's vocals. "I thought the same thing the second I made you do it." They were sharing another moment, a totally awkward, ill-timed moment, both laughing until both Zander and Elyza looked up, noting they had everyone's full-blown attention and sadly no one else joining in their amusement.

Olivia grumbled, "Here we go again."

"Grams, how do you know Templar? Never mind, we'll talk after you finish."

"You're damn right, we will talk, Sparky. Do not

move a muscle, Templar. Trust me, I can put an end to them."

"I don't think he could if he wanted to, Grams," Elyza responded still fine-tuning Zander's vocals.

"I could," Zander struggled to form the words. "I am just displaying an ounce of sense in a situation that clearly makes none." Legs crossed, Zander looked up at a man, no, he reneged such a delusion and decided on mountain, trying to figure out Julian. The walking asteroid had two different colored eyes, one the color of jade, the other deep brown. Long, wavy auburn hair parted on the side added to the guy's ruggedness. Any other man trying to pull it off would have looked feminine. This beast had to been around since the days of cavemen. Elyza did say her family had a lot of history.

Now you're being silly, Zander.

Doolittle, there's not an ounce of anything soft or cushy on the guy.

His heart makes up for his looks.

Julian poked Zander's shoulder quickly and backed off. "Where's Elyza? What have you done to her?"

"Uncle Jules, we will talk after. Let Grams work her magic."

Julian jabbed Zander again giving him a hard sideways glance, the veins in his neck pulsing and his chest puffed out. "I don't trust this—you."

Elyza reprimanded him. "Uncle, stop trying to being a bully. You look ridiculous."

"I do not have to try, Lizzy." Julian winked at Elyza.

"Completely inappropriate." Zander snorted, shaking his head. "Don't ever wink at me again."

Julian gave a quick bashful look around the room, his attitude somewhat dismayed. "This is beyond messed up."

"Elyza? Is that really you?" Daelyn stooped down searching Zander's huge black eyes for any clue his cousin really was trapped inside another human. He fell backwards, crab-crawling to get away when Zander's eyes went turquoise again. "Holy crap, this is messed up."

"Are you my freaking parrot now, Dael?" Julian asked, hoisting Daelyn from the floor. "I do believe I said just that."

Daelyn placed a firm hand on Zander's shoulder. "I want her back buddy. Whole."

"Clearly not as badly as I want her…" Zander took a breath when Daelyn's grip tightened. He produced an innocent enough grin. "Out! I meant out." Zander jerked his shoulder out of Daelyn's grip. "Do you mind?"

"Praise the Goddess. Her heart beats. Maybe it just needed a minute. The old ticker has after all been stagnant a century." Olivia stood before her family with her arms raised, bloodied fists clenched, she wore a smile that rivaled a little child eating ice cream for the first time. Tears of joy but more so—relief flowed down Olivia's cheeks until Serina's body began to buck and make an unearthly haunting hiss. The wet, choking sound of a death rattle emitted. The room fell silent.

Prone on the table, Serina's skin a sickly grey, her eyes staring into space, Zander waited like the rest of the room for the woman's chest to rise or fall again… Do something. Anything.

Nothing!

One sob, so miniscule, slipped through Olivia's quivering lips as she tersely brushed an abandoned tear from her face leaving a bloody streak behind. "I failed her, Thomas. I failed our daughter."

One second Olivia Spencer defied death. The next, death pounded down the door, flattening everyone beneath it.

Zander feared his heart would shatter, noting the grief in the older woman's eyes. The loss. The agony. Every drop of pain Olivia and Thomas experienced threatened to drown Zander. Did his parents look like this when he disappeared? Or was stolen? Or given away or thrown away? Did someone grieve over him the way this woman and her family did the cadaver on the table? Was there an ounce of remorse for his life? He doubted it highly.

The tremor in Olivia's hands before Father Thomas took them in his own and pulled her into his keep had tears spilling down Zander's cheeks. Nothing to do with Elyza being an empath trapped inside him.

"Mom? Mom?" Elyza sounded scared. Alone. Uncertain. Desperate. "Momma, please don't leave me."

Zander now understood what it felt like to lose someone you loved more than your own life. Every crushing emotion Elyza experienced so did he. His memories held no one special: No one to love or care for so suffering this was most uncomfortable.

Others in the room dropped to their knees.

Zander lunged forward holding his chest. Daelyn grabbed his arm. "What is it Lizzy?"

Zander broke from Daelyn's hold. "Don't!" was the only thing Zander could muster before Elyza came through again, her tranquil eyes reeling in heartbreak. "I can't do this without you, Mom." To Zander, Elyza murmured, "You and I would have made the rest of the world wonder where they went wrong. Thank you for being you."

"No, no, no. no, no little cherub, you are so not saying goodbye to me." Zander stammered, shut his eyes, bent forward holding his chest as if he could hold Elyza in there forever. "Elyza no!" His voice echoed through the chapel. Julian came to his other side, and Payton his back. Zander stiffened, stood erect and cast a plea to Olivia with his last shred of hope. "Not her too, Mistress. Please stop her."

Her damp, auburn locks draped in her face, Olivia huffed to get them from her view. "I cannot make her stay. She has chosen to follow her mother." Olivia clasp her hand over her mouth and choked. "I am so sorry."

"No!" Zander crossed the room to Olivia and dragged her to a standing position. "I will not allow her to leave me. She can't. Elyza is the only person in my entire existence who has ever made sense of me. Please don't leave me, Doolittle. Do something, Mistress." Zander spun to Daelyn completely devastated. "You have her body, right? Can't you get her spirit back in it somehow?" Zander didn't wait for an answer. From any of them. Screw them all. He turned to the doorway that led to where? He'd never been in this mansion before, but Elyza's body was somewhere in here and he would find her and damn the entire lot of them he'd get her back together if it cost him his life doing it. Over his shoulder he cast an angry glance directed at Olivia. "Elyza said you were the most powerful mage alive. Ya want to know what I see? Losers! All of you." And with that Zander turned and headed out in search of the most beautiful person he'd ever encountered. Not two steps into his journey he met the most formidable force of nature he would ever confront.

Two men, identical in looks, brawn and attitude slammed him to the ground knocking the wind out of him, while a third man held Elyza's body draped across his arms. Zander tried to get a breath, but it was as if he was hooked up to a respirator and someone purposefully had their foot on his air hose. Burning pain filled his lungs. His eyes watered while he punched himself in the chest praying to kick-start the lungs. Losing consciousness seemed imminent.

Embarrassment. Well, wasn't this a hell of a way to die?

One of the men, guy A, since Zander couldn't tell them apart other than their clothes ordered, "Get up kid and get back in the chapel. Now!" The man had on jeans and a white shirt with loafers, no socks. The guy's clone, guy B, wore a navy shirt and black jeans, barefoot.

Guy B was nice enough to squat down and pull Zander to his chest then slam him dead center in the back. Guy A leaned in and added a cynical, "That should do the trick." That's when one; Zander now knew what it was like to be a vacuum cleaner being turned on for the very first time and sucking out all the air from a hot air balloon and two: this close to the guy he noticed a subtle difference—their eye color. The man in the jeans with a totally pissed off face had silvery-blue eyes that resembled a torrential mistral and the guy in black jeans that most likely cracked all his ribs had eyes so blue they looked nearly black.

"Thanks?" Zander choked.

"Don't thank me. Move."

The dude carrying Elyza's flaccid body came in a few inches shorter but no less intimidating. The thing that stuck out like a sore thumb was the guy's eyes color, daffodil yellow. His biceps had biceps, he was that ripped. A loose pair of linen scrubs fell to his hips and showed off a six-pack. His wavy sandy brown hair parted on the side landed just short of his chin, which sported a goatee. When he noticed Zander hadn't moved after the direct command from the two men he asked, "Death wish, kid? The two guys are Lucian and André St. James: Identical in everything including life and death if ya get my drift. I am one of Elyza's uncles, Jonah. You want to save our girl? Move. Your. Ass."

Zander heard Guy A, Lucian's voice, rumbling through the mansion, "Elyza Tracey St. James get your dimpled little behind back here immediately. I'm not playing around little girl and don't you make me get your mother involved. I know she's around here somewhere too. I am over and done with this disappearing act."

Sobbing, condolences, and soft murmurs of, "It can't be true," came from a room a little farther down the hall. Zander stopped, his head cocked a little to side, as if that motion alone would turn up the volume, not that he needed it. Lately he could have picked up a feather sifting across the field. In pairs of two others began to saunter out of a room, holding each other for support. Every one of them had stress lines etched into their faces. A few of the women resembled Elyza but there were subtle differences. They were all taller for starters. One woman had curly, long, jet-black hair and eyes that matched guy B, André. And she was almost as tall. The woman latched onto her arm had long blonde ringlets. Her eyes were the lightest blue, like a Siberian Huskie's. When the woman with blonde tresses noticed Zander watching them come toward her, she swung her body in front of the girl with jet-black curls.

That move had mother defense stamped all over it. This family he could respect. They were fierce. Loyal. Protective. Passionate. And hurting.

Another woman came to stand beside the blonde, completely blocking the woman with the jet-black curls. She looked every bit as intimidating as guys A and B did. And she looked exactly like them, except female: Tall, slender, sapphire eyes, porcelain skin, and plump ruby lips. Onyx hair, pin straight, fell in layers down her back. She was beautiful right up until a subtle sneer flashed a lovely double set of fangs.

"I haven't eaten yet kid, and I'm not feeling at all hospitable, so I suggest you move your skinny jeans. I'm Raven. Don't forget me, because if you've screwed up anything here today, I'll guarantee you will be forgotten."

"Yes, Ma'am." Backing up and trying to keep an eye on all the people behind him for his own salvation Zander began to make his way back to the chapel. Coming up fast from behind him a young woman with curly red hair, freckles and cowboy boots kicked him in the shin.

"All you had to do was stop running and none of this would have happened. We could have saved her. You probably killed her. Thanks. If I could end your life for real right now without fear of losing Lizzy forever trust me, you and I wouldn't be having any conversations at all. Once I get her back, you better run. Run a hell of a lot faster than you did two days ago."

"So, you're Shelby?" Zander asked rubbing the new indent in his leg no thanks to a precisely placed boot tip. "You're the one that shot me?"

"They were paintballs, moron. Loaded with potions

to knock you out."

"Well, thanks for that because we passed out and landed in the Garland encampment. Thanks. That was a total trip."

"Here's another trip for you." Her boot reconnected with Zander's opposite leg. As he danced down the hallway groaning, she added, "Someone filled you and my cousin with lead. What the hell happened?"

"I can't talk to you right now. I have to stop her from crossing. She is trying to follow her mother." Not a second passed all the hairs on Zander's arms and back of his neck prickled hearing the most devastating keening burst from the chapel.

Shelby grabbed Zander's arm and started running as fast as she could drag him. "That was Lucian," she said breathy, "Elyza's father, Serina's husband. My uncle. I swear to God if you can't get her back…"

"I know…I know. I'll be a dead man walking."

With zero remorse Shelby clarified, "Nah, just dead. None of us want you coming back here in the afterlife."

As Zander and Shelby pushed past family the sight in front of him stopped him in his tracks. Lucian, Zander guessed, since he hadn't been formally introduced, had climbed atop the altar, lifted his wife's body up over his head and with deep sanguineous tears pouring down the man's cheeks that landed on Elyza's still body beneath him, he decreed, "We have done this dance before, M'lady. I've said it once and I'll say it again, the only thing that can separate us is time and circumstance. Now is not our time and this most certainly is not the circumstance. Not one hundred years from now. Not ever!" Lucian yelled as he thrust her body as high as he could, taunting the gods it seemed. "She's mine. Not yours. Not now. Not ever!" Lucian lowered Serina's body to his chest, her head cradled safely against his beating heart, while Olivia, refusing to release her grasp, held tight to her daughter's purple ankle. He placed his lips on her forehead and whispered, "Listen, M'lady. Listen to my heart. It beats for you. My heart is yours. My life is yours. Follow me home and then our daughter will follow you. Come back to me, my queen." Next Lucian squat down over Elyza's body, still holding Serina's, resting her on his knees. He placed one hand over Elyza's cheek, his thumb caressing her. "Elyza, my princess, I just heard from your big sister, Sydney. She needs you and me and your momma, pronto! She's in a peck of trouble too. I need you. I can't do this thing called life without you three. And then there's some fool running around here searching for you, Lizzy. I'll deal with him later. He will want you here to buffer the repercussions." Lucian looked Zander square in the face and reiterated, "And there will be repercussions, son."

Palms rather slick, Zander glanced around the sanctuary. Not a friendly face to be found.

Chapter Thirteen

"Momma?" Elyza looked around and couldn't for the life of her…almost the moment the thought escaped she corrected it to… figure out where she was or how she got to this place. She huffed or huffed as much as one could without an actual body, up the stairs until she reached an ornate entryway. Something in her gut told her to hightail it back down those stairs. She did not belong here. Every fiber of what she had left pleaded to get back to Zander. Against better judgment she tapped on a horned angel doorknocker, pressed her nose against the cool glass, peeked through and waited. Everyone on the opposite side of the entry shook their heads no and pointed back to the way she had just come. Pretty rude from Elyza's shoes. She looked down at her feet. Make that flip-flop. One. Well maybe there was a dress code to this joint to which she flunked miserably. She did another quick glance at herself and groaned. Naked as the day she was born.

Zander would have a field day if he caught her like this. On second thought that idea sounded heavenly. She took in her surroundings. What was she doing here when her destiny awaited her elsewhere? There was so much left to explore between them, a lifetime for starters. She'd never met a man like him. And knew right here and now if she went any further, she never would.

Through the doors she yelled, "Is my mom in there?

Is this Summerland? Doesn't look like what I envisioned. Y'all look foreign as feck. Did I sound like Sydney or what?" She pounded on the door again. "Hello? Come on! It's not like I'm selling encyclopedias or bibles. This place is probably the reason for both books."

Those on the opposite side of the door began to slowly filter away from the entrance. "Ah, really? Could someone at least let my mom know I'm here? Pretty please? I apologize for being butt naked. I should have planned better. I should have…what?" Elyza glanced around at her surroundings knowing a pout bent her lips. "What should I have done differently?" Perplexed and annoyed, Elyza turned and plunked her butt on the cold marble step, immediately wishing she hadn't. The Polar Plunge she'd done once didn't pack this chill.

Underwear. She. Missed. Them. Dearly.

"Miss?"

Elyza's brow inched upward. She didn't recognize the voice. Feeling totally under-dressed and overexposed she crossed her arms over her breasts and clamped her legs together, for all the good it did. With a slow turn she pulled a backwards glance over her shoulder and took in a young man. Handsome. Came in around five foot eleven. Long brown hair, a beard… neatly trimmed, the most mesmerizing green eyes, wearing sandals, two of them, and a white robe that stopped short of his shins. A length of rope tied the edges of his garb together around his waist. *Fabulous Elyza, you're swearing outside the pearly gates, even if it is in your mind, the guy can probably read minds. You're a damn idiot. You just swore at Jesus. Holy shit. Jesus? Oops, I did it again. Shut up already!*

"Can you tell me your name? We weren't expecting anyone this hour." The stranger's voice had a calming nature to it.

"Are you serious? You really don't know me? Aren't you like the almighty, all-knowing smartest creator ever? This is Heaven, right? I went due North, right?"

The man smiled and when he did Elyza's fear dropped another notch. He answered, "You make me sound like Oscar Zoroaster Phandrig Isaac Norman Henkle Emmanuel Ambroise Diggs."

Elyza managed to pull off an award-winning blank stare. Not because she was going for sarcasm, but because she had no clue who this guy was talking about. If this was Heaven, she was already way in over her head. He leaned in waiting for a response. She bit out a grin. "Am I supposed to know that name?"

"Oz. The almighty."

"Okayyy!" Elyza drawled out with the corner of her lip curled. *Now I'm having a laugh with Jesus. I really have died and gone to Heaven. There's worse alternatives.*

"So again, what is your name?" The man waited as patiently as death for her to stop biting her bottom lip.

"Elyza St. James."

"What is your favorite color?"

Totally blown away that this quiz was going to make or break her entrance to the afterlife she yelled, "Oh come on! Really?"

The man sat down beside her, his elbows on his knees and his head buried in his hands, chuckling. "I had to, Elyza. I am sorry. You look so nervous. Ice breaker. People want me to say it and then when I do, they're in shock."

"You're not the one sitting here butt naked in front of God's son shooting the shit with him."

"Well, it seems we have something in common. I too hung around naked for a few days talking to God while others came to sate their curiosity, to see if a miracle happened. I do suppose it was better late than never."

"You got a raw deal. I am sorry."

"Water under the bridge. Listen, your mother is not here, and you shouldn't be either. She is searching for you. I believe there is a young man you left hanging very much in need of your assistance down below. Your father and uncles can be so imperious."

"How do you know that if you didn't even know my name?"

The man winked at her and stood. "Pleasure, Ms. St. James. I won't be seeing you for many years to come. Live well and love earnestly. Until we meet again."

"Wait a sec... You never actually told me your name. Are you?"

"In your heart you know the answer."

"Lame come back if you ask me. You could be the doorman for all I know. When I get my body and soul reunited and try to tell my family this they'll be like, 'Oh, Lizzy, you were dreaming. You've always had such an imagination...You had one of those out of body experiences. You didn't really meet Jesus.'"

"Elyza, their day will come too. Do not worry what others think or believe of you. You are accountable for all your actions. You are responsible for how you react to others either in a good or bad situation and you are accountable only for your life. Choose life. And always choose love."

Guilt ridden she blurted, "But I set the fire in the hall that caused so many to lose their lives. I was trying to save Duncan, and everything went so astronomically wrong and then Zander in his flat. I—I caused those two men their deaths." Elyza couldn't look at the holy man; mortified she would never atone for her sins. She glanced down at her nakedness. All that was missing was the old hag following her around yelling, "Shame! Shame!"

"Your heart was in the right place. I believe what you did happened in self-defense. Correct?"

Elyza let it roll off her tongue. "Self-defense? Really? I suppose so. I feel like you handed me a get out of jail pass."

"Second chances are what keeps us on the straight and narrow path. Some people have tools they use in situations like the one you were thrust into. There are natural born fighters, others who can talk their way out of Hell—it's truly rare, but it happens, and then there are people with gifts, like yours. Your family has a very unique set of skills, each of you different. You have never used yours to malign anyone, intentionally. But before you do take the road that has no way back, think first. Even a split second will help you. You have a very keen, sharp mind but your ability to control anger needs work."

Giggles flowed as easily as the love growing between Zander and her. Her hand over her mouth, she barely articulated, "Jesus told me I need anger management." Then hysterics followed to the point Elyza ended up with the hiccups. "Even I don't believe this conversation."

The man placed his palm on the side of Elyza's cheek. The slightest graze produced an influx of calm.

With those mesmerizing green eyes he said, "Take care, Elyza. And take care of others around you as well. And no more showing up unannounced. Hey, when you see Xanti Sinclair tell him to study."

"Wait! What? Who? But—" And then Elyza fell, fearing she would never stop, or worse, not wake up before she crash-landed. Damn dreams. When she looked around Lucian had his hand on her cheek tears flowing down his cheeks.

****

It all happened so damned fast.

With what equated to a lightning bolt impaling him, Zander couldn't break his fall.

A sickening thud ricocheted through the floor. Immediate pain ensued. With trepidation Zander went to touch the one thing on his body he still liked, or used too, before smashing his face down onto the unforgiving slab, his broken and bleeding nose. Squinting and trying to be brave, he ran his index finger gingerly under his nose. Blood. Fear jabbed him the way an ice pick ruined a perfectly good hunk of frozen water. He had blood oozing out in a room of vampires.

Officially screwed.

When he cranked his head sideways a mob of unknown faces circled him. Oddly, all were well behaved. No extra flash of fangs hung over lips, no one drooling and thankfully no one vying to shred him to bits.

Yet.

Lucian stood there with those silvery blue eyes rising the way mercury does on a toasty day.

I got this Zander.

The beauty reunited with the beast.

"Daddy, I am here."

The crowd shuffled backwards giving Zander space.

With haste Lucian set Serina's body on the table again and hopped down. He ran his hands over his daughter's face, brushing a few curls from her view. "Baby open them eyes. Look at me."

"No, Daddy, I'm down here."

There Zander sat on the floor with huge turquoise eyes, innocent as the day Elyza was born looking lovingly into Lucian's horrified face. With his hands tossed palms up in the air, Zander managed to drawl out, "She's backkk." He waited through that impervious stretch in time a stand-up comic dreads when no one smiles or chuckles. "Tough crowd."

Daelyn extended his hand. Zander accepted it. Olivia tossed him a wad of gauze. He nodded a thank you and placed it beneath his nose to stop the blood from making more of a mess than there already was.

Using his voice, Elyza thought about everything she'd experienced before plunging in headfirst. "Daddy, Mom is not in heaven. And clearly I didn't pass either. They aren't expecting any of us yet." Zander grinned big... and bat his eyelashes.

"Doolittle, stop!" Zander begged, fighting for what might be left of his dignity.

Noting Lucian with his mouth open and no words forming Elyza shot Zander's hand out. "Don't ask. You wouldn't believe me."

"Lizzy," Lucian hedged, swallowing a gulp, "I don't believe any of this and yet," with his hand out in front of him he took a breath, "here you are, sort of. This is so messed up."

Olivia bent over to Zander, keeping one hand firmly

on her daughter's chest refusing to relinquish the miniscule hold on her soul she still had. "Lean forward so I can touch your nose." It wasn't a question.

Please don't break it again, Zander prayed silently.

"Fool. I'm going to heal it. It is up to Lucian if he sees fit to rearrange it later."

Then the woman with the huskie's eyes spoke up. "Lucian will behave. He hasn't got it in him to harm his future son-in-law."

Both Lucian and Zander snapped their attention toward the woman.

"Wait, what?" And "No!" were heard simultaneously from Zander and Lucian.

With a shrug of her shoulders, Jovan smirked. "What? Don't you of all people, Lucian, give me those thunderstruck eyes."

"Jovan?" Lucian tugged his curls out of his face. "You can't go springing stuff like everyone's future on us like this. Look around you."

"Are you a seer?" Zander noticed a few heads bobbing a collective yes. So there was a chance Elyza would get her life back, Zander would get his body back and they could what? Maybe go out on a date like normal people do?

With an unforgiving gleam to her eye, Olivia latched onto and yanked Zander's broken nose. The more he twisted the tighter she gripped. "Stop fighting me. Stop fighting this."

Sounding rather congested Zander questioned, "Stop hurting me. And what is thisss?" He hissed.

The laugh Olivia produced had others in the room, except Lucian joining in. Lucian appeared to be in as much if not more agony than Zander right now. "Your future, kid. Hell of a way to meet the family."

From the back of the crowded room a gent wearing a gauze turbine held together with duct tape added his two cents. "Like father-in-law, like son-in-law." Zander recognized him as the man that fell from the balcony the night of the fire.

Lucian spun on the guy. "Duncan, old man, I'm going to forgive you this once and blame it on scrambled brains."

Duncan snickered, "He's a giant teddy bear, kid. Don't let him scare you."

Aghast, Lucian added, "I am not a teddy bear." Before Zander knew what hit him Lucian leaned over and cuffed the side of his head sporting a grin with his top lip peeled back exposing the same set of double rowed dents others in the room wore like it was freaking shark week. He gave a little tap to them and winked. "We will chat later."

"It's fine. I'm good," Zander responded all too quickly.

"I'm not, boy." Lucian straightened his stance while he licked his lips. "Grimmy," Lucian tapped his ear and then pointed to the door. Julian opened the door a crack.

Before Zander had an inkling of what was happening Julian greeted the man with blond hair Zander had caught a glimpse of in Trafalgar Square.

"Hello?" The man offered a nervous smile.

Before the stranger could get a foot in the door Julian had him by the scruff of the neck dangling before the choir. "This day keeps getting more and more interesting. Who are you and why are you here?" In an awkward fashion Julian sniffed the man. With his nose crinkled he added, "Mutt," and slammed him onto the ground beside Zander. Landing, the man's leather bomber flapped open showing he wasn't wearing a shirt, that he had a scar that wielded Jack the Ripper's first chop-job signature engraved on him, and lastly, he had a cross just like the one Zander owned. A few, "Ewh," and "dear lords," were whispered seeing the man's scars. Zander couldn't wait to see their reactions if he ever got caught strutting about in his birthday suit.

Something in Zander's gut clamped down even harder than Olivia's stranglehold on his nose when he focused on the cross and then the guy's striking eyes. Regardless of the fact this was going to hurt, he did a double take, turning his head in the direction of the newcomer. There was this déjá vu moment he couldn't dismiss; they were acquaintances.

"Jerk!" The new guy muttered rubbing his elbow and hip. His gaze landed on Zander. Wide-eyed he asked, "You! You literally flew by me the other day. Who the hell runs that fast? Is the lady breaking your nose or fixing it?" He gave a not-so-subtle nod to Olivia.

"Jury's still out." Zander sniffled, wiping his eyes after Olivia finally released her grip. "Do I know you?"

"Nope."

"Are you certain? I feel we've met."

"Again, nope." The stranger extended his hand. When Zander didn't accept it, the new guy pointed to the table Elyza's body lay upon. "You and your lady both looked like crap. You left a trail of blood in your wake, ya know. Guess she went on without you. Condolences, mate."

"You never answered Julian's question. Who are you? Why are you here?"

The new guy pointed to Serina's corpse. "What in

Christ did you do to him? You're a sick lot."

Soft chatter of, "Him?" had the family all shooting questioning looks to one another.

The blond leapt toward the exit shifting into a werewolf easier than men who give away their hard-earned dollar bills when exotic dancers swivel their hips and squat before them.

Unapologetic, Olivia yelled, "Halt!" Moving through space and time one second, the next left hanging there to resemble some taxidermy-stuffed wolf on display by an angry witch with a blackened fingernail. "Look at this mess." Olivia held her hand out and wiggled her fingers. "Do you see what you made me do? I do not have time for this nonsense nor a manicure."

The blond wolf yelped. With a dismissive wave she retracted the hex and down he went, landing on all fours, baring canines. "But just in case, sit until I say otherwise." Tail tucked between his legs he shook it off and sat on his haunches, azure eyes blazing. "Witch!"

Olivia rolled her eyes and gave an encompassing sweep of her hand around the room. "He is here because of all of this."

"You know him as well, Mistress? Did you call him here?" Zander asked.

Olivia gave a very subtle shake of her head. "Yes and no."

Acting more like a caged animal the new guy's entire demeanor flipped. His body stiffened and the whites of his eyes became glossed with a red glare to them. His swishy appendage swatted Zander repeatedly in the face turning him into a bobble-head to escape getting swatted. "Enough." Zander grabbed the werewolf's tail. "Do ya mind?" Then Zander realized he'd literally just grabbed a werewolf's tail and although he knew without a doubt he should be freaking out, he had other things to freak him out.

The room went black. Zander couldn't breathe. Couldn't scream. Couldn't react. He was having a night terror mid-day wide awake. Paralyzed by pain and fear, his memories said he'd done this before. He'd gone into some dark corner of the universe where a lock hung rusted on a door, and he never had the key. Until now. He reached for the lock, red and brown sediment caked on the metal. He scraped at it until the eroded metal crumbled into the black hole, he now existed in.

Elyza asked? *What is going on? I can see what you see and this is petrifying.*

Trust me lil cherub, if I could scream I would.

You are not alone.

He knew she was there, with him, trying to add strength, but this took fear past the extreme. With his grip tight on an illusory door, Zander inched it open to a splinter of a view. Strobe lights flickered. Screams, the ungodly ones that forever torment a soul, echoed through the chamber. Chills burned his spine. Willing the courage to spare a glance at his body, he wished he hadn't. He was but a child with his intestines dangling like links of sausages at the open market. A gutted pig died with more dignity. And he was wide-awake. Pain swathed him. He couldn't move. He'd been given a medication to paralyze him so he could see and feel everything as he died. There was a small medicine vile, with a label of Pavulon along with a syringe on a bedside table, along with bloodied instruments.

He knew if he stayed with this vision it would be his last.

When he mustered the strength to flee, he made the mistake of taking in all his surroundings. In between the flickering lights he noticed a second toddler in no better shape than he, bleeding, screaming, fighting for his life, restraints on his arms and legs. The toddler had blond hair and blue eyes. A sound to his right made him jerk in that direction. They weren't alone. A woman sat curled up, knees to chest in a corner rocking back and forth wailing inconsolably. Blood saturated her. Zander couldn't tell if she had injuries or had a hand in his and the other child's mutilations. When she turned and looked at Zander, he noted raw pain in her red-streaked eyes. He'd seen her before. The woman in the hallway with the double row of fangs, Raven.

Zander, let go of his tail now.

Elyza! Is that...

No. I'll explain it to you in a bit.

The moment the new guy ripped his tail from Zander the nightmarish memory faded leaving him with a lasting impression of what Hell entailed.

Panting, as saliva bubbled at his lips, the wolf demanded, "Don't touch me. Just let me go. You people are freaks."

"Dude," Breathing hard, Zander hesitated, uncertain of what he saw, "did you see that?"

The new guy tried playing it down, but his reaction said volumes. "Don't touch me ever again," was all he said while he scooted away from Zander.

Zander, what is happening?

I got nothing, Elyza. Did you see that?

Yes. And that wasn't my Aunt Raven.

Let's keep this between us for now.

Olivia bent over and whispered in Zander's ear,

"Don't let it freak you out. You will be fine."

Or we will just keep this between the three of us, Elyza.

The corner of Olivia's lips went up. *Atta boy. You're catching on.*

In an attempt to put some distance between whatever passed between the two men, Zander changed the subject. "Are you bleeding blind? Serina isn't a 'him' but a 'her'. Wrong sex, mate."

"I am not the one blinded by the obvious, mate." The wolf gave off a low warning growl.

"You don't scare me. Your canines are mute in comparison to him." Zander pointed to Lucian who kindly bestowed the same foreboding snarl Zander received earlier. Hierarchy, or self-preservation prevailed with the wolf bowing his head in surrender.

Overjoyed, Olivia squealed, "Her heart is beating again. Both sides. Praise be. We got our girl back, Thomas." Olivia took in the strange young wolf with intensity blazing behind her eyes. "Have you figured out why you're here yet?" The blond wolf shook his head no. Laughter burbled out before she placed her index finger atop Serina's chest and drew a zigzag line from her collarbone to her abdomen. Red smoke filtered out beneath her movement, while her skin meshed before Zander's eyes to flawlessness perfection and in doing so, stunk up the room.

Serina's flaccid body twitched once, twice, and then without warning she sat upright. The scar where her heart rested faded before Zander's astonished eyes. Euphoria filled the chapel.

"Serina, speak to me, lovie. Tell me you're okay. Tell me you remember me." Olivia gave a snarky glare toward Zander, before she placed a tender caress on Serina's cheek.

Serina's cheek twitched, her fists balled up, changed from an ugly shade of purple to white while her body stiffened. Being a fast learner Zander wiggled back. The odds of further frenzy seemed quite doable. "Ah, Mistress? I really don't see this playing out the way the same way it did in your head."

Jonah whispered, "Death wish for sure, kid," while a few others gasped.

"How dare you."

Olivia didn't appear any better than Serina once Zander stated the obvious. "Just saying. You screwed up the spell." Zander crossed his eyes and with a toss of his hands palms up he continued, "I might as well finish digging my grave. I believe you were going for the heart and soul incantation. They are, after all, intertwined as are the vines and roots that seep far below the surfaces to connect with the waterways and ley lines to the universe." Hearing, "This kid will never live long enough to see if Jovan's premonition comes true," he gulped down any further sagacity and added his award-winning smile that got him nowhere with Elyza when they were back at his flat. "I got nothing on where that came from. Nothing."

With his stoicism stagnant Lucian pleaded, "Please don't tell me Elyza fell for that stupid grin. Let me kill him, Olivia? We will get Lizzy back somehow."

"Patience, Lucian, is a virtue. One at this moment I sorely lack. Make nice with your new son-in-law." A splinter of a smirk curled Olivia's lip.

Hearing a few snickers, Lucian glared at his comrades daring anyone to make another sound.

Elyza blurted out, "What exactly did I miss?" making Zander cough and rub his throat.

"The usual. Your aunt has been playing with her magic eight ball, Sparky, and asked if you and your prisoner would live happily ever after."

Elyza waited for her to finish but Olivia scrunched up her nose at Lucian.

Oh, crap.

Doolittle?

Silence for a hiccup in time.

You hesitated, Doolittle.

Umm, no, it's good. I mean I knew you were special. You must feel so fecking awkward. I'm so sorry.

I'll live. I hope.

Serina cleared her throat and with measured determination she resembled the second hand on a clock: Tick one-she cast an abandoned glance toward her parents, Olivia, and Thomas. With both her bloodied hands across her chest, unshed tears filled Olivia's eyes. Serina's remained dry, hollow, mocking, her chin held high. Tears welled in Father Butler's eyes while he pat Olivia's back, whispering, "You did it, Liv. You saved our girl. The gods have seen fit to save our beloved angel."

Serina took in a hefty breath, her chest hitching halfway through. Exhaling, a whistling shriek had everyone cover their ears. Her voice raw, Serina muttered, "Pretty certain God had nothing to do with this." One brow up she winked at Olivia. "This is going to be so much fun."

Tick two-she did a head to toe of Lucian. He smiled, reached for her. Aloof, she jerked away from him. Tick three-she took in her family surrounding her. Her head slanted sideways in an inquisitive fashion, her lips a giant pout and her shoulders slumped. She shook her head a dismissive no and moved on. Tick four-the lone wolf with his tail tucked between his legs again, chanting the Lord's prayer. Squinting, she gave a flippant sneer and moved on. Her sights on Zander, she clutched her throat and looked at Zander and then the new guy. "Help me?" Serina cried.

The wolf blabbed, "This is why you don't dig up pets from the cemetery. People never learn. Never the same afterwards."

Elyza used Zander's voice and shouted, "Mom, I am here."

Serina pointed at the new kid and spit out, "Fraud. Murderer."

Julian once again hovered over the new wolf, Daelyn at his side surrounding the stranger.

And then just as swiftly, those brilliant green eyes of Serina's went to a mucky shade of grey before everyone's astonished expressions.

"Your mother is not well. Ignore her ramblings," scraped its way free of Serina's lips.

Without realizing it, Zander held his breath.

Breathe handsome.

Easy for you to say, Doolittle. You don't have the queen of the damned giving you the stink eye. Not you Mistress, if you're eves dropping.

That was actually funny, kid. Olivia spared a nod at him. *Keep an eye on your brother, Zander. My daughter does not trust him.*

My what? My who?

Olivia never answered him.

This non-response was not what Zander expected,

but then so far nothing was going as expected, and why would it? If anything, he had an entire scene playing out in his head of mother and daughter embraced, reunited, once Elyza got her own body back, the two of them laughing, with the ultimate culmination of Serina accepting Zander as a part of the family and Lucian not wanting him dead. The situation right here and now seemed laughable. Instead, Serina's head dropped backwards, and her mouth opened. Some sinful wail followed along with pungent black vapors. The renovated paintings Jovan finished? The room looked like a smudging gone awry. Hearing so much about Elyza's Aunt Jovan on the bus ride to the mansion, Zander spared a fast peek in Jovan's direction to catch her reaction. Pissed. She looked royally pissed.

Index finger jabbing at the ceiling, Jovan mouthed, "Really?"

Julian went to comfort his sister. "I'll help repaint it, Blossom."

"Suck-up," Olivia added at the last second.

"It was worth a shot," Julian quipped.

"You're all bleeding insane," Zander blurted. "You have a dead body in front of you, Elyza. Remember her? And yet you find time to jest? I want my girlfriend back. Now!"

And there it was. Out loud for the world to see. For the universe to have its way with. Or Lucian. Zander Templar announced his intentions for a woman. A woman who had yet to reconcile with herself.

Awww Zander, I can't wait for our first real date either, even if my dad can. Elyza giggled into his soul.

Then just hop back into your body, little cherub. You can do it. And we can vamoose on out of here.

If I could I would.
What's stopping you?

Elyza didn't want to think about what was stopping her, let alone admit it. Fear. She hated herself for allowing the ridiculous emotion to control her. Fear of loving another person and giving them everything only to lose yourself in the mix. Romances, relationships, love took work, commitment, faith and hope. What could she offer Zander? What did she have right now? Fear, that she was indeed dead. That this ghost gig was her lasting legacy.

Serina pointed to each person in the room. Her actions mirrored those of Zander when Elyza controlled him. Protested. Riddled. "I've died and gone to Hell twice it appears," Serina's phantom speculated. "I found the company in the actual Ever After less hellish than to those whom I am surrounded by now. What have I ever done to deserve this? I'm stuck in a house full of cursed St. James's?"

Lucian muttered, "Not. Humanly. Possible," while others numbly nodded and moved in closer to have a look.

Serina—the marionette. Zander now understood why the wolf referred to her as, him. Serina and Zander now shared the same affliction, possessed: Serina by a demon, him by an angel.

Age-old question answered—animals can really see spirits or possessed people. Zander hedged a peek at the wolf and before he could ask, the blond offered, "Yeah, you reek like old man cologne, and raspberry shampoo. All that's missing is the shiny bubble gum flavored lip-gloss of the 70s. You are so possessed, dude. So messed up. I'm not your brother and don't ever touch me again."

"I don't reek like old man cologne. And the shampoo smells delicious."

The wolf pawed at his nose. "Corpses smell and taste better."

Julian, Ethan and Daelyn all nodded a united, "Yes." Daelyn added, "Bay Rum, Zander? I believe great grandfather still wears the same stuff."

Father Thomas pointed to Daelyn with a confident smile. "Olivia loves the scent."

Olivia rolled her eyes as she patted Thomas's hand. "I love you. That's what matters. Now shoosh, I have work to finish."

Olivia weaved designs in the air, her lips feverish in an ancient tongue of Manx. Zander studied language in HMR prison while he worked on his degree in journalism on the off chance he ever ventured into Scotland, Ireland, the Sidhe or the Highlands in search of Fae, Nessie, Dracula's lair, all of which were seemingly more real than anyone ever realized. The Manx language had become like the saber tooth tiger, extinct. Supposedly the last human to have spoken the language passed on to higher grounds well before Zander's time, but not the queen of sorcery here in front of him orchestrating something. The charm Olivia created would have been tough to replicate but for some reason he understood everything she said and did, which kind of freaked him out and at the same time, well, still freaked him out.

"Grams, what the hell? What did you do to her? Mom?" Elyza forced Zander into a standing position. She made him reach for her mother, but Olivia gave a stern head shake, no, swatting Zander's hand away.

"Don't goad the gator, Sparky. Serina isn't herself

right now. A lot like you. Templar, later you will explain how you trapped my granddaughter. If you ruined any chance in hell of getting her body and spirit reunited, please be assured I'll escort you there personally. I can only deal with one heap of you know what at a time."

"I want to know how you know about my scar and why you called this guy—" Zander pointed to the blond wolf—"my brother. And I didn't trap Elyza," Zander started to explain but Elyza butt in.

"I jumped him, Grams. To be clear, not the kind of jumping Savanah pulled on Ethan, Daddy. Not yet anyway."

His eyes clamped shut, with his hands over his ears, Lucian sighed. "Elyza, I can't unhear that. And I didn't need that visual."

André mimicked Lucian in his actions and nudged Savanah. "Really, Savvy? Lizzy, I can't either."

Savanah glanced at her mom shaking her head. "Papa, it was a long time ago. Let it go."

Jovan tossed her arm around André's shoulder. "Savanah, he's not Elsa, love. He has no idea how to let things go."

"You are all insane. In-fucking-sane! I'm out of here. Lady with the blood up to her armpits, to be clear, I don't have any siblings. The lot of you need to be locked away. Naked lady on the table that's possessed, I'm not a fraud or a murderer." The blond wolf stood, shook his fur out, thrust his tail into Zander's face one last time and darted out the outer chapel door. Halfway to freedom Serina grabbed her chest and fell back on the table, turning blue before everyone's eyes.

"Stop him!" Between Olivia throwing a barrier of some sort and Lucian and André taking the wolf down to the ground the kid didn't stand a chance. The moment the wolf was dragged back into the chapel Serina took a forced breath.

Zander took on the life of a church mouse, not making a peep. Olivia ran her index finger back and forth over her lips ruminating. Her entire attitude changed and not necessarily for the better. When she set her sights on Zander a sense of dread settled over him. "What is it, Mistress?"

"Walk outside. I want to test a theory."

"Grams!" Elyza protested, "You can't play with mom's life like this."

"Sparky, we need to know if these boys are directly tied to your mother's lifeline. If so adjustments will need to be made."

The wolf cleared his throat before he proclaimed, "Lady, I'm not an adjuster. And you freaking bloody kidnapped me."

Olivia slammed her fist on the table. "Kid, my sinuses are being accosted by wet dog odors. Lose the fur coat. You walked in here of your own free will. And how dare you talk to me with such disdain." Olivia strut right up to him. Her face a blistering red, the veins in her neck pulsing, she put her hands on the wolf's shoulders, dug her nails in and yelled, "To me of all people."

Zander stood. He looked at Jonah, Julian and Payton for a reaction. The three of them stepped back.

Julian placed his arm on Zander's shoulder and whispered, "Don't move."

The wolf shrieked before he flopped on the floor. Writhing in pain, his bones cracked and reshaped. Zander's gut clenched as he watched this metamorphosis unfold. With an inquisitive glance, no one else even flinched.

Zander recognized something in the wolf. Felt his pain. *Is that your empath, Doolittle? Feeling sorry for the dolt? It really sucks.*

No. That's all you.

Ok. And crap. This meant they shared some sort of bond along with Serina, the evil side to her. A union to the wraith holding her hostage. He knew without a doubt the moment he left these walls Serina would need an eleventh-hour miracle. Something he'd never ever thought of himself as. The only thing Zander had ever been dubbed was a useless waste of sperm from one of his foster moms. "Okay, Mistress. I'll be right back. I promise." Zander waved his hand over the half man-half wolf panting on the ground. "I really don't want to watch this anyway."

"I have no doubt you will return," Lucian cautioned, as he made his own hand gestures of hand to the throat throttling him. Zander got about fifteen feet from the chapel before the Mistress yelled, "She's down. Get back in here."

Fabulous, Elyza. Wolf boy and I are related to the demon holding your mom prisoner.

This doesn't make you the bad guy, Zander. Maybe you're a really distant relative.

I have a feeling no amount of distance will help.

Back in the room Zander looked over all those he would soon call family. If Jovan's premonition held truth. If Lucian didn't off him. If Elyza made her way back to her own body. Not one friendly face met him. Despair settled over him the way a coffin's lid slammed shut for the very last time.

They're scared, Zander. Put yourself in their shoes.

These guys—my family, have been together over a century. One person gets a paper cut and we all whine. It's called family.

Elyza, I get it, truly, but here I am, a new guy, waltzing in wearing a pair of borrowed yellow rubbers with his own little captive spirit and then finds he is somehow linked to the devil in disguise.

You're a bit of a diva, Zander, but I get it. Need to borrow the vocals, again.

Without apologizing Elyza went on a rant. "Pops, Gram, Gramps, everyone, could you all hold off on the preconceived notions you're all conjuring up right now. I may have only known Zander a short time at best but as you can see, I trust him with my life, and that alone should be enough. The guy next to him? Someone might want to lend him a pair of trousers. There's a bit of shrinkage going on down there since Gram sheared him." Zander's thumb showed some reluctance as it was forced into pointing to the nude guy's man-scape.

Jovan stepped up and made a hand gesture and before the wolf boy knew it, he had a pair of red and green plaid pants on with a V-neck red cable sweater. The guy bounced to his feet in disbelief. "How?"

"You just went from being a man to a wolf back to a man and you're asking me how I fashioned a pair of pants from thin air? A simple thank you would've sufficed."

"Thank you?" The young man looked completely puzzled.

"That's right," Jovan quipped as she returned to André's side.

The young man groaned, "Look like I belong on St. Andrews Links as a cadet."

Olivia pointed to Zander. "Jovie…for Goddess's sake, the kid in the Wellies and skinny jeans has more fashion sense than what you mustered up. Not much more…" For a split-second Olivia smiled and then went back to her daughter. She placed her hand over Serina's forehead. "Now that you are once again in the land of living, even if you act otherwise, I have to get a feel for your health. No words, no fussing. And no casting spells, little girl. I know you can hear me. I know you are in there being held hostage. I'll get you back. My word or the devil may have my soul."

Serina's masculine shade retorted, "Pretty sure he claimed your soul eons past."

"I have no doubt some day you and I will dance through fire but till then shut up." With her head lowered Olivia slammed her powers back into her daughter. One gasp later Serina was flat on her back staring blankly at the ceiling.

While the mistress checked out her daughter, Zander did the same of the new wolf, "What is your name?"

"Alek."

"Alek, you ok? That transition looked like getting run over by a Mac truck would be more fun."

Alek bit out, "I'm fine."

"Do you have a sir name?"

"Bond."

Elyza burst into hysterics at Zander's expense, making him wipe under his eyes and then shake out his hair with a slight finger fluff to get stray strands from his view.

"That's messed up," Alek exclaimed keeping his distance. "Your eyes go from black to turquoise depending on which one of you is speaking. Messed up!"

"Seems to be the general consensus," Zander countered.

Elyza continued, "Bond and Templar. How much of a coincidence is this?"

Olivia warned, "Elyza, there are no coincidences. That deadbeat vampire should not have had a soul left to possess my daughter with. I still need to know how you knew the spell with the memory tag. That spell is as ancient as time. I don't trust you or, your little friend."

Yes, Zander decided the most powerful mage ever had a funny bone because she tried to sound exactly like Scarface.

"Well Hallelujah!" Olivia threw one arm in the air, praising the higher powers, if there were any higher. "I am so glad I was able to entertain the boy." She crooked her index finger to Zander beckoning him to come in closer. He declined with a subtle shake of his head. "Yes, I read minds. If I don't get the answers I need your head might wind up on a pillow somewhere. That would be funny. Lucian would laugh."

Lucian did laugh. Uncontrollably. "Ah Liv, do it now?" he asked with his hands clasped in prayer. "Spare me the manure that comes with this kid?"

She finished her inquisition with, "Speak now or forever hold your arse." She nodded to Alek. "Why are you here?" For the second Zander was off the hot seat.

Alek sputtered, "For lack of a better explanation, I followed the blood trail you left in Piccadilly yesterday. I went to the cemetery and then that hospital that blew up. Don't know how you got out or why I am here. I should probably go. I have no idea who the possessed dickless chick on the table is. Sorry. Freak coincidence her heart kicked when I left. She looks half dead anyway.

You all look seriously up to your elbows in ya know, body parts, hearts, and black freaking charms. Surprised there's no skull on the alter."

Zander tapped a finger to his head then pointed to Alek's head. "There could be if you don't shut up."

"Not funny."

"Do I look like I'm joking?"

The only saving grace in this situation? At least Olivia wouldn't hurt him since he'd been given the daunting task of keeper of her beloved granddaughter's soul. Nothing to fear. His cockiness returned.

"Dear child, do you recall the beautiful, good witch? You know, the nonthreatening wench who dropped a house on her sister over a pair of freaking shoes? What makes you think once I have my granddaughter safe and secured in her body, I shan't do something grander?"

Cockiness now limp, Zander's shoulders slumped.

Olivia pat his thigh. "Yes, you should think about it. I know Lucian is."

"Go, Liv," Lucian yelled from the sidelines. "A woman after my own heart."

With a decided glance, Olivia set her sights on Lucian. Only one side of her lip curled into a smirk. "Dear son-in-law, when we first met, I wanted your heart skewered. Don't ever forget this."

"I don't think she will, Luce," André added, elbowing his twin in the ribs.

Olivia focused on Serina once more. "Do you know everyone here, Serina? I'm asking Serina, not the freeloader within."

Serina's inner demon answered, "Madam, and I use the term as loosely as you are, what in the name of Lucifer did you do to me?"

Before Zander could stop himself, words blurted out, "Is it just me or does anyone hear a crossover voice between Demi and Darth. Dominating yet demure." Not even finished saying it, all eyes landed on him. He probed, "Anyone?"

"Tell me you did not label my wife a dominatrix." Not only did Lucian step into the uncomfortable zone but so did Julian and André.

Oddly, Ethan sided with Zander. "Easy big guys," he said as he made his way between the men to block Zander. "I kinda thought the same thing."

"Eth, you stupid son-in-law of mine," André jabbed him in the shoulder. "Never ever side with the newbie. Have I taught you nothing?"

Ethan snapped, "André, it has been eons since there's been a new guy in this house to side with. You and Lucian put gargoyles to shame, scaring everyone off. It's why not a one of the kids have brought anyone home."

Jovan added, "Ethan most likely recalls the formidable atmosphere to which you all subjected him to when we first met him."

Ethan snorted and opened his mouth, but Savanah squeezed his fingers together until he uttered, "Uncle," giving his wife a full-blown pout.

Savanah whispered, "Don't make it worse," while she rubbed his knuckles. "Momma knows she instigated most of what you endured, Ethan."

"That doesn't make it right," Lucian added.

Serina's sprite changed the subject. "What year is it? Why is everyone here so oddly dressed? Or should I say undressed? Is this an orgy?" She started inspecting her body. A huge huff erupted when she reached in between her thighs. "Could someone please tell me what happened to my balls? Who castrated me? How am I to participate if this is an orgy? Why am I downtrodden with udders? For Lucifer's sake, they are mammoth. Wait! What's this? Nipples!" One minute panicking she'd been turned into a eunuch, the next? Euphoric. She took but a moment to pinch each nipple. She smiled. Everyone else cringed. "I can't believe I am stuck in the stuffy doctor's body. What happened to mine? Find me a surgeon. I need a pecker, not tits." Serina glanced at her reflection in one of the windows and winced. "And a barber. I look like the bleedin' French Sun King with all these waves."

With the softest murmur, Serina barely managed, "Over my dead body."

Serina's inner shade came back with, "So it seems this already happened, or I wouldn't be stuck here in this booby trap, would I?"

Lucian lunged at his wife, his eyes completely black, fangs gleaming. At this point every cruel and inhumane experience Zander ever faced in the big house of HRM seemed trite. Trivial at best. His new soon to be father-in-law, if Jovan's premonition held water, frightened the living daylights out of him. Julian, André, and Ethan dove after Lucian, all fighting to restrain him from killing his wife accidentally. The four men went down in a groveling, fisticuffs frenzy. Lucian emerged from the rubble and brushed his clothing off, grumbling, "Get off me. I want his fucking heart out of my wife this very second, Olivia. If you don't take it out, I'll rip it out myself and give her a new one. Yours. And my new son-in-law here will help me do it since the little bastard knows more than you do!" Lucian latched onto Zander, dragging him to his side.

"You'll do no such thing, St. James." Serina's freeloader spirit lifted a delicate finger and aimed it at Lucian. He went rolling down the aisle taking Zander down as well. "My body now. To do with as I see fit." The incubus even tweaked her nipple again."

"Jovan, dress her now," Lucian demanded while he scuffled to get up.

"Oh, this will be so much fun, Serina. So much. Do you know what I can make you do to yourself? Expend you till you really truly want to die and then bring you back from the brink of death just to do it all over again. You and your family of ingrates ripped out the wrong heart and chopped off the wrong head. You'll wish you died on that cross all those years ago." Serina's hands went to her crotch and then she flipped them palm up, empty. "The wrong head. It's payback time. All I ever wanted was Raven. Where is the beauty? Still alive? She didn't die of boredom around the lot of you, did she?"

Lucian and Zander made their way back to Serina's side. On the outside Serina had the face of an angel, an appearance that by no means would ever cause another ill will or harm. The perfect illusion.

Books and covers. Zander had a whole new appreciation for the phrase.

Zander gripped Lucian's forearm. "She's still your wife, Sir. Take a step back. We will get the devil exorcised. If we don't? You can use my heart because it won't be any good to me if I break your daughter's."

Double-edged fangs snapped in Zander's face. "Deal."

Barely able to speak, Serina begged, "Mom, help me? Lucian, if you can't kill him, then do this, kill me. I can't live with this sinister maggot worming around within me." Serina latched onto Lucian's wrist. "I mean it. Promise me."

Lucian attempted to console her but as he wrapped his arms around her, he became air born going twenty feet across the chapel, landing over the back of a pew.

"I don't get Raven, you don't get Serina." The demon within his wife raged.

Jovan and André rushed to Lucian's aid while Olivia questioned, "I compelled you to silence, Serina. How? There isn't a witch on this planet stronger than I."

In Serina's new baritone brogue, she answered, "Go way back in time, Olivia. Who was your biggest foe when the leprechauns and banshees were starving due to lack of crisps? My mum I believe. People forget about her because she died giving birth to the village idiot, my asinine brother Xanti, but she equaled your powers. Best them if the stories were true."

"Lies," Olivia quipped.

"Those powers were passed down to Xanti and me. That idiot couldn't handle being a magical vampire let alone brush his teeth. Pity my mother's life ended tragically. She was a direct descendant of Lilith. Bet you didn't know that."

Lucian mused, "Well that would explain the hideous quagmire of demons."

Before Xavier could add another word, Olivia swanned her way around Serina stopping beside Lucian and Zander. "Dreadful her last moments, how she turned a frightful shade of indigo." Olivia closed her eyes and let out a long-drawn breath of air. "'Twas as if someone pinched her wick till the flame extinguished. No one at her bedside to hold her trembling hand. Hear her final pleas for help. Her useless husband out whoring. Her children locked up in the brink for pilfering. Rumors were as such your dear papa had a mistress of his own to tend to. I pray no further depraved spawn came of such a tryst. Your mum died a lonely bindle stiff. The wench reaped what she sowed."

"How do you know of such things?"

Olivia produced a grin, wolfish in nature. Her appearance went from a lovely well-kept middle-aged woman to a side of her Zander never hoped to see again. "Who do you think her midwife was?"

Dead for days, it didn't matter, Serina bounced off the table, and landed on her bare feet. Arms flailing, hands groping the air, she lunged for Olivia.

Zander attempted the same maneuver he'd watched Olivia pull a few times so far. "Halt!" He even added a few hand gestures in there to add to his unbridled talent. Seemed simple enough. It worked for Olivia. Serina spun on Zander, her hands now locked around his neck, her legs wrapped around his waist.

Not so simple it appeared.

"You may be more imprudent than my brother," the incubus spit out. "Oh, I do fancy this position, boy."

Both unnerved and repelled, Zander pleaded "Get her off me," with his voice now higher than Elyza's could reach.

Lucian tapped Serina on the shoulder. "Sorry, M'lady." With a preempted apology he entwined his fingers in her hair and tugged her off Zander with a loud whelp. "Serina, when this is said and done, you're getting a haircut. That was too easy. To the demon within, had your sinister desires about our Raven not played into it there's no telling where you'd be now."

"Dead, Lucian. He'd be dead, dead, dead, dead!" Raven seethed stomping toward Serina with an unforgiving rage in her eyes. "Go back to Hell, you detestable rat."

"You first, Beauty." Serina did some sort of head bob/blink aimed at Raven, sending her backwards into André's arms.

Something felt terribly maligned to Zander. Something he couldn't quite put a finger on. Well, considering the fact Olivia went and pulled off a classic Frankensteinian maneuver to reanimate a corpse using a heart transplanted from a century old dead vampire on a woman that essentially had been pulseless, heartless, without oxygen for two plus days, some might have even called—dead... what else could go wrong? And that they, Zander, wolf boy, and the incubus shredding the insides of Serina, were somehow magically connected. And yet, even with all that something remained off.

That's when the bottom of the ride fell out from beneath Zander's feet.

"Go get her tiger," Serina's evil inner twin nodded from Zander to Olivia.

Before he knew what was happening, new upper dents cascaded down into Zander's lower lip introducing him to his new lease on life. "Holy mother what is happening to me?" Zander grabbed Olivia's forearms to pull her closer, but he squeezed too hard, his nails lengthening before his horrified eyes and digging through her flesh. The scent of blood hit his senses the way a sharpshooter pierces his targets, spot on, so he squeezed a little tighter.

"Let me go, boy."

Zander followed the sound of her pulse and settled

on Olivia's throat, a map of pretty blue roads, all leading to a dead end.

"Don't be stupid, son," Olivia cautioned. "Look around you."

He had tunnel vision and couldn't see farther than that one little juicy vein pulsing a little too fast. Stupidly Olivia struggled, which only heightened Zander's desires. His turning came with a few hidden features he'd only ever seen in movies; super speed, super strength, finely tuned hearing, a voracious appetite, a keen sense of smell and utterly poor judgment.

With his hands steeled around her throat, he tugged her closer and opened his mouth. Between his endorphins amped up and his blood rushing so loud, it drowned out all the chaos of everyone screaming, "Stop." About to break in the new choppers his neck snapped backward.

Everything hurt. After clearing his vision, a mob of angry faces stared down at him. This predicament made him wonder about Jimmy Hoffa being buried alive, having a gang of mobsters stand around waiting for the cement to harden, laughing at his expense. Zander had no idea how long he'd been out. Could have been days, years, or seconds. Felt like eternity. Zander's need to touch body parts was overcast by the inherent need to survive. If he moved a single muscle fiber right now, it could be his last, Elyza inside him or not. When he finally mustered up the courage to flinch, his hand jerked, an empty, crumpled bag of Type O negative blood clutched in his grasp.

Did I just define bat shit crazy? Elyza?

No response.

Did you leave me again, Doolittle?

A small burning in his gut made him rub his belly. *Is that you or acid reflux? I'd hate to think you're inside me stewing away. I promise we will fix this.*

Zander, you suck at spells. Like totally suck. Halt? Did you honestly think it would work? Be that easy? Do you have any idea how complex those spells are?

Umm, don't forget my protection spell at my apartment.

And I won't even mention the fact you tried to eat my grandmother. You tried to eat her, Zander. So, somehow you're related to Sinclair. Blood doesn't dictate who you are. Families come in all shapes and sizes. Look at mine, but if you ever allow that evil incubus to control you again, I'm gone.

Come on, Elyza. The past few days have been hellish to say the least. I went from being this easy going, happy go lucky ex-con looking for a job, trying to not go back to jail to being a kidnapping, priest impersonating, jewelry heisting, possessed vampire that will most likely go back to jail before the end of the day if I'm not heartless first. A little compassion would be much appreciated.

He had a point. Elyza sunk a little deeper into her protector reflecting over the past calamities. She said some harsh words to him. And she certainly wasn't without fault. They were both under duress, but she needed to tread lightly, even if her own situation seemed dire. The obvious issue at hand, her body and soul and the fluent connection she'd been stripped of. How did she reconnect to her body? What would happen if she couldn't? She couldn't—wouldn't go down that avenue right now. Then there was mommy dearest. Her mom needed a different heart before Xavier's vile spirit destroyed her from the inside out. Then came her father, less than tickled with her choice of possessions. Well, one way or another he'd have to get used to her choice in mates. She smiled for a stolen moment. In mates versus inmates: yes, her dad would be peeved once he found out about Zander's previous housing arrangements but finding out he had Sinclair's blood thrumming through his heart? There were two elephants in this tiny chapel. The circus would be coming to collect them soon enough. And she was the ringmaster. If she'd never taken the modeling job none of this would ever have happened.

And you and I would never have met, Elyza.

I'm sorry, Zander. I got you into this mess. I turned you into an astral plane without your consent.

I'm rather positive I've been some sort of ass long before today.

You said it, not me.

If I didn't want you slinking around my heart and soul I could blast you into the next galaxy.

Yeah, okayyy! Then do it. Please. I got you shot. Probably put you back on the police radar, ruined your probation—again, all my fault.

Nah, lil cherub, you seem to forget I'm the klutzy caveman who tossed you over my shoulder and kidnapped you.

Rescued me.

Kidnap—rescue… Chip, crisp… But if the cops do show up rescue sounds so much better. I know everything we've seen is incomprehensible, but we'll get it straightened out. Are you holding up?

Holding up or holding on? I'm along for the ride. I have everything and everyone I need and want in my life right now. In this room. Well, minus wolf boy, the ghoul my mom's babysitting, and I need my sister back.

Elyza, other than death nothing in life is guaranteed. Lives are meant to be dynamic—maybe not this dynamic but you know what I mean. We evolve and adapt or we as a society perish. I'll be damned before I allow you to perish on my watch. You and I have some serious unfinished business. A date. A kiss or two for starters. Not that I mind you tickling me from my insides. I mean how many people can say that has happened to them? But one embrace where I get to wrap my arms around you and feel your warmth against me? Snuggle you in as close as I can to me and inhale your wild essence, while your lips move against mine would be a fantastic ending to a rather tumultuous few days. And maybe not having your pop dismember me before, during or after would be a blessing too.

We will get there. Eventually. My Aunt Jovan said it herself.

"Welcome to the dark side, Zander." Daelyn startled Zander when he offered him a hand up, his face a mask of stoicism.

"How long was I out?"

"A good day."

"And ya left me on the floor?"

Daelyn winked at him and grinned. "Ten minutes max. Who's got him covered for his next feeding?"

"Sounds like a daunting task." Zander mumbled trying to get his footing and losing.

Ethan stepped in and grabbed Zander when he went sideways, catching him before he fell. "It means for the next few days until you stop acting like my father-in-law did when he turned, you'll need a steady supply of blood."

"Ethan! Stop tossing me under the bus." André appeared aghast, his eyes wide, jaw hung. "I did no such thing."

Gibberish and much hullabaloo came from Lucian, Julian, Payton, Jonah, Raven, Jovan and even Serina had a second to let her true personality come through arguing with André over his turn. For a moment Zander got to see the lighter side to this family and what it meant to be a part of one. This interspecies group truly loved one another, flaws and all. Jovan tossed her arm over her husband's shoulder and gave him a squeeze. "André, you tried to eat all of us. At the same time. You were out of control." She zoned in on Zander and concluded, "At least you tried to take out only one of us. The one with the biggest attitude of us all, but go big or go home, right?"

"Mistress," Zander had to find the will to make up for nearly killing Olivia. He held his chin high when he looked Olivia squarely in the eyes. "I apologize. I don't know what came over me."

After a moment of uncomfortable silence Olivia spoke, the playfulness she'd displayed throughout this quandary vanished. "Zander, the demon got in your head. Enthrallment. It is a lot like a child being browbeaten or a dog being forced to fight. They will do whatever it takes to get in the good graces of their tormentor to stop the pain and suffering, losing themselves in the process. Brainwashing is another definition. You'll need to work on your skills to block this. Like right this instant or else none of us will be safe."

Grunting, Serina started gouging at her flesh. "Get

this thing out of me before it makes me into a monster."

When the doorknob creaked, Lucian mumbled, "Now what?"

The chapel door opened bringing with it a drastic drop in temperature.

A tall, emaciated gentleman filled the doorway. The tip of his shoe did an exploratory tap inside the chapel. When he didn't get blasted backwards from the entryway a smile of crooked fangs lit up his face. He proceeded to enter as if he owned the home. "Splendid, my welcome has never been revoked. One cannot be too presumptuous." With a simple flick of his wrist his top hat landed on a coatrack. He slid a pair of sunglasses, the red lenses splintered on top of his head, like a headband, pulling back a wealth of jet-black hair. He gave a courtly bow to his audience. Beneath his arm a small black kitten purred contently. The little fur ball even wore a top hat, with black silk strands tied below his chin to keep the hat in place, his ears popping out through two holes in the hat. A tiny pair of red goggles sat strapped around the hat's brim, steampunkish style. The man placed the cat on the altar beside Olivia.

Chapter Fourteen

"Good afternoon, all." Since I was in, I proceeded to promenade up and down the isle of the chapel taking in all the faces of a family I have attempted to avoid, forget, pretend didn't exist over the past century, and sadly, so it seems, I failed at. They all look the same. Well, I do suppose the whole immortal gig has something to do with that. My obvious jubilance left a glorious distress on all those watching. Was it seeing me? Had they hoped to never see my handsome mug again either? Or the fact I flitted within a consecrated sanctuary? Hello! This is me we're talking about, Mr. Flamboyance leaving those huddled in here with a look of annoyance. Most people think vampires aren't allowed in churches. News flash. Look around. This entire chapel has a nest of vamps, a pack of lycans, a fallen angel, not to mention a coven of sorcerers filling the void and even with the lot of us there's still probably less sinners in this room than any other given Sunday here. I stepped farther into the room and took up a seat on the bench beside Olivia. She made her aversion clear when she scooted away from me as if I were a diseased rat. This is not my first circus. I am well attuned to what people see, think and feel in my presence. Jealousy.

Hovering beside her daughter's body, Olivia appears wild, shooting sparklers from her fingers at me. At me... trying to freeze me. If I hadn't seen it with my own eyes, I would never have believed it. This is the woman who never loses her cool? Her control more disciplined than my deadly bite? It would take more than her child's play to halt me. I've had years to plot, years to learn how to overcome the mind control and dominance others seek. My biggest hurdle for freedom had been the brimstone cuffs and silver spikes. My jailers are sadists. After I got my little red head, Murph, to see things my way, well tippity tap, tippity tap, Xanti got his freedom back.

Olivia glanced between the cat and me and shook her head. "You've got to be kidding." She went to shoo the kitten off the table but the animal hissed, his fur now fluffed out, back arched. My poor baby. I've never had a pet, so this is all new to me. I have this overwhelming sense to protect him even though I'm certain the rascal can handle himself. My little kitten stuck his nose in the air, sniffing before he produced the tiniest roar. I never thought I'd be a cat person, but this little fella is a blessing after so many years of forced solitude. And I'm rather certain the table scraps he's been given the past day or so far surpass to the measly crumbs we'd barely survived from in the museum. I named him Purcy, due to his soft, lulling purr.

"I wouldn't piss him off, Olivia. He's got a nastier bite than most of the scavengers in this room."

"That would be due to the fact your kitten is jaguar. Not a domestic cat."

"Oh my gosh! This explains the bit of the wild side he has." I couldn't help but giggle. I proceeded to pull up the sleeve of my jacket and show off red inflamed scratch marks along with a few teeth marks marring my flesh. Noting all the confused expressions I received I explained, "Okay, the teeth marks might be others I've encountered over the past twenty-four hours, but the scratches are all him."

"And I wasn't referring to you placing the mousetrap beside me, Xanti. I was referring you having the sheer audacity to show your face within these walls."

I thrust my arms out and up to my sides and went down on one knee shouting, "Surprise!"

No one seemed rattled other than the young man I'd seen in the Square running full out with a woman bouncing in his arms bleeding out. It was then I noticed the said bouncing bleeding girl spread out on a table. She'd seen better days if I do say so. The young man blurted out, "What the feck?" and then covered his mouth with a shocked guise.

Elyza stop censoring my vocabulary.

That was all you. Guess I am rubbing off on you.

I stood, straightened my trousers and smiled. "I'd cover my mouth too son, if I sounded so delicate. You possessed boy, or just have a very feminine voice?"

"A bit of both it seems."

"Keeping it all in the family I see. Good afternoon, Father Butler." I gave a gentleman's nod to the portly gent. Olivia's eyes popped. Time to stir the pot a bit. "So nice to see you again."

"Thomas?" Olivia's neck snapped in his direction. "What is he talking about?"

Stammering for an explanation, the old man went for a white lie of sorts. Guess it's part of his genetics being a fallen angel and all. "I went to visit Xanti occasionally at the museum. To keep tabs on him."

"He dowsed me in holy water every damned time he came in, is what he did, knowing full well I could not fight back and that the holy H20 might as well had been acid rain." I tugged a hunk of hair away from my ear to show off one of many hideous scars.

"I did this in good faith, Xanti." Father Thomas made the sign of the cross over his chest.

"You keep telling yourself that, you sadistic devil."

"It is the truth," the man answered adamantly. "I was hoping to convert you so that if this day ever arose, you would not venture down the same misguided path of your father and brothers."

I laughed. "How absurd you sound. You're nothing more than a philistine. So, it is done. There is a change in the air, is there not? I have waited a lifetime for this day."

"Who in Hell are you? What kind of name is Xanti?" The man with the effeminate voice asked me.

I smiled. Okay I cheesed again. I tossed a finger toward Serina. "I am brother to the spirit occupying the poor waif over there. And you?"

"Zander."

"Village idiot here. The one my brother spoke of. The last Sinclair standing. Xanti Sinclair! Not so stupid after all, am I, Xavier? Saddened immensely though. I truly believed we would have a reckoning for the books, but I think brother, you might just wind up in a slush pile. I planned this day for a century and for naught it seems. You're nothing more than a bleeding ingrate."

"Brother!"

His annoying voice held a strained staccato. I know fake when I hear it. If only I had learned it the day Dad coffined me. You never see betrayal coming from family.

Serina opened her arms for an embrace, grinned at

me, but the moue on those dried, cracked lips lacked complete sincerity. Just once I'd like to be the recipient of a heartfelt smile, a hug where no one wanted to crack all my ribs. Am I asking too much? Is no one of this earth happy to see me? I don't know, maybe I am being too judgmental, or too sensitive. Technically Serina died, really died. It tends to put things in perspective upon reawakening. And since Xavier is possessing Serina, maybe she held back on the joy of seeing me. Maybe she's royally pissed with her new roommate. If 'tis the latter, I cannot find blame.

Like her father, Thomas, Serina also popped into the museum to see for herself that I'd been detained years past. We had a nice one-sided chat. She wished me dead. If she read my mind, she would know already in fact I had died a million times over pinned up in that black tin casket. And that I wished her the same fate, a slow, mind-altering, soul-gouging deterioration where she wished she were dead but just couldn't die.

Santa might be real after all. I got my wish. Xavier can make all those around him suffer to the point they wish they were dead. Trust me.

Using Serina's voice, Xavier marveled, "I can't believe you heard me, Xanti. Or better yet, that you're even of this earth. No, really, how in this world did you outlive all of us? You possess the stealth and brain of a cockroach."

So much for the Mistresses' quieting spell, Elyza. She's losing her touch.

Death wish it is, Zander. Olivia sent that message back to him.

Gram, be nice. He's actually right. None of your charms are working on Xavier or mom. Let Zander try.

270

He did a protective spell at his apartment that I was unable to breach.

His 'halt' spell sucked, Elyza.

Stop talking as if I'm not right here. I've never been in a situation like this before. Ya know possessed or becoming a living leach. Let me try.

So now I am a leach? Elyza produced a prickly heat throughout Zander's system leaving him to run his hands up and down his arms and legs.

May you suck me dry, my little leach. In the loveliest of ways. I meant me being the leach, by the way.

Nice save. Obscene but nice.

I await the day.

I bet you do.

Enough of the innuendos you two. Stop the foreplay and focus.

Sorry, Mistress.

Not sorry, Gram.

I watched the young man and Olivia intently looking at one another and my curiosity piqued. I knew they were having a mindful chat, yet I'm unable to tune in. This irks me. I've always been very good at eves dropping, until now. Anyway, Serina went to embrace me again but I despise the very notion of Xavier's hands being anywhere near me. Call it years of being niggled, put down, abused, and an undue lack of trust on my behalf. Instead, I punched her in the face. Boom! Dropped the bitch to the ground. Words burst from my jubilant mouth. "Get up so I can do that again. Do you have any idea how good that felt? A century in the making, Xavier. Lord how I loathe thee." I bounced around in a circle, jabbing air punches better than the butterfly dude of the 70s did. Out of thin air, I've been surrounded by a wall of testosterone. Thank you, God.

If churches looked like this every Sunday their offertory collections would overflow.

This is my type of fair fight, three against me. While the boys and I squared off, Olivia, Jovan and Savanah rushed to Serina's aid.

As for my current predicament, I can see why women ogle over this clan. Muscles on muscles. Broody, mesmerizing eyes, pouty lips, endowed with man parts that makes men, men. And a few of them butt naked, along with silky locks to tangle your fingers in and tug into submission. Oh, wait a minute, that would be mine getting tugged out. Atop of me are Lucian, Julian and Jonah kicking and biting. Yanking me up with a garrote-like hold around my neck, André dragged me out of the rubble and slammed me up against the wall.

"Don't let his feet touch the ground, Ands," Lucian barked, fangs gleaming.

While I struggled for freedom, Olivia cast a malign glint my way and flicked her blackened fingernail towards me and mumbled, "Balls to the wall," and then said, "You can let him go, André. He is the new poster boy for the choir."

Pretty certain my heart stopped. My dignity plummeted. "Honestly Olivia? I will end your miserable existence one way or another when I get down." I tried not to panic but what twisted fate has brought me full circle to wind right back to being on fucking display for the world to see or poke fun at? It's as if I never freed myself from the museum. I vowed to never return to that living purgatory and here and now I've been cast the same fate only worse, in a chapel full of St. James's. How God must despise my being. Damn me to Hell and back and fuck me, my cheeks are wet.

"Liv, let him down. He's bleeding out. He's sweating red."

My biggest foe just spoke on my behalf? The wolf I want stuffed and mounted then chained outside? Ethan of all the pups on this planet shows mercy? Jesus I must appear frenetic.

"What did you do to him? You people are all sick." That came from the blond dressed like a caddie, who honestly doesn't look much better than I currently feel.

"Not till I have my girl back in one piece."

"Mom?"

From the bird's eye view I currently hold of this quagmire, I watched the young man massage his throat and attempt to make his way to Serina, but Lucian wrapped his hand around his wrist shaking his head no, not to go another step forward.

Lucian cautioned, "Pick your battles wisely, Elyza."

The kid jerked his wrist free of Lucian's clutch, scratched his head and thought for a moment. "Salt? Sea salt if you have it, sage for smudging, some blessed water or rosemary oil, and fennel. Enough fennel for everyone here." His voice dramatically deepened. Hmmm.

"It is fine. Just go about your business as if I am invisible, not stuck up here like outdated wallpaper. You're dead, Olivia. You just don't know it yet. Retribution will be merciless. What are your intentions for Xavier? Will it hurt?" I had to know. "If it brings any discomfort to my brother and Serina I am all for it."

Olivia raised those judgmental eyes of hers to me and smiled. Trust me, no cheesing on her part. That damned blackened fingernail pointed in my direction again and before I could even think about tossing a protection spell up, I'd been struck with what appeared to be a bolt of lightning. "I'm giving you a manicure when we're done here. I'll chop every finger off."

This time she had the audacity to pour on a grin when she sent another zinger my way.

That did it! Now I'm smoking hot. Literally. I have black smoke oozing from my nose. When I went to give her my two pence more smoke rolled from my mouth. She's charred my insides.

Zander whispered to Elyza, *Makes me wonder what Xanti's true intentions were/are coming here in the first place if he doesn't care for his brother?*

So far it appears to gloat. Until Gram's shut him down.

You mean nailed his carcass to the wall.

Keep an eye on him, you two, Olivia intervened. *I have a feeling he has more up his sleeve.*

Olivia pointed to Payton. "There are bundles of sage in the dry cellar. Can you grab that along with the fennel and sea salt? I ask this of you because you know the difference between salt and sugar." To Ethan, Olivia lifted an ire brow, her expression jeering.

"Love you more, Liv," Ethan tossed back.

"Thomas, you're up. Holy H_2O. Go get some."

Thomas pat Olivia's shoulder and headed out of the chapel with a distinct limp.

"That stuff better not be for me." I yelled.

Olivia raised her voice to Thomas, "Don't forget the flask."

"That one, I'll share." I attempted a smirk, but no one is paying attention to me.

Daelyn gave a surprised, "Hold on! I have that, Liv. Be right back."

"What's the flask for?" Zander asked. "Not the best time to start day drinking. Or, well, maybe it is?"

Elyza answered him. *The flask has healing powers from Grandpa's days from being a white-lighter; blood from the archangel Raphael. His blood is infused into some wine to make it go down a little easier. It's like a liquid band-aid.*

Why didn't they give that to your mom in the first place?

She still needed a heart…

Zander laughed at his foolishness. *I need a brain. Who's short on courage?*

Alek. He's tried to run twice now.

With nothing better to do than hang out I watched Zander now that he had all the materials he needs. He's crafted a circle around Serina with the salt and then lit the sage and walked the perimeter of the chapel allowing a smudging. The little shit purposefully came to a standstill in front of me and whiffed burning sage under my nose. Next, he anointed the windows and doors with holy water. He gave each of Elyza's family a trace of fennel to hold onto and then he approached Serina. "Fennel seeds are for memory and to repel interference from outsiders," he explained, while he made certain the candles remained lit.

The kid knows his stuff. I'm impressed but miffed I'm not included. Maybe I shouldn't have punched Serina… Nah! It was so worth it.

Zander decreed, "Deny the light required by this sprite. Serina, continue the good fight. Fear not of being impolite. You need to settle the score to make things right, to reunite heart, mind, body, and soul. Make yourself once again whole—"

I interjected. "Wait, I know this one. The spell is to cast away evildoers, sprites and to reunite body, mind and soul. Won't work, but good luck. That defunct heart of my brothers is cursed through eternity. You'll all end up in Hell. You first Olivia. Please put me down?"

The boy never broke his concentration and kept on point. I admire his determination. Guess the fennel is working."Despite his innate need for triumph you have the foresight to second sight. Send this demon back into the night along with his evil plight. Lead him from your noble birth right."

Like I had any other choice, I watched the dynamics play out without me. Serina, with my brother's vile ego trapped inside her, lay motionless. I clocked her good. She is breathing. The jiggling breasts being a direct giveaway each time she inhales. No earth-shattering miracle came forth. No salient beast ripped its way from within Serina's host. No alien exploded from torn flesh attacking the first thing in its path. Not even a bloody hiccup.

What a letdown. No ah-ha moments like when King Arthur yanked a sword from a stone and gave a triumphant, "Hoorah," and then passed out because he couldn't handle the sword's power, or when Regan spun her head in circles during her exorcism and painted the room pea soup-green. To this day that scene makes me laugh. But this? I find this entire scenario disenchanting. Lucian remains solid in front of Zander protecting him…or so he believes.

With murky grey eyes, Serina lifted her head and began rubbing her jaw and cheekbone. Her speech a bit garbled, thanks to me, she muttered, "Do not ever touch me again, brother." Interesting, Serina's eye color changes when my brother speaks or does something. Need to remember that.

Xavier's rant continued. "You never did play fair, brother. You hit like a girl. This spell is child's play, Zander. I'll be free soon enough."

Olivia gasped and, in that moment, I had my freedom. Her concentration broke. The almighty witch of the world failed. This is my *Hoorah* moment.

Speaking of let downs… I licked my lips as I slowly slid down the wall to land squarely on my feet. "Kid with the very feminine vocals"—

"Zander, for the last time." He took in the fact I was once more eyelevel with the rest of these ingrates. "Ah, Lucian?"

Zander's eyes are now the most alienistic-blue I've ever seen. I don't even know if that's a word, but it works. He is the definition of possessed. Ghost hunters would be running around changing their shorts after five minutes in this place. Serina/Xavier sat with her legs swung over the side of the table, sitting so not-lady like, doing the new phrase, a man-spread, showing off what most women back in my day coveted or used as bargaining chips to further their careers or relationships. Then Zander cast a queer eye my way. I adore his black eyes much better. They are exactly like mine… Well, well, well. Jigsaw pieces are coming together. The blue eyes are so St. James's. Poor, poor Lucian sat there with the same confounded expressive baby blues. There is nothing I adore more than watching dreams diminish.

Serina or my brother Xavier, became restless. Guessing since the eye color showed mop-water grey Xavier had control for the moment. He flexed those scrawny thin ankles, looked at his feminine arms and made a huge pout when he went for the showing off the guns, or the anatomically correct version—biceps. Serina's are more like those cap guns children used to play with when children were allowed to be children.

"What am I supposed to do with this body, Xanti? This is more up your alley."

He never had the quality of patience. Or a filter. He was and I guess, will always be a prisoner to instant gratification. The past few decades have taught me time is on my side. "They have surgeries these days, brother. If you feel you are locked in the wrong body of a sex you do not meld with, the physicians can alter a few defects, although your defects are too many."

The mob stirred. Can't blame them really. Lucian and his identical shadow André conspired with their brothers-in-law, Julian and Jonah. Any other day of the week the four men are formidable adversaries but today? I stroked my sideburns… I'm feeling lucky. "You cannot blame this on me, or my brother, and you cannot harm him without doing irreparable damage to his host, your precious Serina. This storm is all Serina's fault."

Jovan asked, "And you had naught to do with this, Xanti?"

I scratched my head and thought about it. "Eh! Can I make a suggestion? Clothing would be a good start to cover her naughty bits. I find them distasteful and an unpleasant distraction. Mind if I give it a go? I haven't truly done magic in forever so this might be hit and miss."

"It's a trick. Stop him," Julian yelled as he moved closer, towering over me.

Nipping this one in the bud. "Grimmy is it? Is that what they call you? I am in a mood at the moment. I did ask politely." I took a step back and held my hand in front of me. I knew the universal signal to stop. Mr. Grimmy did not. I drew from my inner reserve a sliver of my power and shared it with the so-called reaper. He fell backwards and landed in a pew, eyes wide, jaw dropped. "I have more where that came from. Next one will send you into Purgatory or beyond. I mean no one ill will here. I only came to say a righteous farewell to my departed brethren." With my eyes closed I heard the family tittering amongst themselves what could I have meant. Honestly? It's not rocket science.

First things first. I moved my hands as if I was running them along Serina's curves, to which she has an overabundance. At last, Serina no longer resembles some sacrificial chic in a horror flick, but she now sports a lovely white jacket, laces wrapping around the curves of her backside with sturdy knots locking her arms in place. Keeping those menacing fingers from weaving any remiss curses my way. My motto—trust no one, especially my brother. And a St. James even less. I won't even mention a pissed off witch. A pair of tidy whities with today's day of the week, Funday, embroidered on them, contains her bottom half. If she didn't look completely put out when the kid did his spell, well she took that rage to a new level after I fashioned her outfit. I can imagine myself doing fashion week in Paris next spring. Dear lord, I have a bucket list. Clean house and then have my own little catwalk. Now I have that stupid tune in my head, but it is true… I'm too freaking sexy. I strut myself to stand a few feet away from the beehive protecting their possessed queen.

"Get this thing off me and if you think a little salt and this straight jacket is going to keep me contained think again, dickless."

"You might want to rethink your words, brother. Mine works swimmingly. I had a very pleasant dusting off last night and sadly yours is six feet under in a pile of dust." Serina's plus one didn't have a comeback. There is a first time for everything.

"That wasn't Xavier talking. That was me."

Oops, I missed the eye color change. "Serina, it is for your own safety. Trust me. If you or Xavier were to try any spells or charms or whatever you call them—"

Someone in the back of the chapel yelled, "Minor misfortunes." That was followed by, "Ugh!" Guessing someone got elbowed for speaking to me. If our families didn't have such polluted waters running beneath the bridge this crew could be entertaining. "If I were to be the target of your minor misfortunes our cheerful reunion may take a different path."

Olivia huffed out, "Are all Sinclair's bleeding morons? Neither of you will ever harm my daughter. Ever!"

Both Xavier and I opened our mouths to speak but Olivia took the stage. "It wasn't a true question. Rhetorical in nature. So you three," Olivia pointed to myself, Zander and Alek, "if you haven't figured it out yet, why you were all mysteriously drawn here today," Olivia walked to within a foot of Serina and tilted her daughter's chin up, "it is because you all share a bond with the demon keeping my daughter hostage." Brushing her hair behind her ears, Olivia continued, "Zander, don't shoot the messenger. Me. One of these two ingrates is your father. Same to you Alek. There's a long story so I'll cut to the quick. You were born conjoined. Ripped in half when you were toddlers and separated for the past twenty-one years."

Not so much on sounding manly Zander proclaimed, "No fecking way," in a very pitched, distressed cadence. He jerked his attention between Xavier and myself, and then Alek. Assumingly at a loss he tossed his hands in the air without trying to further his vocabulary. Then, as if desperation amped up the adrenaline he asked, "This is a joke, right? We are nothing alike. It's impossible. Night and day here. Blond hair, blue eyes, and black hair, black eyes, doesn't follow the laws of nature."

Sat there with his arms crossed Alek reiterated, "Nuts! Every last one of you is nuts. Can't say it enough it seems."

"Do you see anything in this chapel that follows the law of nature? How could it? You two are an anomaly. One of you hold the gene to turn into a wolf as your mother did, Alek, and the other, well Zander, you had your debutant party earlier this afternoon, so you have the vampirism gene. You also carry the power of magic, and you resemble Xanti so I'm guessing he is the sperm donor. Alek, you have your mother's features. The eyes mostly. And the blond hair."

I interrupted Olivia, "The woman I impregnated had black hair. We thought it was Raven."

"Haven't you ever heard of dye, Xanti?"

"Are you serious?" Zander has this wide eyed dumbfounded look about him.

The innocence his face holds almost makes me want to lie to him, but family is the one institution you don't lie to, no matter how ugly the truth. You should be able to tell them everything, including your darkest moments. Mine was about to come. "Zander, Alek... Xavier and I are your fathers." I can't help but laugh. "This is such a

Darth moment." Funny tears rolled down my cheeks.

"I have a father," Alek stood up and headed for the exit. "You people belong on a reality show for the insane."

Olivia held her hand to Alek. "Please sit. You will want to hear the end of this. I know when Zander pulled your tail you both went to a very dark place. Observed things you'll never be able to explain. The woman in the corner of that room covered in blood was your mum."

"Is she still alive?" Zander asked.

With a subtle nod yes, Olivia added, "But no one has seen her in years."

Alek poked Zander's shoulder. "Dude, you're drinking the punch."

Olivia continued. "The scars on your chests... they're from your mother ripping you apart and damn the consequences. Your mum belongs to a pack that goes way back in time, ancient bloodlines that keep to themselves. Her pack believed in abstinence prior to marriage and to marry only within the pack and if a new pup is born out of wedlock, or rape, well let's just say the baby pays the price. Xanti over here did the only thing I have ever seen in his existence, I would call noble, or an attempt at parenting. When you boys were born Serina had been summoned to do surgery to separate you but attempts on your lives kept happening. I'm guessing it was the pack trying to kill you. Serina couldn't get close enough to do the surgery. We were told by the couple who had you, your mum died giving birth to conjoined twins. Apparently, this is not so. The couple ambushed your mother and kidnapped you. It's unknown if they saw her trying to kill innocent children and intervened or if their intents were viler than hers. When your mother caught up with all of you, she killed the couple who had you and basically eviscerated the two of you. Xanti got there and rendered her unconscious and did what he could magically to save you. He ran with you both to the nearest hospital. Some of the witches in my coven summoned me to heal you, but for some reason every time I put my hands on one of you, I was blown out of the park, literally. I don't know how I even stopped the bleeding. And you, Alek, were flip flopping between a pup and a baby faster than someone playing with an on/off switch to a light. Never seen anything like it. It was as if you had two entities fighting for control."

Chapter Fifteen

Xanti smiled, one chipped fang caught on his lower lip. He looked Zander in the eyes. "That was when I'd broke out of the museum and yes, went on a killing spree trying to find you boys. Museums are very educational. You hear a lot when people think you're a harmless decoration collecting dust. One of the wolves in the non-petting portion of the museum told his pack about the plot to kill you both. I broke out and found you and dropped you two off at hospital. Then I placed a protection spell and memory spell on you boys so no one would find your true identity. The crosses you wear carry the spell. Guess it worked rather swimmingly if I do say so. Just to be square I do know both of you." Xanti pointed to Zander. "Took me a minute to figure it out but then all the pieces filled in nicely." Then he pointed to Olivia, "I am not the moron people believe me to be. I wanted the boys to grow up in loving homes, something I never had. I didn't want them to be the next back-alley freak show I'd become."

Lucian spoke up, "Spare us the poor woe is me tale, Xanti."

"How does Xavier fit in here?" Alek asked as he took a seat on a bench beside the door. "And just because I'm asking doesn't mean buying this crock. My father's going to love this when I tell him."

"Who is your father, Alek?" Xanti asked.

"You had a fight with him in Trafalgar Square. Devon Badcock."

"Are you serious? Of all the ingrates in the world to raise my boy, him? He treated you like a rodent."

Slick in sarcasm Alek added, "I never said he was gonna win the father of the year award."

Olivia grabbed Thomas's hand and sidled up in between Lucian and André. "That menace has had it in for us since Savanah, you know…"

Elyza borrowed Zander's vocals. "Savanah was one of the targets at the runway show. Long story on how I know this. Mom jumped in front of her, saving her."

Savanah clasped her hand over her mouth holding back her shock. "Auntie, please forgive me."

Olivia answered, "Savanah, love, do not blame yourself. Cambridge is a louse and up to no good."

"You mean Badcock. He changed his Sir name. He's not smart enough, Olivia," Xanti added.

Olivia tossed her hands in the air. "Well, we didn't think you were smart enough either but here we are."

Xanti walked to within a hair's distance from Serina and whispered in her ear, "I think your mum just called me smart." He did an about face to Alek and Zander. "A century ago Xavier and I shared a woman. All of her. Afterwards I froze the fruit of our loins. I used this to impregnate your mother. I know, I'm surprised as you two it worked but you two are living proof. Even Ethan can vouch for my cunning mind."

"Cunning? Xanti, you drugged and raped an innocent woman. And I'm gonna go out on a limb here and hedge a wager you killed a few people around here in the past few days."

"Not rape. I did not rape her or hurt her. She was

more than willing."

Ethan protested, "He said/she said. Compelled? Sound more politically correct? You have been and always will remain delusional."

"Not rape. That was what Donovan and dear old dad, Xier did. Even Xavier. I'll apologize to you Raven, for my brother's past indiscretions at the university."

Raven stormed up to Xanti. "Indiscretions, Xanti? He nearly killed me. He went all Korowai on me and tried to eat me alive, kind of like Zander on Olivia. Must run in the family. Xavier stole everything dear to me. My innocence. My virtue. My security. My desires. My dreams. Your brother is a merciless villain."

"Korowai?" Alek asked.

"Korowai, a cannibalistic tribe in New Guinea." Olivia answered matter-of-factly, like a contestant on a game show.

"Again, I apologize for Xavier since he seems to be tongue-tied."

Serina's eye color went murky grey. "Raven, I am right here. I loved you. I believed you loved me. Once I get a new body we can try again."

Serina's shoulders started to go up and down and then she broke out in a fit of laughter, tears streaming down her cheeks while her eyes changed to green again. Serina shrieked, "If someone doesn't get this demon out of me, I will rip this organ out myself. And get me out of this straight jacket."

Xanti placed a slender hand on Serina's thigh. Serina shot a seething glare to remove it. "Hang on a sec, Doctor. I'm still attempting to mend my sullied reputation. We, the boys mum and I, parted on amicable terms."

Ethan added, "And by amicable you mean, she ran out of there screaming for her life?"

"She may have left in haste but there was no screaming."

"Which means you either removed her tongue or spelled her."

Jovan interrupted, "I can't believe I'm saying this but he's telling the truth."

Xanti gave a nod to her. "Thank you. Ethan, it pains me so to this day you think so little of me."

Ethan air jabbed his index finger at Xanti. "Xanti, I couldn't think less of you if I tried."

"Then 'tis a good thing I'm not here to mend bridges. I never saw her again until the day she ripped the boys in half," Xanti caught his breath and with a bit of cockiness added, "and her hair was still black. As for other innocents the past few days? Killed is such finite word, Ethan. Shall we say resurrected?"

His fingers ticking off a number for each newly turned vampire, André asked, "How many, Xanti? How many have you resurrected since you escaped? This is exactly why you were caged. You are the reason people—"

"Enough!" Xanti cut him off. "You mean fodder, André. Decorate it by any name you wish that seems politically correct since this is the new era of over-sensitive crybabies and coddling half-grown adults. Humans are beneath us and there isn't a living entity in this room that can argue otherwise."

Zander turned to Xanti. "Did you kill the priest a few days ago? I'm about to get tossed in jail for that."

"Wish I could say that was me. I do have one priest on my checklist I need to even the score with though."

Xanti winked at Father Butler. "We'll dance soon, you and I."

"And there he is boys and girls, the true Xanti Sinclair. Humans are fodder. You heard it yourself." Ethan pulled his cell phone from his pocket and punched in 911. "You're done. I have no idea why I cared you were bleeding out a few minutes ago." Ethan stormed out of the chapel with the phone to his ear.

Lucian added, "You're insane."

"Define insane, Lucian. Living centuries seeing people think they control the world, where they kill off those they fear? Those they never meet, pass judgment with the single plink of a gavel? Those with no superhuman powers, no speed nor agility, nor reasoning in life or death. What makes humans super? Tell me."

Olivia answered, her voice most decidedly weary, "Their ability to love. Compassion. Forgiveness. Integrity. All of which you lack."

"In order to understand all these weaknesses, you must first be shown them." Xavier voiced over Serina. "Our father wasn't exactly one to throw compliments at you, but stones or daggers, well? With each kiss came blood—ours. Xanti always received the brunt end of it, not that he didn't deserve it. Donovan sat upon a pedestal, untouchable. Can I please speak to Raven now?"

An all-out group, "No," resounded through the room.

Xanti interrupted Xavier. "I have my two boys, my sired line I must attend to shortly and one more thing to take care of before leaving this vagrant lot of you. Would you like to know the one thing I find completely comical in this situation?"

Halfway back into the chapel Ethan gave a roll of his hand to Xanti. "By all means, continue. We all know you love to hear yourself babble. Tic toc, you're on the clock."

"Ethan, I have waited for today through seasons of wither—"

Ethan interrupted him, "Don't you dare start singing that song. If you kill that song, I kill you."

"Huh?" Julian asked perplexed.

"The guy thinks he's a one man show."

Thomas pointed to Xanti. "You are a cancer. Nothing more. You kill off your host each time you feed. It's what cancers do. They take up residence in a body and feed until there's nothing left and then they die because they aren't intelligent enough to figure out that killing their host leads to their demise."

"Well then you disgraced, broken angel, take a close look at your precious daughter. Serina has the worst cancer of all inside her. One that isn't curable. And your loving partner, the wickedest witch of the world, placed it there. What are you going to do about it? And you stupidly believe humans will open their arms to you and accept your inner demons and help you find a cure for vampires and lycans? Hand over their precious hard-earned money? Their children to nibble from? Can ya see it? A line of little kids waiting to go get their neck ripped open so we can survive. Humans are worse by far. Delusional. You'd die if you knew half the things I do about the museum I'd been locked in. They run an assembly line of people through the displays. Problem being it's one way. People go in and never come out. That's humans for you. I'm going to close that house of horrors once and for all. And would you like to know what I find hysterical about this entire mess? You have such hatred for my family. I honestly feel the same but they're my family so I can make all the disparaging remarks I want, but you don't get too. Right here you have your granddaughter trapped in my son and from what I overheard they're to be a thing? What could be worse than a St. James having a Sinclair child?" A small snuff broke from Xanti's lips. He tapped Zander's shoulder adding, "I guess we will soon find out."

"Lizzy?" Lucian's colored faded. "Were you pregnant?"

"Daddy!"

"You're more maniacal than your brothers." Savanah looped her arm through Ethan's. "A leopard doesn't lose his marks, no matter how he covers them."

"I've never pretended to be anything other than who you see, Savanah. You tried to kill Cambridge—Badcock."

"Self-defense."

"Olivia murdered my mother moments after delivering me. One can see why our father would hold animosity toward me. He was left with the burden of raising an infant—"

"Monster." Father Butler decreed.

"What makes any of you better than I?"

Silence filled the cathedral.

"That's what I thought. Too late for remorse people."

Something in Zander's gut held a pang of sorrow for Xanti.

Doolittle, how do you get through the day? Experiencing all your emotions since you hitched a ride with me, quite frankly is exhausting. Feeling everything.

I'd cordoned myself off from the world with the exception of family, until I met you. You act as a buffer and take the edge off the pain and anxiety.

You can't live like that either, little ghost.

Alek waved a hand. "At the risk of sounding like a broken record I have a family. No Cain or Abel here. Just Alek, getting ready to leave this house of horrors once and for all. I have a father. Have had as far back as I can recall."

Zander asked pointedly, "How far back? If what these people are saying holds water—"

"That glass shattered, Zander. These people you've surrounded yourself with are all in need of padded rooms."

Zander pressed further, "Alek, how far back do your memories go? I know you saw the same thing I did when I grabbed your tail. I was four."

"How do I know you didn't plant those images in my head? You seem to fit in rather well with this crew."

Zander's eyes went to turquoise, and Elyza spoke up. "Because he doesn't know how to yet. He hasn't got it in him to hurt a flea, which in your case might prove helpful."

Chuckles filled the room. Elyza continued, "I, on the other hand, have an unmanageable temper so don't attempt any rash movements."

"Trust me, we've all seen it. You killed all those people in the hall. It was the worst thing I've ever witnessed."

Raven asked, "Why were you there?"

Alek's eyes narrowed, his tone snotty, he answered, "Public affair, remember? I was one of the fortunate ones to get out."

Zander's gut hurt. What Alek said to Elyza hurt her on the deepest level. Guilt was already eating at her over the fire and the lives lost.

Lucian spoke up, "It was an accident. My daughter would never harm another person."

"I'm okay, Daddy." But she wasn't. Far from it. Alek was right. She'd killed countless of innocents because she couldn't control her temper. Maybe being stuck in someone else's form was a blessing in disguise. She didn't have the powers to start a fire. Or evanesce. Or kill people. Or live.

Doolittle, it's ok. Those who love you know you would never intentionally hurt anyone, even the flea beside me. Your father spoke for everyone in this room.

Is that your way of telling me you love me? Elyza was attempting to lighten the mood anyway she could. She needed it more than she realized.

Zander hiccupped. *I just told you we all believe in you and...*

You said loved.

Can we address this after we get your mom and you reconciled with your bodies? After we figure out if I have a new family? One that seems to be at direct conflict with yours?

Whatever!

No. Not the whatever word. That's not at all what I meant, Elyza.

Whatever, Zander. I'm a foolish ghost hoping to keep a relationship alive anyway I can with a man that remains in the land of the living. I get it. You don't want to tie yourself down to a deadbeat any more than you have to, to a spirit who had no right to hop a ride home or invade your intimate space. I'm sorry.

It's insane in this room right now, Doolittle. There's so much going on I can't wrap my head around it all. I think we fell down a rabbit hole. This guy claims to be my father who is probably a complete sociopath. The guy next to me, my conjoined twin who's not-really identical at all... Please? Don't take my words wrong. I need a moment to breathe.

Take all the moments you need.

Doolittle—

And with that, Elyza shut the door to their conversing. She loved him. Hands down. She knew it. The connection they shared went deep in her soul, but he dismissed it, her. He was right about one thing though, she had get to the bottom of this debacle and get out of his body and back into her own. She could no longer share his space. If this continued, she'd combust. Or he would and she couldn't bare hurting him any further.

"Kid," Olivia pointed that blackened fingernail at him, and he ducked, "you're an idiot. You better find a way to fix this and fast." With everyone wearing puzzled looks Olivia explained, "He told her he loved her and then reneged it."

"Can I kill him now, Liv?" Lucian asked. "You break my daughter's heart, I break yours, kid. If you mess up any chance of her getting back in her body, I will be your new keeper."

Jovan crossed to Zander and placed a hand on each shoulder and stared him in the eye for what seemed like a very uncomfortable eternity before she spoke. "They will work it out. He knows what he must do to save Elyza. Don't you, boy?"

"I do?" But he didn't. Without moving a muscle Zander gazed around the room. Yup, all eyes were indeed on him and being the center of attention was never good. He knew Jovan had a message for him but what? Why couldn't women just say what they thought without making men run a scavenger hunt for clues? Women!

André asked, "What does that mean, Cherié? That sounded cryptic."

"Can we please get my sister whole again? Humpty is starting to smell like the proverbial rotten egg over here." Jovan spun, her face stern, she nodded to Daelyn. "Hand me the flask Dael. It's past time."

Xanti tugged the hanky from his jacket pocket and waved it. "Before you poison my brother can I have my final say?"

"Dear lord, do you never shut up?" Lucian groused.

Xanti headed over to the stained-glass window to pick up his kitten who had entertained itself pussyfooting along the sill. "How about you all sit silent for a moment." Before anyone could argue Xanti added, "May silence be golden as my confession is spoken. My spell is woven, your words and actions now stolen. Please remain quiet, compliant, do nothing rash nor defiant. I truly mean no one here any ill will other than the fool I called brother. We are gathered here today to rediscover, what happens when you mess with the wrong bloody Sinclair."

Xanti's hex proved its weight in gold. Everyone in the chapel stood more solid than marble chess pieces. "Isn't it splendid when a plan comes to fruition? Please, allow me to digress to a dark time in history, when the witch hunts were still in full swing." Xanti walked to within inches of Serina. "My entire existence I have loathed you, Serina, and yet now oddly I find myself compelled to kiss you because had you not cursed Xavier's heart for eternity, I never would have found the poor slug and he'd still be rotting in a grave." He spun to take in his captive audience. "I too saw Serina on the cross the night you-Father Butler, lost your head to my brother's merciless sword. Nice work with the reanimation Olivia. Necromancy is definitely your forte. That was the night Donovan possessed you, Xavier, and then jumped out just before your lumpy noggin rolled down the hill into the cemetery. It was all rather comical. Raven's hacking out your tongue totally made my day. It meant I wouldn't have to listen to your whiny voice ramble on about Raven and how she didn't love you and you poo-hooing all night over it. Do you blame her in hindsight, Xavier? I'd ask if you ever grew a set of balls but even now, you haven't." Xanti pretended to wipe tears from his eyes. "Xavier, mister all mighty vampire, daddy's favorite blood sucker, got one upped by his brother and then beheaded as he lay at Raven's feet beseeching her to run away with him. I stood in the crowd wowed beyond any orgasm as chaos consumed the lot of you. Then you, Serina, asking for the heart of the man that murdered your father. It was as if God pat me on the back and said 'Xanti, there is such a thing as karma. Watch this bitch play hardball.' When Lucian plucked your vile heart from your headless corpse Xavier, I too cursed it, just as I did every day of your vulgar existence. I placed a memory hex on the defunct organ so if and when you were resurrected, it would call to me so the last person you would see in your miserable life was me, as it should have been. Guessing this is why Alek and Zander are here too. Sorry you both got dragged into this."

This guy is damaged, Elyza. Please talk to me. I think I can get to him. How's this sound? Being powerless requires a mindset of defeat. We shall not be browbeat, filled with hatred or deceit. Those whom you love you do not mistreat. Repeat after me, by the powers engrained in me, we are free, mind, body and soul. No chains. No constraints. Your powers over us are useless, rootless. We are bound by no man, nor beast, and above all you the least. Elyza? Please talk to me. You can ignore me all you want after today.

Can you tap into his mind? You're supposedly blood bound to him if he's telling the truth. Do you believe him?

I do. Olivia jumped into their conversation.

Gram! Seriously? You are the worst ever snoop.

I love you too, Sparky. Zander, get to work. Elyza help him to share it with the others here so we can all chant it.

Done.

Between Zander, Elyza, and her family they each focused on Xanti and chanted the unbinding spell Zander created.

Xanti babbled on clueless. "There's a bit more, I am afraid." Xanti took calculated steps to Serina, his eyes darting around the room taking everyone in, fangs still draped over his bottom lip.

"Yes, Xanti," Zander approached Xanti as everyone closed the circle.

"Well, well, well…" Xanti turned, a half-smile, sort of Grinchy in appearance spread across his face. "My old, pickled heart has warmed for the first time in an epoch. No, wait, Xavier had the pickled heart. Mine is more mummified. Anyway, you prove yourself well. A true Sinclair through and through. Good job, son. You broke the spell holding you prisoner. Now all you have to do is save Serina from my brother. Good luck with this. Do you know the difference between a virus and a bacterial infection? Bacteria eventually die with meds. Viruses go into hiding. They never truly bite the dust. Resurface whenever, wherever the time suits their needs."

Gurgling, Serina fought to say, "Untie this bleeding straight jacket now. And don't allow Alek to leave. He was at the crime scene of the dead princess I went to just before the show. Kid, did you kill her? You know more than you're letting on."

Julian and Jonah had the exits to the chapel covered before Alek could get a foot out the door.

"Not me, lady. I wasn't there."

"Liar!" Jovan explained, "I'm the walking lie detector in the house, kid. You utter one more untruth and I'll let the boys have their fun."

In Serina's next breath Xavier's personality emerged. "Lucian darling, please undo these constraints. I'm feeling fit to be tied, and I'd so love to give my brother a welcome home hug. Pretty please?" Serina bat her lashes at Lucian laughing. "Not doing the trick? Darn. Anyway, I was just about to make my acquaintances. If this isn't the oddest conundrum ever. Here I sit in a female's body and here you, Elyza, sit in my son's body. If this doesn't qualify as a giant enigma nothing will. Tell me girl, do you think about sex differently now? How's it feel to have a cock? I know I can't wait to find out what it feels like with studly over here."

Lucian's color returned tenfold. "I know you're

trying to bait me. Won't happen. Someone has thirty seconds to find a solution to ridding this beast or else."

Making a Pfft sound, Serina rolled her eyes.

Alek confessed, "I didn't do what you think I did. Yeah, I was at the crime scene, but it was right around the corner from my dad's office. I wanted to see what all the fuss was about and I'm sorry I went."

All eyes landed on Jovan for confirmation. "He's telling the truth."

The distant sound of sirens drew everyone's attention to the window. With a quick pace Jonah made his way to the door and looked out. "Xanti time to go back to your time capsule, I mean casket."

Making a break for it, Alek sucker punched Julian in the face, knocking him backwards. He leapt over pews and plowed his way through Jovan and Savanah knocking both ladies to the ground. When he jammed his left shoulder into Raven to shove her off balance, his forward momentum hit a brick wall.

"Kid, how you have lived this long is a miracle. I've taken years of self-defense classes no thanks to your fathers." Raven held Alek's arm behind his back while her other hand dug into his scalp locking his head in place.

Struggling, Alek muttered, "Lady, I've learned a few things too living with a monster." When he shifted back into a wolf Raven lost her grip on him. He disappeared into the mansion.

"Never mind him." The horror Olivia's voice held resonated throughout everyone.

Time stopped. Life came to a standstill. Jovan screamed something inaudible. Savanah passed out and hit the floor. Ethan dove after her but missed. Thomas grabbed his chest with one hand and slumped over sobbing, his other hand latched onto Serina's ankle better than a home tracking device. Lucian dropped to his knees, every vein in his throat pulsing, his chest heaving, fighting for each breath. André looked between Lucian and Jovan and didn't know who to go to. Daelyn caught Zander just as his legs gave out and held onto him while Elyza used Zander's voice screaming, "No!" over and over again until silence expanded the walls of the chapel.

One second earlier Serina had life. A totally bollixed to the max life full of uncertainty but she had life. In the next tick of the clock Xanti yanked his hand from Serina's chest and held the heart of his dead brother high for all to see while Serina gasped one last time, her eyes wide, filled with shock, hatred and defiance. "Damn. I so hate my impulsiveness. I'm sorry. I got caught in the moment. I had such plans for you, Xavier, but I couldn't allow you to do the things you planned to Serina. How odd is that, that I give one scintilla of a thought of her. Must be getting sappy in my old age." Xanti shrugged one shoulder and continued, "I told you my face would be the last one you ever saw, brother. Just when you think you have everything you want in this life never forget it can be taken at any time by anyone. No second chance for you, Xavier. This is for never having my back. Never protecting your little brother from the monsters. For you being a monster. Olivia, this one's for you too, for the same reason. This is for killing my mother and ruining my family. You took someone I could have loved. I took someone you did love. Father Butler, I had other ways I'd envisioned your demise, but honestly, this, today, tops all my other plans. I get a two-for-one deal. I get rid of one demon and watch two others suffer. Payback, I promised, and I always keep my promises. And I did it in a church, so my quest is complete. Your house of holiness has a giant hole in it now, or do I need to point it out?" Xanti poked his index finger around the new wound in Serina's chest. "Lucian, you asked someone to fix this. You're welcome. Raven, three times will not be your charm or my curse. You had a hand in both my brother's demises, not mine." Xanti brought the pulsing organ to his nose and gave it a sniff. With a tentative tongue he licked the side of the muscle and immediately scrunched his lips together in distaste. Noting repulsion and disgust in everyone's face, he laughed. "For Pete's sake, lose the grimaces. I'm not going to pull a Khaleesi, but this thing is definitely rotted. Watch." Xanti squeezed the organ with all his might. The muscle broke apart under his strength and oozed between his fingers as if the muscle were naught more than ground beef. Greyish-black fluid and gooey matter sprayed in every direction. When done, he lobbed the clump of mangled muscle onto the floor next to Lucian's feet. Worms slithered from the debris across the floor. "Almost done." Xanti swirled two fingers in a circle and drew from his power and pointed to what once was a heart and incinerated what remained of the organ and anything wiggling away. Serina flopped backwards on the table, her body convulsing as her pale complexion went through various waves of greying as her life ceased.

Chapter Sixteen

The door to the chapel swung in, cops converged, guns drawn. On entering, each officer paused, looked around the room and then between themselves. Disbelief and fear became evident with their wide eyes and misconstrued facial expressions. Attempting to make sense of the madness they ran blindly into, one of the men uttered, "What the fuck?" The other three men echoed the phrase like a piss poor choir at Sunday mass.

Xanti stepped in front of Zander, placing himself in a direct line of fire. "'Tis impolite to burst into one's dwelling without introductions. Please take a moment to present yourselves so we may know how to tag your bodies afterwards."

Obscenities echoed a few more times.

"I'll start since it seems the cat got your tongue. Over here we have," Xanti gave a sweep of the room, "the St. James', an illustrious quagmire of do-gooders. And then there's my son and I, Sinclair's." Xanti added a bit of compulsion to his words. "Your turn."

One of the officers responded, "That's Brody." He pointed to a short man with a huge appetite, then he said, "MacBeth," and pointed to a tall beefy man, with blood-stained trousers and shoes. "He's been on call today cleaning up a crime scene down below the Tower."

Xanti aimed a bloodied finger at the cop doing all the talking. "Your name, Sir?"

301

The cop answered, "Hallewell. Mr. Sinclair, you will be coming with us now. And where were you last night?"

"Fighting for my life down below the Tower as well. Such a coincidence, is it not?" He broke out in a snuffle of giggles. Ignoring all the weapons aimed at him, Xanti turned to Zander. "Every relationship has a few bumps in the road. Will you join me, Zander?"

MacBeth aimed the laser's red dot on Xanti's chest. "Buddy you aren't going anywhere. No one move."

Forever cocky, and blindingly fast, Xanti moved a foot to his left and smirked. "Keep up with me boys."

Elyza screamed, "He killed my mother. Ripped her heart out. Kill him."

Brody asked, "Who said that?"

"Our window of opportunity diminishes rapidly, Zander. You with me, son?" Xanti wiped his hand down his pants leaving blood stains and held his hand out to Zander. To the cops Xanti suggested, "Do give him a second, boys. He has a split personality, and the little misses is trying to wear the pants."

Don't you dare touch that hand. Please tell me you aren't thinking of going with him, Zander please tell me you aren't thinking that. Dear lord, he just ripped out my mom's heart. He's a monster.

He's my father, Elyza. He has been treated like his life never mattered one day.

And now you see why. Hello! Sociopath.

Doolittle, what happened to you? Where's the compassion?

No. Tell me you're not, you can't side with that maniac.

Elyza, I've never had a family. Never been a part of

one where I was accepted for me. I have a father. What happened to you being an empath and understanding people's emotions or life situations?

What happened to the, what the fuck part of him ripping my mom's heart out, did you miss? You have a family here, with me.

I can't leave him.

Like father like son, Zander. You just ripped my heart out. Goodbye.

All it took was one moment in time. One bad decision. Siding with the enemy. Elyza's departure may as well have been a cannon ball being blown from his chest taking his heart with it. Zander now understood all too well how Serina felt being heartless. He'd never encompassed such loneliness or misery.

MacBeth demanded, "There are two dead bodies here. Someone needs to start talking."

Jovan shot her thumb over her shoulder to the hallway. "One got away. Looks like an oversized white wolf. Most likely rabid."

MacBeth pointed to Serina's body. "Dammit, that's the coroner, Dr. Spencer. She and I worked the Princess's crime scene. I had some info for her."

Olivia held her chin up, wiped tears from her cheeks and pointed to Xanti. "He killed my daughter."

Officer Hallewell added, "Thought she died at the show? Looks like the model didn't make it either." The cop moved cautiously, shimming his way through the pews of the church, being careful not to contaminate the room for any evidence. Xanti followed.

"The guns—wooden bullets or silver? Asking for a friend." Xanti toyed with Hallewell.

Officer Hallewell suggested, "One wrong move and

you'll find out."

Jovan raised her voice and seethed, "Don't trust him."

Officer Brody took a step toward Elyza's body. Lucian bounced to his feet towering over the man, his hand protectively on Elyza's stomach. "Touch her and there will two heartless corpses in this room. We are in the process of mourning her."

His tone snooty, Brody mocked, "Well then, that explains all the blood and Dr. Spencer's heart missing, doesn't it? No caskets. No embalming. Blood spatter everywhere. Not buying it. Arresting everyone in this room. Hallewell, call the bus. Give the Garlic gang a buzz too for back up. We need silver, Vervain, and a few cages."

Laughter erupted in the chapel. Xanti pat his chest catching his breath. He stroked one of his fangs before asking, "Are you unaware the garlic encampment was sauteed?"

Brody's nose turned flaming red. "Get everyone to the station so we can get statements and figure out what the hell happened. The girl on the floor, is she dead too?"

Ethan brushed Savanah's hair from her face. "No. She has a condition called Myotonia Congenita. If she's over stimulated she basically turns into a fainting goat."

Savanaha's eyes fluttered. "Lovely way to put it, Eth." She snapped her hand out. Ethan helped her stand. "I'm not dead but I know someone who will be soon enough." Savanah glared at Xanti.

Xanti licked his lips slowly taking Savanah in. "Oh, you're a feisty little witch. I can see why Badcock and Donovan adored you or wanted you dead. I can see it going either way."

Ethan nudged Savanah. "Can you and your mom do your blinkity-blink flash of light thing?"

Zander cleared his throat and tossed his hands in the air palms up. "Blinkity-blink thing?"

Jonah answered him. "It's a mind eraser. Blinding flash of light reroutes the brain and makes one forget what they saw."

"Holy crap! MIB was real? The neuralizer?"

Massaging between his brows, Ethan gave Zander a blank stare. "Where do you think they got the idea?"

Zander produced his shoulder shrug.

Brody wore a half snarl while he kept checking his phone. When he looked at Savanah with a steel gaze he scoffed, "Won't work. We have contacts that block the intensity, but feel free to try. It'll only get you tossed in the clink that much faster."

Xanti waved a hand in the air. "Well, this has been lovely reminiscing, but I must flee. Zander? Last chance."

"Don't you dare do it." Olivia pointed at Zander. "Don't you leave with my Sparky."

With two long strides Xanti came face to face with Hallewell. Before the cop could defend himself, Xanti looked him dead in the eye and said one word, "Surrender," leaving the cop to resemble a mannequin. Xanti latched onto his throat. One loud crunch severed his day. He dropped the dying man and strut back to Zander's side wiping his mouth off. "So much for the contacts. Idiot. It's that easy, son. No thoughts. Just do it! Just make sure you have your running shoes on. Those girly boots won't make do."

Gun shots had everyone diving behind pews, running from the chapel, searching for cover. Savanah yelled, "Kevlar," as Olivia followed with, "Shield."

When the smoke cleared, Savanah popped her head up from one of the pews. "Everyone all right? Dael? Answer me."

"I'm fine, Mom." Daelyn got up and hugged Savanah. That's when he noticed Lucian sobbing and Zander limp on top of Elyza's body. "Uncle Lucian?"

Lucian wiped his eyes and shook his head no. "Zander? This cannot be happening." Lucian jiggled Zander's body, but nothing happened. "Fucking wake up boy!" André and Raven were beside Lucian in a heartbeat both with their arms around him. "He's not moving. Is he dead? He's got my Lizzy trapped in him."

Daelyn checked Zander's body. "Two fresh bullets, two other holes and he's burning up. He needs the hospital unless, Liv, you can heal him? I know it's a lot to ask in light of everything, but Elyza's within him."

Blocking the outdoor exit, MacBeth yelled, "Brody?"

Julian made his way to the officer slumped over in the corner. "He's been shot."

MacBeth's voice went through the roof. "Friendly fire? We killed one of our own?"

"There's no we, MacBeth." Olivia's voiced in angst. "You shot him. You shot your partner. And that monster—" She pointed to Xanti — "killed Hallewell and my daughter."

Lucian strut to the cop, picking him off the ground and shaking the man accused, "You are more heartless than my bride. Open firing on a group of people mourning." André and Julian came up on both sides of Lucian while Raven placed her body in direct line of fire of another cop coming in from outside with his firearm drawn.

"Move lady." The cop nudged Raven with the tip of his gun. "I don't want to, but I will."

Raven made a slight snigger. "You'll endure a slow death if one bullet pops from your gun." Raven took a quick glance over her shoulder. "Luce, let Macbeth go. I'm not about to lose you too today, brother."

Lucian begrudgingly released his hold on the officer.

MacBeth stumbled, putting space between himself and Lucian. "Where's Sinclair? He was here two seconds ago. How did he do that? Tear this place apart. Get a bus here for Brody and Hallewell."

"And Zander," Lucian demanded.

Olivia answered, "Brody's gone. Hallewell too. MacBeth, your bus can't save them, but I can. For a price." Olivia was quick to find a scrap of paper and jot something down on it and hand it to him. "Read this and don't lose this."

When the EMT walked in, his first and last words were, "What the fuck?"

Chapter Seventeen

Olivia sought out Savanah and Jovan. *I need help.*

Being an elemental witch, Savanah discretely slipped her shoes off and drew from her powers calling to the earth. She held the power to give life to plants, flowers, trees, tap into the waterways and ley lines if she needed to, to use the earth's resources at her discretion. She also held a darker power she vowed to never use again after she used her magic on Devon Badcock once, trying to make him go back to the ash from which he'd risen. They were third cousins by the blood and three wasn't anywhere far enough in numbers.

Jovan's powers were a cross between a psychic witch and an elemental witch. She could read people's minds, see their auras, see through lies, scry into the future, and create things from thin air.

Olivia was just plain exhausted and needed help. She spent about thirty seconds reckoning the dead and bringing life back to two men who were in the wrong spot at the wrong time. When Xanti called her a necromancer he was spot on.

Earth and vines, entwine. Create a cocoon that shall not release these men anytime soon. Cause no harm. Do not make them feel alarmed. Hold them in peace until I say release. Before MacBeth and his men knew which way was up, they had thorned vines entwined around their legs and torso with blooms of lavender giving off a tranquil aroma. Savanah stood back admiring her handywork.

Jovan muttered, "Mimic the Emperor's new clothes," to leave the officers butt naked.

"Really, Mum?" Savanah rolled her eyes toward her mother then turned and looked at Olivia. "Liv? What is it?"

Olivia held both her hands to Thomas's cheeks sobbing. "It's all fun and games until someone gets a heart ripped out. I have loved you, Thomas, from the second I saw you standing in my grove in the same predicament as these cops now stand, butt naked. Thomas, when we met, you were confused, your wings broken and bloodied. You were so angry with God. So angry. Swearing at him, using a language I'd never heard, but I'm guessing you were cussing."

"That was the day I fell from grace. Best day of my life, my love. I met you. What a ride we have had, my belle."

"Guys, come on, we don't have time for reminiscing. Liv? Grandpa?" Savanah pat the older man's hands, who remained glued to Elyza and Serina.

Olivia reached out to Jovan and held her hand. "Jovie, you're in charge for a bit. Hold the fort down. You'd mentioned something to Serina about getting to the heart of the matter? Get to it. Savvy, even though you are not my granddaughter by blood I have loved you as if you are. Daelyn, same to you. You two and Elyza and Sydney have given me purpose in this life. Thank you. Get my Sydney home safely."

Ethan piped in, "Liv? What the heck? Hang on, as long as you're in a sappy once in a lifetime mood, what about me?"

"Learn the difference between salt and sugar and we'll talk. Otherwise, we won't."

Ethan grunted. "Savvy, we are in trouble. She didn't crack a smile or wink or burn the house down."

Still unresponsive and draped over Elyza's body, Olivia tapped her finger to Zander's butt. Sparks sizzled and he stirred. "Get up. Time to finish what I started, smart-ass. Get my granddaughter's spirit reunited with her body." Olivia turned her attention to Thomas. "Until brighter days, my lover." Leaning in, Olivia kissed Thomas on the forehead. "Promise. Don't let go."

"Until then, my belle." Thomas stood up and with one hand tore his shirt open exposing his hairy chest and his Buddha belly. He closed his eyes and whispered, "Don't wait so long the next time."

"Promise."

Ethan blurted out, "What the fuck are you two doing?"

One second of calm and then the tsunami hit. The first wave Xanti obliterated Serina's heart. The second surge ended with Olivia plunging her fist through her own chest wall and extracting her heart, beating, bleeding. Horrified gasps filled the chapel as everyone dropped to their knees and grabbed the person's hand beside them to make a circle. Hysterical, Thomas yelled, "No! Liv! It was supposed to be mine. Not yours. You can't do this. Not like this. What have you done? How are we to save you?"

With her color rapidly draining from her face and her voice shaky, somehow, Olivia managed to say, "What any mother would do for their child if they could, give her my last, dying breath. Don't you let go of me, Thomas. You are my anchor." Her body reeling in shock,

Olivia's hands shook as she placed her heart in Serina's chest. "Lucian, foolish imbecile of a son-in-law, I can see why my daughter chose you to cherish. I love you too. Zander, you're up."

His eyes glazed over, seeing double, Zander asked, "What did I miss? What am I up for? Why does everything hurt so badly?" He glanced down at his feet and noted blood leaking from his gut. "Not again."

Bloody tears streaming down his face and his voice cracking, Lucian pounded his fist onto the table so hard Serina's, and Elyza's bodies bounced. "No Liv. You don't get to do this. You don't get to say good-bye to me, or anyone else. Not today. Not tomorrow."

Olivia's knees buckled. Duncan ran to the woman and picked her up from the floor. He draped Olivia's body on the table beside her daughter and granddaughter. Thomas pulled a chair to the end of the table. He crossed Elyza's right foot over Serina's left leg and then Serina's right foot over Olivia's left leg so all three were connected. Not looking any better than Olivia, he sat down and leaned over the table, his arms spread across all three women. "Wake me when this nightmare is over."

****

Bleach's pungent stench accosted Zander's olfactory senses. *Funny*, he thought, *HRM cell block H keeps copious amounts of the stuff on hand*. Without opening his eyes, he knew exactly where he was. How he got there was the question. And now it was not the least bit funny.

He went to roll over but found his arm restrained. Go figure. They were kind enough to leave one arm free in case he had an itch somewhere the nurses weren't willing to scratch for him. Did he stick his head out from under the cover and look around? Did he open his eyes? If he kept them closed, he still retained deniable plausibility he hadn't been magically transported back to Hell. If he peeked out from beneath the covers, he had to deal with the fact his get out of jail free card had been revoked.

"Templar, welcome home."

Zander nudged a blanket aside. The overhead fluorescent light made him squint and wish he'd stayed shrouded. "Day and time? Can you turn off the light? How long have I been here?"

"Twenty-four hours. I'm Carmen. You lost one day. Nearly lost your life. You were extremely febrile and anemic to the point you needed four units of blood, but I do suppose old bullet holes coupled with new bullet holes and sepsis will do that to a person. It is a miracle we aren't planting you right now."

Zander tartly added, "That's me, a walking miracle. Any chance anyone has come to see me? A beautiful little woman with raging blue eyes and long silky black curly hair?"

"You're in jail, Templar. No one bloody cares if you rot here. The police recovered the jewels from a locker you rented at the airport. All of them. They even have you on tape wearing the priest's bloody clothes."

Zander feigned a brilliant smile. "So, they have their scapegoat. I want to see my barrister. Do I have one? When can I get out of here?"

"You'll be in infirmary a few more days. Our surgeon dug out four bullets. Somebody doesn't like you."

"You mean someone doesn't want me telling their

truths."

Elyza? Can you hear me?

An uncomfortable awareness gnawed at Zander's gut while he waited for a response. Her soul no longer resonated within him. The bullet holes he'd been left with didn't compare to the cavernous pit his heart held. Hindsight—Jovan gave him a riddle on how to get Elyza out. Apparently choosing a deadbeat dad over a ghost was the golden ticket. Now, how to get her back?

Zander didn't know if Serina made it after he somehow performed a ritualistic not-so-medical heart transplant. That was one for the horror books. Then he laughed at a fleeting idea, a title for a book he'd soon write: Romancing the Necromancer. Unfortunately, reality took his thoughts back to his last moments in the chapel.

Was Thomas still slumped across his three ladies? He'd placed Serina in a holding pattern after the transplant to give her time to heal. He did the same to Olivia until they figured out where to get another heart. He hadn't had the chance to get Elyza's soul and body reunited. Timing being everything he'd collapsed immediately following the charming curse, so he had no way of knowing what went down between then and winding up in Club Fed again.

Not knowing totally sucked.

What sucked even more? Jovan's bogus hocus pocus bologna about Elyza and him having a happily ever after. Jovan had to be the worst fairy godmother. What kind of person dangles love in front of you and then snatches it back?

A witch. To which Jovan was one. So, there he had it. And here he lay, cuffed to a bed in a place he'd vowed to never ever wind up in again thanks to a witch, or more like a coven of them.

Moving about the room Zander's nurse spoke up, "Templar, play nice with your roomie. The kid went on a killing spree, claiming he is a distant relative of Vlad. Tore out the throats of five people in one home. He's a bit of a nutter, so mind your p's and q's. He would have normally gone over to the Garland's hospital, but the place magically exploded. You wouldn't have anything to do with that too, would you?" The nurse shot Zander a knowing glare.

"I'd love to take the credit for that, but 'twas not my doing." That was all Elyza's work.

The nurse tossed her stethoscope around her neck, grabbed her laptop, and walked out. Alone for the minute he glanced around the room. On a white wallboard he read the synopsis of his life to date: Handle with extreme caution.

If only people had followed that rule when he was an infant.

Zander continued reading his white board: Diet: Blood. One pint of blood every four hours until teeth recede. "Are you fecking kidding me? Fecking? Am I fecking kidding me? What have you done to me, Elyza?" His heart ached when no response came. Silence was not golden in the least. He needed Nitroglycerin on this board for a broken ticker. Ah, but there was a Vervain and Silver nitrate drip every twelve hours, as needed for restless leg syndrome. "If this isn't the joke of the century, restless leg syndrome. Covering up the true reason. Keep me from flying the coop. Vancomycin… Really? They're actually treating my infection? Hmmm." With a few grunts Zander attempted to lift his legs. The struggle was real. He half-expected to find cement booties. He missed his yellow, faux fur lined mud kickers.

Hearing a grunt, Zander turned his attention to his roomie. The kid had brimstone and silver cuffs binding his hands and feet. His memory shot back to the first time he saw Elyza in his flat. How beautifully pissed off she was with fire in her eyes. Made complete sense to him now. This poor kid beside him would be at the nurse's mercy if anything itched. A leather mouth guard with silver spikes pointed inward put pressure on the kid's lips so he couldn't draw his lips back in preparation of feeding.

Feeding. There's a word Zander never thought he would use in his vocabulary with casual indifference. "Fecked up. I said that on purpose Elyza."

The boy beside him had two festering holes in his neck. Looked sore as hell. Smelled worse.

"So kid, you got a name?"

The kid aimed a finger at the white board on the wall opposite the bed he lay in. "Oh, sorry. Forgot you've got the lip lock on." Zander read the kid's board, "Murphy. Do people call you Murph or Hannibal? That mouthpiece reminds me of him."

The kid nodded yes. *Can you read minds?*

"Did you just ask me if I can read minds?" The kid's head went into bobble mode nodding yes. "I kinda thought that only worked on people who shared family or were sired by the same monster."

The kid rolled his eyes. *Yes. Zander, I read your board too. We have to get out of here. The nutjob that turned me is your father. Irony at play here. I removed the pear of anguish from Xanti and let him free and now*

315

I have it on me. We can communicate because of him.

What happened to you?

Seriously dude? Look at me. What do you think happened? Believe it or not, there's scarier monsters than vamps out there. Look, tonight there's a masquerade ball put on by the museum I used to work at. The ball is a front for all kinds of black-market shenanigans. Things range from getting food for the animals they breed and sell for fighting and hunting. It's beyond perverse. Dog fighting taken to a new extreme. They lock up random people and drain them for blood products and then turn them. They sell the blood laced with heroine underground to anyone and everyone including vamps and once they get them hooked, they clean out their accounts and estates and kill them and sell off their organs. Cash cow extraordinaire, dude. Recycling to the max. They sell precious art and jewelry on the black market to the highest bidders and report it stolen to claim insurance money, and another lucrative enterprise? Human trafficking. They have my sister. They told me as long as I keep my mouth shut and do my job, they won't kill her. This is me, keeping my mouth shut...technically...Pretty sure my sister would rather be dead than be a sex slave. I overheard one of the head honchos at the museum going off about tonight's party before I dined on him and a few of his family members. That's when my stomach started turning inside out and I wound up here because I couldn't get out of my own way.

About to ask Murph a million questions alarms began to blare. To Zander's horror, the kid started convulsing. Blood squirted from his ears, ran down his nose and red tears dripped from his eyes. "Help!" Zander yelled. "Somebody help!" Not a moment passed before the drape between the two beds closed.

Murph, I'll get your sister for you if you don't make it. I promise. One way or another.

Get who? "Time of death thirteen, thirteen. I'm going to sit with the body a few minutes. I knew his family."

Once the room cleared Zander asked the doctor, "How did he die? He was fine two minutes ago."

The curtain edged back a bit. "Poison."

Zander gasped. "How?"

"It happened when he took one of the museum manager's blood last night."

"No, I mean how did you get in here? Why are you here? How did you know? You're no doctor."

"No, but I play one occasionally with friends. Though honestly, I'm much better at giving last rights."

Zander gave Xanti a blank stare.

"You lack a sense of humor, son. I went back for Murph last night, but I was too late. The kid didn't stand a chance. The top officials at the museum have been ingesting scant amounts of grain alcohol and ethanol for years in case anyone ever tried to kill them. It's got a technical term called mithridatism. You can build a tolerance to it but ingested in large quantities, like say, draining someone's blood? Well, it'll kill even a dead person. You want to stick around and see how your fate plays out or come with me?"

"I don't trust you. Everything I have heard and seen about you leads to a stake in the heart. And I won't even mention Serina."

"You shouldn't... right off the bat. Like that pun? I did Serina a huge favor. She'd have killed herself eventually trying to live with that maggot in her."

"Did Serina live? Have you been back?"

Xanti shook his head no.

Zander's heart skipped a beat or two. Even though fear filled him, he needed to know the answer. "No—she didn't live or no you haven't been back?"

"That's not what you truly need the answers to, is it? You can't feel Elyza any longer and you want to know if she lived. I am sorry, son."

Zander collapsed backward on the bed and yanked the covers over his face, tears flooding his vision. "Get out."

"Zander, allow me to finish. I am sorry. I do not know if she made it. I fled for my life. Something you need to do now. These people have a case stacked against you. They will kill you eventually. Come with me. We need to hit the museum for some fancy clothes if we're going to crash a masquerade ball."

"Are you insane?"

"Redundant query."

"I can't evanesce. Elyza barely could."

Xanti picked up a set of keys, a cell phone, a wallet he'd dropped on the bed and tucked all but the keys into his jacket pocket. "Those cuffs burn like the dickens. Here." Xanti took the key and undid the cuff.

Zander pointed to the items Xanti just stashed. "I don't want to know, do I?"

Xanti cheesed big. "Come on." He tossed a bag at Zander. "Think quick." The bag hit him in the face.

"Thanks."

Xanti laughed. "Forgot you were all numbed up."

Inside the bag were a pair of jeans, trainers, a shirt, and a hoodie. Zander didn't know how to read the man. He seemed earnest with his intentions, going against everything he knew about the man. Once again books and covers popped into his thoughts. Dressed he said, "I don't think I can walk yet."

"Not an issue," and just like that Zander's cheeks were flapping in the wind and the HRM bastille became a distant memory.

Chapter Eighteen

Hogging the entrance to the door waiting for his brother and wife to walk up the drive, André yelled, "Did you get it?" Jovan pulled a small red and white cooler into his view and jiggled it.

Lucian yanked the container from Jovan. "Precious cargo, Jovan. Geez!" He gave her a reprimanding glare before finishing, "Looks more like a picnic."

André wiped beads of sweat from his forehead and rubbed his jaw. "Picnic from Hell maybe."

Lucian bumped into his twin. "Has Elyza shown any signs since we left?"

André shook his head no. "I'm so sorry. Zander's back and he is ready when we are."

"How?"

"His father, if one can call him that, dropped him off after he broke him out of jail."

"This should be fun." Lucian walked away shaking his head.

****

Candles illuminated the chapel. Zander made certain the candle's colors represented the circle of life: silver for stability, brown for protection of family, white for healing and protection, pink for reconciliation of soulmates, red for strength, blue for truth and healing, purple for astral travel, psychic manifestations, and spirituality, and finally black for banishing negativity.

He'd drawn planetary sigils in chalk of the moon to represent family bonds, for remembering past lives. Pluto's symbol of rebirth also took up space on the floor and table. The sun's pictogram of the horned God brought health, power, and victory. Venus's symbol represented love, passion, friendships. Bundles of sage combined with petals of lily, rose, lotus, chamomile, and poppy burned to cleanse the air. A bowl of opals, moonstones, citrine, diamonds, and rose quartz overflowed with their untapped energy. Silver dishes held water and coarse sea salt to help purify both the family and the room. The earth's endless resources always amazed Zander. At the end of the table holding Serina, Olivia and Elyza's bodies sat a little red cooler where Father Butler looked as if he might need a transplant too.

Payton pointed to the container. "Well, at least it's not a canning jar filled with black charms like the last one." A few, "Blessed Be's," followed.

His nose scrunched, Ethan asked, "Did we buy stock in a candle company?" Savanah kicked his shin giving him a wide-eyed shut the hell up, glare. Ethan gave his bride an indignant glance and rubbed his leg grumbling, "It's really pretty. That's all I meant. Is that pumpkin spice? Honestly?"

Zander gave up a half grin. "It masks the odor."

"Not really, dude. Not really," Ethan added still tending to his shin.

Daelyn came up between his parents. "Zander, have you felt her? Has she surfaced?"

All eyes upon him, Zander couldn't make eye contact with anyone and begrudgingly shook his head. "Not since I chose the dark side. I had to. It was the only way to get her back in her own body."

"Well played," Daelyn chided. "You have balls. Hopefully it worked. If it doesn't, I will crush them."

Shelby butt in with, "No, that pleasure is all mine if this doesn't work."

Lucian tapped Shelby's shoulder. "No budging the line, Shells. He's mine if this goes south."

Rocking back on his heels, Zander drawled out, "*Okayyy!* Let's do this. I combined a spell to get Grandmother, mother, and daughter back on this side of the daisies, in their own bodies."

Everyone crowded in the circle, each placing an arm on the next person's shoulder and held the other person's free hand creating an eternal ring. Father Butler nodded to the flask at the head of the table. Three shot glasses were filled pink wine next to the bodies. "As soon as Zander finishes this and before any of them have a chance to speak, pour the sacred fluid in their mouths. Plug their noses so they must swallow it. Pretend they're a little kid refusing their meds. The fluid will seal the charm." Father Butler gave a weary grin. "Go on Zander, just do it. Bring my girls back to me."

One deep breath in and out for nerve control, Zander began. "This is for Serina St. James and Olivia Spencer:

There is one heart, each of you share a part.

This heart I now impart,

Will give you both a fresh start,

To live apart, until the end of days and always remain each other's counterpart,

Mother and daughter.

One's fire to the other's water.

Today we bring back to you—life, love, health, laughter, memories,

Of old and new,
A fresh beginning for the two of you.
Until the end of days.
In all your gallantry,
Return to your family."

Zander sprinkled a few drops of the water from the silver dishes over both the women and then wisped the burning sage and herbs and flowers over them. With gentle, steady hands he picked up the heart from the cooler and placed it in Olivia's chest. Gathering his strength, he unleashed a searing stream of energy through her. The heart jumped and then slowly began to pump on its own. Showing no emotion, Zander closed the wound, weaving his fingers above her in a healing spell, just as he's seen Olivia do with Serina. His hands interweaving patterns, he continued, "One is for love, Olivia and Serina. Never doubt anyone's love for you. You will both love again. Fiercely. Passionately. With your new hearts. With your family. For your family." A blaze of power arched and slammed into both corpses. "Two is for laughter, ladies. You will laugh again. With us. With your family. At us, myself excluded." Zander spared a glance at the family and gave up the tiniest smirk. "Heard that from the Mistress." A third surge of power blasted the body, making Serina's back arch and flop back onto the table. "Three is for health. Your health will be restored. Flawless. Absolute perfectness shall reign. You shall live long lives with your families." One last power surge blasted from Zander's fingertips. "The final intention is to restore memories, to allow new ones. No Abby Normal brains allowed." A few chuckles broke the strained silence.

Thomas pointed to Olivia's hand, her finger's

twitching. "Quick, poor the shot down her throat."

Savanah reached over and grabbed the small glass. She opened Olivia's mouth and plugged her nose. "Sorry, Liv." One hiccup later, the liquid vanished. Lucian reached over Serina's body and did the same thing seeing her stir. After a few minutes of tears and hugs Olivia and Serina lay side by side holding hands, quiet, alive, waiting patiently for Zander to resurrect Elyza.

"Two down... One to go. Please reform the circle." Zander took one step to stand before Elyza. After dipping a cloth into the water, he ran the material over her face, carefully, brushing her curls back and smoothing her hair out.

"For Elyza—What was once lost has been found.
To this body, Elyza Tracey St. James you are bound.
My heart, my soul,
You say borrowed, I say stole.
I ask you here, to share my life.
I ask you now to be my wife.
Rejoin me here on this side,
Where forever you will be my treasured bride.
My dear bonny lass,
With that ever so tiny dimple on your ass,
Walk with me barefoot in the grass.
Trust in me,
I'll be your sanctuary.
Tell me these words, 'It is you I want to marry.'
Our souls have mingled.
I know you felt it too, how they tingled,
No longer single.
As one. This is no easy feat.
So, when our lips do meet,

I beg of thee,
Set yourself free.
Make yourself whole, body, mind, and soul.
Stand side-by-side forever with me.
This is my wish for you and I, so mote it be."

Zander placed one hand over Elyza's heart and his other beneath her head then sent her an influx of his power to kickstart her heart and brain. When nothing happened, he added a second surge of magic through her.

Unease and dead silence encased the space, all fore Lucian's stern tone asking, "You saw my daughter's ass? You just proposed to her? Seriously?"

When Zander peeked up, he wished he hadn't. The term bated breath had never held a truer meaning. There Zander stood in a circle of vampires, werewolves, and a witch or two, maybe more, who knew at this point.

Please find your way back to me.

Foot tapping, sweat oozing from every pore, Lucian blurted, "My baby's not moving. Not breathing. Well, so much for the wooing spell. Just kiss her already. It worked for André and Jovan."

Jovan burst into nervous hysterics and André blushed to an incinerating red. "You didn't honestly tell him it worked?" Jovan wiped tears from her eyes while she waited for her husband's response. "André?" Lucian stood behind André giving her the head bob.

"Well, it did, Cherié. You are standing here due to true love's kiss. My kiss."

Jovan tossed her hands in the air. Zander stood there with a dumbfounded glaze, not knowing what to say, if anything. This family seemed to be the root of ADHD. Tangents. Mazes. Turn circles that no one knew how to navigate. Not a one of them could stay on point.

Jovan defended herself, "I had a simple case of amnesia. My soul remained intact, heart still pumping, but by all means, we are out of options, so just plant your lips on hers, and end this charade since your spell worked as well as Olivia's."

"And it started with a little kiss like this," André leaned back and sang the lyrics into Lucian's ear. "Stress breaker."

Lucian grabbed his twin around the neck. "Keep the day job, brother," he added absent of any humor. "Kiss her. Now!" Lucian's grin held an unhealthy appetite.

Zander blurted, "How have the lot of you survived? You're the definition of the clown posse."

"Pour the shot in her mouth first," Father Thomas directed. "Make sure it goes down."

"Little cherub, forgive me." His hand ever steady, Zander placed the shot glass to Elyza's lips and allowed the liquid to drain in. The fluid pooled in her mouth and dribbled out down her cheek and into her hair. Tears filled Zander's eyes. "I've lost her."

Shelby broke the circle and strut to Zander's side. She leaned into his face and coolly stated, "Fucking kiss her now."

He leaned down to Elyza's cool body and whispered in her ear, "I wanted so much for us. I wanted our first kiss to be inti—"

"Bloody hell, boy, just do it," Raven yelled.

Not another second was wasted. Zander planted his lips over Elyza's allowing every ounce of his power, courage, will and determination into their kiss. When her mouth moved beneath his, tears fell. And then he followed.

****

"Hey, Mr. Thaumaturge, wake up."

"Mister who?" Zander asked, his voice groggy.

"Thaumaturge. The miracle maker. Come on, we have a party to attend. One could call it my coming out party." Elyza lay beside Zander on a daybed in the sunroom, stroking his hair, wearing a grin gods would envy. She couldn't help but smile. She had her life back. She had the man of her dreams beside her and a world of wishes to accomplish with him.

Zander whispered, "If I open my eyes and you are but a dream I will perish."

"No dying today. We've done enough of this lately. Now is our time to live. Open them gorgeous orbs for me." Elyza bent to him and kissed the tip of his nose and then his lips. His response demanding, she slid her tongue softly over his mouth and gently probed. He met her, adding a bit of oomph behind it. He teased her a bit, gnawed on her bottom lip and stopped. "Are you like dead certain we didn't die and go to heaven, because right here, right now, it feels like it."

"That's the cheesiest line ever. Get up you two. Save the sex for later. We have a mission to accomplish." Daelyn approached the daybed and leaned over and kissed Elyza's head. "If you ever pull a stunt like this again, I'm not turning into an ice pop to free you. I'm completely over igloos."

Elyza reached up and grabbed Daelyn's hand. "I love you too, Dael."

"You both need to eat. Payton went all out and put on a smorgasbord to die for." Elyza shot a look to Zander, eyes wide. Daelyn asked, "Too soon on the deadbeat jokes?" Elyza chuckled. "What is it?" Daelyn asked.

"Did you see it too? In the secret garden, Zander?"

"Whoa!" Zander brushed his hair from his face and sat up, taking Elyza with him. "I thought it was a dream. So, we either had the same dream or we both went…"

"We were so in a secret garden."

"Guys, I hate to disappoint, but we found you in the graveyard. Not really so secret. Come on. Let's go rescue Sydney."

Chapter Nineteen

Other than an occasional nicker, horses stood resilient in the evening drizzle in front of their coaches waiting for the intricately detailed wrought iron gate to open. With Zander's fingers looped through hers, Elyza peeked out behind the old tapestry curtain. The Victorian gothic mansion at the end of the drive held grandiose illusions. Beautifully alluring on the outside. Twisted, nefarious realities within. Castles and prisons, she thought. Both are made from stone and brick, only difference being one has a better interior decorator.

Three stories of white brick set the framework of the building with high peaks of black slate roofing, a tower on each end, the garret's windows all stained glass. Three balconies rested beneath the center front windows of the second floor, all designed with trefoil molding in each pane. Lavish overflowing flower boxes draped down to the ground from the balconies made a quaint bower for teatime. A huge fountain took up the center of the courtyard. Water cascaded from the top of a winged angel to three lower tiers. One of the wings on the angel dangled broken. A fallen angel sculpture. Elyza found it oddly intriguing. On the backside of the property the River Thames flowed. Elyza was betting a lineup of yachts waited for their owners after the party.

"A burlesque themed party. How amazing—"

Elyza put her finger to his mouth to shoosh Zander,

but instead he kissed each finger. "That backfired," she laughed. She gave a slight tug to regain her hand. "It would be amazing if it were for any other reason."

"Have I told you how fecking..." Zander gave a slight pause watching Elyza's smile pour over her face. "Nailed it! Amazing you look? Steampunk is my new favorite style. Those shoes belong in a shoe porn magazine. I've never seen a stocking worn over a shoe, and who knew diamonds could be sewn into them? They are the sexiest things I've ever witnessed."

"Sexier than this?" Elyza teased, slightly raising the hem of her dress.

Nibbling on his pouty lip Zander grunted. "Just how far up your legs do they go?" Zander walked his fingers up the length of her leg and inched his way beneath her dress.

"The only thing better is when I take them off for you later."

"Later?" Zander shook his head no while he ran his hand down the length of her leg trying to take a stocking down. "Are the gems real?"

"Yes. Daddy made them for me, but I still love the flip flops you designed for me."

Zander's smile met his eyes. "Me too. The layers of lace on your gown, shorter in the front, longer in the back, covers that dimple..."

Elyza's jaw dropped. "Do you want me to set fire to you here and now?"

Laughing, he reeled her in closer. "My little cherub, I'm already burning up. Trust me. There is nothing you can do to make me hotter."

"Challenge accepted." Elyza leaned in and kissed Zander's neck, grazing him with her teeth. She waited for a response, a deep inhalation, a jerk, his body stiffening, but nothing happened. Not getting the reaction she'd hoped for she pulled away with a coy look. "Anything?"

"Need to try a bit harder." He broke into hysterics and returned the favor, kissing her neck until his fangs started poking through. He pulled back in haste. "Oh, no!"

"Breathe. I trust you. If you want to try this, I'm game. It might help keep your control when we get inside anyway. A little snack never hurts. No telling how long we'll be stuck in this carriage." Elyza bat her eyes playfully.

"Sweetheart, that is my signature move. Find your own ya little thief, but seriously, what if I can't stop?"

With a subtle shift, Elyza reached around and pulled her hair to one side, exposing her neck. "I can stop you. You won't like it if I have to use force, so when I say stop, you stop."

"So, stop is your safe word?"

Shaking her head and laughing gently, she answered, "No dear, it's yours."

Zander slid his hand beneath her chin and studied her, his demeanor changing. "I didn't save you just to kill you. We've been through more life-altering circumstances than anyone should ever experience."

"We are here, Zander. Flesh and blood, alive, because of sheer will and love. And a wee bit of magic. No one will ever steal this from us again. I need to thank you for saving not only my life, but my gram's and mom's. What you did, was nothing short of a miracle."

"How's your mom and gram been since the magical transplant? I would think it would mess with people's minds. I know it did mine."

"My mom's been a bit broody. It's a lot to take in. Gram is gram. She seems bubbly though like she has the excess energy of a teenager. I don't know if Gramps can keep up with her. She's a bit out of character. I guess they need time to come to terms with everything."

"What about you, little cherub? You feel any different?"

Elyza gave it a moment before she answered him. "I do miss having a penis." Her laughter filled the carriage.

"No worries, you can borrow mine anytime, day or night."

Fist pump in the air, she whispered, "Sweet! Honestly though, I'm appreciative. I took life for granted thinking I had immortality on my side. I will not make that mistake ever again." Elyza ran her hand across his cheek and through his hair while she leaned in and kissed him. He melted beneath her mouth, reacting the way she wanted, needed him to, until his stomach started to tighten. She sent a quick thought to him, *This is natural and in no way should cause discomfort.* His stomach relaxed. "You will not toss cookies on this gown. Understood?"

"Mm-hmm." His lips shifted and caressed the length of her neck, placing small kisses and nips here and there, but stopping when he found her pulse.

"I'm all yours, Zander. Until the end of days."

His voice raspy with need and his finger sliding over the vein in her neck, he asked, "Did you hear everything I'd said to you when I was trying to save you and your mom and the Mistress?"

"Yes, I believe I did. We shared one heart for a time. I knew how you felt without words. That day I jumped into you I gave you my heart also." She barely finished saying this when Zander's fangs pierced her flesh. Sweet euphoria rushed through her. Liquid fire ignited her in a way she'd never experienced or dreamed of. That 'O' she'd teased of with her sister and cousin days past was on the verge of rupturing her shell. Zander's hands explored her, slipped over the curves of the corset she wore, over the length of her arm, then over her thigh, moving upward while he drank her in. Very breathy Elyza confessed, "I can't breathe, Zander. This is the most erotic moment in my life. Don't stop."

Zander released her and licked her neck where a few drops of blood trickled down. "I promise, my little cherub, I will never stop, but I want our first time to be filled with time to explore, to enjoy one another."

Elyza wasn't having it. She needed him more than the air she breathed. She'd learned incredibly fast over a few days span the value of life and living it to its fullest. She'd died. She'd ghosted. She took an unexpected trip to Heaven and had a chat with the big guy. And got sent back to live her life. Today, not tomorrow. Not later. Now. She reached down and began undoing the buttons on his breeches, and smiled at the reaction he had, all wide-eyed and his fondness for the situation reaching critical mass. "Anticipation is overrated where spontaneity is underrated." She straddled him and while kissing him, she slid her hips over him.

Zander reached behind Elyza and gathered her dress, slipping his hands beneath, to the curve of her derriere. "Commando? Dear lord woman, you are going to kill me."

"I have a spell or two to resurrect you."

"Pretty certain the erect part has already been

achieved."

"Stop wasting time, I see someone opening the gate. There's six carriages in front of us."

"No pressure," he chuckled.

"I beg to differ." Elyza reached between her legs, wrapped her fingers around his manhood and guided him to where the sun didn't shine. "You can lead a horse to water, but you can't make him drink it."

"This stallion is parched beyond reason, love." In one swift plunge he filled her in ways she couldn't imagine. The pleasure of him being inside her, stroking her in the most intimate manner brought tears to her eyes. A need like none other drove her, rocking her hips back and forth while he pressed harder into her.

****

"Spontaneity it is!" In one fluid roll, Zander had her beneath him on the unforgiving hard carriage seat, with layers of lace, satin, and tule all around them. He took the lead and with some well-earned control, he continued to press into her. His lips skimmed her neck, and lower to her breasts, or what her corset allowed to show. "The corset, I can't wait to take it off you later. This is the tease of a lifetime." Her arching her back and moaning, "Harder," fueled his desire and with little notice her core began a series of intense spasms, gripping him, causing his release. When they both caught their breath, he placed one final kiss on the tip of her nose. "This, right here, you and I, Elyza Tracey St. James, until the end of days."

Elyza winked at him. "You drive a hard bargain, in every sense of the word."

In the midst of making themselves presentable, the carriage door swung open. On the opposite side stood

Serina and Jovan. Zander went three shades of embarrassed, patting down his hair, and making sure body parts were concealed.

"Like mother like daughter." Jovan pat Serina's back in jest.

Elyza responded, "I wouldn't have it any other way. I love you, Momma."

"I love you too, Sparky."

"Momma, you've never called me that. Only Grams."

"Hmm, maybe my mom's heart rubbed off on me." Serina reached for Elyza's hand and kissed her palm. "In a few moments we enter Hell for a second time, my littlest love. Keep your minds open to our channel. Zander, I realize you and Xanti have a way to communicate but none of us trust him. He killed me, even if he is claiming to be the savior killing Xavier, I was a package deal."

"I will take caution, Serina, but in earnest, he got us this far tonight, invites to the ball, the layout of the mansion, and who to expect. Second chances sometimes are the first step to healing."

"That's a good line, kid. How long did it take you to think that up?" Jovan asked, her face half serious, half joking.

Zander grinned. "All day. I knew the conversation would come up. I just didn't think it would be thirty seconds after…"

Elyza blew out a breath, running her fingers through her hair. "Carriages ladies. We're up."

****

The foyer had to be fifty feet in length, with rooms

off to each side. The ceiling stood easily twenty feet in height. Archways with gilded crown molding held chandeliers in front of each room opening. Witch balls were sporadically hung along the wall with horse skulls on each side of the ball.

Squinting, Zander gave a discreet waggle of his index finger to the odd items.

Elyza answered, "They prevent magic or spells or incantations. How did you not know that?"

"Uh, I did. I was just pointing it to you. Going to be tough if we need to do any magic."

People dressed in elaborate period gowns from the seventeenth century fused with steampunk accessories, danced through the halls. Some women adorned masks, while others used a handheld fan to disguise themselves. A few paraded about with parasols. Men wore masks or had their faces painted to retain anonymity. The bird mask one gent wore that became famous during the Plague creeped Zander out. The blood dripping from the tip of the beak didn't help.

A crossover between Burlesque and baroque music echoed through the estate. Performers wore poofy, cotton candy styled wigs in a rainbow of colors with blindingly bright costumes. Musicians played viols, or mandolins, or kalimbas, or the lute, or the saxophone. One lonely artist flit about playing her violin. Her talent so beyond extraordinary, Elyza could have watched her all evening. She danced a cross between ballet and jazz as she performed. Her music brought the room to a silent standstill to regale in her passion. She wore a deep maroon velvet corset, and a black tulle tutu, army boots and tights that had runs through them. Her entourage of dancers dressed similarly. Their synchronized steps made Elyza wish she'd finished dancing lessons. There was no realm in this universe where having two left feet did anyone any good.

In the drawing room two cellists sat side-by-side, their attire befitting of French Nobility with their rich embroidered velvet tailcoats and breeches, white hosen, and shoes with a lifted heel. The crowd before them danced an exaggerated version of the minuet. They played one of Elyza's favorite songs from the 90s. "I think I've been thunderstruck," she stated in awe of their passion to regale her. She leaned back into Zander's open arms and enjoyed the moment.

Except for bowties, waiters were shirtless. They wore satin shorts with white velvet trim down the sides. They were so 70s fashion era. All that was missing was the knee-high tube socks. Elyza had a few pictures of her dad and uncles dressed as such. Blackmail photos for a rainy day. Other staff members wore bowler hats, rich tapestry tailcoats with matching breeches for the men or thigh high stockings for the ladies. Bite marks and years of abuse decorated the wait staff's flesh. Unconsciously, Elyza reached for Zander's hand, finding it a welcoming comfort.

With his lips to her ear, Zander whispered, "I had no idea this lifestyle existed. Always thought it lived only in the pages of romance novels."

Elyza smiled. "Where do you think authors come up with their stories?"

"I want to be an author when I grow up. Writing is all about the research." Zander bat his lashes at Elyza.

Elyza elbowed his side and kept walking.

"I'm kidding, sort of," trailed after her, "but I even have a title to a book."

Elyza swung to face Zander and wrapped her arms around his waist. "Will I be in it?"

Zander bent and kissed her nose. "Maybe. I'll probably kill you off in the first chapter." Her gasp had him laughing.

They entered the rotunda where a round table sized for King Arthur, adorned with an endless supply of food and drink took up much of the room. The ceiling was a cast of a wrought iron dome, the windows all stained glass, the floor made from mirrors, reflecting everything, including what you did or did not wear. Zander was quick to point this out to Elyza. "Keep your legs closed."

She swatted the back of his head, tipping his top hat sideways. "You weren't saying that ten minutes ago."

Lucian followed with a more enthusiastic swat to Zander's head that sent his top hat to the floor. "I can't unhear that either."

"Still not sorry, Daddy." Elyza put her hands on Zander's shoulder and swung him around. "Look up." Above them two women were doing acrobatics from swings. Their skintight costumes of silvery-blue leather accentuated the female form. Both outfits held wings of deep indigo feathers giving the illusion the ladies could fly. Their faces were painted to represent the blend of Day of the Dead and Mardi Gras. When they repelled to the floor right in front of Elyza and Zander, and then sprang back to the ceiling with a simple tug of the rope, Elyza gawked. "So cool."

From the second floor, a well-dressed man made his way through guests, shaking hands, making small talk as he descended the staircase. He grabbed a microphone from one of the musicians and tapped the tip of it, making a shrieking sound. "Welcome all, to my court. Tonight, we have a little something for everyone. No one shall leave disappointed and if you do, it is not by my fault. In a few short minutes we will hold our private auction to raffle some precious pieces off to the highest bidder, so I hope your Bit Coins are ready to get chomped on and if the auction is not to your satisfaction, then feel free to chomp on the staff. All are willing." He waved his deformed hand to the crowd the way the queen gave her signature waggle.

Lucian inhaled sharply. "What a phony."

"Who is he, Daddy?" Elyza asked.

"Devon Badcock."

With a light step, Xanti walked up behind Lucian and whispered, "Don't freak and don't spin about and please don't kill me. I promise you no harm this night."

Stiffly, Lucian responded, "I cannot afford you the same courtesy, Xanti. I suggest you walk as far from my family and myself as possible."

Ignoring him, Xanti skirted around the family to come to a standstill before them. Now donned in an off the shoulder silk and satin mantua, with a matching petticoat, something Marie Antionette once fashioned, minus his black chest hairs peeking out from under the cloth, Xanti spun and pulled up the hem of the gown showing off a pair of heeled shoes with large satin bows. "They make a delightful click." He pat a white wig atop his head, straightening it. His black eyes were showcased with black eyeliner and shadow mastering the smokey-eyed look.

He was met with the family staring at him. "Truly? It's a costume party. Have you never cross-dressed before? It's liberating. Nothing, and I mean nothing inhibits your balls from swaying freely."

"Shut up and ewh," were exclaimed at the same time from Serina and Jovan.

Xanti reached for Elyza's hand, but she stepped behind Zander. Lucian and André blocked him. "I mean her no harm. My purpose here this evening is to see to my son's wellbeing."

Zander pointed between Xanti and Elyza's eyes. "I think you could take pointers from him, Elyza."

Elyza's eyes almost popped out of her head. "Are. You. Fecking. Kidding? You did not just say that."

Lucian rolled his eyes. "Kid, you're about to take over my nickname of imbecile."

Xanti smiled, his fangs getting caught on his lips. "Hello son. Hello Elyza. You are looking better, now that you have an actual body. I do hope to get to know you. I can help with the makeup if you desire."

A loud snort escaped Elyza's throat. "Are you for real?" She looked at Zander. Her voice a few octaves higher she asked, "Is he serious? Dude, you killed my mom."

Xanti scrunched his nose and looked Elyza over. "Really? You're still miffed? It was naught more than a minor technicality."

Elyza countered, "I don't think I'd call plunging your fist through someone's chest and extracting their heart a minor technicality."

"And yet here she stands beside you, her mental faculties intact, no thanks to yours truly." Xanti bowed. "Serina, we have never been friends—"

Serina stopped him there. "And we never will be."

"I did what needed to be done for the sanctity of life. Do not take it personally. My revenge has been sated.

None of your family had the courage to do it. You look better now that your naughty bits are covered and your color returned. If Xavier's heart remained within you, the vile soul would have been cancer's evil twin within you. I hope you feel better?"

Serina scratched her head in thought and looked at Lucian and then Elyza before she spoke. "I've been back in the land of the living less than twenty-four hours and no one other than you bothered to ask me how I am. How is it the one person"—Serina caught her breath— "I loathe, is the first one to show compassion? Most likely because everyone fears my answer. Xanti, I am missing the most important part of my being. Ya know, feeling kind of like my heart was ripped out of my chest while it beat…" Xanti went to open his mouth and Serina held up a finger. "Don't even! You ripped my heart from my chest, Xanti. The heart has two functions. Life and love. Both with different memory sets. Only half of my heart is functioning, the half keeping me upright. I have to figure out the whole love thing portion again."

"Serina?" Lucian reached for his wife, but she stepped back.

Tears welling in her eyes, Serina said, "I'm sorry. It'll be fine, Lucian. I need time."

Scratching his chin, Xanti replied, "Gosh, I didn't really expect an answer. You're alive and you have your family. Be thankful. But let's not forget your original heart was blown to bits in the Hall Royal, so technically—"

"Shut up!" Lucian grabbed Xanti by the shoulders, but Elyza stepped between the men.

"Not here. Not now, Daddy. Let's get Sydney and live to fight another day."

"Until a new dawn then. I only ask that you let me take Devon down." Xanti pulled away from Lucian and reached for his coin purse. He held his hand out. "I promised you entrance to the events. You'll need these." In his palm sat a heap of gold coins. "Take them." When no one reached he jiggled them. "They aren't laced with poisoned. Damn, I wish I'd thought of that earlier."

Zander grabbed them from him and passed them out. "Thank you."

The tinny squeal of Devon's voice caught their attention once more. "If everyone would follow me to the rib vault, please? Once you've deposited your entrance coin into the box and all the coins are counted, bidding shall begin, and the pieces revealed." Devon swept his hand in the direction of two armed guards, one on each end of the table where all the jewels Zander had been accused of stealing were displayed. "We have London's finest here this night protecting the heirlooms."

Inside the room an ornately ribbed, vaulted ceiling showcased paintings of Dante's Inferno, depicting all the levels of Hell in each bay. Elyza pointed. "Those guards are the ones that stole the fecking mask and Hope Diamond from me. Nugget and Dick junior. They're the ones who shot mom."

Serina looked long and hard at the two men before saying, "We will deal with them another night. MacBeth is here too."

"I don't know if I can wait that long, Momma."

Lucian ducked his head. "MacBeth thinks you're both dead. Keep the masks on. I'll be back in a few minutes." Lucian grabbed André's shoulder and they disappeared into the crowd.

Elyza leaned into Zander, placing her lips close to his ear. "Zander can you undo those charms and make the witch balls shatter? Chances are good Sydney is locked up better than the Tower gems."

"It makes no sense. The cops said they had me on tape stealing them and stuffing them into a locker, and now they're here for an auction?"

Xanti grabbed Zander's arm. "They will get absurd amounts of money tonight and then tomorrow pass a tape with you stealing them to the precinct, where the same bad cops will arrest you again for breaking out of jail."

Serina flicked Xanti's hand from Zander's arm. "We will get the jewels, Sydney and clear both of you. We will get the video of Zander somehow."

A little breathy, their suits somewhat disheveled, Lucian and André returned with drinks for everyone.

"Daddy? What's up?"

"Let's just say Dick Jr and Nugget are more secured than this mansion is." Lucian and André cast a glance at one another and high-fived each other.

Zander grabbed Elyza's hand. "As my dad always says, 'It's best you don't know.'"

"I never imagined saying this, but for once your dad is a wise man." Jovan added, "Let's make sure we can communicate."

Serina sent a message to the group. *Ever thought about casting an exposure spell?* She waited for a response.

Elyza's lips twisted. Lucian coughed. Jovan looked at her feet. André bowed his head and made the sign of the cross over his chest.

"Really?" Serina huffed, "Ye of little faith! Let's make everyone spill their hearts, in a literal sense, Xanti.

Not physical."

"Killjoy," Xanti responded wearing a lopsided grin.

"Serina," Jovan grabbed her arm, "let's not try anything rash."

Serina bit her lip, her one eyebrow creeping toward her hairline. "Of course, Sister." Serina twisted away from Jovan's grip and stepped behind Xanti. She tugged his ear lobe, and whispered, "Abomination,.."

"Bollocks!" Xanti gasped and rubbed his ear. "Xavier?"

Serina spun to him, her grin a mix of mischief and malevolence. "Toying with you, Xanti. Or, maybe I'm not." Serina stopped and put her hand on Xanti's shoulder. "Oh my gosh I've got it. Xanti, thank you. You stated viruses never die. We've been going about this cure all wrong for vampirism and lycans. We need to quell the virus, control it since we can't irradicate it. Genius." In a fluid turn, she headed off on her own. "Spell time."

Xanti asked, "What just happened?"

Elyza shoved Lucian in the same direction Serina headed. "That's Momma doing nothing rash, Daddy. You're going after her, right?"

Serina sauntered off chanting, "No more illusions. No more confusion. Remove the mask, so we may go forth with our task. Bring to light those basking in the dark, so we know who to mark. Now is our time to embark to remove this faux hierarch, to expose him as he is, the true pock hidden in mock. Masks and facades drop your shields, true identities are now revealed."

His feet in forward motion, Lucian looked back over his shoulder saying, "I'm pretty sure that's not my wife. Your mom has never cast an exposure spell...because the end result would be her exposing herself as the worst witch ever, other than her healing abilities. Now your grams? She's almost more flamboyant than your soon to be father-in-law."

Xanti curtsied toward Lucian before adding, "Yeah, I'm one hundred percent certain that's not Serina. Think part of Xavier may still be lurking inside her too."

"This is so fucked up," Jovan mumbled.

"Mouth, Grandmom," Daelyn added as he approached the group.

"Whoa! Where'd you come from?" André tossed his arm around his grandson's neck and reeled him for a hug. "Why are you here? Everything okay at home?"

"I sifted in with Shelby. You know we love a good party."

****

About to dagger Devon, the stake Serina held slipped from her grasp and fell to the floor when a man stepped in front of her. "Avery?"

Catching up, Lucian choked asking, "Son?" He reached for the man.

An emaciated, tall man with short dirty blond curls and huge brown eyes stepped back. He whispered, "I haven't been related to you in eons. Walk away now. Leave the party. All can see you. All know you are here thanks to your spell, Serina."

Serina whispered, "We thought you died."

He responded, "Everyone here thought you did as well. Guess we both have our secrets."

Serina shoved Avery with all her force knocking him off balance. "Nothing. What happened to you?"

"Keep your voice down." Avery St. James kept his demeanor calm as he nudged Serina and Lucian away from Devon and the crowd. When Avery had them somewhere a little safer, he grabbed Serina's hands then took a breath before explaining, "I met Devon during the First World War. I'd been fatally shot. I understand your hatred of him, but just know if you kill him, I'm a package deal, much like you were with Xavier. Devon has Sydney. I can't do a thing to save her. That whole sire-line, compulsion BS. Don't come after me. I have orders to take out anyone should there be a rescue attempt." Avery dropped her hands and walked away without another word or glance back.

Serina followed regardless. *The day the princess was attacked, I saw you. Are you honestly into human trafficking? Did you know the princess is related to Devon? Was it you who killed the priest? You may not be able to help Sydney but tell me how I can.* His pace faltered for a step, but he regained his momentum and walked away.

The spell Serina cast no longer lingered like stale cigarette smoke. Masks lay abandoned across the floor, concealing makeup ran in lines down faces, wigs came off... game on. She dragged Lucian back to her family.

"I have a plan. It's going to get messy. Xanti, you're going to love this."

****

"Do I get to kill anyone?" Finally, after a century, the woman said something that piqued my interest. The unhealthy side, the one most vegans would hold a massive protest over.

I've had so many designs of ending Badcock I've lost count. Sitting idle and allowing old dreams to die hard is no longer an option. Now, stuck in my head, is that ridiculous phrase, *Yippee Ki Yay, mother*...I need to focus, stay on point. I jammed my hand in my pocket and twirled around a small vile of what I like to call, Dumbfounded. I made the potion earlier. Payback's going to be epic. Stood there on his high horse, looking down his bumpy, crooked nose, Devon thinks he is better than everyone, thinks he is in control. Time to pin the tail on the ass. He appears thoroughly put out that his masquerade is coming undone. And yet, he proceeds with the auction, assuming no one can touch him. We all know what happens when someone assumes…This is me not assuming he's assuming…I'm actually giddy.

"The coins have been accounted for. Let the bidding begin." Devon pointed to a wall where a large maroon velvet curtain lifted. "The creatures will be the last items for auction. Look them over to make certain of your choice before bidding. All sales are final. You break it, you buy it." The crowd roared with anxious laughter.

It was as if we had front row seating inside a brothel. A curtain revealed a wall of thick glass and behind it, separate cages, each holding a young woman or man. All naked. All posed like wax statuettes on a pedestal that spun in circles.

One hand fisted, the other he slapped over his mouth, Lucian turned his head in revulsion. "I'm going to kill these bastards. Sydney's up there."

"We will get her back, Daddy," Elyza grabbed her father's hand and gave it a squeeze.

I pointed to the petite red head in one of the cages. "She's coming with us too."

Before anyone could add any disparaging comments, Zander spoke up. "She is a friend," and gave a nod to me. My heart melted. I do believe it's a first, having another person have my back. And then I saw

Alek. "Aww Christ, my boy's up there too."

Lucian made me his focal point. "We have our work cut out for us. A truths, Xanti." I nodded back to him.

The lone bedazzled sandal Elyza wore was the first item to sell. It'll be a nice talking point on my mantel when I get settled in a home. I cataloged who the items went to so later tonight I could pay them a visit. If nothing else, I will clear Zander of wrongdoing through blood, sweat and tears. Theirs, not mine. The booby and snap trap Elyza wore at the Hall Royal sold for fifteen million to a singer who'd made it big in the eighties and then fizzled out of fashion when her body did in the late nineties. Hollywood is so judgmental. I paid her sixteen million for the outfit and told her it's a shame she was such a material girl. After I'd shared a drink with her, okay, from her, I got my money back too. Let's see how she likes being on the giving end of blood lust. There seems to be a new strain of vampirism out there these days. Hollywood's elites, or so they've crowned themselves, seem to have gotten mixed up in human, and child trafficking all for a little chemical in the blood called adenochrome. Supposedly, stealing blood from a child leads you to the Fountain of Youth... I don't want to burst anyone's bubble, but I am one of the original Fountains of Youth. You want immortality, come see me, not some baby. God, I love being a vampire.

The Iron Mask, from King Louis XIV's era came up for grabs. There are so many stories behind it, with the truth yet to be discovered. What would a king do to retain his reign? Stuff his older illegitimate brother in a mask and lock him away in the Bastille? I met the Sun King a few times. Wouldn't put it past the pretentious bastard.

That little artifact will be in my custody before nightfall. I have high designs for it. Speaking of which, the Hope Diamond is now on the chopping block. Will someone's head fall prey to the cursed thing again? Who here has three hundred fifty million or more to blow on a chunk of coal? Two males, both dressed as clowns took home the hunk of sparkles, but with its curse, who would have the last laugh?

Me. That would be me. I'm going to pop some balloons.

Badcock hoisted the illusive blue diamond mask stolen from Elyza high in the air. The room sounded like a mass orgy of 'Oohs and awes' upon seeing the tiara. "Let us take a moment from time to delight in this magnificent piece that has coveted centuries of life, love and loss. It once belonged to Dracula. Bidding begins at one million. Close your eyes to imagine the allure of being the center of attention as you shine beneath its splendor."

I'm having a hard time believing Drac isn't here to retrieve his bling. A frenzy of bidding ensued. Two million soared to twenty million. My adrenaline spiked. One gentleman, reedy in stature, his hair wispy white, watched the room and the dynamics play out. His silk suit and shoes could equal the going price of the mask. He oozes power and wealth. He waved his number thirteen flag each time the bid increased, driving the price skyward. When the price of the mask reached forty million, lucky number thirteen bowed, conceding to a woman, small in stature, overdone in jewels and gold. The way he watched her gave me a shiver and honestly that takes a lot. Beginning to think the bidding will continue off the venue.

As I stand beside this dandelion of a man with wispy hair, unease agitates my gut that we are acquaintances. And then it hit me. Or he did.

Bastard blindsided me. Sucker punched me in the chest so hard the wind sailed from my lungs and my ship sank. In my next breath he hoisted me off my heeled shoes making us eye level.

"Xanti, did I say you could leave the museum? You swipe a few mothballs?" He sneezed in my face. My entire being shuddered. I am totally skeeved. I despise respiratory fluids. Go figure.

"Dracula, you're looking well. A little thin, but well. I see you went blond. The color is a stark contrast to your eyes. Can I borrow a hankie?" I cheesed big, not that it did me a damn bit of good.

"Heard you've been up to your old games." The prince of darkness flashed his pristine fangs my way. "I am disenchanted to hear the misfortunes the St. James's have endured as of late."

"They're all fine." His caustic look said he didn't buy that line. Drac intensified his glare, tapped his fangs together and grinned. With that, I spilled the beans. "Okay, Serina is acting like Ragan with a few different personalities, but I didn't cause it. I did your basic exorcism and took out the vilest one, my brother. Please set me down. People are pointing."

"Let them point. I want you and I to be the focal point for the moment. If you've ever wanted to atone for your past indiscretions now is the time, Xanti."

"It is why I am here. Not so much the atoning part, but I want Devon's head no longer attached to his neck." After an awkward moment of Drac sizing me up and down, I asked nicely, "Please set me down?"

Drac launched me sideways into one of the guards. And there you have it. Always think twice about what you wish for. Trying to get my feet beneath me, not so easy in women's shoes, hands grabbed me, tugged away at my gown, restraining me as all sorts of obscenities filter out from the guard and myself.

"Get him!" The guard yelled in my ear.

One bloke rushed over and sat on my chest while another jabbed me with a loaded needle of what I believe is Silver Nitrate since I can no longer feel my extremities. My adrenaline is skyrocketing while my inner clock idles like a car in a traffic jam. I'm overheating.

What a surreal combo. Stuck in limbo watching Armageddon. Drac went through the room faster than a toddler trying to escape with an object he shouldn't have. People ran for their lives, others didn't budge, frozen in fear. One by one heads of all the staff in the manor rolled past me. Drac left no one to clean up the mess. I glanced about the room. Hope he didn't leave me here to mop up. He wiped out anyone with strings attached to the laird of the house, I guess. I don't get it, he takes out thirty or more people and I'm the one locked in the museum for a quarter century. Where's the justice? The golden goose who purchased Drac's mask is stood in a corner shaking while he looms before her, his arms stretched to her sides, trapping her in place. Thinking she won't like the ending to duck-duck-goose. The flock I'd started out with tonight? Think they flew south for the winter.

Bleeding lot of them left me as a patsy. Go figure. And here I thought we'd bonded. Serina said something about me loving her plan? Guess I missed the sarcasm in her voice. The party in the rib room ended. Poorly for most. I'm watching Drac now with Devon pinned against the wall, whispering in his ear, eyeballing him in a very unhealthy fashion, like Devon's his midnight snack— better him than me. Devon sort of slides down the wall with a blank expression. Seems we were left here on purpose as a match of wills. Who will walk away the victor? Drac glided across the shiny glass floor my way. He's more fluid than water. He squat in front of me with that grin dentists probably died for. His knees didn't even crack. I'm slightly annoyed. Everything on me groans when I move.

"Your fate and future rely in your hands, Xanti. Do not make me regret this. Take care of your family and if you harm another St. James member, well, I'll leave you to your imagination." A glimmering rainbow mist appeared beneath the lights as he vanished.

Those glowing red hot coal eyes of Devon should have been a warning to any other moron but here we are, facing off. My hands have that insatiable tingling sensation you experience after having a tooth anesthetized as it wears off. In my pocket, I loosened the cap to the ampule of the Dumbfounded and I waited.

Devon hasn't flinched. He could be stalling or incapacitated. I straightened the remnants of my once lovely gown. It is beyond tattered. Museum's going to be miffed.

"How the mighty have fallen, Badcock." I received a blank stare.

"Not a step closer, Xanti." Pfft! I shuffled a bit faster toward him, not because I was going for speed, but because I barely had control of my legs.

Devon's jugular vein pulsed away. Reminds me of a blocked colon, the shit trying to force its way through, getting backed up and making parts of the encasement bulge. He might spring a leak unless I get to it first, which means the end result is he's going to spring a leak.

"What a sight you are. I'm going to have to thank Drac the next time I see him."

"There won't be a next time, Sinclair. I have your son. If I'm not here at sunrise he gets put down."

"Get up. I want a fair fight, none of this sissy stuff."

"But that's all you know." Devon gave me a weak head bob and splayed his hands gesturing, whatever!

Well, now I know he can move. Acting like an injured bird—pussy. He sprang on me like he was a freaking leopard, all claws and teeth barred. For once, I was ready. I blew the powder in that gaping hole of a mouth, his nose and eyes. Down he went a second time. The look of utter astonishment in his eyes I shall forever cherish. Pink frothy bubbles gathered along his jaw making it look like a beard. I might have a new favorite color.

"I'm going to go save the day, Badcock, while you rot." The monster curled up in fetal position, gibberish filling the void. "I'll give the poison a little more time to work its magic. I have a surprise for you. You'll love it." Now I sound like Serina. I fished out some extra-large zip ties I'd stashed for a rainy day from my purse and secured his hands and feet together. Where's he going? Nowhere! Adding a few drops of Hawthorn oil over him for my own perverse pleasure, I sauntered away with my head held high. Tippity tap, tippity tap, Xanti's got his mojo back.

****

"The fuzzy haired guy, Elyza, who is he? He was at the Garland's slaughterhouse. He's headed this way."

"That's Drac—"

"—Ula?" Zander gulped and grabbed Elyza's hand and scooted around to her front. "Get behind me."

Elyza shook her head and stepped back to his side. "I appreciate such a noble gesture, but I can take care of myself."

"Good evening, St. James's clan. Nice to see you made it, Serina and Elyza. And I don't mean to the party."

Lucian held his hand to the most notorious vampire ever. They exchanged a shake followed by a hug. "Thank you for supplying all the blood the past days to us. You risked everything going to the Garland's encampment. You are a true friend and life saver."

Dracula laughed and clasped Lucian's shoulder. "That's a first, me being called a life saver. And most likely a last."

Stood with his jaw parted and not blinking, Zander let out a slight burble while he continued to squeeze Elyza's hand. "Just when you think your life can't get any weirder."

Elyza leaned in and whispered, "Can't feel my fingers."

Zander really laughed then, to the point he'd become the focal point of the conversation.

Lucian offered, "This is Zander—"

Drac cut him off. "Sinclair. I know. I had a nice chat with your father. Come see me next week, kid. I need a ghost writer for a book I'm conjuring up and since you and Elyza have the inside scoop on ghosting...I think you'll be a perfect match." The tall lithe vampire smirked, his ever-pristine choppers resting on his lips.

Elyza snickered. Zander remained twinning as an

ice sculpture.

Drac pat the young man on his shoulder. "I get that look a lot. I'm used to it. Anyway, I hope to hear from you soon, Zander. One more thing, you'll need to dismantle the binding spell to release the prisoners. I have every confidence tonight's favors shall rest with you. I bid you all adieu." With an affable bow he vanished, the golden girl stuck in the corner with him.

"That wasn't my finest moment. I totally turned into a star struck geek." With a shoulder shrug, Zander laughed it off and then took the lead. "Break these binds, intertwined and woven like vines. No longer needed are safeguards. Drop them like a house of fallen cards. Goddess, release our family from this calamity. Show us a clear path, so we may exit without a bloodbath or be the victims of a psychopath's twisted wrath."

Elyza added, "Make us all bullet proof. And the lot of us fireproof." She gave up a grin. "I'm completely over getting shot and if my temper flares, I want us all protected. No repeats of the shit show from a few days past."

From the second-floor balcony people pointed between Elyza and her family and the victims caged. Who was the main attraction? A loudspeaker startled the bejesus from her. Zander flinched as well.

"And once more, we have a true fallen angel with us. Let us begin the bidding."

"Are you fecking serious?" Elyza screamed, her voice echoing through the room.

"Why do I know that voice?" Zander asked.

Serina gasped. Lucian turned in a circle searching for the person speaking. "Where are you, Avery?"

"Avery?" Elyza spun facing her father.

Serina whispered, "Show us that which you conceal. Dissolve any and all bars of steel. All locks, unseal. Any weapons you now hide will leave you cross-eyed if not immediately dropped to your side and kicked curbside. My will is so, I shall not be denied. So mote it be."

"Momma, you sound more like Gram than she does."

Fighting and losing to hold back tears, Serina confessed, "I have her heart, and memories. I'm not certain this good or bad."

"I have you and that's all that matters." Elyza leaned in and kissed her mom's cheek.

Avery approached the group holding a large talon blade. "I was hoping it wouldn't come to this but the lot of you are bleeding insufferable. I told you to leave."

Baffled, Elyza waved her hand in Avery's face. "Hold up! You can't possibly be the loser my parents sang praises about for over a century, held vigils for, cried themselves to sleep because they had no idea you lived? Wow! What a letdown."

"I see you have your mother's free spirit. Not to worry, it will be broken." Before another word was spoken or spell cast, Avery had Elyza snugly against him with the tip of the blade to her throat. "You get to choose, Serina. My dear sweet sister, Sydney, or your own flesh and blood, Elyza." Avery pointed to the glass wall. "Let's see if you can find Sydney first, shall we?"

Momma, your last spell was shite. There's still something working against us.

Lucian ordered, "Avery, if you harm either of them I will make certain we finally have your body to mourn come sunup."

With the slightest pressure behind the blade, Avery

nicked Elyza's throat.

"You bastard!" Zander yelled. Lucian grabbed him as he lunged. Blood began to trickle down her neck. And then it stopped. Avery put more force behind the tip of the blade. Elyza started to bleed and again the wound healed.

"Serina, I see your powers have improved. Always believed you had to physically touch a person to heal them."

Serina said nothing. She stood stoic with a menacing grin.

"You fucking hurt her and you're dead, dude." Zander's rage filled his eyes with fire.

"Easy kiddo." Avery taunted, "You don't remember me, do you? You were kind enough to deliver all the gems to the locker for me. I am your probation officer. We'll talk later. I bet Elyza, you don't recall me yet either? I'm the one who handcuffed your fiery little ass up and gave your boyfriend here a good bonk on the head."

Zander questioned, "You're my probation officer? How is that even possible?"

Avery produced a grin that made Zander's gut curl. "Let's just say prison is run by those who run Hell."

Elyza spared a glance at Zander. *Well, at least we know what the feck happened to us and why.*

"Your brother, Zander, is getting euthanized in a few hours. See him up there in that cage? Did you find Sydney yet, Serina? The next cut goes deeper. I'll keep slicing till her head comes off. I truly don't mind. I enjoyed taking the princess's head from her shoulders. And. Yes, Devon knew who she was. You think he wanted a reminder of all he'd lost hanging around, touting her royal life and shenanigans in his face?" Avery sliced Elyza's throat leaving her gurgling.

Within a split second the blood stopped again. "Very impressive." Avery swung Elyza to face the glass enclosure holding all the women. "Eeny, Meeny, Miny, Moe, hurry up and pick or this one's a dead little hoe."

Struggling, Elyza found a waste of time. The man had a death grip on her and wasn't afraid to use it. The blade in her throat being a no-brainer. She looked over all the young girls trapped in the enclosures. All of them wore masks concealing the top half of their faces. Two girls had long blonde, curly hair, both were petite, and both had a tattoo of crescent moon with a tiny star on their hip. The same birthmark she had. God damn Sydney for getting the same tattoo as her birthmark. Either girl could be Sydney. There was only one difference between the two. Lipstick color. One girl slathered an outrageous neon pink shade over her mouth and the second girl had sunset coral plastered all over her face. *Sydney, I made you a promise. This is me keeping it.*

Elyza sent another message. *Momma, Sydney made me promise she would never get caught dead in that putrid pink shade of lipstick, so choose wisely.*

Chapter Twenty

Xanti peeked over the edge of the balustrade and waved. "Hey! I'm back," preempted a woman's body being dumped over the balcony that clipped Avery and sent him sideways. "I found a witch doing witchy stuff preventing other witches from doing their witchy stuff so get to it witches."

With not a second to spare, Serina and Zander repeated their spells to break the wards to free the people trapped in the glass enclosures.

Busy crawling for her life, Elyza turned on Avery, her hand red and glowing, she launched a fireball at him. Dodging the blaze, he went at her again. The next orb hit his well-padded doublet. Avery snagged Elyza to him and grabbed a pitcher of something wet and poured it down the front of his clothes. "Choose Serina. Who lives to see another day? You think you're so in tune to playing God, choose one now. One of these two blonde babes is your daughter. What's your favorite color? Pink or coral?"

Sobbing inconsolably, Serina wiped her eyes and looked at Lucian. "I can't choose one life over another. They're both someone's daughter. If I choose one, the other dies."

Avery started counting, "Three, two, one..."

Serina pointed to girl in the pink lipstick and said, "Goddess forgive me."

With Elyza unable to move, Avery yanked the girl wearing the coral lipstick to his other side, entwining her hair through his fingers. He kicked the one in the pink lipstick in the ribs so hard she went down wheezing. "Choose again, Serina. This time blood or borrowed?"

"I said the other one," Serina sobbed.

Zander couldn't breathe. He was about to lose the love of his life, the one person who gave meaning to his existence. Looking between Lucian and Serina, they stood side by side holding hands, frozen with fear. He understood more than he should in that moment. Jovan came to stand beside Serina as André threw his arm around Lucian's shoulder.

"What did we ever do to you, Avery?" Serina let go of Lucian's hand and took a step forward toward the glass enclosure.

"You never found me. I was right under your bleeding nose, held hostage by the biggest demon on this planet. Screw all of you with your ridiculous *all for one* mentality."

There was no warning before vines burst through the floor, spiraling around Avery's legs, climbing higher around his torso. Stammering for balance, Avery plunged his fist through the blonde's chest and yanked her heart out. He drew the mangled organ to his mouth and bit a huge chunk out before he tossed the remainder to the floor. Vines continued to entomb Avery until he looked like a spider's next meal trapped in a web. Serina collapsed keening in shock. Lucian went down beside her inconsolable.

"Momma, forgive me." Taking a deep breath with her focus solely on Avery, Elyza had to put an end to this. Avery passed the point of no return. He'd killed innocent people and Sydney might be one of them. "Avery, you have forsaken everyone's trust. Your actions throughout your life have been unjust. Momma may have an issue putting one life above another, but you are about to become a stain in this rug, brother. Ashes to ashes, return to dust. Burn you, I must." Playing catch with a ball of fire, Zander jumped in front of her.

"Hold on there, tiny Jedi rhymer. Don't you have an anger management class to attend? Take a drink of water and put out the fire. Let me do it." The looks she gave him said he might be next on the firing squad.

"Zander, Elyza, do not stain your souls over this maggot. Allow me this pleasure. Go live your lives together." Before another word was spoken or sound made, Xanti along with Avery and his tangled web vanished.

Zander spun to Elyza. "What the bloody hell just happened? Where did he go?"

Wide-eyed with shock, Elyza stood silent, broody, rubbing her neck. "I can't believe I almost did it again. I would have killed him, Zander. Tiny Jedi?" Elyza shoved Zander backwards off balance. She didn't know whether to laugh or cry. Crying won.

"But you didn't," Serina offered.

Sniffling, Elyza answered, "Only because Zander and Xanti saved the day, Momma."

Stepping over broken glass, Alek sluggishly made his way to them. A few feet away he toppled over sideways, his hand reaching for the girl in the pink lipstick. "Is she okay?"

Lucian made his way to the girl Avery murdered. Shaking and his vision diluted with tears he fumbled getting the mask off. Gasping, he buckled over crying.

Wiping his eyes he looked at Serina. "It isn't Sydney." He took his jacket off and covered the girl's body.

Both Elyza and Zander headed for the girl with the pink lipstick curled in fetal position wheezing. Alek growled a warning. Zander removed his tux and placed it over the girl in the pink lipstick. Zander held his hand out to Alek. "We won't hurt her. I promise. She's safe. You're both safe."

Jovan fashioned a pair of jeans and a blue hoodie for Alek. He looked up at her and in between tears barely afforded her a nod.

Syd?" Elyza wept as she removed the mask from her sister and tossed it aside.

"Sissy?" Sydney sounded incredibly drained. Bruises painted her black and blue. Uncontrolled shakes ravaged her body.

"We got you now." Elyza laid on the floor and curled herself around Sydney and held her. "Momma, get over here and help her. She isn't breathing right. Auntie Jovan, she needs clothes. Where's Daelyn and Shelby?"

"Here." Daelyn stopped in front of them out of breath. "We were tending to the other victims. And we may or may not have put holes in every freaking boat out back so no one can escape. And we unhooked all the horses from the carriages and gave them a nice little pat on their rumps. Let their owners have fun rounding them up."

"That was all my idea," Shelby added as she got down on the floor with Sydney and Elyza. She scooched in and tossed her arm over both girls so they melded into one group hug of ugly crying.

"Syd, I'm going to take all your pain from you. Your entire body is giving off more bad juju than Chernobyl did radiation."

"Sissy, no. You always do so much for everyone else, always buffering our hurt or disappointments or loss but no one looks out for you. I can deal with this. I have to."

Elyza wiped tears from her sister's face. "Syd, I think pink is your new color."

Sydney threw her arm around Elyza's shoulder. "And here I thought you never paid attention to anything I said. I told you I'd never be caught dead in pink."

Half crying, half laughing, Elyza tried to lighten the mood, "I usually don't." She hugged Sydney and kissed her forehead and discretely absorbed what she could of Sydney's distress and anxiety. "I love you."

Sydney twisted to look at Elyza. "Lizzy, I said no."

"That was me not listening to you." To Serina, she shook her head. "Momma, you picked the wrong girl. She could have died."

Serina knelt beside the girls and placed her hands on Sydney's ribs immediately sending her healing powers. "I knew he would choose the opposite. Avery would never hurt his baby sister. My beautiful Sydney," Serina cried, "I never thought I would see you again." She looked at the deceased girl. "I'll never forgive myself."

"Momma, I don't know how you're alive, but I've never been more grateful you are."

Jovan joined them. "You aren't responsible for the girl's death, Serina. That was all Avery. We will find her family and at least offer a proper burial." With the twirl of her finger, Jovan whispered, "Clothes," and just like that Sydney matched Alek in her attire.

"Sydney?" Alek made his way to his knees and inched his way closer. "Are you okay? Did they do anything to you before we were paraded out like animals?"

Grabbing Alek's hand, Sydney's eye dripped tear after tear. With quivering lips she asked, "Can we please get the fuck out of here?"

André pointed to the exit. "There's an extended limo out front. Come on."

Spotting Xanti, Zander brushed Elyza's hair from her face and placed kiss on her cheek. "Be right back."

Xanti stood in a far-off corner watching the reunion with a petite, red-haired girl stood at his side. He had wrapped her in pajamas with a long dinner jacket over them and tucked her protectively beneath his arm. Approaching Xanti, Zander extended his hand. "Thank you for everything you did. I mean it. The entire night would have gone sideways if it weren't for you. I see you found Murph's sister?"

"Yes. Zander meet Siobhan. I'll escort her home tonight and check in on her on the morrow." She didn't move, blink, or respond. "Later, I will ask if she wants her memory erased. It's her choice. She's in shock and is heavily drugged."

Zander nodded. "You can ride with us. There's room. Will she be okay?"

Xanti shook his head no. He reeled Zander in and gave him a huge hug. "Trauma comes in many forms. I believe the survivors tonight can attest to this. Good night, son. I have a busy night ahead."

Peeking at his dad from the corner of his eyes, Zander asked, "Is this where I ask if I want to know what things?"

Xanti laughed, all fangs. "I'll stop by soon. Go be with your girl. And take care of our Alek."

****

Feet from the limo, a bevy of cops rushed Zander and Elyza and surrounded them.

"Hands out where we can see them," an officer shouted as another cop circled behind. Lucian and André hastily made their way to them.

"What is going on?" Lucian demanded, "That's my daughter and her..." He struggled for the right term, "Boyfriend."

The cop behind Elyza spoke up. "Yeah, your dead daughter. Nice reanimation. No closer you two. This shit just freaks me out. We have orders to take them to the station for questioning regarding a jewelry heist and a murdered priest."

Peaking around Zander, Elyza said, "It's okay, Daddy. We'll go. We don't want any more trouble." Mentally Elyza screamed, *'Get us a barrister immediately.'*

Chapter Twenty-One

Stuck well past sunup in a cool, dimly lit room, Zander trumpet tapped his fingers on the table while Elyza's nervous knee bounced beneath it. This was it, his last bit of freedom before the silencing sound of a cell door slammed with him on one side, while his hopes and dreams died on the opposite. Beside them, his barrister bit his bottom lip, huffing nonstop, running through all the evidence stacked against him. Zander had been charged with the priest's death and the missing jewels. At least Elyza was off the hook. How did this go so utterly wrong? He was innocent. The video of him with the jewels was damning. But the video that surfaced of him literally swapping his bloodied, shredded clothes for the priest's, as the man lay mutilated on the floor was beyond damning. Footsteps drew closer coming down the hall. Elyza squeezed Zander's hand.

"Can't feel my fingers, little cherub." Zander gave her an ill-fated smirk.

"It's going to be all right. Trust me." Elyza squeezed his knee.

Four men entered the room, the DA, the Judge, and two officers. Zander looked at Elyza from the corner of his eye. *Mac Beth? He's dirty as Hell.*

Elyza set her sights on MacBeth and sent the man a message:

On judgment day as the gavel pounds the wood, you

will do as you should. Before the jury rules, you will confess to the knowledge of the theft of the jewels, the deaths of innocents and Zander's case will be overruled. You will divulge Devon and Avery's twisted plot, to make certain they are caught, and if a body does not swing from a silver garrote, if when the final bell doth toll you have not complied your head will roll, by my hand be it told.

"Mr. Templar, we hereby reprimand you—"

"Oh God, Elyza," Zander mumbled, "I love you. Live your best life."

MacBeth started choking and coughing, interrupting the Judge. "My Lords, I, I um, I must confess this case is not as it seems…"

An hour later, Zander was certain his mug shot mirrored the bewildered appearance of MacBeth as the cop was led off in handcuffs. He didn't see that one coming until Jovan and Olivia stepped into the room, both appearing guiltier than MacBeth.

"I did, Zander," Jovan added, reading his mind. "How does it feel to be a fully exonerated free man, with no anvil hanging over your head?"

Grinning ear to ear, Zander asked, "Does that include Lucian?"

Jovan looped her arm through Zander's and walked toward Olivia and Elyza. "I'm not giving up all my secrets. Where's the fun in that?"

Olivia gave Elyza a bear hug. "Nicely done, Sparky. Your gifts are expanding."

"Grams, I don't know what just happened. That incantation popped into my head. I wasn't aware Macbeth had any involvement."

"When you were ghosting us, you remained able to

see and hear everything. You sensed your mother's unease in his presence, and you watched me hand him a slip of paper, the invocation you just read. You finished what I began. That is all."

Zander tossed his arms around Elyza and Olivia getting in on the hug. "Let's get out of here."

Olivia ducked under his arm and headed out of the courthouse. With a glance over her shoulder she said, "See you at home."

Elyza ran her hands through his silky locks. Before he knew it, she'd jumped into his arms, wrapping her legs around his waist. She puckered up smiling. "Plant one here. I love you, Zander Templar."

"Sinclair, Zander Sinclair, and I love you more, Elyza St. James."

"Shut up and kiss her already. What is it with you?" Jovan walked away laughing.

Zander was rather confident that their kiss made every other kiss in the history of kisses pale in comparison. Her lips against his, soft, smooth, plump, meeting his demands ignited his passion as her fingers ran through his hair. Zander drew back, his heart sated.

"What is it? Why did you stop?" Elyza asked, now pouting.

"Two things. I don't feel sick anymore when I think about…you know…"

"Sex. You can say it," Elyza giggled.

"Sex!" He swung the two of them in a circle, jubilant beyond words. Breathy he admitted, "And here I worried you were going to catch us on fire. You're so hot."

"I promise not to incinerate you if you promise never to stop kissing me." She gave him her version of the sidewinder stink eye.

"Deal," he mumbled through another long kiss.

Walking into the manor Zander and Elyza were handed an envelope from Serina.

"What's this, Momma?"

"An invitation to the museum. Get cleaned up. We're headed over in a few."

****

Zander, Elyza and most of the St. James's were greeted at the entrance to the museum by an exuberant Xanti. The man had a hard time containing his elation as he paraded the family to his old neck of the woods, as he called it. Donned in a wig befitting the Sun King and a cloak of off-white velvet embedded with jewels, that most likely belonged to King Louis, Xanti stopped and held up a white gloved hand, where a gold ruby ring graced his index finger. "This is where I spent a quarter century." He pointed to the black tin casket holding a man strapped down with spiked bracelets secured inside the casket. A black burlap bag with holes cut out around his eyes rested over his head. A silver garrote snuggly rested around his throat. "This is where your son, Avery, will do the same. He has time on his side. It's an olive branch I was never offered. He can either choose to turn his life around when released or you can deal with him if he chooses the darker journey. His bond to Badcock still needs to be severed. Now, follow me please."

Uncharacteristically, Serina approached Xanti. Elyza went to grab her, but Serina smiled and took her hand. "It's ok, lovie." Serina looked Xanti in the eye and said something no one ever would have expected, especially hence the circumstances leading to this. "Thank you."

"I really didn't see that one coming," Jovan professed.

"Let us not falter in this moment. There is more. So much more." Euphoric, Xanti led the way to the area of the museum holding French artifacts. "You're really going to love this. It's my favorite." He turned and cheesed. In the center of a glass vault sat an elaborate Baroque throne, the side arms carved to resemble half a woman, half animal. At the back of the rectangular piece leaves and a crown of gilded gold were shaped. On a red velvet cushion rest a man wearing the mask that always plagued King Louis XVI's reign. "If you want the identity of the man now behind the illustrious mask, take a guess." Xanti's impatience got the best of him and he blurted, "Badcock. It's Badcock. Where's he going? Nowhere!" Xanti spun in a circle doing a little jig, before he concluded, "Bastard's gonna rot there for the world to see. I have this place hexed to the next millennium. You're welcome!"

Zander asked, "How?"

Through giggles, Xanti wiggled his brows and straightened his wig. "This is one of those better off not knowing situations. One last thing, Elyza, Le Bijou du Roi, has been returned to its rightful owners. Now, if you'll all excuse me, I have a museum to run. Son, I'll pop over before sunup."

"Xanti," Elyza reached for his hand. With a weary look he accepted her offering. "You need to study to get through the Pearly Gates."

Xanti bent over laughing. "Impossible."

"Nothing is impossible in this family." She smirked and grabbed Zander's hand as Xanti led them to the next exhibit.

"Smile when you leave, The Last Laugh exhibit. There's a photo waiting for you."
****

Opening the door before the bell rang, Raven gave the vamp on the opposite side a caustic glance. "Oh Jesus, now what?"

Xanti tipped his hat sideways with a curt bow. "Good morning, Raven. Where are you headed, and so early? The sun has yet to rise."

Raven barely turned her head, deciding whether or not to waste her time with idle chitchat. "Morning constitutional."

"Well, you are dressed more for a funeral."

"Am I?" She smiled, her fangs peeking out from under her ruby lips.

"Whose?"

Raven sauntered out the door donning her favorite shade of black. "Yours!" With unfathomed speed Raven crossed to Xanti and plunged her fist into his chest. Reeling in shock and pain she stepped back from him, holding her hand, her fingernails broken. "A metal chest protector? Well played, Xanti."

"I'm done underestimating the women in your family, Raven."

Without looking back at him, Raven offered, "Maybe there is hope for you yet. Until we meet again."

"Looking forward to it, Raven."

"You say that now." Raven's laughter trailed behind her. *Zander, your dad is here.*

Out of breath and with a huge smile he couldn't get rid of, Zander made his way to the front door.

"Good morning, son. Hope I didn't wake you or interrupt."

Zander gave the man an earnest smile. "What's up? Wanna come in?"

Xanti shook his head no. "It's about time I see the sunrise. Believe I am well past due."

An arrow pierced Zander's heart. He'd just found his father. They had so much to catch up on. "Dad, no. You forgetting something? You're not one of the vamps that has a magical daylight ring, and there isn't enough SPF in any lotion to keep your leathered-up hide from frying." He stepped in front of Xanti stopping his advance toward the park. "No, seriously. We just met. You can't say goodbye."

Xanti sidestepped Zander and laughed. "When has this ever stopped me from doing something stupid?"

"Clearly, after all these years you never found an ounce of common sense."

Xanti held his hand out. "You coming? I made a daylight necklace. I want to try it out."

"You've been watching too much television. Hang on," Zander retorted, "let me grab the fire extinguisher and let Elyza know."

****

Cozied up by a fireplace that didn't require a few tuppence every so often to run, Zander hit the jackpot. In Elyza's bedroom they snuggled beneath a warm blanket. He smothered her with kisses from her neck to her nose, pausing long enough to sweep a few stray strands of her curls from her face and gaze into her eyes. It never ceased to amaze Zander of the overwhelming sense of family within these walls. It blew him away that he was a part of it. How had he gone from being a loner with no family on parole to finding the most brilliantly beautiful woman alive to spend his days and nights beside? He had a brother. Alek and Sydney were keeping very much to themselves, and no one pressed the issue. They'd talk when they were ready. Zander had a father, Xanti—one of strangest men he'd ever encountered, but the guy would stop at nothing to protect those he loved, and he now had Elyza's crew. Just as protective. Just as quirky and ever present in their lives.

"How did I get so lucky?"

"Oh, so you're feeling lucky?" Elyza wiggled her eyebrows playfully. She slid out from under the covers and stood. With the snap of her fingers the night dress she wore disappeared leaving her in only a tiny pair of black satin panties and black lacey bra. She gave him a little spin before she turned and strut to her closet.

"No—hold up. Don't go anywhere. Let me get my fill of sheer perfection for a moment. I want, need to engrain this vision of you into my memory. I'd chase you but I can't walk. Something is in the way." He pointed to his groin and bat his eyelashes.

Elyza laughed but kept walking into the closet. When she came out, she had a black bat-shaped teddy bear, complete with little fangs and a red silk cape in her grasp. "This is for you. You now own a teddy bear. Grams also told me when your birthday is. You and I share the same day. June sixth. How cool is that? We are so going to party!" Elyza handed him the bat. Before he could get a word in, she had Zander down to his birthday suit. She straddled his lap and smiled. Running her finger up and down his thigh Elyza teased, "Remember telling me I was a lousy vampire when I bit your bum?"

Zander nodded, his grin growing wide while his manhood sprang to action. "I said your aim was horrible."

Elyza changed positions and dipped her head to rest on his thigh. Glancing up to him, she said, "I'm going to fix that right now," as her fangs descended.

A small burst of giggles followed one gasp as Zander dug his fingers into the side of the mattress and held on for the ride of his life.

Elyza licked her lips. "Cheers to happy endings."

A word about the author...

Jaclyn Tracey's life began on an American Air Force Base by the North Sea in England, giving her dual citizenship to both beautiful countries.

She grew up in the resplendent city of Saratoga Springs, NY. She is married with children, and four dynamic grandees.

Jaclyn is a Registered Nurse who saves lives by day and shreds them during full moons. She's written paranormal romances, a few YA fantasies and also a few children's books. Her website is:

http://www.edensbower.cloud